"Stark and honest, *A Quiet Cadence* masterfully captures it all . . . from the individual courage, sacrifice and dedication, through the black humor, dread of combat, and fear of failure, to that special unbreakable human bond that stands the test of time. Powerful, it brought back many names and memories for me."

—**Gen. Mike Hagee, USMC, 33rd Commandant of the Marine Corps, A 1/1 Vietnam**

"Mark Treanor has written an extraordinary story about the Vietnam War in 1969 on a par with *Matterhorn* and *Fields of Fire*. The narrative follows PFC Marty McClure, USMC, during the war in fierce and brutal ground combat, which is compelling. What is then unique is Mark's telling of life after combat and the post-traumatic stress (PTS) that accrues to every single individual who has ever been in a firefight. We are far behind in addressing PTS issues for our combat veterans. Mark's incisive writing does a great deal to illuminate its reality and the urgent need to address it. Please read this book. You won't be able to put it down."

—**Adm. Mike Mullen, USN (Ret.), 17th Chairman Joint Chiefs of Staff**

"A riveting look at what soldiers have experienced from Vietnam to Afghanistan. In *A Quiet Cadence*, they live through intense combat then return to civilian life to struggle with memories of dead or horribly wounded friends while successfully pursuing careers ranging from shopkeeper to surgeon. A story of resilience and recovery, this book brilliantly describes characters who struggle but nonetheless get on with their lives—like most veterans do."

—**Jan C. Scruggs, Esq, Founder of Vietnam Veterans Memorial, Chairman National Selective Service Review Board, Army rifleman in Vietnam**

"*A Quiet Cadence* is a riveting account of a young Marine's combat experiences in Vietnam and the indelible effects in its aftermath. Mark Treanor brilliantly captures the physical and emotional trauma of close combat while masterfully weaving in timeless lessons about leadership, courage and camaraderie. Simply put, this is as relevant to veterans today as it was in the '60s."

—**Lt. Gen F. C. Wilson, USMC (Ret.), 12th President, National Defense University**

A QUIET CADENCE

A NOVEL

Mark Treanor

NAVAL INSTITUTE PRESS
Annapolis, Maryland

This book has been brought to publication with the
generous assistance of Bill and Kay Valentino.

Naval Institute Press
291 Wood Road
Annapolis, MD 21402

Library of Congress Cataloging-in-Publication Data

Names: Treanor, Mark, date, author.
Title: A quiet cadence : a novel / Mark Treanor.
Description: Annapolis, Maryland : Naval Institute Press, [2020]
Identifiers: LCCN 2019056325 | ISBN 9781682475065 (hardcover ; alk. paper)
Subjects: LCSH: United States. Marine Corps—Fiction. | Marines—United States
    —Fiction. | Vietnam War, 1961–1975—Psychological aspects—Fiction. |
    Post-traumatic stress disorder—Fiction.
Classification: LCC PS3620.R4346 Q54 2020 | DDC 813/.6—dc23
LC record available at https://lccn.loc.gov/2019056325

♾ Print editions meet the requirements of ANSI/NISO z39.48-1992
(Permanence of Paper).
Printed in the United States of America.

28 27 26 25 24 23 22 21 20   9 8 7 6 5 4 3 2

This novel is dedicated to the veterans of all our wars and their families. They have given so much and asked so little.

Acknowledgments

A special thanks to Adm. James G. Stavridis, USN (Ret.), who believed in my manuscript and brought it to the attention of the Naval Institute Press; and to Bill and Kay Valentino, a Vietnam Marine CH-46 pilot and his wife, whose generous assistance helped bring this book to publication. During the writing of this book, I received helpful advice from fellow Vietnam veterans: Col. John McKay, USMC (Ret.), and his wife, Margo; Lt. Col. James McNeece, USMC (Ret.); Dave Warvel; Bill Jayne; and from my son, former Marine captain Adam Treanor.

Phyllis Brill read and typed more drafts than she'd like to remember, and Steve Brill, Vietnam vet and her husband, not only helped throughout that process, but also was often my personal IT guide. I would also like to thank the staff of the Naval Institute Press, particularly Rick Russell, Jim Dolbow, Rachel Crawford, Robin Noonan, and their staffs, and Ann Boyer, my copy editor.

Finally, and above all, a special thanks to my wife, Claire, reader, typist, and encourager. Writing can be a lonely and uncertain endeavor. With her at my side, I was never alone.

Though fueled by fact, this novel and the characters in it are fictional. Any errors in this book are mine alone.

1

SOMETIMES THE GHOSTS TALK to me still. Forty years ago, they came frequently; in my thirties and forties and fifties, not very much. They've visited some in recent years, and, mostly, that's okay.

The dream frightened me for a long time. I couldn't tell if my old friends accused me or wished me well. Sometimes they seemed to look to me for answers I've never had. I searched for a long time for a way to make peace with them and what I'd lost. My best friend and my wife helped me with that. Corrie lost a great deal more than I did in Vietnam, at least physically, yet helped me remember what was good. Patti lived with much of what I brought home and saved me more than once from the dark.

I've spoken very little of my war and the turmoil that followed, and over the years nearly no one has asked. Most men my age celebrate Woodstock and Haight Ashbury, reminisce about sit-ins on campuses or protests in the streets. They still marvel at their luck in the draft, or, depending on their audience, boast of or bury the deferments they received. My decile of the Sixties Generation grows old having said little to our children about times very different for us.

Recently though, even us old guys sometimes hear, "Thanks for your service." Sort of faint echoes of the well-deserved cheers greeting our troops coming home from our most recent wars. My guess is they'll find it difficult, too, to grapple with the truths they've learned. We have more in common than they may know.

I'd like my kids to understand the events that changed their old man forever when I wasn't much older than theirs are now. Sometimes I think they believe my memories of those charged days were surgically removed along with the bullet in my back. Not that I blame them; I haven't exactly encouraged questions about my war or its impact on me. But I remember it all, a gift and a curse. Remembrance across decades is like looking through a telescope; sometimes people and events in the distance come into the sharpest focus of all.

The pictures come to me in extraordinary detail, like photos my brain took but couldn't erase. Sometimes frayed at the edges with things in the middle I wish I'd never seen, though there are some photos I would not want to lose. I remember the odors, the heat and the wet, the exhaustion and fear. I can still taste the bite of gunpowder, the terrible ferric sweetness of blood. I can still hear the cacophonous noises, the voices, the argot, the silences; it's as though they're next to my ear. What a profane, crass gang we were.

I remember the pain and the joy when I returned to the World. The hopes and the nightmares. The shame of what I did to get my first job, the one I'll retire from soon.

I remember the love.

My family and friends know me as a man whose most violent moments generated fast tennis serves. How do I explain that when I was very young, I plumbed the depths of depravity without knowing if I'd find my way back to sanity's surface? I can describe the camaraderie of shared misery, but can I also relate the excitement, the pride, and the love without downplaying the horror and terror that nearly drove me mad? What about the craziness in the years after the war?

Patti thinks it's important that I tell the truth. She knows little of my story, but she's probably right. She's usually been.

I think it's time I tried. I know that too many men grow old basking in selective memories of their youth. But I don't believe much in glory, though I wouldn't trade anything for my time in the Corps.

Unless it was to save the forever young men who march front and center in my sleep.

That dream always begins in silence, an absolute vacuum of noise. Then only a faint, distant sound, the *whup-whup* and *thrum* of an approaching medevac bird. Quivering in the air, a muted tremor of cries. A shroud of gunpowder-infused fog covers all. Then my old friends emerge from the swirling pall and walk toward me, their eyes never leaving my face. They step to a cadence I sometimes strain to hear.

Lately, Pius John's spoken for all six of them. "Tell them now, Mick," he says. "Tell them the truth."

This, then, is their story, and mine.

It begins on the day I saw the dead man above the trees.

2

THE HELICOPTER ROARED AND squealed and shook as it flew. The ceiling of the CH-46 was open, a tangle of black wires and dull aluminum tubes glistening with a lubricious sheen. The chopper smelled of JP5 and hydraulic fluid and gunpowder. Brown splotches spread across the metal floor like the aftermath of a toxic spill. It was good that I didn't know then that blood stains metal. Every time we lurched, I grabbed the web seat I sat on, convinced we were falling out of the sky.

The door gunners leaned over their mounted .50-cals. and studied the rumpled patchwork quilt of rice paddies, tree lines, and hillocks unfolding fast below us. I wondered if they'd be able to spot anyone firing at us, certain that hordes of bloodthirsty, wiry brown men glared up at us with slanted, fanatical eyes. I wondered whether a bullet could penetrate the helicopter's floor.

Four of us were headed to the bush. Havey, Timmons, and I were new guys, in Vietnam five days, all of it behind wire. Lance Corporal Woodson was on his way back out to Bravo Company after R&R. None of us would complete a full thirteen-month tour.

Waiting on the airstrip, Woodson had tried to smile at us new guys. It looked like the effort made his face hurt. Even ragingly hung over, he was strikingly handsome. If it weren't for his faded uniform and beat-up gear, I might've guessed he was a movie star, part of a USO tour visiting the base for a few hours.

"How ya doin'?" I said.

Woody nodded very slowly, as though movement might cause a disaster inside his skull. "Wonderful." He tried again to smile, but all he produced were some crooked wrinkles around his lips and eyes. "Long as you've got your health," he said quietly. His eyes smiled at that. It didn't make sense to me, but I didn't ask.

I wondered if the crate of mortar rounds he sat on could explode. If we got rocketed, there wouldn't be enough left of him to fill a C-ration box. But then, I thought, standing beside him, if those rounds go up, there won't be enough left of me to make a bad impression. Welcome to war, I congratulated myself in an attempt to calm my nerves. Just like John Wayne or Gregory Peck, the stalwart who doesn't blink in the face of possible death.

It's amazing how foolish you can be when you're nineteen.

Havey was a black kid from Mississippi with a cherubic face and ears like ginger snaps glued to his head. He talked in such a falsetto, if you looked away you might imagine you were talking with a twelve-year-old girl. He was a nice guy, but I didn't trust him. He wanted to do the right thing but struggled to do about anything right. That could get someone else killed. His mother talked him into enlisting, signed the papers with him since he wasn't eighteen. She thought after the Marines, he wouldn't get picked on so much. I've wondered if she ever forgave herself.

Timmons was the sort who could be all by himself in a sound-proof room and still piss somebody off. He thought he was a tough guy, too cool to have much to do with another boot like me, though I was squared away and we were both PFCs. He joined the Marines because his girlfriend's old man had won the Navy Cross on Guadalcanal and owned a construction company now. Timmons planned to go home a hero, impress the father, marry the daughter, and take over the business. His attitude made me as nervous as Havey's ineptitude. A guy aiming to be a hero could get people around him killed. Given what he did after we went to the valley, I'm pretty sure Timmons' plans didn't work out.

The three of us had been sent together to Bravo Company's headquarters tent when we first got to Hoa Binh. First Sergeant Miller and his clerk were the only people who worked at the field desks under the baked canvas. The rest of the Company was out in the bush. They were always out in the bush. In front of the tent, a large wooden sign painted scarlet with a gold Marine Corps Eagle, Globe, and Anchor stenciled in each corner said

BUSH BRAVO
WE COUNT THE MEAT

"Welcome to Bravo Company, men," Top Miller greeted us. His salt-and-pepper flattop and deeply lined cheeks gave him a hard, no-nonsense look, but his eyes were kind. I thought of him, at the time, as a pretty old man. He was probably thirty-seven or -eight. The Top was a few months into his second tour in his second war. "You're joining the best rifle company in the Marine Corps. You've got a lot to live up to." He looked us each in the eye. "I'm sure you will."

I hoped he was right. But how could I know until I'd actually seen combat?

The clerk, a short-timer rifleman named Landau who stayed in the rear to help with paperwork after he got out of the hospital, didn't look up. A scar ran from his temple to his chin. He kept raising his hands high as he pecked two long, thin fingers at his typewriter keys. First Sergeant Miller said Landau would get us checked in. The Top smiled, actually looked pleased to have us with him.

"I'll see you men again before you go to the bush," he said. "Right now, the Company's in a pretty easy area. We haven't gotten any kills there, but haven't taken any casualties, either. That could change. It's gonna be hotter than a freshly fucked fox in a forest fire today, so drink lots of water. Welcome aboard."

After the Top left, Havey said, "I wondered 'bout the sign outside. What's it mean?"

Landau stopped typing, gave a single cock of his head as if to say, "Damndest thing I ever heard." He seemed to measure Havey, then looked at Timmons and me to see if we were screwing with him. I was pretty certain I understood the sign, but wasn't going to say anything. Timmons looked back at Landau with a grimace that mocked Havey and his naivete.

Landau apparently concluded that the new guy wasn't pulling his leg. "Body count," he said. "When Bravo finishes with the gooks, all that's left is dead meat. You'll see soon enough."

Havey's eyes looked like fried eggs gone bad in the middle. Timmons rolled his eyes and pooched out his lips as though the answer had been intuitively obvious. I didn't say anything.

It was silent in the tent for a couple minutes except for the clack of Landau's poking at the typewriter like a convulsive pianist. When he looked up, the sudden movement of his scarred face was like a light beam slashing through the tent. I wondered if I'd have scars like his before I was through. "You're all going to First Platoon," he said. "Gungiest platoon in the Company. *Dinky dau*, crazy, the whole bunch. McClure, you're going to be Lance Corporal Garafano's assistant gunner. He's the gungiest of them all." Landau shook his head as though amazed. "Loves to hunt gooks. Damn near died when he was wounded, still couldn't wait to get back to the bush." He added as though to assure me, "When the shit hits the fan, you'll be happy to have Garafano beside you."

Havey looked like he wasn't understanding half of what Landau said. Timmons grinned.

"In fact," Landau looked at all three of us, "when you guys go to the valley, you'll be damn lucky it's First Platoon you're with."

"Are we going for sure?" Timmons sounded like he couldn't wait. We'd already heard stories. Crawling with NVA; booby traps all over the place. Timmons, gonna be a hero and a construction tycoon.

"Top thinks so," Landau said. "Probably a few weeks from now." He grinned. "My ass will have skyed home by then."

"Garafano's last A-gunner rotate home recently?" I asked.

Landau looked at me like I'd sprouted a gargoyle on my neck. "He was killed last week."

———

Lieutenant Mangan sat in the dirt writing a letter. He had holes in his green T-shirt and a rip in one knee of his trousers. "Welcome back, Woody," he said. Woodson looked like someone was performing a root canal through the top of his skull.

"Swell to be back, Lieutenant."

"Let's hope we don't get hit tonight, looks like your head might explode."

Woody nodded slowly, as if moving faster might set something off between his ears.

The lieutenant put his writing gear in a plastic bag, then stood up. "Who's the 0331?"

"I am, sir," I said. "PFC McClure."

Mangan looked at me for a moment, sizing me up. He was twenty-two or twenty-three, but I thought of him as older, probably because he was an officer and I was a nineteen-year-old PFC. Probably, too, because his eyes conveyed a hard weariness that seemed much older than the rest of his sparsely stubbled face. "Good," he said. "We can use you."

He turned to Havey and Timmons. "You're both going to First Squad. I'll introduce you to Corporal Harding." He looked at Woody and pointed. "Landon's hole's over there." He smiled a little then. "You can get there on your own?"

"Sober as a judge, Lieutenant."

"You must have some bad judges in Delaware."

We walked behind where First Platoon was dug in along a third of the Company's perimeter. Beyond the hill, paddies crisscrossed by dikes and bordered by tree lines seemed to stretch on forever. The hilltop itself was a raw, muddy moonscape studded by torn boulders and pocked by deep fighting holes and shallow straddle trenches. It wasn't yet 8:00 a.m. but it had to be in the nineties. Mist rose in ghostly vapors from the baking mud. Down the hill, shredded shards of trees groped skyward like the wretches in despair on the cover of the Dante's *Inferno* I was supposed to read during my freshman semester at UVA. In the thick, wet air, I could smell napalm-charred wood. I wondered what the Top really meant by an easy area.

The lieutenant asked where we were from. When I said Towson, just outside Baltimore, he said, "Ever eat at Haussner's? I did a couple times when I was at Annapolis. Great chow."

"Yes, sir. Amazing desserts." I thought of asking if he'd made it to any Orioles or Colts games when he was at Navy, but he didn't really seem interested in small talk.

Corporal Harding shook hands with each of us but didn't smile until the lieutenant asked, "How's your wife doing?"

Harding broke into a wide grin then. "Great, Lieutenant." He scratched at a fester of gook sores on his arm below a brightly colored Eagle, Globe, and Anchor tattoo. The sores looked like leprosy to me.

"Not long now."

"Just a few weeks, sir. I'm betting he's a boy."

"Any new pictures?"

Corporal Harding glanced at the three of us. He grinned again at the lieutenant. "Not in her condition, sir. Not that I'm sharing anymore." I found out later his wife used to send him polaroid nudies of herself. She had an EGA tattoo like his, too.

"Don't blame you for that." The Lieutenant's smile faded. "I'll leave you with your new people." He pointed. "Havey and Timmons, right?"

"Yes, sir," Havey said. Corporal Harding cocked his head like a Doberman trying to figure out where the squeak came from in a new toy.

"Right, Lieutenant," Timmons said.

Harding pivoted toward him. "That's 'Yes sir, Lieutenant.' Got it, Marine?" I half expected him to get right up in Timmons' face. I wondered if he'd been a DI before Vietnam.

"Yes, sir." Timmons didn't sound like he was trying to be cool then.

"Let's go, McClure. Find the Pope." I had no idea what the lieutenant meant by that, but I wasn't about to ask.

We approached a fighting hole where a thickset, muscular Marine sat in the mud on a tattered piece of cardboard, an M60 machine gun beside him. He had a stubble of dark hair, a couple days' heavy growth of beard, and a thick, drooping mustache. He wore only scarred, filthy boots and faded tiger-striped shorts. Dog tags, a rosary, and a crusty green towel hung around his neck. He was sunburned a deep bronze, except for the pink scar-ropes crisscrossing his chest like ritual markings on an aborigine warrior. He was watching a can of franks and beans bubble over a flaming chunk of plastic explosive.

My god, I thought. Garafano even looks like a barbarian. What the hell am I in for now?

"Hey, Pope," the lieutenant called.

Garafano looked up and smiled. His eyes looked genuinely happy. "Hey, Lieutenant. Sorry for not standing. Can't knock over the feast." He pointed to the steaming can.

Lieutenant Mangan waved off the comment. "Lance Corporal Garafano, meet PFC McClure, your new A-gunner."

Garafano reached up a sinewy, thick arm encrusted with runny sores and swallowed my hand in his. "Welcome to shit city," he said with a grin.

3

PIUS JOHN GARAFANO WAS HIS real name. "My mom named me after a couple popes. I come from a pretty religious family," he said with a look that indicated he might be telling an inside joke. "When my dad had cancer my senior year in high school, I promised God that if He'd cure him, I'd become a priest. Prayed my ass off. Didn't work worth a damn. But I entered the seminary anyway. Lasted a year, then joined the Marines." John grinned like he'd played a pretty funny joke on himself.

He wiped the crusty green towel over his head and chest. The rosary around his neck caught in the threads. John untangled the beads and looked at the crucifix. "Who knows, things change. I could go back. Did you know Ignatius of Loyola was one hard-ass officer in the Spanish army before he became a priest and founded the Jesuits?"

I didn't.

John grinned again. He had terrible breath. "The Corps and the Jebbies have a lot in common—self-sacrifice, service to the down-trodden and oppressed." He looked out over the rice paddies beyond the hill. "Lots of those around here." He absently rubbed his finger-tips across the raised scars on his chest like strumming a ukulele. I'd half expected a wild-eyed killer; he sounded more like a social worker. Even now, all these years later, despite what we did in the valley, I think he might've been a fine priest, or anything else that involved sacrificing for other people.

We turned two ammunition cans upside down on a sleeve of C-ration cardboard and put the machine gun in front of us on another piece, then sat in the broiling sun talking and cleaning the gun. John's clothing and boots and gear were faded and worn. I looked like I'd bought up every new sale item in an army-navy surplus store. I envied his dark Italian skin. I had the Irish McClure clan complexion, arms a boiled-lobster red and my face the texture of a deeply embarrassed birch tree. John had been in-country four and a half months, counting the four weeks he spent in Japan recuperating from wounds.

He was inspecting the bolt and operating rod when he asked if I'd brought a toothbrush.

"Sure," I said.

"Two?"

"Just one."

"That'll do!" He looked as though he were about to unwrap a birthday present. "Man, that's great. I had two but lost the one I used on the gun a few days ago, so the teeth lost out again. We can share yours until more come in a supply pack." Under the ammo can, the cardboard made a mucky, farting sound in the mud as he bounced up and down.

He wasn't kidding. For the next four days, we used his toothbrush to clean our weapons and mine on our teeth.

It turned out we had a lot in common. Catholic high schools, sports, altar boys when we were little, Boy Scouts—neither of us made Eagle. John had to cut back on everything except football to help his mother and sisters when his father was sick. I'd dropped out because with football and lacrosse, student council, a job in an auto body shop on weekends. and plenty of parties, something had to give. "Camping out with a bunch of guys in uniforms on weekends came in low on my list of fun things to do," I said.

John laughed, "Guess you got over that."

John's dad had been a Marine in World War II. After John decided to leave the seminary, enlisting seemed like the right thing to do. My dad had been on a cruiser during the battle for Okinawa. He didn't talk much about it, but always said the Marines were the bravest men he ever knew. I believed America was doing the right thing in Vietnam. Fighting the spread of international communism. Domino theory and all that. As a college freshman in 1968, I hated hearing classmates brag they'd get deferments until the war was over, or forever, whichever came first. My country was at war; shouldn't I do my part?

I stewed about that over Christmas vacation, though I didn't say anything to my parents. Back in Charlottesville in January, I bungled my way through exams. A week later, I dropped out and enlisted.

I hitchhiked home to Towson to tell Mom and Dad.

"Jesus, Mary, and Joseph!" Mom yelled. A small woman, slim with dark brown hair, she came up out of her chair like a sparrow puffed up for a fight. "You must be kidding me!"

Dad sat forward in his chair. "No, Marty, you didn't. You're smarter than that."

"Tell me your father's right, Marty. You didn't, and this is not one damn bit funny."

I picked up the burning cigarette Mom had dropped on the braided rug and handed it to her. "No, Ma, I did."

"Don't 'Ma' me." She took a deep drag on the cigarette. I looked down at the new burn on the rug.

"I know you've both worked hard to send me to college."

"My good God!" Mom said.

"But there's a war on. I thought you'd be proud. At least Dad would." I looked toward him for support. His eyes looked like he'd been stripped to be flogged.

"Can't you wait until you graduate? Then if you want to go into the service, you can do it as an officer."

"I already enlisted, Dad. I go to Parris Island on the seventeenth."

Dad sagged as though the air had been sucked out of his slender frame. "I was afraid you'd come home to tell us you got some girl in a family way. That would've been bad enough. But drop out of Virginia to go to Vietnam . . ." He'd not gotten to go to college, had worked at Bethlehem Steel over twenty years.

"There's a war on." Mom sounded like she was mocking me. "And my only child wants to go fight it? Jesus, Mary, and Joseph." She walked out of the room fast—I supposed to go cry.

Dad lit another cigarette and sat studying the floor as if something there might tell him how I, or maybe he, could've gone so wrong.

"They calmed down in a day or so," I told John. "But it got pretty tense before I left. I don't know what was worse, Mom yelling or crying, or Dad looking like he might."

John laughed, "You got off easy. Pasta Mama threw a bowl at me. She never calmed down. My sisters had to keep her from killing me before I could come here." He looked serous for a minute. "What we do to our mothers," he said.

John talked about life in the bush. Patrol formations, where the lieutenant wanted the gun teams for ambushes, assaults, interlocking defensive fires at night, and for when we searched villes. "Not much happening around here," he said. "No contact in days." He sounded like he was being deprived.

We were almost finished cleaning the gun when John glanced around at the Marines on our side of the hill. He looked as though he were about to welcome me into his secret club. "You're gonna love these guys. The Skipper calls First Platoon 'the frat house.'" He bent over the M60 again and began to spread viscous white lubricating fluid across the feed pall. "Most educated infantry platoon in the Marine Corps, he says. A year of college, sort of, for me. Doc Matheson has two years, an associate's degree. Corrigan actually has his bachelor's. Gio named him 'the Professor.' Now we get a semester from you. These guys have balls, too. Most of them."

"Why isn't Corrigan an officer?"

"He got his draft notice, so he enlisted in the Marines. They tried to get him to sign up for OCS, but he didn't want to do more than two years. Going to law school when he gets out. Figured he'd be safer with Marines than going to war with a bunch of draftees. Smart man, the Professor."

I couldn't tell if John meant that or not.

"'Course, they're not all like that," he said. "We've got plenty of guys my mother would say are from way across the wrong side of the tracks." He cocked his head. "I guess there's tracks farther out than the ones we lived across." John looked directly at me for a moment, then gazed away, a suddenly contemplative look on his face. "It's an interesting thing," he said, "being in the bush, doing what we do." He hesitated. "Or maybe I should say, have done to us. You can lose your bearings, if you're not careful."

The former seminarian seemed to be talking about a moral compass of some kind, but I wasn't sure what he meant. I waited for him to go on.

"Sometimes it takes real courage to make the right choices out here. I'm not talking just physical courage. I mean not letting the darkness that can get inside you take over." For a moment, John looked like he was studying some pattern in the mud to the side of the gun.

It would be a long time before I truly understood what John was talking about—the choices you make at the margins, some might even say at the far edges of sanity. And what I learned then has amazed me the rest of my life.

An explosion suddenly erupted from the hill to our east, the noise rushing at us a sodden roar, as though sound waves had been wrenched from the mud and hurled through the thick air.

I bolted upright, looked around frantically, then tried to hold absolutely still, anxious, embarrassed, waiting for John to react. He gestured for me to hand him a belt of rounds from the top of another ammo can, slid the M60's bolt home, then wiped his lubricant-shiny fingers on his shorts. "Let's go see what's up." I thought I saw concern in his eyes.

A South Vietnamese Army company had been encamped on the lower hill a quarter-mile away until earlier that morning. Marines milled around behind First Platoon's sector of the line staring toward the hill like they were waiting for a demolition derby's next blast of cars around the third turn.

John put his hand on a man's shoulder. Virgil Landon turned around. He had a mouse face—round cheeks, bright brown eyes, a sharp nose, and oversized yellow front teeth. A wispy brown mustache curled down past his upper lip. "How you doing, Gnat's Nuts?" John said. "What's up?"

Landon didn't say anything, just nodded and smiled as though he'd just been blessed. He'd never fired a rifle before boot camp, but was the best marksman in the platoon. "Shoot the nuts off a gnat from five hundred yards in the offhand position," Gianelli claimed. Landon rarely spoke. He seemed frightened of words, as though a teacher had ridiculed something he'd recited in class and he'd been reluctant to speak ever since.

"Holiness!" A scrawny kid held up his hand.

John slapped him five. "*Que pasa*, Rudolpho?"

"Booby trap, man. Gooners doin' gooners. That's the best." He did a sort of little jig. Everything about him was purple, the granny glasses perched on his blade-thin nose, the cheap stone in the silver ring on one hand, the veins that throbbed at his temples and stuck out beneath the baked tan all along his ropey arms and down his legs and under the gooey, crusty sores on his shins.

"This is our big bang man," John said. "Rudy Gianelli would stand in a long line to see something blow up. Meet Marty McClure, our newest gunner. Gio's our other gunner. Cavett there's his A-gunner."

"Welcome to the armpit of the world," Cavett said. He had a sour expression on his face. He was a short, densely muscled fireplug with a pocked face, drooping brown mustache, and a skull on his upper arm with the words "Death Before Dishonor" tattooed under it.

Gianelli stuck out his hand. "I am an artist, my man. I have a deeper appreciation for explosive things than the rest of these savages."

Corporal Harding shook his head as though he were dealing with a kid who couldn't help himself. "A fucking con artist. What're you going to do when you get back to the World, Gianelli? Blow something up each week, just to hear the bang?" He looked at John. "That was pretty big."

Pius John nodded, clearly disgusted. "Could be villagers scrounging up there. Women or kids might've triggered it." He said villagers often searched for food or anything else they could use after Marines or ARVN units left an area.

"The ARVN made their hat this morning," Harding said.

"Bastards probably booby-trapped their trash." John was angry. "They don't give a damn that booby traps can't tell the difference between VC and civilians."

"Civilians?" Cavett looked like John had just said "priest" when he should've said "prostitute." "What the fuck, Garafano? There's no such thing."

I wondered if this was some of the darkness John had started to talk about.

"Bullshit, Cavett." John shook his head. "Villagers just want to live in peace. That's why we're here, remember?"

"Thanks for explaining that to me. I've been wondering why Lyndon Baines sent my ass here to get shot at while they sit out there hoeing their rice, not giving a shit if we get blown away. Civilians, my ass."

"The mothers and kids we see in the villes, Cavett. The old people. They just get caught up in the war."

"Shit." Cavett waved a thick arm dismissively. "The women and their little bastards and the old half-dead ones set booby traps themselves. Those that don't never warn us where they are, even though they fucking well know. I got no sympathy for 'em, man. I am too short for this shit."

"You're full of shit's right." Harding looked at me and shook his head. "Cavett's got so much time left, he almost makes you look short, McClure."

"One hundred seven and counting, people. Eat your hearts out." Cavett glowered.

Gianelli pulled his purple granny glasses down toward the tip of his nose and frowned over the rims. "Cavett, I've had these socks on longer'n that." He pushed his glasses back up and studied the far hill.

Three more Marines walked over to us. Woodson raised a hand to greet the rest of us, but didn't say anything. It looked like he still couldn't stand even the sound of his own voice. John introduced the giant beside Woody as Lance Corporal Jackson, the Third Squad leader. He walked with a long, rolling stride, like a beardless Paul Bunyan who'd spent years at sea. He and Woody had been best friends since kindergarten. Against all kinds of odds, they'd ended up in the same rifle platoon in-country. "Mike Jackson, Seaford, Delaware," he said.

I felt like I had to crane my neck back to look up at him. "Marty McClure, Towson, Maryland."

"Nearly neighbors." Jackson grinned. He had stubble like wall-to-wall carpet, and mischievous eyes, like a giant looking to play or for trouble—or who might think they were one and the same.

The third Marine, Cloninger, was short and wiry with a beak for a nose, a long scrawny neck, and dark, bulging eyes. He had a dog-eared paperback dictionary tucked into the waistband of his shorts.

"How's it hanging, Buzzard?" Gianelli said.

"Elegant." Cloninger grinned. He had snaggled, chipped teeth.

"Getting through the *E*s, Buzz?" John asked.

Cloninger spit a stream of tobacco juice. "Exactly," he said with a straight face.

He told me later he'd been given a choice of enlisting in the Marines or being tried for manslaughter after he'd knocked into a coma a guy who'd insulted his girl. The guy was really big and blonde and full of himself and had called Laura ugly, so the Buzz hit him in the face with a chair. Kicking Blondie in the balls first had helped. Cloninger visited him in the hospital before he shipped out for Vietnam; it'd seemed like the Christian thing to do. Blondie was still in a coma. He didn't move when the Buzz tickled his feet.

"Decent time on R&R, Woody?" John asked.

"The best, Pope." Woodson looked like the grin on his face hurt the inside of his head. "Screwed, blewed, and tattooed. And here I am with nothin' left but double digits." He cocked his head mockingly at Cavett, moving slowly as he did. Cavett glowered but appeared to think better of whatever he was going to say.

An enormous explosion bellowed from the lower hill. The surge of sound rolled over us like a squall.

Cavett dropped to the ground. All around me, people swore or yelled, then there was one collective startled gasp of amazement as the noise crested and we saw a man fly straight up in the air thirty or forty feet above the tops of the trees on the far hill.

The body hung at the apogee of its climb, spinning lazily, arms and legs akimbo, a black-clad pinwheel turning against a thin blue sky. The thunderous roar of the explosion still echoed around us as the man folded into himself, fingers reached up to toes, head tucked to chest, a graceful, swift, unhurried movement, like an Olympic diver performing an inverse jackknife. Then, still in its tuck, the corpse plummeted to the earth through a filthy gray cloud of smoke and dirt and debris billowing up above the tree tops.

Gianelli stripped off his sunglasses as though he expected to get a clearer look. "Holy shit! Seven-point-three for technical merit."

"Nine-point-oh for difficulty," Corporal Harding added in an awestruck voice. "Damn."

"Tommy, did you see that?" Jackson exclaimed. "Whoee, that boy could dunk."

Woodson was bent double at the waist, hands clamped over his ears. He rocked side to side as though trying to stifle clamoring cymbals inside his skull. "Aaaah, aaaah, aaaah," he murmured. I couldn't tell if he was moaning or laughing.

John frowned toward the distant hill, his eyes shifting from the tree line toward the point in the air where the body had stopped flying upward. "Satchel charge," he said. "Too big for anything else." He shook his head. "Bastards."

"What a waste." Corporal Harding looked offended. I wondered if he was talking about the man, or the satchel charge.

Marines continued to stare as though they expected an instant replay, some confirmation that what we saw had actually happened. I was glad no one was looking at me, watching to see how the new guy reacted. I'm sure I gaped slack-jawed, astonished by what I'd seen.

"Well, it wasn't one of us," Corporal Harding said. "That's a good thing."

"Might've been some VC that didn't get the word from one of his pals that set it." Jackson sounded like he was trying to convince himself, without much hope of success. "You'd have to love that idea."

"Gooners doing gooners. Couldn't get enough of that," Gianelli agreed. He and Jackson exchanged unenthusiastic high fives.

John shook his head. "That would be cool, but not likely. The ARVN probably mined the trash, and that guy up there . . ." he raised his head toward the sky above the far hill, "was probably just a farmer."

"Fucking gooks," Cavett said. "One less to worry about."

Cloninger nodded. "Extensive number left."

I felt a strange constriction in my chest. I'd never seen anyone die before. The man in the air had been close enough to see clearly, but far enough away that I felt detached from his death. I wondered whether he'd been an enemy or one of the people we were there to help. If he'd been a Viet Cong, I supposed I should feel good seeing him die. But if he wasn't, if he was just a farmer like John said, what was I supposed to think of that?

And what was with people's reactions? John seemed to be the only one who was really bothered. The others seemed not to care that a man who was probably an innocent had just met a violent death. Was this the darkness John had been talking about? What kind of people was I going to be dealing with for the next thirteen months?

And me? Part of me knew I was supposed to feel worse than I did. But it'd been fascinating, surreal, to see him fly above the trees. People laughed, and I'd laughed at what they said. Seven-point-three for technical merit; nine-point-oh for difficulty. That boy can dunk. Why'd I been so fascinated instead of upset? The old Irish Catholic guilt kicked in with that thought. I pushed it away. I hadn't actually enjoyed seeing him, I told myself, I was just amazed.

I couldn't foresee there'd come a time when I'd arrive at a much darker place.

4

THE VILLAGE CONSISTED OF a dozen hootches in an area the size of a circus tent. A central path ran the length of the ville and a couple smaller trails led through bamboo and palm thickets to surrounding paddies and fields. I felt like a little kid walking for the first time into an ominous, rank, and bedraggled big top not knowing if the big cats were loose or caged. Thatched huts, thick stands of bamboo, women and kids in the shadows, animals stirring in pens. Where would I take cover if we took fire? Where might it come from if we did?

My first patrol shouldn't be a big deal, John had said yesterday. The villagers in the area weren't openly hostile, and in the past couple weeks, few VC had been spotted.

"We'll still be damn careful," he said. "Never can be sure somebody hasn't planted a booby trap where we're likely to walk, or that a couple gooks aren't going to take shots at us, then make their hat before the lieutenant can bring supporting fires down on them." John grinned like TR talking about San Juan Hill. "We'll be careful, and we'll be fine."

He meant I'd be fine. "Looking forward to it," I said. I didn't want him to think I was nervous. I thought I hid it pretty well. Nineteen and bulletproof—bad stuff happens to other people. I was actually looking forward to my first firefight, my first test in the big leagues. I admitted to myself that if it could be pretty small, though, that would be good.

Alongside a pathway into the ville, a water buffalo half the size of a pickup truck watched us with rheumy eyes from inside a flimsy, three-rail, bamboo pen. I wondered if an M16 could stop something that big. Further down the tree line, piglets rooted at the engorged teats of a filth-smeared, fly-covered sow. The sharp stench of rot and manure assaulted my nose and mouth. As the squad ahead of us moved into the ville, the water bull bawled a sudden, despondent moan that ratcheted up my apprehension like the here-it-comes music in a scary movie. I gripped my rifle even tighter than before, my finger taut above the trigger, my thumb pressed against the safety. Was he going to attack? Had he alerted men who would? The animal glared at me as we passed by.

Focus, McClure. Worry about VC, numbskull, not animals.

I heard my first cackle of high-pitched, sing-song chatter as women and kids scurried toward their hootches. Outside one home, two young women squatted alongside three toddlers watching an older woman examine one kid's foot. He cried softly. The babies were naked from the waist down. The two young women had ebony hair and faces like calfskin; they were barefoot and wore form-less baggy black shirts and pants. When they saw us, the women grabbed the kids and, with a burst of excited chatter, disappeared into their hootches. The air around the thatched huts was tainted with the sweet-sour smell of damp thatch and the pungent odor of fermenting fish.

I saw no men in the ville, except for one ancient papa-san, gnarled and bent with coarse gray hair, a wispy mustache, and a goatee of long, silver strands. His skin looked like brown wrapping paper balled up and smoothed out a hundred times. He leaned with both hands on a twisted stick, shuffling about without apparent purpose. An old woman, her face like corrugated leather stitched around deep-set black eyes and a few betel-nut-blackened teeth, grabbed his arm, sputtering at him vehemently. He shook his head and said something. She walked slowly to her hootch, then squatted in the doorway, her knees nearly as high as her chin. She reminded me of the old black women with sunken faces and stooped shoulders we'd brought Thanksgiving baskets to in student council. I felt sorry for her.

I followed John toward the field at the far end of the ville, where we'd provide security for the search. I smiled at the old woman. She looked past me. The old man looked like a bewildered gray heron trying to lift an arthritic neck to focus beyond where we were going.

John scoped the far side of the field. He'd bought binoculars in Japan when he was recuperating from his wounds. He was the only enlisted man in the platoon with a laminated tactical map, too. "I'll keep an eye out," he said, "if you want to watch what's going on in the ville."

The search appeared methodical and businesslike, as though both Marines and villagers had been through the drill many times. The mama-sans and their children squatted or paced in front of their homes. Marines stabbed thatched walls and roofs with rifle muzzles and bayonets, shook out clay pots, pulled aside reed sleeping mats to search for bunkers of weapons or explosives or medical supplies. Staff Sergeant Gilles moved hootch to hootch, watching the search, his shotgun crooked in his arm like the trustee for a docile chain gang. The platoon sergeant reminded me of a panther, all sinew and smooth movement, except for a slight bounce when he walked. His skin was so black, it seemed to have a purple sheen. He had nine brass tacks in the butt of his twelve gauge. His older brother had been killed at Hue the year before; Gilles wanted revenge. I figured if he didn't have the shotgun at the ready, there wasn't much chance anything bad was going to happen in the ville.

Two women with a pair of infants and a young boy squatted in front of the closest hootch. I could never tell how old the women were in Vietnam. Most seemed to be olive-skinned girls in their teens or early twenties, or weathered, wrinkled women of indecipherable age, someplace between thirty and sixty. These two might have been mother and daughter. They both had babies at their breasts. The young girl had rounded features and smooth skin and didn't look more than sixteen; the other was wrinkled and dusty and dried up.

I'd never seen women nursing before. I stared at the young mother's small, full breasts. When she switched the baby from one to the other I could see her nipple glisten wet. I caught my breath and then was instantly embarrassed and hoped John hadn't heard me. I focused quickly on the older woman. There was nothing to excite me there. I wondered if the fuzzy-headed infant sucking desperately at the leather pouch of her breast was likely to starve. I felt like I'd walked into the pages of a *National Geographic* magazine.

Between the two women, a little boy squatted naked in the dirt. He was cute, copper skinned with a shock of black hair and wide, dark eyes. Staff Sergeant Gilles squatted beside him, tousled his hair, and talked softly to him. The little boy watched him warily but didn't shrink from his touch. His mother or sister, I wasn't sure which, kept her eyes on the ground and kept nursing her infant. Sergeant Gilles looked up from the toddler once and smiled at her. He didn't look at her breasts.

I felt sorry for the little boy and the two women with their babies as I watched Marines search their home. A couple of them leered hungrily at the younger woman and exchanged comments with each other I couldn't hear.

Farther down the path, Doc Matheson knelt on the ground examining a cut on another toddler's foot. Three mama-sans squatted around the corpsman and the crying child, the women chittering a backup chorus of praise or lament to Matt's rhythmic bass, "It's okay, baby, it's okay." I hoped all the villagers understood we were there to help them.

The search turned up nothing. Lieutenant Mangan kept lookouts in place and gave the rest of the platoon fifteen minutes to relax. "Stay with the gun a minute," John said.

He handed the two nursing women and the little boy squatting between them discs of C-ration chocolate. The women looked at John as they took the candy, but neither smiled.

A blurb of chocolate drool ran down the boy's chin, but his blank expression never changed, even when John gently stroked his head. He reminded me of my cousin's two-year-old; how he stared at you sometimes like he couldn't figure you out when you handed him a toy.

They might live in thatched huts and nurse their kids in public, but they're probably not really much different from us, I thought as another woman walked out of her hootch and stepped off to the side of the path. She pulled one leg of her shorts aside, squatted and peed a stream in the dirt. *Well*, I said to myself, *there are a few other differences, too.*

"Where're the men?" I asked when John came back.

"Probably a couple off in the fields," he said. "Tending the rice. Mostly older ones." He shrugged. "Maybe some younger ones are farmers, too. But some are probably fighting us. Some may've been killed by the VC for not siding with them. We've probably killed some who did. A lot neither side's killed by now are VC."

"What's that make these women?" I thought of Cavett yesterday arguing there was no such thing as civilians.

"Caught in the middle. Not real happy with us." John ran the swatch of crusty green towel around his head and face.

"What does that mean? Do they set booby traps?" I looked over at the women again, wondering if I should feel sorry for them anymore.

"Not much around here. Marine units move through here often enough that most villagers don't want any problems with us. Mostly, they just tend the rice and the kids, wait for their men to sneak back once in a while."

"So how do you tell the good villagers from the bad?"

John shook his head. "You can't always."

"Then why'd you give them candy?"

John shrugged and smiled. He pulled his kabar out of its sheath and examined the blade; he kept it honed like a razor. "Women, kids," he said, as though that explained it all. He began to scrape the dirt from under his fingernails with the tip of the knife. "Maybe if we treat them decently, keep the real bad guys away, they'll have some peace for a change and remember it was us, not the VC, who helped them." He smiled. "One way or the other, they're human beings, like us."

"But what about their VC husbands?"

John surprised me. "Some of them might be decent people too. Their leaders sure aren't, but I'd guess a lot of them are kind of like us. Just doing what they believe they ought to do."

Behind us, Staff Sergeant Gilles suddenly bellowed. "What the fuck you mean you forgot, Willis?" Every cord and vein in the platoon sergeant's face strained as he got up close to the heavyset Marine's nose.

Willie gaped at him. He was like a big old dog that thinks even slower than he moves and just wants to be near you and have you say something nice to him once in a while. A Vermont farm boy, Willie was more comfortable around cows than people. Cows didn't cuss him out when he messed up or make fun of him when he said or did something stupid, and Willie did that a lot. He always got upset at himself then, but I only remember him being angry about someone calling him on it once, much later, after he announced he was going to marry a whore.

"You get that fucking can back, Willis, you read me?"

Willie nodded, but said, "I didn't want no ham and fuckers anyhow, Sergeant Gilles."

"I don't fucking give a rat's ass if you feed every kid in this entire fucking country, Willis! But don't leave the goddamn can so his mama can stuff a fucking grenade inside it with the pin pulled and a trip wire tied to it."

Understanding began to spread across Willie's broad face. "I forgot . . ." he said slowly.

"Some Marine gets his fucking leg blowed off, you'll fucking wish you didn't fucking forget, Willis. Get the fucking can back, got it?"

Beside me, Corrigan chuckled. "Gotta love the sarge. Everything but a gerund." I laughed, but realized, too, that the platoon sergeant didn't believe these women were friendly.

"Yes, sir," Willie muttered, his head lowered, only his eyes raised to watch as Gilles turned and glared toward the group of us.

"Old Willie doesn't keep his shit together," Woody said, "the lieutenant's not going to let him go on R&R in a few weeks."

"That dude gets to a whorehouse in Bangkok, he won't know whether to shit or go blind." Prevas had really long arms and legs. Sitting there with his knees up in the air, I could see why Gio called him the Grasshopper. "Willie may not leave anything for the rest of us," he said.

The platoon began to get ready to move out. I picked up my rifle and hefted the can of machine gun ammo. The sunlight was so intense it seemed to bounce back off the stubbled, cracked earth where we were heading next. It made the clumps of trees along the way shimmer and pulse.

Suddenly a small stand of bamboo forty yards beyond us burst open and a man sprinted toward the trees further out.

I was closest to him. I just gaped.

Legs high, driving, kicking up spurts of dirt as he ran. Like a barefoot hurdler in black pants and flaxen shirt.

"Get him!"

"Kill him!"

"Shoot, McClure, shoot!"

Before I could even bring my rifle up, Landon pushed past me and fired twice, *pap-pap*.

The man pitched forward on his face.

Gnat's Nuts lowered his rifle, turned toward me, and shrugged. "Snooze," he said.

Gianelli slapped me on the shoulder. "Snooze, you lose." He looked toward the body. "Pow-pow, motherfucker! Nobody tell you it's walk don't run to the nearest exit?"

"Decent shots, Virgil," Pius John said. "Dead center."

Landon looked like a fourth grader whose favorite teacher just gave him an A.

Around us, a chorus began.

"Good shootin', Landon."

"Nice shot, Gnat's Nuts."

"Jesus, McClure."

"Hey, McClure, you get buck fever?" Timmons yelled. Why the hell was another new guy picking on me for a mistake? I wanted to punch him in the face but was too embarrassed to say anything.

Lieutenant Mangan looked like it was all he could do to keep from beating the ground with his rifle. "Knock off the grab-ass, people!" he roared. "Sergeant Gilles, get security set up again! Take a team and check where he came from." He spun back toward the village. "Squad leaders! I want this goddamned ville searched again. And I mean you check every fucking clump of bushes, people. Every fucking clump!"

He whirled toward me, so close I could smell the weeks of filth and sweat in his clothing. "Pay attention, McClure. You hesitate, Marines get killed. Talk to him, Garafano." The lieutenant turned away, yelling for his radioman.

In the ville, the old papa-san swayed on his crooked stick. He stared past us while the old mama-san chattered and pulled at his shirt. The women and kids had vanished.

Pius John put an arm around my shoulders, gave me an encouraging tug. "You're okay," he said. "It takes a while to get the reactions down. The lieutenant knows that; he just doesn't like surprises."

I shrugged his arm away. It was bad enough that I was a screwup; I didn't want anyone thinking I needed comforting, too. What the fuck was that man doing in the bushes? Why didn't any of the women warn us? Why didn't I shoot him when people yelled at me to?

The lieutenant and Smitty, his radioman, and Woody's fire team walked toward the man lying in the dirt. The lieutenant and Smitty had their rifles trained on him.

"Let's go have a look," John said.

The lieutenant rolled the man over with his foot.

When we got there, the dead man stared up at me with eyes already gone glassy. He was twenty-five or thirty-five or forty-five, I couldn't tell. Shiny black hair fell over his forehead toward pencil-thin eyebrows. His thin black mustache and goatee surrounded tobacco-stained buck teeth. His mouth was slightly open, lips drawn back in a grimace, as though he'd felt something very painful just before he could ask the question that seemed half-formed in his shocked expression.

I stared at his face for a long time. Then I looked down across his body. His callused feet looked strangely relaxed, as though he'd just settled down for a nap. His shirt was plastered to his middle by bright red blood. The dirt that clung to him when the lieutenant rolled him onto his back was now maroon mud.

Lieutenant Mangan said, "No weapon, Landon?"

Gnat's Nuts shook his head. "Jack rabbit."

"That's right, Lieutenant," Woody came to Landon's defense. "Not even time to yell *lai dai*, sir. That son-of-a-bitch skyed out for a big man's ass."

The lieutenant bent down and ripped the shirt from the corpse's shoulder.

"Shit, Lieutenant, that's a goddamn gook if there ever was one." Woody sounded as though he couldn't believe he had to explain the facts to the officer. "Look at the strap marks." The man's shoulders were chafed and calloused; he'd spent a lot of time carrying a heavy pack recently. "There's probably a whole shitload of ammo or explosives hidden around here. Fucker should've stopped running if he wasn't a gook."

"Ease up, Woodson. I know he's a goddamn gook." Lieutenant Mangan turned to his radioman. Smitty stood at the dead man's head looking down into his face as though he were waiting for the corpse to ask him a question. "Call it in," the lieutenant said. "One confirm."

I stared at the man's face. My God, you die fast, I thought. Two holes in the belly, and you're dead before you hit the ground. Why the hell were you here? Setting booby traps, scoping out ambush sites? Maybe he was related to one of the villagers. A VC. Damn good we'd killed him, I thought. I wondered if he could've been the father of one of the toddlers I'd watched.

The dead man looked angry and puzzled, as though he wanted to ask, *Why? How did this happen?* As though he'd tried very hard to do something right and just found out he'd blown it all with just one mistake he didn't quite understand and didn't quite believe was his fault. My mistake was embarrassing. His killed him.

I looked over at Smitty. He'd just finished calling in the sitrep. He dropped the handset into his flak jacket pocket, shrugged to adjust the radio on his back, and took a pack of Kools out of a plastic case. He held them out. I shook my head. I wanted to say, *Thanks, I don't smoke*, but my mouth was so dry I couldn't make words.

"You okay?" he said. He lit his cigarette.

I nodded. I really wasn't. I'd screwed up not shooting, and now I felt sick looking at my first bloody corpse. I'd never seen a dead person up close before, except once at a wake for a high school friend's grandfather—a little, ancient man, waxy and powdered and rouge-cheeked in a velvet-lined, walnut box. Worse, I'd let everyone down, including myself, and I didn't know why. Smitty flicked out the match and let it drop. It landed on the dead man's face beside his nose, just beneath one of his wide-open eyes. A wisp of smoke curled up past his eyebrows and disappeared. Smitty didn't notice.

I felt the bile rise in my throat. I was afraid I'd lose everything in me right there, in front of everyone.

I choked it down and stood looking at the ground beside the corpse. When I looked up again, Smitty was watching me. I couldn't tell whether he was angry or puzzled. He took a deep drag on his cigarette, looked down at the dead man, then back again at me. Finally, he blew out a stream of mentholated smoke and spoke in a matter-of-fact voice.

"Don't worry 'bout it, McClure. Everybody feels the way you do the first time they look at dead gooks." Smith took another drag on his cigarette. He paused, and the silence between us seemed to contain a search for some truth. "You see some dead Marines, you'll get so you love seeing dead gooks."

I didn't believe him at the time.

5

WE SAW NO ONE TO SHOOT AT FOR two weeks after Landon killed the running man. We patrolled a part of Bravo's area of operations on most days. For eight or ten or fifteen hours, we walked in baked slow-motion, inhaling boiled air and sucking fetid, halazone-laced water from sun-poached canteens. We searched the broad rice paddies and the small villes for several clicks around the hill, sometimes staying out all night, lying in ambush near trail crossings where enemy troops might travel. On nights we were out, I got no sleep, though no one triggered our ambushes. On other nights, it was two hours on watch in the hole; two hours on my air mattress—we called them rubber ladies—two on, two off, all night long.

For several days, I beat myself up about freezing. What if I panicked whenever the shit hit the fan? Maybe I wasn't cut out to be a Marine. Maybe I didn't have the killer instinct the other guys had. I worried about what the old hands thought of me. None of them took me to task.

Timmons was the only one who tried to rag on me. Another new guy! In line to get our Cs a few days after I froze, he said, "Hey, Buck. If I get spiced beef I might be willing to trade."

"Buck? What's that supposed to mean, Timmons?" I hated his cocky look. I knew damn well what it meant, and I wasn't about to let him hang a nickname on me.

"Buck fever, McClure. What the fuck d'you think?"

Would Timmons have handled the running man any better? It didn't help that I imagined he would. The man with the plan. Going to be a goddamn hero and a millionaire, besides.

I squared off in front of him, hands clenched at my side. "I hear that word from you one more fucking time, Timmons, and I'll knock your teeth so far down your throat you'll have to shove a toothbrush up your ass to brush them."

He threw up his hands as though dismissing the whole thing. "Take it easy, McClure. Can't you take a joke?"

"Fuck you." I picked up my Cs and stalked away.

Jackson had heard the whole exchange. "If you need to lend him a toothbrush, I've got one I'll trade you for those spare socks." His boots were size 15; I wore 8s. He'd kidded me about wanting my socks before.

"Soon as it snows, I'll lend them to you for ear warmers," I said. It felt good that one of the most respected men in the platoon thought enough of me to kid around.

I told John about the exchange with Timmons that night, standing to in our hole. "I'm just praying I won't do something dumb like freezing again," I said.

"Don't beat yourself up. Only one guy in history never made a mistake, and they nailed him to a cross."

On patrol the next day, I thought about that conversation with John. The paradox made me smile. Leave it to Pius John. Jesus was perfect; you're not; forgive yourself for making a mistake. Forgive yourself for not killing a man.

Despite my efforts, that first patrol stayed in my head for a while. Not just my screwup, but the dead man, himself. His eyes—that puzzled, angry, embarrassed look. As if he'd just found out that the dumbest move he'd ever made was his last, too. Dead before he hit the ground. Dead before I'd even reacted. *Snooze, lose. Pow-pow, motherfucker. You get to love it.* I didn't think I ever would.

We crisscrossed the AO in a random pattern so the enemy wouldn't know our path. Some days took us where villages had been but were no more, where small stone pagodas stood unkempt, untended, scarred by bullets and bombs. Beyond them, graves had long settled into solid, grass-covered dunes. On most patrols, we went through villes, small clusters of hootches where women and kids and old men watched warily as we searched their homes. Usually, our searches were careful but not destructive, and the villagers seemed anxious but not threatening. We saw fighting-age men a couple times at a distance out in the fields. The lieutenant scoped them through his binos and saw no evidence of weapons. John said there were still a few brave, or at least stubborn, farmers left around who hadn't been killed or gone off with the VC.

One ville, not far from where Landon killed the running man, was my favorite for a while. Captain Brill went there with us on one patrol. We called him Captain or Skipper or the Six for his radio call sign, Bravo Six Actual. Sometimes we called him the Old Man, though not to his face. He may have been twenty-seven years old. He'd been an advisor on his first tour, so he spoke Vietnamese. He squatted and talked and ate nuoc mam with an old man while we searched the hootches. Beyond the two of them, a little boy flew a gigantic cockroach on the end of a string. Its wings made a racket above his head like a wooden spoon in a blender. I've never seen any kid happier with something from Toys 'R' Us.

An old mama-san squatted back on her haunches outside a hootch. She appeared to be grinning at us, but her face was so wrinkled and loose, I couldn't tell whether she was smiling or her creases just fell together like a crumpled burlap bag. She slowly reached up an arthritic hand, and Jackson put a cigarette between her fingers. She brought her hand down slowly, as though savoring a treasure, and placed the cigarette delicately in her toothless mouth. Jackson lit it for her. She closed her eyes, and the smoke wafted out her nose and drifted like a veil over her face. It was like looking through fog at a deeply etched wooden mask.

A toddler wearing only a stained, torn T-shirt ran past the old woman, chasing a rooster and a couple hens. His little penis sproinged along as he ran back and forth. I worried the rooster might turn about and deprive him of his appendage, but neither the old lady nor any of the other women near us seemed the least bit concerned about the boy or his imperiled anatomy.

"Don't worry if your fly's not buttoned up, Cavett," Gianelli called. "That rooster won't bite worms that small."

Cavett flipped him the bird. "Fuck you, Gianelli."

"Stand in line, babycakes. Uncle Sam's been fucking me ever since I joined this green machine." Gio's scrawny shoulders shook as he laughed. We loved his antics, but he was always his own best audience.

When the search was done, we took turns filling our canteens at the village well. The captain was still with the old man. As I approached the well, another little boy looked up at me with raised, hopeful eyebrows and mimed smoking. He might've been eight or nine.

"Sorry, pal," I said. "I don't smoke, but maybe that man over there can give you one for your mom."

Woody grinned at the little boy, then at me. "You've come to the right place, Little Beaver," he said. He handed him a Marlboro. The boy tore the filter off, stuck the cigarette in his mouth and waited. Woody gave him a light. The kid inhaled deeply, stuck out the tip of his tongue, picked a shred of tobacco off it, then exhaled a billow of smoke. I would've choked. He took another deep drag and grinned back at Woodson.

"Like Big Jim says," Woody laughed, referring to his dad. "'Long as you've got your health.'"

One young woman in that ville was very pretty with fine features and olive skin not yet turned to saddle leather and teeth not yet stained black from chewing betel nut. She watched as we refilled our canteens and splashed water on our faces and necks at the well.

Willis filled his helmet, then put it on and stood there grinning like a hound just emerged from a pond. "Nice work, Willie," Woody said. He pulled a bucket and poured it all over his own head and chest. I half expected Willie to wag his tail. It was fascinating watching them together; slow, well-intentioned Willis and the All-American Boy. Most of the good-looking jocks in my high school wouldn't give guys like Willie the time of day.

I envied guys in the platoon who could wear nothing under their flaks but a tee, if that. I sunburned so easily that on most days I wore my utility blouse with the sleeves rolled down to my wrists and walked all day inside a wet oven. I was so sunburned I had my green towel draped under my helmet to cover my neck and part of my cheeks. "McClure of Arabia," Woody said when he saw that. For a while, Gianelli referred to me as "the Arab." Fortunately, the name didn't stick. Once he started calling me "the Mick," that did, which was fine.

The pretty girl stole glances at us at the well. A couple times I saw her smile, and once she giggled at our antics. "I bet she'd like a good time with a Marine," Woody said. He gave her a big smile. "Good time, boom boom?"

The girl smiled shyly at him, clearly not understanding what he said.

"Not enough morphine in my bag to calm you down when the lieutenant cuts your balls off, you try something like that," Doc Dorsey, First Platoon's other corpsman laughed. He patted his many pockets as though he'd lost something important.

"There were some young ladies that looked a lot like her in Bangkok that thought it was a good deal."

"They thought your dollars were a good deal," Jackson said.

"Spoken like the old married man that you are," Woody laughed. "You need your attitude adjusted, Mikey. Other parts of you, too. How many days until you meet Dottie in Honolulu?"

"Twenty-three and a wake-up."

"Always a one-woman man. If it were anybody but Dancing Dottie Delight, I'd say you lost your mind." The three of them and whatever girl Woody was with at the time had gone dancing nearly every weekend in high school.

"Jealousy, jealousy," Jackson laughed. Woody had been his best man.

"You guys need to stop talking about women," Corrigan said. The Professor had a mock-serious look on his face. "Some of us got forever before we go on R&R, and Woody's done nothing but talk about gettin' laid since he got back. I'm exhausted. I been awake two straight weeks."

People were laughing now; we knew Corrigan would come up with something but had no idea what was coming next.

He lit the stubby briar pipe he smoked. "Maybe I could get some sleep if listening to you all didn't give me a hard-on that stretched the skin on my forehead so tight I couldn't close my eyes."

John walked over to us. "Hey guys, get this." He sounded angry. "I was just talking with the captain. He said the old man asked if we were French. Think about that. These poor people have been fighting communists longer than we've been alive."

"Poor people, my ass," Cavett said.

As we left the ville, I saw the old mama-san Jackson had given the cigarette to. I still thought she was smiling. It was hard to be certain with her worn catcher's mitt of a face. I smiled at her and gave her a thumbs-up. But her face looked like a carved witch's mask.

6

O N ONE OF HIS CHECKS OF the lines, the lieutenant caught Willis asleep on watch around 3:00 a.m. Willie had a welt under one eye the next morning where Corporal Harding hit him when he found out the lieutenant had discovered him asleep. "Life has consequences, Willis," Harding said. "Yours are on the way."

Willie spent the first couple hours that afternoon after our short patrol carving at the hard earth with an E-tool, digging a long, deep slit trench for First Squad to use as a head. "You want to act like a shitbird, Willis?" the lieutenant said. "Digging a shitter in the sun might help you stay awake in the dark."

"Willie's damn lucky," John said. "Some officers would've written him up, taken his PFC's stripe and a month's pay. He'll need that money for R&R in a few weeks."

Naked to the waist, soaked with sweat, Willie muttered and shook his head like an old bull mastiff as he swung the small folding shovel like a pick. When the lieutenant finally let him stop digging, he sidled slowly up to the edge of our group like a big, wet, smelly dog who knows he's been punished. Armed Forces Radio was playing rock and roll over the portable Landon carried in his pack. A used PRC-25 battery bigger than the radio itself was taped to its side. When the batteries for the platoon's tactical radio didn't have enough juice for communication, they had plenty of power for the Zenith. Willie thumbed the dirty blue rabbit's foot his sister had given him and eyed Lieutenant Mangan sitting by himself, heating his Cs. The lieutenant was wiry, with the athletic grace of someone who'd played lacrosse at Annapolis. Even relaxing, he looked like he was ready to leap into action. Willie looked like he was worried Mangan might.

Jackson and Gianelli walked over to us, Gianelli almost jogging to keep up with Jackson's long, rolling strides.

"How's it hanging, Willie?"

Willis grinned. "Good, Jax. The lieutenant made me dig a shitter. But I'm better now." He looked again like he'd wag his tail.

Jackson clapped him on the shoulder. "Glad to hear it. Got to stay awake, hear?" Willie nodded, then hung his head. Next to Jackson, he looked like he wasn't full grown.

Gianelli pointed at the can bubbling on my rock stove. "Hey, McClure, that spiced beef?"

"Just traded Smitty for it." I'd given him the Kools I'd gotten in my Cs.

Gianelli began patting his pockets. "What do you want for it?"

"Is that your Doc Dorsey imitation?" I said. "Sorry but no deal. Paid for it and about to put it away."

"A lot of streets named after you, McClure. Every fucking one says, 'One Way.'"

"Be My Baby" began on Cloninger's radio. "The Ronettes, Mikey!" Woodson yelled. "They're playing Dottie's song!"

Then Woodson and Jackson were on their feet doing a gyrating boogaloo, boots shuffling and stomping in the dirt, arms pumping and flailing. I wasn't surprised that Woody had dance moves, but seeing giant Jackson with those tree-trunk legs and size-fifteen boots dancing nimbly in rhythm to the rock-and-roll beat was something I wouldn't have guessed. People formed a circle around them and clapped and hooted and cheered. Willie laughed so hard I thought he'd pee himself. Even the lieutenant was laughing before the two were through.

My second week with the platoon, and I was watching two Marines dance. I was amazed. Given what Landau said about First Platoon hunting gooks, I wouldn't have predicted in a million years I was getting a ticket to *Bandstand*-in-the-bush. In many ways we were still kids, even if the Marine Corps said we were men.

Staff Sergeant Gilles flipped through the envelopes he'd alphabetized. In front of me in line, Havey got nothing. I stepped forward, tried to keep a stoic look on my face.

"Nothing yet, McClure." The platoon sergeant studied my face, taking the temperature on my morale. "Who you expecting to hear from?"

"My folks, maybe a friend, Staff Sergeant."

"Did you write them from Hoa Binh when you found out you were coming to Bravo?"

"Almost two weeks ago." I hadn't meant for that to come out so plaintively, but I'd written to Mom and Dad and also to Spence Burke, my long-time best friend, who was still at UVA.

"You'll be getting mail soon. Count on it. Sometimes the back-and-forth can take almost three weeks."

Havey and I walked back across the top of the hill. "Sure do wish I'd get mail," he said.

"No joke."

"People back home, they proud I'm a Marine. The grown-ups. But Mamma will worry. I write her every couple days. Just tell her I'm fine. Wish I'd hear she's gettin' my letters and doin' fine her own self."

I hadn't really thought about my own parents doing fine while I was in Vietnam; I just assumed they would. They'd worry about me, I knew, but they worried about me when I drove to the beach. At home on leave before I deployed, all I wanted to do was sleep late and spend time with friends home from college on weekends. It didn't occur to me that a few hours talking at the kitchen table or just watching TV with Mom and Dad would've been some comfort to parents waiting for their son to go off to a war that had already killed thirty thousand young men. "I guess my folks worry about me, too," I said. I didn't actually think much more about that. I just wanted letters telling me what was going on at home, any news about my high school or UVA friends.

"Listen to this, guys, listen to this." Corrigan waved a letter, motioned for people to gather around. "Got a letter from Carter, this is great." I'd never seen the Professor so excited. He shook the pages as though he'd been notified he'd gotten into Harvard Law with a full ride.

"How's he doing?" John asked.

"He's in the hospital in San Diego. Going home soon."

"Good," said John. "He'll be better near his wife and daughter."

Corporal Harding didn't say anything, just nodded.

John looked at me, then at Havey and Timmons. "Carter was in Third Squad. Lost a leg to a booby trap a few weeks ago. Good guy."

Havey's eyes got bigger. I hoped the odd, flushing shiver that ran through me didn't show on the outside. Timmons was listening, but except for an attempt to hide a nervous swallow, you couldn't tell how interested he was.

"Listen to what Carter said about Jakobic." Corrigan was grinning like he was about to unveil something fun.

"Jakobic? What about that sack of shit?" I was startled by how angry John was.

"You'll love this." The Professor bounced up and down on the balls of his feet as though he couldn't wait to dive in. "He's in the same ward as Carter."

"Fuck he still doin' in a fuckin' hospital?" Ladoor, a black Marine with biceps like bowling balls, looked like he was about to punch somebody.

Corrigan laughed out loud. "Wait, wait. This is good."

"Fucker shot hisself to get back to the World," Woody said to us new guys.

"Did he get court-martialed? Don't people go to prison for that?" I asked.

"No one was around. Claimed it was an accidental discharge. We all knew the bastard did it himself." Corporal Harding looked like he'd beat Jakobic to a pulp if he had him with us now.

"Acci-fuckin-dental, my ass," Ladoor growled. "Black man do that, they court-martial his ass."

"The lieutenant wanted to, Ladoor," Cloninger said. "The lawyer at Hoa Binh said there wasn't enough evidence."

"Been a black dude, they'd a found it."

Cloninger shook his head slowly, spit tobacco juice to the side. He didn't like blacks, or at least Ladoor.

Corrigan put his fingers in the middle of one page. "Carter says 'Jakobic fucked up big time.'" The Professor read slowly, as though he wanted to make sure the class understood. "'He thought shooting a little hole in his foot wouldn't do much but hurt. Man, did he blow it, so to speak.'" Corrigan looked up and grinned as though to say: That Carter, what a sense of humor. "'They took it off at the ankle.'"

He looked around the group. "Jakobic's foot," he said.

"Of course."

"Right."

"Good for him, the son of a bitch."

Corrigan continued, "'Then that got infected, so they took it off higher up his calf.'"

"Oh, man."

"Yes!"

"Bastard deserved it."

"'Now he's only got one leg, just like me.'" The Professor looked up from the page. The spark in his eyes had dimmed. Carter had been a good friend. He finished reading. "'Man, do I love watching that asshole hobble.'"

John clapped. Actually clapped. Woodson laughed out loud. Several others did, too.

"Poor guy," Havey said, a puzzled, concerned look on his face.

"My ass," Corporal Harding glared at him. "Fucker deserved it. People with balls out here getting wounded and killed, and fucking Jakobic hurts himself on purpose. Fuck him."

"There it is," John said.

"Like my old man always says," Woody began, and the old hands' chorus finished the line: "As long as you've got your health . . ."

I had trouble falling asleep that night. I didn't know how people could laugh at a Marine who'd lost his leg. It seemed so much worse than joking about an unknown dead man flying above the trees. Maybe Jakobic deserved what he got, but I couldn't imagine life without one of my legs. I understood, at least in theory, that could happen to any of us. Hearing about Carter losing his made the possibility seem much more real.

I said a small prayer, *Dear God, please don't let that happen to me.* Then I added, *Or to any of these guys I'm with. And please help Carter recover.*

I had no idea what that meant. How do you recover from losing your leg?

I didn't pray for Jakobic. He'd done it to himself, and I couldn't imagine a worse way to let your fellow Marines down. Still, laughing at someone who'd live his life without one of his limbs was hard to understand.

I thought about what John had said about darkness getting inside. I hadn't expected to find it in him. My last thought as I finally drifted into sleep was that I wanted to be like the old hands, but I was afraid that one day I might be.

7

"**W**E'RE GOING TO THE VALLEY in about a week and a half," the lieutenant told the platoon. People exchanged looks. There were a few muffled oaths, a low whistle, the whisper of feet and butts shifting in the dirt. John gave me a thumbs-up. I nodded, though I wasn't sure why.

"We'll go to Hoa Binh first. Four or five days from now." Heads nodded approvingly. There were a few quiet "All rights" or "Hot damns."

"Hot showers, hot chow." The lieutenant smiled slightly. "Might even be some cold beer. We'll be there probably four or five days. We'll clean and check weapons and gear and get some rest. There won't be much after that."

"Livin' the good life," Willie chortled. It wouldn't have surprised me much if he'd said something about living off the fat of the land. Woody gave him a thumbs-up then looked around for Jackson. He was standing behind the rest of us, half turned toward the lieutenant, his head cocked as though he were trying to listen with a good ear.

"Who else's going to the valley, Lieutenant?" Corporal Harding asked.

"Captain said probably most of the regiment. It's a damn big place."

"Christ on a crutch," Corrigan said. "The whole regiment? What do they think's in there?"

Mangan looked at him for a moment, then around at the entire platoon. "All the gooks in the world. They just don't know where they are."

"Try ever'where," Glass said. Several of the old hands agreed with that.

The lieutenant nodded. "Probably. The big deal is some sort of headquarters. Maybe a big underground complex like they found outside Saigon last year. No one knows for sure. The captain says all they know is there's a shitload of gooks. It's our job to find them and destroy them."

No American or South Vietnamese infantry units had been in the valley for over a year. The reconnaissance teams inserted in the last several weeks hadn't located any headquarters or complex. But there were a lot of NVA. No matter where they went in, the recon Marines got shot up and had to be extracted before they found anything.

Fullerton spit a stream through the hole between his teeth. "Sounds like they're going to have us chasing ghosts, Lieutenant."

Havey caught my eye. He looked scared.

Lieutenant Mangan shook his head. "No ghosts. Just gooks. Killing them and bringing the valley under control is what this op's all about." He paused for a moment and everyone waited. "I'm not going to bullshit anyone. This is going to be tough. But it's a chance to kill a lot of gooks, and maybe even secure a big area."

John nodded in agreement.

"Think they'll chopper us in?" Prevas asked. The Grasshopper carried the platoon's blooper, the M-79, a squat, shotgun-like weapon that fired HE or flechette rounds. He wanted to go to college when he got out, then become a basketball coach.

"Think Raquel Welch will hump my pack?" Corrigan said.

"Hump this, Professor."

"You people think you're in the Army?" Staff Sergeant Gilles jumped in. "There aren't enough fucking helicopters in the entire Marine Corps to move the whole regiment."

"Really think it'll be the entire regiment, Lieutenant?" John asked. Mangan nodded. "They told the captain at least two battalions."

Woody shook his head. "Must be a million gooks out there."

"I'll need a butler to carry all the ammo I'm gonna want on this op," Gianelli said.

"I am way too short for this shit," said Cavett.

"We count the meat," Timmons called out as though he were starting a cheer on a high school football team. I don't know why he did it; it was stupid. Only a couple weeks in the bush and he'd decided he was cool enough to brag about killing enemy with guys who actually had.

"Shut the fuck up, new guy." Carlton looked like he wanted to punch Timmons' lights out. He was eighteen, had a pregnant wife at home. "You don't know shit. You never been scared shitless. You never had to crawl after a man and not be able to . . ." Carlton stopped in mid-sentence. He suddenly looked embarrassed, like he'd broken a serious, unwritten rule. "Just fuckin' shut up."

"Don't get gungy on us, Tycoon." Woody spoke surprisingly quietly. "We'll count the meat. But sometimes when the shit hits the fan, we are the meat."

When the meeting with the lieutenant broke up, I went over to where Doc Matheson and Jackson were arguing in whispers. The right side of Jackson's face was swollen and red; he looked like he'd crammed a tennis ball into his mouth.

"How long've you had that?" the corpsman asked.

Jackson shrugged. "A day, maybe two," he mumbled.

"Interrupting anything?" I asked.

"Nothing good." Matt sounded exasperated. That was unusual for him. "Why didn't you come to me before now?"

The squad leader shrugged. "I been rubbing bug juice on it. It helps some."

"Jesus Christ, Jackson. Insect repellant on your gums? You'll poison yourself." It was one of the few times I'd heard Matt swear.

Jackson's breath smelled like he'd been gargling kerosene. "Jeez, Jax," I said. "You're lucky you haven't set your face on fire lighting a cigarette."

Jackson grinned at that, sort of. His eyes were bright with pain.

"You've got a bad infection in there. You need a root canal or the tooth pulled or something." Matt shook his head. "You need to go to the rear, see a dentist."

"Could you pull the tooth?"

"Are you kidding me? Without anesthesia?"

"Couldn't hurt more than it does now, Doc." He looked like high voltage was running through his skull.

"Oh yeah it would. Jax, molars don't just jump out like baby teeth. Besides, even if I could do it, which I can't because I don't have the tools, you'd have a hole your Orioles couldn't dig themselves out of."

Jackson chuckled as much as his face would allow. He and Woody were Orioles and Colts fans, like me. Matt was a hometown Boston fan. He knew the name of every player through third string on the Red Sox, Patriots, and Celtics.

"Whoa, Doc," I said, "your Sox have more holes in 'em than Jackson's."

Jackson tried to grin. Laughter in his eyes, he nodded at me as if to say, *Good one.* He spoke slowly to Matt. "Only a few more days until we go to Hoa Binh, Doc. Can you just give me something 'til then?"

"If I were you, I'd go in on the next bird."

"C'mon, doc. Just a few days. I should be with my squad."

"I'll give you something, but if that doesn't go down tomorrow, you need to go back on the next morning's bird."

"Thanks, Doc. Don't rat me out to the lieutenant."

"Tomorrow night, Jackson. You check with me then."

Our patrol the next day took us back to the ville where the captain told the old man the week before that we weren't French. We'd just set up security for our search when the lieutenant saw Jackson's face. "What's with that?" he said. I couldn't tell if he was angry or just surprised.

Jackson looked like a kid caught cramming his old man's chewing tobacco in his cheek. "Just a sore tooth, Lieutenant. Doc Matheson gave me some pills. He said the dentist at Hoa Binh can fix me up when we go back."

"You look like you need to go back on the next bird." I still couldn't tell from his expression if the lieutenant was angry or concerned, or both. He looked like Jack talking to the giant at the top of the beanstalk.

"You said we're going in a couple days, anyhow, sir. I don't want to leave the squad."

"One of your fire team leaders can take over. It's only a few days, like you said. There isn't much going on around here."

"C'mon, Lieutenant." Jackson sounded like he couldn't open his mouth enough to let his tongue work. "You don't want my knuckle-heads runnin' loose without me here to corral 'em."

The lieutenant smiled a little at that.

The plastic bottle of insect repellent under the rubber strap around Jackson's helmet was almost empty. The lieutenant was probably so used to people smelling filthy and coated with bug juice that he didn't notice Jackson's breath.

"I don't want you getting an infection that keeps you from going to the valley. We'll need you there a hell of a lot more than here."

"I'll be ready, Lieutenant, I promise."

"We'll talk when we get back to the hill." The lieutenant turned and went to watch the search. Jackson gave me a wink. I could tell that tooth hurt like hell.

When our search was completed, Woody offered a cigarette to the old man the captain had eaten with. He stared at it, then looked away. The old woman came and took him by the arm and turned him back toward her hootch. I didn't see the pretty young woman at all.

L EE, THE POINT MAN FROM Third Squad, led us away from
Checkpoint Three, a small field on the flat top of a low hill surrounded by thick brush. He found a small crease in the thorny scrub,
eyeballed it for any sign of a trip wire, then stepped through the break
like he was walking barefoot on glass. On the other side of the bushes,
he peered around, scoping distant tree lines, the next ridge line, the
ground in front of him where he would walk. Then he began walking
slowly down the slope looking for any signs of an ambush as he went.

The gun teams stood to the side while the first riflemen started to
move out of the field. When the point squad was through the brush,
the lieutenant and Smitty and Staff Sergeant Gilles would go, then
the gun teams, followed by the two docs, then the other two squads.

The next two men in the fire team followed the point. Each moved
slowly through the break in the brush, looked all around, waited for
the man in front to get ten yards down the slope, then walked forward.

Jackson waited to follow the next Marine through the break. He
gave me a little grin; it was all he could manage. "Think about those
socks, McClure. There's new holes in mine. I'll make you a deal." His
breath reeked like petroleum. His eyes glowed with pain.

"I'll check the going rate."

Jackson turned and looked intently toward his first fire team
as they moved down the slope. All business again, it was like he'd
never smiled.

Sturmer stood next in line to go after Jackson. "Hold out for spiced beef, McClure. And peaches."

Jackson stepped into the opening in the scrub.

The roaring, howling explosion blew me to the ground five feet from where I'd been standing and then there was a blow to my legs and everything I could see and smell and taste and feel and hear seemed to whirl into a vortex filled with enormous pressure and bellowing, pounding noise.

What seemed like a very long time passed, but probably only seconds. I struggled to lift my head, to move my arms and legs. The roar inside my skull was like a thick tar making it impossible to move, then the thunder in my head became a loud, numb background to blurred, clamorous questions pushing their way through my brain: *Am I hurt, oh sweet Jesus, what happened, can I move? Why can't I move my legs?*

I was flat on my back, legs splayed out at crazy angles to my knees. *Oh Jesus, my legs are wrecked, when will the pain start, oh God not my legs!*

A revelation began to ooze through my brain. I could feel my feet! *Those aren't my legs, they're Sturmer's.*

He was splayed face down across me. I rolled him off me as gently as I could. Acrid, begrimed haze hung all around us, yellow and gray and searingly pungent. It burned my nose and mouth and the scraped, sunburned skin on my face. But I could feel my legs again.

Sturmer moaned.

I yelled, "Corpsman! Corpsman!"

Sturmer's eyes were squinched shut, his face a mask of blood and dirt and snot and spit. The thighs of my trousers were splotched with blood. I didn't know if it was his or mine. I heard my own voice as though it were in a distant room, "Corpsman! Corpsman!" I felt no sharp pain anywhere. I could move all my limbs in slow motion. My entire body was a dull ache.

I pushed myself up to my knees beside Sturmer. His whimpering sounded way off in the distance. Blood dripped from his face and made shiny inkblots in the dirt. Doc Dorsey dropped down beside me. He began to wipe blood away from Sturmer's face and throat. "Help Matheson," he said.

Matt stood beyond me staring at the opening in the thorn bushes. It was much larger now, leaves and gnarled branches shredded and burnt. "Sometimes they come in pairs," he yelled. "Help me check it out, people. Come on people, help me look for more booby traps." He sounded like he was talking through a megaphone filled with oil.

I tasted blood in my mouth. My head felt like my brain had expanded and was searching for an opening to escape my skull. I was still on my knees, trying to comprehend what was happening around me, like looking at one of those pictures where the object is right before you but your eyes have to adjust, scan slowly, calibrate little by little, until the obvious becomes gradually recognizable. Beyond Matt, I saw Jackson's helmet on the far side of the opening. His rifle lay in the dirt, pointed toward us.

Then I saw Jackson. He lay to the side of the opening, jack-knifed face down over a scorched, twisted thorn bush. One hand dangled from a branch. His fingers opened and closed slowly, tentatively, like an infant trying to wave bye-bye to the M16 two feet away. The brush around him was burned, the opening he'd been the fourth man to step into, mutilated and charred; wisps of gray smoke rose like ghosts from the burned grass to his front. He was stark naked from the tops of his boots to the bottom of his flak jacket. Shreds of his trousers lay scattered like camouflaged confetti across his bare legs and over the branches beside him. Halfway up the back of his thighs, a pink, bloodless groove cut across the width of each of his massive legs. He looked as though someone had gouged him out with a melon scoop.

I struggled to my feet. The thunder receded in my ears; I could hear more. Smitty was calling for a medevac. Pius John and Woody and Matt were bent over at the opening, searching for trip wires or detonators. Sturmer pressed his fingers beneath his eyes, his panicked voice reaching higher and louder. "No, God, no! Jesus, no! I'm blind I'm blind I can't see, no don't let me be blind!" He looked as though someone had stuck raw bacon to his face with barbeque sauce. Bright blood oozed through his fingers, seeped down through the hair on his arms.

"Put your hands down. Keep them down, Sturmer. You're okay." Dorsey talked fast, trying to keep him calm. "You're gonna be okay, Sturmer. The blood's from your forehead, not your eyes. You're not blind."

"That's affirmative, Bravo," Smitty said into the radio. "We have two wounded. At least one emergency. We need that bird now."

Jackson groaned. A low, hushed, guttural sound. "Aarrgh . . . aarrgh . . . aarrgh . . ." His hand opened and closed slowly, grasping at something even he couldn't see. He groaned again, softly, as though he didn't want anyone to hear him cry out. Then, almost as though he were whispering to himself, "Please, people . . . please hurry. . . ."

The plea was worse than the explosion, a quiet, urgent, brave entreaty that would echo in my brain long after the explosion's roar had faded in memory.

"We're hurrying, Jackson. As fast as we can. We'll get you fixed up, man. I'm coming, I'm hurrying." Doc Matheson's calm, urgent assurance was a promise, a plea in itself.

John, Woody, Corrigan, and I carried Jackson back into the clearing, struggling under his weight. We laid him gently on his belly on the poncho Gianelli unrolled. He was so long his face was almost in the dirt on one end, his bare legs stretching from the knees down beyond the makeshift litter on the other. His thick, muscular legs had no blood on them at all, as though the deeply scooped groove across each thigh had been cauterized. Matt shot him with morphine. "Dave, I need help!"

"You're okay, Sturmer," Dorsey said. "I'll be back. Sergeant Gilles has you, he'll finish bandaging you."

The lieutenant got the rest of the platoon into a loose defensive perimeter around the clearing. John and Woody got Jackson's flak jacket off. Woody kept talking quietly, urgently. "You'll be okay, Mike. You'll be fine. The bird will be here in a few minutes, Mikey. Hang in there, big guy, you're gonna be fine."

The two corpsmen wrapped field dressings around Jackson's thighs. There was no blood on the bandages. They checked his back, turned him up on his side; Dorsey checked him for other wounds while Matt stuck an IV needle in his arm and began a saline drip to help stave off shock.

"Smitty! Where's the chopper? Where the fuck's the bird?" Woody yelled.

"It's coming. It's on its way."

"Hurry them up! Jesus."

The morphine took hold of Jackson; he muttered unintelligibly. The only word I could make out was his wife's name. "Dottie," he whispered again and again. "Dottie. Dottie."

Woody held Jackson's hand, talked to him quietly. "Hang in there, Mikey. You're gonna be good."

"Bird's coming, Jax," John said. "I can see it now. You're out of here soon."

Morphine had quieted Sturmer too. He wasn't talking or crying any more. His forehead and one eye were covered by field dressings. The rest of his face looked like it'd been painted a syrupy red. His eyes were closed tightly, as though he were sleeping through bad dreams. Or praying hard.

Staff Sergeant Gilles was back in the center of the field. "Never mind what's going on over there, goddamn it, people! Keep an eye out. Gooks may come looking for us now. Turn around, goddamn it, turn around! Watch over there! Keep an eye on that fucking tree line! We got a bird coming in! Let's keep an eye out, people!"

Lieutenant Mangan stood in the middle of the field, the radio handset up to his ear again. Smitty stood near him, the cord running from the PRC-25 on his back like a tether to the lieutenant. The platoon leader looked all around while he spoke into the radio. "That's affirmative, cold zone. Right now, we have a cold zone. Over."

The lieutenant listened as the medevac helicopter repeated back that the landing zone was not under enemy fire. He spoke again. "Affirmative, Blue Dragon. Two wounded. One emergency. I say again, one emergency, over."

I watched the helicopter grow from a speck in the thin blue sky to a dot to, finally, a CH-46 rushing toward us.

The lieutenant listened again. "Roger that. I'll pop smoke. You identify, over." Standard procedure: if the enemy was on our radio frequency, they could pop their own smoke and lure a helicopter into an ambush. Mangan tossed the smoke grenade downwind in the field. A red cloud billowed and spread to the lower end of the clearing momentarily obscuring part of Second Squad. Marines coughed and gagged before the wind carried the acrid red vapor upward.

"That's affirmative. Red smoke. You have us marked, over."

The *whup-whup* and *thrum* of the rotors became a roar as the helicopter came down fast over the tree line and settled heavily into the center of the field. The rotor wash threw up a storm of dirt and rocks and twigs and exhaust. Woody, John, Staff Sergeant Gilles, and I carried Jackson, his rifle, and gear across the field and up the ramp. Doc Matheson jogged beside us holding the IV bag. We laid the big man on the stained deck of the chopper as gently as we could. Jackson still wasn't bleeding. The corpsman on the helicopter took the IV and hung it from a hook on the fuselage. I ran back down the ramp and across the field and took a knee with John near the opening to the slope.

Sturmer shuffled to the chopper, his arm around Doc Dorsey's shoulders. As soon as he was aboard and Dorsey was running back across the field, the rear ramp went up, and the bird rose fast, the blast of its rotor wash pelting us again with debris.

The blood pounded in my head. Bits of scorched camouflage cloth waved like tiny castle flags from Jackson's thorn bush. Down the slope, the Marines who'd passed through the opening unscathed were on a knee in the grass. They kept stealing looks back toward the rest of the platoon as they watched warily around them for any sign of enemy all the noise might have attracted.

I couldn't keep my eyes away from the despicable, burned little banners fluttering on the scrub. I saw Timmons staring toward the hole in the brush too. He looked like he wanted to run away.

Lieutenant Mangan walked toward the opening, talking to the company commander on the radio. "That's affirmative, Six Actual. The chopper just took off and we're headed back to your pos." He listened. "Roger. Out."

The lieutenant gestured for me. I stood up slowly, hoping that the quivering of my legs wasn't noticeable. "You alright, McClure? I saw you on the ground. You weren't hit, were you?"

"No . . . I mean yes, sir, . . . I wasn't hit. I'm fine."

He looked me hard in the eyes. "Good. Get ready to move out." Lieutenant Mangan turned back toward the center of the field. Smitty nodded at me like I'd just passed a test.

"Let's go, people!" the lieutenant yelled. "We're moving out. Same formation. Third Squad in the lead. Garcia, you're the squad leader for now. Fast, but goddamn careful, people. Let's go."

The rest of Third Squad, the lieutenant, Sergeant Gilles, and John—nine Marines in all—went slowly through the opening one at a time. Each eyeballed the ground and the thick bushes around it before stepping into that burnt hole in the brush. Nine people, not counting the three before Jackson, walked through unscathed. But every fiber of my brain and body screamed at me, warning me not to go. Sometimes they come in twos, Doc Matheson had said.

I forced myself to step forward toward the break in the brush. I kept my eyes on the ground, then on the charred branches festooned with their obscene ornaments of tattered, burnt cloth. I looked intently for trip wires, anything that could give me a clue there was another booby trap waiting to get me. Sweat soaked my clothes, burned my eyes. My mouth was so dry, I could barely swallow, my breath so shallow I didn't know if I could talk. My nose burned, clogged with the odor—or recollection of odors—of gunpowder and blood and helicopter exhaust. I was amazed that my legs didn't buckle. *Jesus, help me,* I thought.

I stepped forward into the scorched hole in the scrub.

9

I KEPT SEEING PICTURES OF STURMER'S legs angled out from my knees, his blood-coated face. Those bloodless pink grooves in Jackson's thighs. When John finally woke me, I was too grateful to be embarrassed that he'd stood two watches instead of getting me up.

At dawn, we got ready to go back to the ville. "We'll teach those fuckers a lesson," Carlton growled.

"We don't know it was them," John said. "Anybody could've set that booby trap."

"Fuckers were the only ones around," Carlton said.

"Bastards must've set it. Or knew where it was and didn't warn us," Cavett said. "Wax all those fuckers. Every goddamn one."

"There's nobody but old people and young mama-sans and kids in these villes." John shook his head as though he couldn't believe what he was hearing.

"Do a couple, it'll send a signal to the rest. Don't fuck with us again." Carlton nodded vigorously, agreeing with his own solution. I'd heard him talk about being a dad, said he wanted lots of kids.

Cavett shook his head. "I am too short for this shit."

Gio looked at Cavett, but didn't say anything. Woody listened to the entire conversation, worry about Jackson etched on his face. He didn't say a word.

Just before we moved out, I was alone with John. "Who do you think planted the booby trap?" I asked.

"Might've been VC in the area." He shook his head. "Might've been people from one of the villes."

"Old men and women and kids?"

"We've been lucky to now. But you never know."

I thought about how I'd written home, saying we were just policing up the countryside, helping the villagers.

"You never know," John said again.

The gun teams and Second Squad stood watch around the edges of the ville while First and Third Squad conducted the search. I heard children crying and, several times, a high-pitched chittering of Vietnamese from women and once a Marine yell, "Shut the fuck up, mama-san!" I heard crockery breaking and metal pots being thrown. When the pretty young woman joined the others herded onto the central path, I saw a fresh welt under one eye. I half expected to hear gunshots and was afraid that I would. I heard the lieutenant yell, "Carlton! Knock it off! Search this fucking ville, people, but do not terrorize these villagers." I heard more children and mama-sans cry. The old man and the toothless old woman with the catcher's-mitt face sat on the edge of the group looking like they were carved out of wood.

The search found no weapons or anything to make a booby trap from. I wondered if we'd made more enemies in that village than we'd had before.

Willie was last in the column as we were leaving the ville. He Zippoed a hootch.

Smoke wafted up from the thatch like filthy steam; flames blazed along the roof's overhang. A knot of women and children huddled in the central path, crying and lamenting loudly. The old mama-san squatted on her haunches, holding her head, wailing in a high keen as she watched the home burn. The old man shuffled toward the village well, a pot in his hand.

Corporal Harding had Marines tossing pots of water on the flames by the time I got there. Willie stood off to the side, chin on his chest, helmet at his feet. He had a reddening welt under one eye. He pulled his filthy blue rabbit's foot out of his flak jacket pocket, worked it with his thumb.

"Six Actual's on the hook, sir," Smitty said.

The lieutenant took the radio. "That's right, Six. A hootch caught fire during our search."

He listened, then, "That's affirmative. As soon as we're back at your pos."

He tossed the handset back to Smitty, spun toward Willie. "Willis, I'm gonna have your ass." Lieutenant Mangan pointed at Harding and Woody. "Corporal Harding, you and Lance Corporal Woodson bring Willis to me as soon as we get back to the hill. Every fucking one of us is going to see the captain, got it?"

The ville smelled like someone had burned something spoiled.

Woody pulled Willis off to the side as the platoon formed up to move out. Willie looked up past his Neanderthal brow toward his fire team leader. "Willie, what the fuck did you do that for?"

"For Jackson, Woody. You know."

"For Jackson?"

Willis nodded as though the size of the arc his head made would show his good intentions. "He's my friend."

"Jesus, Willie. No one cares about Mike Jackson more than I do. But you don't see me burning hootches, do you?"

"I bet his wife does."

"What?"

"I bet his wife cares more about Jackson than even you."

"Goddamn it, Willie. Don't ever burn another fucking hootch unless I tell you it's okay."

Willie looked like having Woody swear at him hurt more than the blows he'd gotten earlier. He still worked the rabbit's foot. "If you don't want me to give no payback, Woody, I won't."

Pius John intervened. "Willie, would you burn down someone's home back in Vermont because one of your buddies got hurt, even if no one knew who did it to him?"

Willie looked up at John, then back down at the ground, struggling with the question.

"You know you wouldn't, Willie. You don't want to get in trouble for doing stuff like that. Or get Woody in trouble for not controlling his fire team. Right?"

"Okay, Pope." Willie sounded reluctant. "But home's different, you know? Home's not gooks."

The captain busted Willis from PFC to private, fined him two month's pay, and turned him back over to Lieutenant Mangan. Willie spent the next several hours filling in the shitters behind the lines and digging new ones for the platoon. Sergeant Gilles wouldn't let him stop digging long enough to put a wet cloth on his black eye. Watching him hack at the hard earth this time was different from when he had to dig after he'd fallen asleep on watch. People felt sorry for Willie this time. Fucking gooks. Two men hurt, and no payback.

When the captain finished chewing him out for not controlling his fire team, Woody had asked if Top Miller had radioed out any update on Jackson's condition. The first sergeant had no word yet. Doc Dorsey was sure Sturmer would be fine but that he wouldn't be back. He had less than thirty days left on his tour. He guessed Jackson would be okay, too. Doc Matheson didn't speculate; he didn't say much at all. The strain couldn't have been more visible on Woody's movie-star face if he'd been projected up on a drive-in's wide screen.

When he made the rounds later passing out salt tabs and malaria pills, I asked Matt what he thought. He wasn't sure.

"What do you mean, Doc?" I said. "Those were mean-looking gashes, but he didn't even bleed a drop."

Matt took off his glasses, ran his long fingers over his angular face and hatchet blade nose. His eyes usually seemed to blend a tentative urge to smile with ever-present concern. There was no hint of a smile now. "I hope so," he said. "Those were pretty deep. We did all we could, I think." His eyes seemed to say he didn't know if he had. Or whether anything he could've done would've been enough.

I needed Jackson to be fine. Those gashes would hurt like hell, and he'd be stiff as a board for a while. But when I compared the scars over John's heart and lungs to those two bloodless furrows across Jackson's thighs, I was convinced he'd be back with us before too long. I'd see him carry on again with Woody like they had when they boogalooed to Dottie's Ronettes song.

How random it all seemed. John's chest all torn up but he's fine. Three men walk through a break in the brush line unscathed, and Jackson trips a booby trap. He and Sturmer get torn up by shrapnel; I'm next to them but not hit, though I'm picked up and thrown down five feet away with Sturmer dropped on top of me.

I stuck my hand deep into my trouser pocket and felt the rosary beads Mom gave me before I left. Maybe it wasn't as random as it seemed. Though why them, not me, I had no clue.

Willie was still digging when Smitty came running. "Garafano!" the radioman cried. "Pope! Where's your gun?" The tall, rangy black Marine gasped for breath.

John nodded toward our hole. "What's happening, Smitty?"

"Grab it. The lieutenant's got gooks." He lit a Kool and blew a long billow of smoke as he tried to catch his breath. The sultry air seemed suddenly mildly mentholated.

"Where? How many?"

"Other side of the hill." Smitty pointed. "Two. The sniper team's out with Third Herd. The lieutenant told the Six he thought you could ding 'em."

Pius John grinned like he'd been awarded a prize.

When we got across the hilltop, Lieutenant Mangan and Captain Brill were studying the distance through field glasses. Smitty lit another cigarette and pointed toward a dike a long way out from the base of the hill. "Fuckers must not know we're up here," he said through a cloud of smoke.

"Cap'n," John nodded to the Six. Then he said, "What do you have, Lieutenant?" John had his own field glasses out of the case.

"Two NVA," Lieutenant Mangan said.

The captain didn't take his eyes away from his binoculars. "Can you do 'em, Lance Corporal Garafano?"

I could barely make out two figures at the edge of a tree line way out from the hill. They had to be nearly a thousand meters away, almost beyond the effective range of the M60.

"Probably, sir. I'll sure try." John handed me his binoculars, knelt down, and rested the machine gun on the scarred trunk of an uprooted tree. He motioned me down beside him. "What's the map say, sir? About nine hundred meters?"

"Nine hundred, maybe nine fifty," the lieutenant said. "Hurry, Pope."

I linked up ammo belts. My mouth was suddenly dry; sweat trickled down my back.

John adjusted the elevating knob on the rear sight again, raised the feed cover, and satisfied himself that everything was in order. His movements were fast and fluid, like a doctor performing surgery—all the time in the world, if you move quickly enough.

I focused the binos. It was like a painting of a pastoral scene—still, soft colors and textures, two faraway figures in muted green clothing without distinct features. The trees behind them were thick and dull green, the wide paddies to their front open, flat, green, tan, and brown. They appeared to have stepped out of the tree line as though the war were a million miles away. They had rifles and carried something tan, maybe packs. Behind me, a murmur of hushed voices, the shuffle of boots as Marines gathered, trying not to disturb John's concentration.

"We're good," John whispered. "You just watch."

I was surprised John didn't want me to help feed the ammo belts but was grateful for the opportunity to observe the target through the glasses instead of having to concentrate on the gun.

I tensed for the roar of a volley.

BAM! John fired one shot.

I'd expected the long, blasting roar of a burst; instead all I heard was one sharp report, as though someone had fired a high-powered rifle, single shot. I knew the gun jammed, though I hadn't heard the telltale *thunk* of a misfeed. "Fuck," I swore under my breath. I dropped the field glasses and spun toward John ready to work whatever needed to be done to clear the misfire. He was frozen in the firing position.

Behind me, Gianelli giggled.

"High left," the lieutenant said.

John adjusted the sights. I picked up the binoculars again. The two men hadn't flinched. At that distance, they probably barely heard the shot and couldn't tell where the noise came from if they had. The bullet that zipped past their heads must've sounded like a fly, if they heard it at all. All of this happened in a fraction of the time it takes me to tell it, but those few seconds were extraordinary. It takes tremendous expertise to squeeze off one round instead of a burst with an M60. John did it to check his aim. I never understood how the lieutenant knew where that single bullet hit.

John inhaled, held it. Then the gun roared, an angry, insistent deep yammer, and a long, fluorescent stream of fire arced toward the two enemy, scores of bullets, every tenth one a tracer creating a laser beam of orange light. John raised and lowered the muzzle slightly between bursts. The orange blurbs of fire slashed side to side, up and down. The two figures jerked and bucked; the earth around them spit, jumped, and flamed as they crumpled like heaps of writhing, smoking green rags, still jerking and bucking while orange flashes danced all around as John riddled them.

He finally let up on the trigger. The gun was suddenly silent, my ears still roared and rang, and we were surrounded by cheers. The two bodies lay still. I stared at them for a long time. When I finally put the glasses down and stood up, John was already standing, the gun raised above his head, acknowledging the applause.

The lieutenant shook John's hand. Then he shook mine. The captain did too. "Good shooting, men," he said. "Damn fine work." I didn't shake with a lot of enthusiasm. I hadn't done much except link up ammo belts, then watch two men die.

John raised the gun high again, pumped it up and down. He threw back his head and roared, a great, joyous bellow that contrasted fiercely with the kind, philosophical tone I'd heard him use so often.

The crowd roared with him.

People slapped each other on the back, exchanged high fives. John had given them payback for friends they'd lost. And with shooting none of them could match.

"Get some, Garafano!"

"Way to go, Pope."

"Count the meat, Pius John."

I walked off to the side and waited while John shook hands like a celebrity in a crowd. Marines began to wander back across the hillside like warrior ants returning to their holes. Some congratulated me, too, like a bench warmer who got to run a signal into the huddle for the big play. I felt pretty sure then that I was going to fit in. But I knew, too, that I'd never become like the rest of them, savages who took such joy in watching people die.

Several of us sat eating Cs or cleaning weapons, shooting the breeze about sports and movies and cars and John's shooting, the most relaxed and cheerful we'd been since Jackson and Sturmer were wounded. Even Woody was enjoying the moment enough to kid with Matt about the Red Sox and Os, though it was clear he wasn't going to really relax until he'd heard that his best friend was going to be okay.

"Anybody got extra envelopes?" Gianelli asked. He was writing on a pad on his knee. Every couple of weeks, his sister sent him pages ripped out of New York City phone books. Gio wrote to random names, protesting the war. "Wrote seventeen in the last two days," he said. "Cavett keeps bitching about crap, and then Prevas joins in and between the two of 'em, I can't concentrate. Must've addressed six envelopes to Agnes Goodbody by mistake. Send her that many letters, I'll have to bring her roses when I get back to the World." He paused for effect. "Probably looks like Cloninger, too."

Doc Matheson came back from the Company CP and sat in the dirt next to me. He glanced at Woody, then looked at John as though he hoped he'd get him out of a fix.

Woody's face lost its color. A sudden silence hung in the air around us. Even Gianelli said nothing. Matt shook his head as though he'd forgotten how to form words. He looked at Woody again and said, "They amputated both of Jackson's legs. Mid-thigh. I am so sorry, Woody. So God-awful sorry."

Woody's face caved in. He began to cry. Gasping, deep sobs, like he was choking on his own phlegm. In the midst of all the wet, terrible sound, I heard him whisper, "Oh Mikey, oh Dottie, oh God . . ."

None of us moved. I felt like I'd been kicked in the balls, a sick, gut-clenching ache in my belly. Jackson! Two fucking little grooves in those mammoth thighs. Cut off both his legs? *Oh my god oh my god.* I fought a sudden impulse to hyperventilate. I had an almost overwhelming urge to yell at Matt, to tell him he couldn't possibly know what the fuck he was talking about. Two clean, pink, melon-scoop grooves. No blood. I wanted to scream: It makes no sense, Doc, no fucking sense! For that you took . . . someone took . . . some fucking idiot someplace cut those big legs off that young giant of a man?

We sat frozen, shocked silent, hurting and sympathetic and embarrassed by Woody's sobs.

John moved over and sat next to him. He put his arm around his shoulders. I half expected Woody to shrug him off or maybe do the opposite, put his head on John's shoulder and cry more. He just sat there with his head bent and cried more softly than before. Beneath the spume of Woody's weeping, I could hear an undercurrent of John's deep voice. "I am so, so sorry, Woody. So very sorry."

A long time seemed to pass as no one else spoke. Then Woody stood and looked at us as though he were begging for answers, his matinee-idol face ravaged and gaunt and bleached dry beneath the tan and the glisten of tears and snot. He said nothing at all. Then he turned and walked away slowly and crawled under his poncho hootch and drew himself up in a ball.

10

HOA BINH WAS A KILN, parched tents and squat bunkers baking behind concertina wire. Red dust billowed from the unpaved street after every truck and tank and Marine on foot passed. It hung in the air, settled like ochre pollen on tents and equipment and men. Every day before we went to supper, Gianelli wrote "Fuck Ho Chi Minh" in the dust down the length of his cot in script like dirty skywriting. A month earlier, the base had been my idea of the OK Corral; after weeks of not bathing, sleeping on the ground, and eating often-cold food out of little green cans, it was the Holiday Inn. I was lucky: most of Bravo hadn't been behind wire for a lot longer than I'd been in-country.

We slept on canvas cots for the first time in weeks or months, and the old hands bitched about the air you could barely breathe, the red silt that stuck to our skin and teeth, and the smell of mildewed canvas and cots previously soaked by other Marines' sweat. And they loved it.

We heaped battered tin trays with mashed potatoes and real butter, mounds of green beans and corn, swiss steak tonged from the depths of bubbling vats. Guys who'd been in the bush a long time complained about the chocolate milk we drank by the gallon being warm and the mystery meat being greasy and the scrambled eggs being runny. And they loved it.

We walked through billowing dust to the showers and used soap and even shampoo under hot water, then walked back to our tents and red dirt clung to us before we made it to our cots. Young men who hadn't felt hot water for a very long time complained about the distance to the showers and the itch of clean skin and the gritty feel of the dust. And we loved it.

We used three-hole latrines and real toilet paper sitting two or three side-by-side for long, sweat-drenched minutes in the hot, dank wooden shacks. Everyone complained of the stench and the splash in the diesel fuel drums beneath the latrines, the reek of the oily black smoke as the contents were burned each morning at the end of the base. And we all thought the shitters beat slit trenches and trail sides running away.

I've stayed in Hiltons and Hyatts and Marriotts, and, once, for two nights, in the Waldorf Astoria. I've never appreciated any of them as much as I relished my time at Hoa Binh after even just a few weeks in the bush.

The captain and the first sergeant threw us a party. It wasn't long before most of Bravo would've blown the baffles out of a breathalyzer. It only took a few beers before most of us could switch gears from dejected to happy. We'd gotten very good at compartmentalization out in the bush. Bad things went in boxes, some of which never got opened again until after we were back in the World.

I remember the Top telling Gianelli to take the purple glasses and rings off. "Staff Sergeant Gilles lets you look like a hippy with all that purple in the bush, that's his call. Back here, you dress like a proper Marine."

Gio grinned drunkenly. "But I'm as improper a Marine as we got, Top."

"Damn close, Gianelli, damn close." The first sergeant smiled, but he wasn't fooling around. "In your pocket. Now. Before I charge you with mopery, dopery, and attempted gawk."

Corporal Harding surprised me.

I was watching Cloninger perched on the end of a table, arms tucked, shoulders hunched, scrawny neck extended, his beaked face rotating slowly side to side. Gio named him well. People laughed at the Buzzard, but some put their hands over their plates when they walked past. Off to the side, I heard Harding ask Matt, "But Doc, do women ever die in childbirth these days?" His speech was thickened by too much beer, but I was amazed to hear a catch in Hard Ass Harding's voice. He caught me watching and turned from the corpsman and strode off.

"First-time-father jitters," Top said. "Lots of us've had those." I asked if he had kids.

"Two boys, two girls." The Top gave his head a quick snap, a mock serious look on his face. "Youngest is two. Ornery little cuss. When I get home, I'll have to teach him to shit in the woods, 'cause he's so mean people worry he'll shit a bear."

Woody asked the first sergeant if he had any updates on Jackson.

"Same as yesterday." Top looked sympathetic. "He's in Japan and his condition's stable. They'll probably fly him to a hospital in the States soon. I don't expect we'll know anything else until you hear from his wife. Or maybe Jackson himself."

Woody shook his head.

"Do you have his wife's address?"

"Yes, sir." He sounded reluctant to admit it.

"Write to her. Just tell her you're checking in, want to know if they're taking good care of him in the hospital."

Woody didn't look like he'd write. "Okay, Top," he said. He sagged as he walked away.

Havey smelled of marijuana when he came back to the party from the "black shack" at the end of the base. The black Marines stationed in the rear who hung out down there had a reputation for insubordination and plotting ways to get back at Whitey when they got back to the World. Ladoor and Glass didn't come back to the cookout at all. That was just as well. Ladoor always seemed pissed at the world in general and angry at white guys in the platoon just because they were white. Glass thought most white people couldn't be trusted, except for the ones in the platoon.

"Fuck, Havey, you smell like you just smoked half the grass on the planet." Timmons didn't hide his disdain.

Havey looked at him blankly. "I didn't smoke no grass."

"Yeah, right. Keep away from me. I'm not getting busted 'cause of you."

"Hang around, Timmons," I said. "Your girlfriend's old man will be impressed when you're in the brig."

I believed Havey, but he did reek. He was amazed by what he'd heard at the shack. "There some brothers there with crazy ideas. Learned all about killing over here, they say. Goin' to take that home and kill lots of white people. Revolutionize, Ladoor called it. That's crazy. I believe in what Doctor King taught, so's everybody in my church. When I'm back in the World, I'll do the nonviolent stuff, but I ain't killin' no white folk. There some crazies out there, but I don't think most white folk want to be killin' me, neither."

I convinced Havey to leave the party and go back to his tent. Nothing good would come of Top or the officers getting a whiff of him.

A little later, Smitty came back from the shack happily stoned. The smell of grass mixed with his menthol cloud. He didn't talk much to anyone, but he never did. He grinned a lot, though, and finished off a bowl of potato chips and a warm beer before John looped arms with him and got him back to his tent too. John taxied a lot of people to their bunks that afternoon. He drank as much as most but had a hollow leg. "Learn to drink doing keggers in the seminary?" I asked.

John roared happily, "Hell no, why do you think I joined the Marines?"

Willie drank as though he had to drench the flames of lust Woody had ignited weeks before regaling him with tales of the talents of the young ladies of Bangkok. "Oh, man," Willie slurred to anyone who'd listen, "I'm gonna have such a wicked good time." He was certain R&R was the biggest adventure he'd ever have. A tour as a grunt was simply the price of admission. He staggered about like a bear with Saint Vitus' Dance, balancing on one foot while he placed his other someplace to his front.

"The boy can dance," Gio laughed.

"Reminds me of a girl I dated in high school," Corrigan said. "Linda Tripps. We called her 'Cuppla.' Built like Willie. Bigger actually, nice personality though. Late for everything except lunch. Every time she had to haul ass, it took her two trips."

———

Woody was slumped on his cot when John and I got back to the tent.

"How can I write to Dottie? I don't have a clue what to say." He shook his head slowly. "Let me know how he's doing? Jesus. I know how he's doing. He wants to die." Woody spoke very quietly, as though he didn't want to hear what he said. The expression on his handsome face was wretched. "I'd rather lose my life than my legs."

"Maybe Mike doesn't want to die," John said. "Maybe he knows he's got a lot to live for. He has Dottie."

Woody sagged more. When he finally responded, I had to lean forward to hear. "I don't know if she'll stay with him."

The statement hung in the air like an odor. I could hardly breathe. Why should she, I thought. Jackson wouldn't be able to run or dance, even walk right. I tried not to think about what sex would look like.

"Nineteen and beautiful and crazy fun. Now her husband's a cripple." Woody got even quieter, as though he couldn't stop his thoughts from leaking into the air but didn't want to hear the words when they escaped. "A freak," he whispered. "I wouldn't make love to a freak . . . Jesus Christ."

"Woody . . . a man's a hell of a lot more than his legs," John said quietly. "Think about it, pal. You and Mike aren't best friends just because you played football and went dancing together. You love him for his brain, for that goofball sense of humor, for how he cares about people. Mike Jackson's a lot more than a pair of legs."

Woody stared at his boots. I struggled to find something helpful to say, came up empty. I was with Woody; if I lost my legs, I hoped I'd die before they medevacked me.

"It's got to be the same with Dottie," John continued. "You know she loves him for a lot more than his legs."

"I don't know if Mike wants to do that to her." Woody looked at John, imploring him to understand. "I wouldn't."

Two goddamn little pink grooves in those tree trunks, I thought. God almighty, how does that happen? With a flush of unexpected anger, I recalled the last thing Jackson said to me was that he wanted my socks.

"His dad went to every one of our games. Just like mine. All their spare time they played catch with us, shot hoops in our driveways. How's his dad going to act now?"

"He's their son, Woody," I said. "They're going to still love him, help him recover." I couldn't imagine anybody's parents doing anything else.

"You don't recover from your legs being gone," Woody said.

"No," John said, "you don't. But you figure out how to deal with it. Like Carter. You don't have a choice."

"He lost one leg. Maybe you do."

"Parkowski lost both. He wrote to Harding and said he was learning to walk again, remember?"

"I might be able to handle it if I lost one leg. I might figure it out, I don't know." Woody hesitated. "But I sure don't want to live if I lose both of them." Tears filled his eyes. "We danced all the time. What's Dottie going to do now?"

"Woody," John spoke so softly I could barely hear him. "You don't want Mike to die."

"He's my best friend, for God's sake." Woody wiped his hand over his face. "But I think he might want to," he whispered. "And I don't know if Dottie wants him to. For his own sake . . . or hers."

I didn't know what to make of what John was saying to Woody. I had no point of reference for thinking about what I'd just heard. What would Jackson's life be like if he lived? How could his wife live with him now? Maybe I'd make it if I lost one leg or an arm or an eye. But if I lost both legs or both arms or both eyes, or my balls, I was sure I'd want to die.

I had a nightmare that night. Jackson wore dress blues, a Purple Heart medal the size of a pie plate on his chest. His white dress cover with its polished bill radiated fluorescence. His swollen cheek flashed like a caution light. His expression stoic, he held the hand of a beautiful girl in a cheerleader's uniform. On the front of her sweater an Eagle, Globe, and Anchor rode the swell of her breasts. Beneath her tattered white veil, her face was all misery and disgust. Jackson's head came up to her waist, his trouser legs, twelve inches long, ended at spit-shined shoes as big as clowns' feet. They were about to step under an outdoor wedding arch covered with glistening black thorns.

"Not there," I heard myself yell, "Don't step there." I bolted up on my cot. No one else in the tent stirred. I lay back down not knowing whether I'd cried out or not.

We slouched out of our tents like teenagers who'd slept late, then gathered in front of eleven M16s bayoneted to the earth, a helmet on each, a pair of boots in front. No one looked sleepy any more.

Father Mullin wore camouflage utilities and a purple stole; his sunburned scalp seemed to radiate heat through his thin hair. Slowly, he spoke the rank and first and last name of each dead Marine.

The priest talked of bravery and duty and sacrifice, the difficult job of defending freedom, the pain we feel when we lose friends, the importance of courage and perseverance and faith. Measured tones, more conversation than sermon or speech. I saw Marines wipe away tears. Until Woody found out about Jackson's legs, I'd never seen a grown man cry. I hoped I never would myself.

The chaplain asked us to join in the Lord's Prayer, to pray for the souls of our departed brothers, for their families and for ourselves. When we finished, Captain Brill walked slowly down the row of upturned, helmeted rifles, stopping and placing his hand on each. A gesture of sorrow and respect and responsibility.

The entire company followed down the line. When it was my turn, I walked very slowly, feeling I should say, or at least think, something meaningful at each shrine: I'm sorry; goodbye; a prayer of some sort. No appropriate words came together inside my head. Just one tumbling, muffled thought: eleven—it's like killing off the entire starting lineup on my high school football team.

I was in the Company headquarters tent the next day to fill out a form listing next-of-kin's contact information so they could be notified if I were killed or badly wounded. The one I filled out before had somehow been lost. "Not planning on using this, right?" I said to the clerk.

"Never do," Landau said, the purple-white slash on his face gleaming under the bare overhead bulb.

Thanks a shitload, I thought. The sign in front of the tent wasn't thrilling like it'd been when I first saw it weeks ago.

The first sergeant held up an envelope and said, "Landau, take this to the Battalion One."

"Will do, Top," the clerk said without looking up from poking at his typewriter.

"Off and on, Marine."

"Top?"

"Off your ass and on your feet. The One needs this now."

Landau laughed, the scar on his face coiling back like a purple snake.

I loved the way Top Miller talked. Off and on. Hot as a freshly fucked fox in a forest fire. A kid so mean people fear he'll shit a bear. Mopery, dopery, and attempted gawk. How many times since have I accused one of my students of committing that when they did something boneheaded?

The phone on the Top's desk rang. He signaled Landau to wait. "Bravo One Fifteen, First Sergeant Miller."

I checked the box on the form indicating my parents were to be notified only if I were killed or my wound was life-threatening. I wondered if Dottie Jackson had been told straight out that they'd cut off Mike's legs? Did she have to tell his mom and dad? If I had a choice, I'd want to let my folks know myself if I were wounded.

"I'm good, Major. And you, sir?" the Top said.

The sirens in the center of the base wailed. Incoming! Top waved me toward the tent flap and stood up, the phone to his ear. Landau was sprinting toward a bunker before I got to the doorway.

"I apologize, Major," I heard Top say. "I've got to run. We've got incoming."

Rockets blasted into tents less than a hundred yards away, the air around me shrieked, roared, lashed like a typhoon in a madhouse. More blasts, even closer as I ran. Screaming tumbling roars, geysers of thick black smoke, debris whirling in filthy clouds. I jumped down into the bunker, hugged a wall, tried to catch my breath. *Don't let one hit here, God. Save the Top. Help the other guys in the platoon. Thanks for getting me here.*

Top Miller jumped down into the bunker.

Thank you, God.

The first sergeant sat down, lit a Pall Mall. His hands didn't shake. "You boys all okay?" he said, like he was making sure we had seats on the team bus to the game.

The day before we went back to the bush, I finished a working party and was going to grab my towel and take a shower. As I walked between the rows of tents, I could hear Cloninger's radio cranked up on the bunker where First Squad had guard duty on the perimeter. The rock and roll made me think again about Mike and Dottie Jackson.

I'd thought about little else the last couple days. I wondered if Mike wanted to die. He was no quitter, I knew. How I wished he'd not refused to leave his squad when he had the abscessed tooth. Would he quit now? Stop eating or something? Could you will yourself to death? I didn't doubt he'd give his life for his squad, maybe he'd think dying would be giving it for Dottie now?

And what about her? What would she do? I knew what people said at weddings: In sickness and in health, 'til death do us part. But, really? Forever, no matter what happens? Would a beautiful, sexy, nineteen-year-old girl even stay with a cripple? Should she? She'd have fifty or sixty years to go. What kind of life would that be? Did she owe Jackson that? What would Mike ask her to do? Would she even listen to him? What would it do to him if she left? How much more pain of any sort could he stand?

My head hurt thinking about all those impossible things.

I was close to the perimeter when I heard the Ronettes begin "Be My Baby." A pervasive sadness drenched me. I pictured Woody and Jackson dancing like a pair of madmen to Dottie's favorite song. It seemed like a very long time ago. I could see Jackson's big, square-jawed grin, those long lumberjack legs shuffling in the dirt to the beat. Then I saw those two damnable pink grooves scooped across his thick thighs and I pictured him lying in some hospital bed, a sheet pulled up to his neck, the form under the sheet ending inches below his hips.

I wanted to turn and run away from the music, from the pictures in my head. But something kept drawing me toward the bunkers. I hoped Woody wasn't on duty. He might go nuts if he heard that song.

I rounded the tents to the Ronettes belting about lovers together forever. John stood looking toward the bunker, a sad smile on his face. "You have to see this." He pointed. Woody was up on the sand-bagged roof, his back toward us. Dancing.

"Jesus. Is he drunk?"

The radio throbbed at full volume.

"Sober as a judge."

I walked to the bunker and looked up at Woody. Baggy camou-flaged trousers and worn jungle boots, holes under the arms of his green tee, bronzed and blonde and so good looking. Like a strangely dressed Adonis on *American Bandstand*, hands above his head, fin-gers quietly snapping, feet shuffling, hips and torso and arms undu-lating. The boy could dance.

He turned slowly, eyes closed, dancing as though he weren't up there by himself. A tear leaked down his cheek.

I knew what was going on inside his head. And for just a moment, I, too, could see Mike and Dottie Jackson dancing somewhere, in some time and place so much better than any they'd ever know again.

11

ALL FOUR OF FIRST BATTALION'S RIFLE companies were in the valley now—Delta to the west of us, Alpha and Charlie to the east. Rifle platoons from each company patrolled from checkpoint to checkpoint, searching, moving forward like pawns on a chessboard, usually coming together to form company defensive perimeters at night, sometimes staying out on platoon- or squad-sized ambushes.

We patrolled across wide, flat expanses of paddies and low hills, through patchwork quilts of undulating green rice and head-high elephant grass stitched together by dikes and thick tree lines and low, bamboo-covered hillocks. On the dikes and moving across the paddies, we were in the open, vulnerable to fire from tree lines and thickets too far away for us to see if enemy soldiers waited in ambush. In the elephant grass, we were even more blind, unable to see five feet into the surrounding walls of green and tan. We trudged warily all day, every day, then dug deep fighting holes before we took turns standing watch under a waning moon or fell into restless, troubled sleep.

We saw no sign of the enemy.

Every night I heard artillery rounds impact in the distance. Harassment and interdiction fires, pairs of rounds, *crump-crump*. I heard them as I stood watch in our fighting hole, heard them as I tried to sleep. Random. A trail intersection or stream crossing or hilltop on somebody's map. Always to the front of us, or off in the distance far to the side. We never knew if they had any effect, never found corpses of anyone killed by H&I.

"Useful as teats on a boar," Cloninger said. He stirred the coffee in his canteen cup with the raccoon penis bone he kept in a pocket.

"Might have a psychological impact," Corrigan said. "You know, Charlie bopping along never knowing if he's gonna get blown sky high, or trying to sleep not knowing if he's going to wake up dead. Might freak him out." The Professor was a glass-full kind of guy.

The Buzzard wasn't. "Like shootin' into tall grass hopin' you'll kill a rabbit you don't even know's there."

Freaked out or not, if the enemy knew we were there, they seemed to want nothing to do with us.

We trudged up a low, scruffy rise and dug in. The night was hot and drenchingly humid, thick with mosquitoes only mildly offended by the bug repellant I rubbed all over my arms, face, and neck. When a sliver of crescent moon or an occasional white pinprick of star hurried through the few breaks in the clouds, shadows skulked in front of our holes. I wasn't sure if I was looking at rocks, trees, or enemy soldiers crawling silently toward us. I spent the entire time I was on watch staring over the barrel of the machine gun, the safety clicked off.

Around midnight John took over, and I lay down behind our hole. The mosquitoes seemed as big as '46s; if they didn't drain all my blood, they might carry me off, save me for a snack. I rubbed more insect repellant on my face and neck. The petroleum smell made me think of Jackson. I wondered when Woody would get a letter from his parents, or his sister, or even Dottie with news about how Mike was doing. I had questions myself that I had no one to ask. How much pain was Jax in? Was he awake enough to know what had happened to him? Could you die from complications after a double amputation? Could you die because you didn't want to live?

I fell asleep wondering if he was still alive. And whether he wanted to be.

I was awakened by a noise in the distance like a dozen hands crumpling paper. It swelled to a static crackle like strings of the firecrackers we used to call "ladyfingers." I grabbed my rifle and ammo and crawled to our hole hoping I wasn't the tallest target inside our perimeter. I slid down beside John. It was pitch black to our front. I hoped no NVA could see my helmet above the ground.

"Delta's in contact," John said. "Sounds like they've stepped in the shit."

I strained to see down the slope to our front, waiting for us to be next. John tapped me on the arm. "There, ten o'clock." The crackling sound of distant gunfire intensified, ebbed, swelled again, punctuated by the low thuds and booms of RPGs and hand grenades. Flashes of light, lines of red tracers, then green, burst from the blackness and streaked through the dark sky.

My chest constricted as if I'd been grabbed from behind. Not far from us, Marines fought in the dark for their lives. My war suddenly became much more real, like I'd encountered something I'd only heard rumored before. I turned from the sounds and the flashes and strained my eyes down the slope to our front, my thoughts teeming. There are gooks out there. Lots of them. Trying to kill Marines. Where did they come from? Are they coming for us?

The firing grew in intensity, died down without stopping, intensified again. A ripping noise like bullets tearing open the dark. Crackles, thuds, booms.

"That's a boatload of gooks," John whispered.

"Think we'll get hit, too?"

"I don't know. There's a lot over there."

"Will we go help them out?" It sounded like Delta needed our help, though the thought of a forced march in the dark into possible ambushes petrified me.

"Too far. Three or four clicks, and a river between here and there. It'd take hours; we'd probably get ambushed, be worse off than them. At least they're dug in. They'll have to hang on until the gooks sky out before dawn."

In the distance, a streak of red tracers erupted from deep in the sky and tore toward the ground. A tearing burp, a loud, deep sound, like the thick membrane of night rent in half.

"Spooky," John said. The big cargo planes armed with .50-caliber multi-barrel Gatling guns could fire thousands of rounds in seconds. There must be a hell of a lot of gooks, I thought. I looked away and stared down front, saw nothing but shadows. I looked back toward the battle. More chains of red light streamed down the black sky. Deep, ripping burps. The crackle of gunfire and *crump* of grenades. Tracers crisscrossing over the ground.

"Get some, Spooky," John whispered.

A streak of green tracers burst from the ground into the sky.

"Gook heavy machine gun," John said. He shook his head—a single, appreciative motion. "They're determined, for damned sure. I wouldn't stick around if Spooky was shooting at me."

My God. What sort of enemy stood and fought in the face of such firepower?

More streaks of red tearing earthward. Green tracers reaching back up.

"Delta must be surrounded."

I felt like someone had rubbed ice on my spine. Surrounded by NVA, could Delta be overrun? I tore my eyes away from the deadly light show and stared again to our front. I sure as hell hoped the rest of Bravo was keeping a hard eye in front of their holes. "How can you tell?"

"The way Spooky's shooting."

"If they're surrounded, shouldn't we go?" I was afraid we'd be told to leave the relative safety of our holes and walk into the darkness, but if Marines were in trouble over there, shouldn't we help?

"Too far," John said again. "If we made it, the gooks would sky out. Or we'd end up with Marines shooting each other trying to hit the gooks between us."

The fight in the distance went on for hours. The red streaks and the staccato burps stopped blasting out of the black sky when Spooky left. The deep thud of artillery began again then. Later the sound of gunfire on the ground slowed, burst out again sporadically, repeated that pattern a number of times, and finally stopped. I heard more artillery rounds land with a distant *crump-boom, crump-boom*.

The gooks broke contact before dawn. We moved toward Delta then. I prayed the gooks weren't moving toward us. Someplace out there was an enemy force big enough to surround and fight an entire Marine company and tough enough to keep fighting even when Spooky worked out.

Every step in the dark filled me with terror. Every bush was a black shape that might be a gook or hiding one I couldn't see. For the first time, I wondered seriously if I was going to die before I was twenty. I glared at every shape and form I could make out in the darkness, tried to think about what I should do if we were hit. What if it came from our left? What if the right? Would I be able to tell in the confusion and noise? *Please, God, please,* I prayed, *let me live.* My entire body was clenched in a knot.

Dawn was worse than the dark. The first faint hints of light made shadows creep and move stealthily, like men with fixed bayonets sneaking toward us in the dim light. My clenched teeth throbbed. I bunched up behind John as we waited our turn to wade into the river. Perspiration burned my straining eyeballs. I was already nearly as wet as I'd be in the stream.

In the thin light, a '46 appeared in the sky. It dropped down fast where I assumed Delta was dug in. Its accompanying gunship circled above. The '46 took off. "They unloaded that fast," I said. "They must think the gooks are still close."

John shook his head. "Nothing came off. That was a medevac bird." Another came in.

The stream was thirty yards wide, waist deep. I wondered if I'd be shot as I waded, slow and exposed. There was no ambush.

We linked up with Delta. I found myself standing next to a Delta Marine, his face smeared with blood and dirt. From the look of his boots and uniform, he hadn't been in the bush any longer than me. He looked barely old enough to be a sophomore in high school, not even stubble poking through the filth on his face. His eyes were sunken deep in his head; a tremor made him look palsied. Baby-faced and a hundred years old.

He caught me watching him try to light a cigarette. I was embarrassed he saw me staring at him. He was embarrassed by my watching.

"Tough stuff," I said. It was all I could think of.

He nodded. He smelled of fear, sharp and sour and bitter at the same time. A smell like a color, filthy yellow-brown streaked with green.

"They came after us." He sounded amazed, still terrified. "We weren't moving, we were dug in for the night. We seen nothing since we got into the valley. Not a single gook. They came after us."

He fumbled with his cigarette, held it between his lips, attempted to steady it with shaking fingers. "So many. We didn't even know they were there until they were on us."

He dropped his hands to his sides, a gesture of futility and grief and disbelief. "They killed Sutter. And Valera. I don't even know how many others." He put the cigarette back in his mouth but couldn't hold his hands still long enough to strike a match.

I fumbled in a pocket and came up with dry matches. I struck one and held it for him as he lit his cigarette. He nearly burned my fingers with its wavering tip. I was embarrassed that my own hands were shaking a little.

I hadn't noticed Timmons standing beside us before. He was smoking, something new. I didn't want him to see my hands shaking. He wasn't looking at me. He stared at the other Marine, fear all over his face.

I looked back at the Delta Marine. "I'm sorry about your friends," I said. I didn't know what more to say about them or what he'd just been through.

He exhaled a cloud of smoke like a deep, ashen sigh. "Thanks," he said. "I don't know how to tell my sister about Sutter."

He looked like he was going to cry.

12

DEAD BODIES WERE EVERYWHERE. Nine Delta Marines in body bags or covered with ponchos lay in a row inside the perimeter. I counted thirteen dead NVA strewn in bloody, torn heaps around just the part of Delta's position I could see. Three of them inside the lines.

Doc Matheson came back from talking with corpsmen from Delta. He said they'd killed over two dozen gooks but had paid a terrible price.

"Eight emergency medevacs," he said. They'd gone out on the first bird because they'd likely die if they didn't get to a hospital right away. The choppers hadn't been able to fly through the artillery or Spooky's fire. "Those pilots have balls; they came as soon as they could," Matt said, distress all over his face. "The first bird took a lot of rounds but kept coming." He looked over toward the row of body bags and ponchos. "Too late for one of the emergencies, though."

Another half-dozen Marines had been classified as priority medevacs—not likely to die if their treatment waited a few hours. They'd gone out on one of the birds I'd seen land as we approached Delta's position. The routines, wounded who'd need lesser surgery and stitches and such, eight or ten of them, still waited near the Delta dead. They could all go out on the same bird. Half-a-dozen Marines with wounds that would heal without stitches were staying in the bush with the company.

I felt a level of fear beyond what I'd known since Jackson was wounded. That had been sharp-edged, focused, almost specific to loss of my limbs or sight. This was blunt, unfocused, but constant, as though the proximity and possibility of death was a weight I carried now and could never put down.

First Platoon began to gather into our patrol formation. "Too damn late," John growled half under his breath. "They're in Hanoi by now. We shouldn't have stayed with Delta so long."

"Where do you think they all came from?" I asked.

We'd searched every day and not seen a sign. We'd been hunting them, but they came after us. No one knew how many attacked. Hundreds, some of the Delta Marines had said in astounded, shaking voices. Out of nowhere. No warning at all. Even the listening posts hadn't detected them before they'd surrounded the company.

"I don't know," John said. "Maybe that complex we're supposed to find. They're probably moving in small units now, make them harder for us to find."

Behind me, Havey said what I was feeling: "It's like fighting ghosts."

"That's bullshit, Havey." Corporal Harding sounded as if he'd just been insulted. "They're just men and we're going to find them and kill more of them." He pointed to an NVA corpse a few feet away. The man lay on his back, eyes closed, gaping red tears in his chest.

"Yes, Corporal Harding." Havey looked like a DI was going to squat-thrust him half to death.

I expected Timmons to have a contemptuous look on his face. He was too focused trying to light a cigarette from the stub of his last.

⸻

We followed a blood trail like muted hounds on a scent. Splotches of maroon on the ground, large, coagulating red spots turning russet like scabs on the earth. They disappeared as though the wounded had stopped bleeding or vanished into thin air.

"Like ghosts," Havey whispered to me.

We searched all day and found no one, then climbed a small hill and dug deep fighting holes. Darkness fell like a trap door slamming shut. By the time John and I'd been in our hole for an hour, the night was so black I could barely see the muzzle of our gun. There was no moon. Low, thick clouds smothered the stars, threatened a downpour that would further mask any movement to our front. John lay down behind the hole while I stood first watch.

I'd never before experienced such darkness, such a sense of being alone in the abyss. I heard no one cough, no one kick a rock or drop something into their hole. Nothing moved. Nothing made noise. There was no murmur of wind in the brush down the hill; none of the usual *thrum* or *scree* of insects or frogs; not even the rustle of rats or lizards or snakes in the undergrowth. It was as though God had wielded the heavy, close night like a soaked blanket to smother all his creatures, blot out the stars, and strangle the wind.

Havey and Cloninger were in the hole to my right, beyond them Timmons and Fullerton, Prevas and Landon to my left, and beyond them, Willis and Ladoor. I could see or hear no one. No sense of their presence, the way you can tell someone is nearby, where they should be, even if you can't see or hear them. Those Marines could have evaporated like the NVA that overran Delta.

I couldn't get the shaken Delta Marines out of my mind. *They came after us. We didn't even know they were there until they were on top of us.*

I stared so intently into the black my eyeballs hurt. I wished John was in the hole with me. I looked toward where he slept. I couldn't see him. I leaned against the back of our hole and glared into the dark. Finally, I could make out a low mound on the ground—John, no more than three feet away. I turned and peered again into the black down the hill and waited for my heart to stop hammering my ribs. An enemy could creep up within less than a yard of my face, and I'd never know he was there.

I clicked the gun's safety off. My hand shook slightly. I told myself it was only the night air against my sunburnt skin.

It was John's turn in the hole around midnight. I lay fully clothed on my rubber lady, my poncho liner draped over me from my neck to my boots, the air like sleet on my sunburned skin. I couldn't sleep. I kept seeing the Marine from Delta, his shocked eyes, his blood and dirt smeared, whiskerless cheeks drained white beneath his tan. I'd never seen anyone under eighty tremble like that.

A flash and blast of gunfire shattered the night, wrenching me out of my thoughts. I tumbled into our hole giving John a whack in the head with my rifle butt as he threw himself forward to peer over the barrel of the machine gun.

I strained to pierce the black, to see anything beyond the painful, bright pinpoints of light that flashed somewhere behind my eyes, to hear any movement beyond the sharp staccato echo receding in my ears.

The thought muddled its way through my fear: No one on our lines is firing.

I could hear Marines on either side of me sliding fast into their holes. To our right, I heard Cloninger's worried whisper: "Where the fuck . . . ?" Then there was no other noise.

Nothing moved in front of us. Nothing made any sound but the blood hammering at my temples.

After what seemed like a very long time, John leaned back from the gun and whispered, "That was from our lines. Someone a couple holes down must've spooked."

God Almighty! I thought. Someone's going to get us killed. What if gooks with a mortar saw that muzzle flash? It had lit up the hillside like a streetlight.

There was movement to our right; I jerked around. The lieutenant's face was inches from mine. "Come with me, McClure," he whispered urgently. "No shooting, Garafano. I think we've got a man down in front."

I followed Lieutenant Mangan outside the lines. I had trouble controlling my breathing, positive the world around me was about to explode. The platoon leader was a hunched-over black form in the darkness.

Ten feet down the hill, a Marine lay in a crumpled, silent heap. The lieutenant gestured to me, then grabbed him under the arms. I took his legs. My arms were suddenly slippery, my nose and mouth filled with the cloying, thick stench of blood and shit and torn entrails. He burped a slow, thick, liquid gargle like blowing blood bubbles through his chest. I fought a violent urge to puke.

The company command post was in an old bomb crater on the top of the hill. We tried not to bump the wounded man on the ground as we struggled toward it. "Corpsman, corpsman, corpsman!" the lieutenant called over and over in a furious whisper.

Matt and Doc Dorsey and Doc Stevens, the company's chief corpsman, appeared as we slid down into the crater. We laid the wounded man on the ground in the middle of the CP. I stepped back and squatted off to the side as the corpsmen tore off the Marine's shirt. They probed and pushed and pulled with desperate speed, wrapped long coils of tape and battle dressings around his torso. Bloody hands flashed and glistened, worked furiously in the red glow of night-lensed flashlights.

The wounded man's hand dropped palm-up in the dirt. His fingers jerked tight then uncurled as though he were trying to grab onto something but kept losing his grip. A black Marine. In the dark rush up the hill, I hadn't seen his face, didn't notice if he was black or white. The corpsmen blocked my view now. Suddenly I needed to know who it was. Havey? Smitty? All I could make out was his hand and part of one arm.

My arms were slathered with blood, warm and sticky and black. A revulsion bordering on terror surged inside me. I began to rub my arms hard.

"Knock it off!" someone whispered urgently.

I stopped rubbing. It made no difference; the blood wouldn't come off. In the dim haze of the red lights, I thought I could see it coagulate on my skin. I wondered if I was losing my mind.

"Jesus, lungs and guts," somebody muttered.

Staff Sergeant Gilles slid into the crater half-holding another Marine. Timmons. Gilles pushed him down to a sitting position several feet away from the frantically working corpsmen. "I didn't know," Timmons babbled. "I didn't know. Oh, sweet Jesus, I did not know."

"All right. Stop. Shut up, goddamn it, shut up," the Company Gunny growled, his voice like gravel in a paper bag.

Timmons didn't stop. A hoarse moan, as though he were begging for torture to come to an end. "I didn't know. Jesus, no. Oh, God, I am sorry."

Lieutenant Russel, the artillery forward observer, scuttled over in front of him, put his hands on his shoulders. "Shut up, man. We'll have all the gooks in the world on us if you don't shut up."

Timmons stopped talking. He started a low, moaning sound, a cross between a growl and a groan.

I still smelled blood and shit and something sharp and vile like spoiled garbage. I began to obsess. *Did the man shit himself when he was shot? Was he coated with crap and the contents of his guts and what's on my arms and are all the gooks in the world going to come at us now and John by himself and me up here without my rifle or helmet or flak jacket or anything to defend myself except my bare hands? Jesus, help me.* I wrapped my arms across my chest and pressed hard to keep the panic from erupting and devouring me.

"Pray with me," Lieutenant Russel said. "Whisper now, whisper. Our Father . . ."

A company radioman looked like he was choking a handset. "Whatta'ya mean all choppers are out?" he whispered violently. "We've got an emergency medevac here! Did you hear me? I said emergency! Over."

Someone moved out of the way of one of the lights. The wounded Marine lay in the flashlights' red wash, torso bandaged and wet. Havey. I choked down a gasp the rotten, acrid taste of bile filled my mouth. *Oh, my God, Havey,* I said to myself. *What happened to you? C'mon, you poor son of a bitch, fight for it, man.*

"...thy will be done..."

Lieutenant Russel whispered the prayer; Timmons followed, out of synch, half a phrase behind him. "Give... day..." It was like background noise in a horror movie.

"...who trespass against us..."

I rubbed my forearms. The blood-matted hair pulled and pinched. *Please, Jesus, please.*

"...but deliver us from evil..."

Shut the fuck up, people. Please, God, make them shut up.

"Come on, man," Matt whispered urgently. "Breathe, man, breathe. For God's sake, please, breathe."

The radio crackled. The radioman whispered angrily, "An hour? I said an emergency! Did you read me, Jackhammer? I said an emergency! Over!"

Crackle. Crackle.

"Forty-five minutes? Can't you do better for an emergency? Over."

Crackle. Crackle.

"Roger. I know about that. But please, try and hurry them up. Over."

"...for ever and ever..."

"I didn't mean to," Timmons moaned.

Matt didn't look up. "Somebody shut him the fuck up. Come on, Havey, hang with me."

Lieutenant Russel still had his hands on Timmons' shoulders, their noses inches apart. He said something I couldn't hear.

Havey's eyes were closed. His nostrils flared like barrels, his entire face scrunched up as though he were in terrible pain, his eyebrows arched in a panicked plea: *Aren't any of you going to do anything about this?*

My view was blocked again as the corpsmen moved frantically over him. The only noises in the crater: heavy breathing, the shuffle of knees in the dirt, hands working on Havey, and Timmons saying "No" when Lieutenant Russel whispered something to him.

And then everything stopped.

The entire CP became very still. No one moved.

Then the corpsmen leaned back, away from Havey. Doc Dorsey shook his head. Doc Stevens looked up at the black sky. Matt sat back on his haunches and hung his head. I wanted to scream and sob and puke all at the same time. I gagged it all back, sat as stiff and brittle as the drying blood on my arms while my guts churned as though they wanted to explode out my ass.

In the muted rouge pall, I could see Havey again, his blood-soaked, bandage-wrapped chest and belly, his open mouth, his closed eyes. The expression on his face seemed to have loosened, as though he were no longer in pain, as though his questions had been answered, or he'd simply stopped asking them.

I couldn't pull my eyes away from his face, his body glistening in the thin red light. I was waiting for something, though I didn't know what. Maybe for some apparition, some slowly rising vapor, his soul leaving his body, floating up out of what used to be him, like something the nuns told us when I was young. What happened when you died? Was it like God hovered above you, hand outstretched like the painting in the Sistine Chapel? Was Jesus standing a little ways off, hands outstretched at his sides—*Come unto me, my little sheep*. Were your grandparents there, like standing on the side of a dirt road waiting to greet you? Did you miss your mother? Your dad? Could you see them?

I wondered again if I was going insane. I clenched my teeth so hard I worried they might break.

Everyone was silent until the Skipper said, "Damn. God fucking damn."

Timmons buried his face in his hands.

"Jackhammer, this is Bravo Six." The radioman's voice was flat and empty, suffused with a weary, generalized bitterness. "Never mind on the emergency evac. It's a routine now. Over."

Crackle. Crackle.

"Roger, Jackhammer. With the supply chopper in the morning. Over."

"Oh Jesus . . ." Timmons moaned.

"Calm down, man. It wasn't your fault," Lieutenant Russel whispered. "You didn't know."

"Who is it? Lieutenant Mangan, he's yours?" Captain Brill asked.

"Yes, sir. Havey. Private Havey."

"The small black guy who was always so polite? High voice?"

"Yes, sir."

"Oh God . . . I am so sorry," Timmons moaned.

The captain looked to the chief corpsman. "Doc, can you use some morphine? We really need to hold down the noise." He turned back to Lieutenant Mangan. "This man yours, too, Mark?"

"Yes, sir. Timmons. Both fairly new guys." The lieutenant sounded as though he had a mouth full of gauze.

Havey lay dead in the middle of us, almost as though he'd been forgotten, no longer anyone needing anything special.

"I've got the morphine, Skipper," Doc Stevens whispered.

"Do it."

"Oh God . . . I didn't mean it." Timmons was getting louder; he began to rock side to side. Lieutenant Russel put a hand over his mouth. Timmons stopped rocking.

Dear God, don't let there be any gooks near us now. We're gonna get mortared; we're gonna get attacked. Don't let us get Delta'd. I wished desperately that I had my rifle, my helmet.

"Take it easy, man," the chief corpsman said. "This will help." He jabbed Timmons with the ampule of morphine.

"Apparently for some reason the dumb . . . the poor bastard . . . Havey, sir, climbed out in front of his hole to take a crap instead of going to the cat hole in back of the lines. Timmons there was in the next hole. He must've just seen someone move in front of our lines."

Oh my god, oh my god, oh my god.

They were the only words in my head.

I walked back to our fighting hole like a zombie with a bad back, crouched over to lessen my silhouette, my arms raised in front of me, Havey's blood on them, a stiff, matted coat. I moved very slowly, terrified gooks would shoot me as I walked in the open, terrified I'd miss our hole in the blackness and walk outside our lines and someone would kill me like Timmons killed Havey.

It felt like I'd gone a very long distance before I made it back to the hole and slid down behind John. "What happened?"

"Timmons killed Havey. By mistake. It was terrible."

"Jesus, Mary, and Joseph."

My mouth was full of flannel. I drank all the water in two of my canteens and one of John's.

I used another entire canteen to scrub my arms. It didn't do much good.

When I finally lay back down sometime later, my brain projected slow-motion pictures of everything I'd seen. Havey's tormented face, his blood-soaked torso, the docs bandaging him, my arms drenched in blood. For hours, the gore-filled pictures slipped slowly across my brain without accompanying words. It was as though horror had left the film intact but expunged my ability to form thoughts, erased all my words as though they'd never been learned.

In the morning, I saw the body bag lying outside the CP like a UPS package waiting for pickup. My arms were stained a foul reddish brown, the hair standing up like bristles on a pig in a slaughterhouse. A thick, vile odor sat in my nose and mouth. I could taste my own blood where I'd worked my tongue against the tooth I'd chipped in a football game my senior year.

A chopper came in. Marines ran through the rotor wash up the ramp and back down carrying C-rats, ammo, a bag of mail. They piled everything on the side of the hill. Witt and Woody and Prevas and Cloninger shuffled Havey's body to the helicopter and laid him without ceremony inside the bird, then ran back through the rotor storm. The Gunny came over the side of the CP crater holding Timmons by the arm. Timmons carried all his gear and Havey's too. The Gunny pushed him up the ramp and he, too, disappeared into the bird.

13

FOR DAYS AFTER TIMMONS killed Havey, we pushed deeper into the valley. Havey had been right; it was like looking for ghosts.

People talked about the incident for only a couple of days. "I feel so bad for the little guy," Woody said.

"What the fuck was it with Timmons he couldn't see another Marine in the dark, for Christ's sake?" Corporal Harding growled.

It could've been me, I thought. I had the M60's safety off when I was on watch. If anyone had moved in front of me, I would've cut him in half. Thank God I wasn't in the hole when Havey went in front of our lines.

I looked down as I thought that, realized I was trying to rub something invisible out of my skin.

"And Havey fucked up," Cloninger said. "He shouldn'a been out there."

That set Ladoor off. "Havey fucked up? Havey dead. Shot by a white boy. You be lynchin' his ass if the other way 'round."

"That's bullshit, Ladoor. And you know it." The Buzzard didn't take shit from anyone.

"One more dead nigger don't make no difference to honkies." Ladoor glared at him.

I thought Cloninger might grab his rifle. "Who the fuck you callin' honky, Ladoor? I liked Havey one hell of a lot better than Timmons. Go fuck yourself!"

"Your likin' him sure didn't keep Havey in the hole, did you?"

"What? I was asleep behind the hole when he got out to take a shit."

"Cool it down, people, they both fucked up," Corporal Harding said.

A day or two later, it was almost as if Havey had never been among us, as if Timmons hadn't been part of the platoon. The only time I heard the shooting referred to again was when Corporal Harding warned a new guy about where he should crap in the bush. In Vietnam we tried to compartmentalize our worst traumatic experiences. Put everything—the sights, sounds, smells, and fears—in a box and put the box on a shelf. It was years before I took some of my boxes down; more years before I stopped opening some of them up. Sometimes, even now, some lids pop off when I'm not expecting them to.

We pushed hard every day, searching for the complex, searching for NVA, finding nothing. Except for an occasional Gianelli wisecrack or a Corrigan-fractured fairy tale about the girls he'd dated, we seldom smiled any more.

We had something to laugh about only once.

First Squad had almost gotten across a knee-deep paddy, the mud grabbing at our boots, when Willie pitched headlong into the muck. He came up cursing and gagging and spitting. The Vietnamese fertilized rice paddies with their feces; no one went face down in one unless the alternative was to get shot. Willie just tripped.

"Jesus Christ, Willis, you smell like shit." Corporal Harding looked at him with disgust. "Skylarking again? How'd you manage to trip?"

"Dunno." Willie hung his head like a brow-beaten basset.

"The girls in Bangfuck aren't going to like you smelling like that," Gio said.

A look of panic flooded Willie's face. He was scheduled to go on R&R soon. "They'll let me take a bath before I go, won't they?"

Corrigan shook his head. "I don't know, Willie, they might just use you as a bad example."

"You don't really think they won't let me shower before I get on the plane, do you?" I was afraid he might actually cry.

Woody held up his hand as though to say, that's enough. "I guarantee, Willie, you'll get a shower and clean khakis before you go."

"I guess Woody's right, Willie," Gio said. "A little soap and water, a little aftershave, those girls in Bangaroo will be waiting for you like heifers in heat."

Willie finally realized that people had been joking with him. "Ah, you guys . . ." he said.

We came to a village different from what we'd seen before. Deep trenches around it, as though people expected to fight. I felt the tension rise in the platoon. The lieutenant and Corporal Harding looked even more focused than usual. Staff Sergeant Gilles prowled the ville with his shotgun at the ready. If panthers carried guns in the jungle, they'd look like that. John and Gio carried their M60s cradled on a hip. For once, Gio wasn't cracking wise. Woody lit a cigarette off the butt of his last. Prevas' eyes looked like they'd been glued open, stuck on wide. He kept the flechette-loaded blooper aimed to his front. I hoped I was hiding my fear.

The villagers watched us in hostile silence while we searched their hootches. "That's good," John said. "They'd have scurried into their bunkers if they thought there'd be a fight."

"Doesn't make 'em friendly," Corporal Harding said.

"Bastards set booby traps," Cavett said.

Harding agreed. "Just because we haven't seen any yet, doesn't mean there won't be any. You people keep a sharp eye, you hear?"

John pointed to an old woman squatted back on her haunches in front of a hootch. He smiled at her. John amazed me. He was filthy and tired and sore like the rest of us, but he was enjoying himself. Gio and John were the happiest miserable people I ever met. "Old mama-san there doesn't look unfriendly, Cavett," John said. "Or that young one beside her." I think John believed that, but it was clear he was poking at Cavett.

"Shit," Cavett said.

We found no sign of enemy soldiers, booby traps, or arms. Nothing except villagers, well-kept hootches, and solid bunkers, all looking as though they were waiting for the worst.

Woody got letters from home three days in a row.

"Mike's mom told mine. They're close friends," Woody said when the first letter arrived. His eyes seemed sunken in his head, bordered by worry lines he hadn't had before.

"Her whole letter's about how terrible it is now for Mike and Dottie and his parents. I mean, no shit, Ma, it's both his goddamned legs. And, of course, she's even more worried about me now. No shit again, Ma, me too."

"Anything about how Mike's doing?" John asked. "I guess your mom wrote before even the Woodsons knew anything."

Woody looked at us, the worry even more pronounced on his movie-star face. "Nothing. But I tell you Pope, I know Mike. I know what he wants."

The letter a day later was from Woody's dad. "Big Jim," Woody called him. He'd been a World War II Marine who'd never talked much about his war. He didn't have any information about Mike, either. "Dad just wanted me to know he realized how much I'm hurting because of Mike. He and mom will do anything for him and Dottie and Mike's parents they can," Woody said.

The third letter Woody got was from his mother again. "She went to see Mike's mom and dad." Woody shook his head. "She says they're devastated. Of course they are; they've got to be. She didn't say if Mike's parents told her anything about him." Woody stared at the date on the envelope. "This is eleven days ago. Who the hell knows what's happened since then? She didn't say anything about Dottie, either, except that she hasn't seen her. Ma assumes she's a wreck. Jesus."

Woody looked like he'd aged ten years since I'd met him a few weeks ago. "I love my mom," he said, "but I don't know if I can even open the next letter I get from her. I don't know how much of that I can take."

Except when Woody told us about letters from his parents, the rest of us rarely talked about Mike Jackson. Sometimes his name came up when someone spoke of guys with a great sense of humor or ones who really had balls. But even if no one mentioned what had happened to him, we all knew it and became silent again.

<hr/>

We moved in platoon column down a small rise toward a calf-deep rice paddy. Landon had point. He moved cautiously, searching for signs of ambush or booby traps. When he got to the edge of the paddy, he stopped, and the lieutenant moved up beside him. Mangan scoped the area with his binos.

John had his out too. A low dike was thirty meters to our front; a couple hundred meters beyond that a ragged green tree line slanted away to the side of a bombed-out pagoda. "What do you think?" I asked. Most of me wanted a fight; part of me half hoped he'd tell me everything looked fine.

"Something feels funny," John said. He put his binoculars back in their case. "Stay close, okay?"

The lieutenant brought the platoon on line so we could bring all our firepower to bear to our front. We couldn't move fast in the muck, so we walked spread out in the open for what felt like a long time.

Loud, sharp, cackling bursts of gunfire suddenly spewed from the tree line.

Things happened so fast they seemed to meld into one turbulent blur of noise and frenetic action and confusion, though later everything that happened next was embedded in my brain with stop-frame, slow-motion clarity.

John was several steps in front of me, going for the dike, his knees pumping like he was running the tires in football practice. He stopped suddenly and looked back at me. "Come on, come on," he yelled. "Get up here with the ammo."

I tried to run. I tried to lift my knees the way John did. Where did he get the strength? I took half a dozen steps in the calf-deep muck, then dropped the ammo can.

The entire platoon surged toward the cover of the low dike, some firing as they sloshed forward. Except Landon. Gnat's Nuts stood shooting from the offhand position as calmly as if he were on a rifle range. I expected him to be killed. He emptied a full magazine, a couple shots at a time, before he ran for the dike.

I searched in the brown churning water for the ammo can.

Gianelli was running forward with John. He turned, too, and yelled. "Come on Cavett. I need those fucking rounds. Come on, McClure, join the party!" Purple granny glasses, purple rings, sweat glistening on his face, he looked like a dope addict at a dance as he yelled, "Get some, First Platoon!"

I found the ammo can, pulled it out of the mud, and struggled forward again. At the dike, John was already firing. He turned and yelled again for the ammo. Standing beside him with bullets snapping around him, Corporal Harding screamed at his squad, "Get up to the dike! Return fire! Move, people, move!"

I tucked the ammo can under my arm like a halfback and tried to run. I'd almost caught up with Cavett when I heard a resounding

CU-WHAP! and he dropped as though his head had been cleaved with an axe.

Gio didn't see him. He kept pushing toward the dike. Cavett lay face down, spread-eagled like a body dumped in a pond. If he wasn't dead, he'd drown. Someone had to get his head out of the water, drag him to the dike. "McClure! McClure! Ammo! Ammo!" Even in the din, I could hear John yell between his short, controlled bursts of fire. I veered toward Cavett.

Then Ladoor was beside me plunging through the water and mud like a water bull on a rampage. "Go to the gun," he yelled, then he was past me and in an amazing show of strength, scooped up Cavett's thickset, limp body, flak jacket, pack, and all, and in one motion threw him over his shoulder and moved toward the dike.

"McClure! Marty! Ammo!" John yelled.

The cacophony of gunfire was bedlam. M16s, M60s, AK-47s, a gook machine gun. I had no clue what targets anyone in the platoon was firing at. All I could see of the tree line beyond that dike I so desperately wanted to get down behind was dense foliage shivering and crackling and thin wisps of smoke rising like gossamer ghosts in the thick green.

I was ten yards from the dike when a line of tracers from an NVA machine gun ripped past my head. Neon blue green flashes like bright blobs of protoplasm at ear level, five or six inches from my face. I had the strongest, craziest sensation that I could just lift my hand, wave "hi" to John, and the bullets would pass through my palm like a Saturday morning cartoon character trying to catch blurbs of bright colored light. In that split second of caricature clarity, it barely registered that dozens of bullets had just passed within inches of my face.

I dropped down behind the dike next to John. The ammo can was coated with thick, foul-smelling mud. I tore it open and began to feed the coiled belt into the feed pall of the gun. *Dear God*, I prayed, *don't let that mud cause a misfeed. Christ Jesus, help us here.*

Ladoor dropped Cavett nearby, propped his head against the dike, then threw himself down and began firing. Doc Matheson ran through the fire and knelt over Cavett.

We half knelt, half lay, bullets snapping above our heads. John raked the trees with a long yammering blast. I lifted the belts up out of the can, let the rounds run across my palm, run smoothly down into the feed tray an inch below my hand. Burst after burst, tracers slashed streaking red fire from us into the tree line.

Then the lieutenant was yelling for anyone without a real target to cease fire, and the platoon sergeant, and then the squad leaders, took up the call, and John stopped firing, and then Gio, and up and down the dike the firing became only sporadic.

Whenever a Marine fired, a blast came back at us. Most of the enemies' bullets went above our heads. A few hit the dike, but no other Marines were hit. If there'd been a lot of gooks there before, it seemed now as though only two or three might be left. I wondered if they were covering for others who'd run off, or maybe the others were dead or too badly wounded to fight. I glanced toward Cavett. I could only see his legs, because corpsmen knelt over him now. I couldn't tell if he was dead or alive.

Lieutenant Mangan took First Squad down the dike to a stand of trees on the left. With a *pop* and *whoosh*, a green cluster flare tore into the air. We blasted the tree line in front of the enveloping squad as the lieutenant and the Marines with him swept in from the left. Then John stopped shooting; there were three or four bursts of M16 fire inside the tree line, then all firing stopped, and then there was a strange momentary silence as though I'd suddenly gone deaf.

Corporal Harding stepped out of the tree line and waved for the platoon to come over.

"I need to check on Cavett," John said.

"Should I go across?" I pointed toward the tree line. I hoped John would say yes. I didn't want to see Cavett's corpse. I rubbed my arms. John told me to go.

Lieutenant Mangan and Smitty were at the edge of the tree line, the lieutenant on the radio, probably calling in a sitrep. Behind them, just inside the trees, Marines from First Squad were looking at something on the ground. As I got closer, I saw Corporal Harding light Woody's cigarette, then his own. They were laughing. I hadn't seen Woody laugh in weeks.

Two bodies lay sprawled just inside the tree line, two more back in the trees. I joined Harding and Woody and looked down at the corpses. One had part of his face shot away. Smashed teeth and jawbone and broken, leaking nose and sinus cavities, one eye bulging out as though ready to explode from its socket and blast through the air like a ghoul's golf ball. My stomach churned.

The second corpse was a woman, an AK-47 next to her, ammunition pouches draped from her neck. I'd heard stories of female NVA or VC, but they'd seemed apocryphal. A woman who carried an AK-47 and hundreds of rounds of ammunition? I hadn't believed the stories before I saw her.

Her eyes were closed. Her lips were raised in what looked amazingly like a pucker, as though she were waiting for a lover's kiss. She may have been in her twenties. Her face was smooth, unlined, more angular than that of any woman I'd seen in the villes. She was pretty. She had full, unconstrained breasts made more prominent by the ammo pouch straps crisscrossing between them, her nipples incongruously hard. It had been a long time since I'd seen an attractive woman. I wondered if she was just knocked out, whether she might awaken and those breasts stir before my eyes.

Then I looked down her body and saw bloody coils of intestines spilling from beneath her torn blouse like glistening snakes.

My stomach lurched. I turned away.

Smitty's prediction that I'd grow to like looking at dead gooks wasn't yet accurate. But I didn't feel sorry for these, even the woman. They'd tried to kill us. Probably had Cavett. And I remembered what happened to Delta. I remembered Jackson. I didn't enjoy looking at dead NVA yet. But I was definitely in favor of killing them.

Pius John was laughing when he finally walked up to me. I thought that was weird, he'd just come from Cavett, who was most likely dead or at least badly wounded. "Flake's got more luck than a cat with all nine lives left and a rabbit's foot around his neck," John said.

"He's okay?"

"He will be. A round must've gone through something or lost momentum when it ricocheted." He shrugged, gave a short laugh. "Had to be mostly spent when it found Cavett. Missed his thick skull by a millimeter when it lodged between his helmet and liner." John laughed again. "Knocked him out cold, but he's come around. He'll have a headache like he's been beat like a drum, but he's okay."

"Fuckin' Flake," Corporal Harding said. "He was damn near as short as he says." He nodded toward the two bodies. "Come here, Pope, look what we've got."

"Damn," John said. "She a nurse?"

"Nope. No medical gear, not even bandages. She had an AK-47 and lots of ammo."

"Damn," John said again. "I've heard of that but didn't think it was true."

"You see the tits on that woman?" Woody said. "Regular Sophia Noojin Loren. Reminds me of one of the girls I dated in Bangkok." He made quotation marks in the air with his fingers when he said "dated."

That was met with a chorus of pleas not to continue, a few threats if he didn't stop.

"No, no, Woodson . . ." Corrigan sounded as though he'd found a way to combine begging with a demand. "I'll have to carry my dick in a splint if you're going to tell more of your R&R stories. Some of us aren't going for a very long time."

"I'm going pretty soon. Bangkok. Like Woody." Willie grinned his loose, rubbery grin.

"Can you imagine old Willie all liquored up in a whorehouse in Bangfuck?" Woody laughed. He'd apparently put Mike and Dottie Jackson into a box for at least a little while.

"Willie, they let you find out about sex, man, none of those girls may be any use to the rest of us when we get to go." Corrigan's thick mustache seemed to droop more.

"Ah, you guys," Willie said. That was all he ever said whenever anyone kidded him about being a virgin. He hadn't been smart enough to lie about that like half the platoon probably had.

Everyone seemed to have forgotten we were standing over a couple of corpses, including a woman with a pretty face and nice tits. I wondered if this, like the joking after the dead man flew through the air or the cheering after John killed the two from the hill, was more of that darkness he'd warned me about.

We left the bodies where they lay. Bloated black and blue flies were already swarming on their wet parts.

Lieutenant Mangan wasn't happy. He was pleased with the four kills, but he'd wanted more and had hoped we could capture an NVA alive so we could send him to Intel. The rest of the platoon was happy. Four confirms and only Cavett hit, and he'd be fine. That was a win. I felt damn good about the day. My first fight; I did okay, and to my way of thinking, the Marines had won by a mile.

I thought then about those blue-green blurbs that had flown past my face. There must've been a dozen or more tracers, and there were eight or ten more bullets between one tracer round and the next. I marveled at that. Maybe a hundred or more machine gun bullets had torn within a few inches of my head, and there must've been hundreds or thousands more bullets flying around me with all the firing that had gone on. And in the middle of it, I'd had that insane notion that I could have let the tracers pass through my hand like cartoon lights.

I was suddenly chilled by retroactive fear. But then I felt happy. Life and luck couldn't be as random as they'd seemed—not after two close ones now. Somebody up there was looking out for me. If that gook gunner had sneezed or burped or flinched or otherwise jiggled the barrel of his machine gun, he would've blown my head off. But he didn't!

For a little while, I forgot about Havey and Delta and Jackson and Sturmer and basked in the powerful feeling of being a combat Marine. *Hot damn*, McClure, I thought. *The luck of the Irish. You'll be just fine.*

My descent into hell began the next week.

14

THE EARTH BELCHED A SHARP, roaring blast. It evaporated every other noise and filled the air with filthy smoke and debris.

The booby trap Corrigan tripped blew off his foot and ripped the meat from above his severed ankle to ten inches below his knee. When the acrid gray smoke cleared, I saw him writhing on his back, near the front of our column. The bones in his leg stuck out like the bloody tines of a crushed tuning fork. He held his mangled stump up in the air with one hand, clutched at the dirt with the other as if he was struggling to keep from being torn away again from the earth.

He began to scream, his shrieks climbing a hideous scale, breaking at the top, followed by a moaning gulp for air, then beginning again. They felt like molten tin rushing through my ears, filling my sinuses, making my teeth and cheekbones throb. I wanted to cover my ears but couldn't in front of the others. I squeezed my eyes shut so hard my sockets throbbed. My chest and stomach felt burned inside.

The two corpsmen tied off Corrie's leg. They knelt beside him, knees dark with his blood, bloody hands moving fast with tourniquet and bandages, checked his femoral arteries, his torso, his head and neck for other wounds. Harding cradled Corrie's head in his lap, and Sergeant Gilles tried to hold him steady while Matt hit him with morphine and ran an IV into his arm. The two docs said little as they worked. They'd performed that choreography together too many times.

It seemed to take a long time before the morphine quelled Corrie's screams.

He lay motionless, his eyes partly open in a dull gawk, his normally taut face flaccid and deflated. The tip of his tongue inched out as though seeking comfort from his dirty straw mustache. Below his trousers, his pallid leg ended in blood-soaked bandages lying in coagulated maroon dirt. My stomach clenched at the stench of gunpowder-charred meat. Corrie murmured something, as though he were trying to push unintelligible words into coherent sentences. It sounded like he was whispering "Mom."

Even after the helicopter took him away, I could see Corrie's truncated leg and tortured face, smell the blood and burned meat. For the rest of that day and into that night, his screams seemed to linger in the air. When I squeezed my eyes shut trying to block out their noise, I saw bloody, jagged bones like snapped-off pipe stems slathered with gore. The echo of that day stayed with me. Perhaps because that's when I began my descent toward a depth of depravity that appalls me now, though one that seemed common, nearly unremarkable, nearly necessary in that violent world.

<hr />

We saw no enemy the day Corrie lost his leg. Or for days after that.

We searched the small villes we came across, used an interpreter to question the inhabitants, found nothing, learned nothing of use. John said the villagers had little choice. If the enemy thought they cooperated with us, they'd be killed. Or maybe they'd already taken sides.

We patrolled farther into the valley each day, not knowing who was friend or foe and finding no one to pay back. I kept seeing Corrigan's bloody, shattered stump, kept hearing his screams.

Cloninger walked point. A new guy who'd joined us the day after Corrie was wounded was next in the column. O'Grady had red hair, freckles and a round face. "I'm naming you Leprechaun," Gio said. "If you had buckles on your jungle boots, I'd be searching for rainbows and pots of gold."

Cloninger stepped off a paddy dike. He stopped, wiped the sweat out of his eyes, scoped the distant tree line, then took one step forward in the shallow water, and felt something tug at his boot. He yelled, "Trip wire!" as he threw himself into the muck.

The wire yanked a grenade out of a hole carved into the side of the dike. When it pulled free of the dirt, the grenade's spoon flew, releasing the detonator fuse. About four seconds later, the grenade exploded, sending shrapnel ten or fifteen meters in every direction. The Buzz was already spread-eagled in the paddy, his body half-covered with water, his face in the mud. He wasn't touched.

Behind him, the new guy had started to step off the dike as the grenade popped free of the hole. The blast knocked him backward; shrapnel tore into his legs, groin, arms, and face. His blood splattered and ran all over his face, down his arms, hands, and thighs. It darkened from bright red to maroon as it mixed with his sweat and turned black as it soaked into his clothes. It coated his skin in splotches and streaks, making it impossible to tell freckles from blood.

While we waited for the medevac bird, Willis lit a cigarette, handed one to me. He was up next on point. "Too bad 'bout the Leprechaun," he said slowly. "Prob'ly shoulda ducked."

"Yeah," I said. I didn't feel like talking.

"Shoulda ducked the fuckin' war," Cavett said. "Fuckin' country."

"Don't forget about being short, Cavett." Gianelli sounded weary and worried, not at all like the wisecracking Gio I was used to.

"Fuck you," Cavett said.

I expected Gio to respond with his usual "Stand in line, Uncle Sam's already fucking me," but he just rubbed the purple stones in his rings against his trouser leg then studied the biggest one as though he expected it to reveal the answer to some unspoken question.

"He was lucky," Doc Matheson said. "Could've been killed."

"Family jewels okay?" John asked.

Matt nodded. "Lucky. He got shrapnel every place else."

Cavett shook his head. "Havin' to check his pecker. Jesus, what a job."

I was surprised to see Matt smile at that. "Just medicine, Cavett. There's worse things to do." He looked at John again. "He's one damn lucky guy."

"Luck of the Irish," John said. He looked at me and smiled, but his eyes were troubled.

I nodded, but didn't say anything, afraid my voice would break. I kept seeing the blood running all over O'Grady's face. I saw Corrigan holding his bloody shattered leg up in the air. I saw Jackson's bare ass jack-knifed over the bush and the two pink grooves in his big thighs.

"Fuckin' gooks," Cavett said. "Three days, two booby traps." He dragged hard on his cigarette. "Two people all fucked up."

"Give it a rest, would you, Cavett?" Prevas said.

I agreed with Prevas, though I didn't say anything. I'd never heard him angry before. Cavett refused to let go. "The little freckled dude had only been here a few days," he said to no one in particular. "I am way too short for this shit."

"Cavett," Gianelli said. "Why don't you just shut the fuck up?"

That was scary. If Gio was frightened, what'd he think might be next?

We saw no one to shoot at that morning.

As we moved out again, we heard the faint crackle of gunfire to the east. Up and down the column, heads raised like hounds sniffing the air. The noise was very faint, very distant. It ebbed, seemed to stop, then shivered again in the air. It sounded like someone across the street at home was raking leaves.

We searched a small village an hour later. No explosives, no weapons. Nothing but women and kids, who eyed us with suspicion, and two old men, who watched us with rheumy eyes and faces so devoid of expression they could've been cut from brown canvas bags.

The land mine Cavett stepped on that afternoon tore his left foot off just above the ankle. Almost. It hung by tendons that stretched pale white like tentacles dangling in the blood pool soaking slowly into the ground between his leg and his stump-filled boot.

Doc Matheson and Doc Dorsey worked fast again. Twenty minutes after Cavett stepped on the mine, he lay bandaged, white-faced, silent, waiting for the chopper, a cigarette dangling from his lips. A tourniquet girdled his lower leg; saline and plasma drips ran into his arms. He hadn't said a word since he stopped babbling when the morphine took over.

He stared at the blood-soaked, bandaged mass of his lower leg and still-booted foot. The corpsmen had bandaged his leg, wrapped gauze around tendons writhing like white worms in his blood, wrapped more bandages around the boot with the ripped chunk of ankle sticking out of it, then used a piece they sliced from Doc Matheson's poncho liner to swaddle the entire mass. Blood seeped through the camouflaged blanket and glistened in the sun.

"You were right, Cavett," Gio said. "We shoulda believed you, short-timer. Headed back to the World." He took the cigarette from between Cavett's lips, flicked the ash, and put it back in his mouth. "They'll fix that foot up good as new. You'll be kicking ass in all the bars while I'm still getting mine kicked over here."

Gio tried hard to sound convincing, but even in a morphine haze, Cavett had to know the doctors would finish taking off the foot when he got to Da Nang. The clenching sickness I felt in my stomach was more from that thought than my revulsion at the blood seeping through the bandages on his leg. Cavett's eyes were sunk deep in his head; they looked like the light had dimmed behind them. He stared angrily at his bandaged foot, as though he'd decided his boot was to blame for what'd happened to him.

We saw no enemy the day Cavett had his foot blown off and the new guy was ripped up by shrapnel. We didn't see anyone to shoot at for the next two days, either. No one to pay back.

I think that's when I started to go a little nuts.

15

STAFF SERGEANT GILLES HANDED Woody a letter from Dottie Jackson. Woody looked like he didn't know if he wanted it or not. He went off by himself and read it, then came over to where several of us were eating our Cs.

"Dottie says Mike's doing . . ." Woody hesitated. ". . . okay. He isn't in much pain anymore."

"Good."

"That's good news."

Woody nodded. "She says his spirits are good. He wants to get going with prosthesis, but the doctors say he isn't ready yet."

Jackson wasn't going to give up. I didn't know how you lived like that, but I felt an unexpected wash of relief to know he didn't want to end his life. I still wondered what Dottie would do. I supposed it was too early to know. Maybe she didn't even know. I hoped she'd stay with him at least as long as he was in the hospital, maybe at least until Jax learned to use his fake legs.

"Is he still in San Diego?" John asked.

"Yeah. They hope they'll send him someplace closer to home."

"I think there's a Navy hospital in Philadelphia," Matt said. "I know there's one in Bethesda, near D.C."

"Is his wife staying in California?" Corporal Harding asked.

I wondered what Hard Ass Harding would do if he lost both legs. And what would Bonnie, that centerfold wife of his, do if he

114

did? They had a baby on the way, too. I wondered whether Corporal Harding worried about losing a limb. He didn't seem afraid of anything in the world.

Woody shrugged. "She's there with him now. I don't know; I hope so."

———

A rushing black sky opened into a downpour like someone had torn open the clouds. It felt like I'd walked into a dimly lit room with wet cotton in my ears and a dark veil draped over my face. I couldn't tell who walked point a dozen men away. I could make out Prevas partway back in the column, because even hunched forward against the slashing rain, he was the tallest man in the platoon.

The booby trap he tripped sheared his leg off at mid-thigh. Clean off, as though done with a guillotine or surgeon's knife. There was a sudden roar, so abrupt, so loud, so violent, it seemed as though God had yelled, and Prevas vanished into a cloud of flame and dirt and smoke while his severed leg blew above the blast and flew through the driving rain spinning flatly, boot, calf, knee, part of thigh, like a boomerang thrown by a giant.

The leg landed outstretched thirty yards away. It lay there like it'd been left by mistake.

Woody helped the corpsmen tourniquet and bandage Prevas' stump, shoot him with morphine, run IVs. A few yards away, Corporal Harding was on his hands and knees swaying like a wounded bull in front of a matador, blood spouting from his nose. John ran to him.

Smitty was already calling for the medevac. The lieutenant told the other squad leaders to set up the usual. "You know the drill, people. Let's hurry. First Squad, go with Burkotich." He pointed. "Ladoor . . ." The big black man turned and stared at him. "Get Prevas' leg. It's over there."

Ladoor's scowl deepened. "What?" He sounded like the Lieutenant just told him to shoot himself in the foot.

"Prevas' leg. We're not leaving parts of Marines out here."

"Why me?"

"Because I told you to, Ladoor. Get the goddamn leg."

"I don't want to carry no fuckin' white boy's blown-off leg. That's sick."

"Ladoor . . ."

Cloninger had been watching. "I'll go, Lieutenant. Prevas is my bud."

"Go. Hurry. The bird won't wait for it. Watch where you walk."

Mangan turned to Ladoor. "I'll deal with you later, Ladoor." He spun, looked at the men working on Prevas, then headed to where Harding was up on one knee.

Ladoor glowered at the lieutenant's back.

"Fuckin' niggers," Cloninger muttered half under his breath as he turned toward where Prevas' leg lay in the grass.

"What you say?"

I was afraid Ladoor was going to raise his M16.

Cloninger turned back toward him. "Fuck you, Ladoor." The Buzz had his rifle in both hands, one finger near the trigger guard.

I was half scared to death they'd have a shootout right then and there. I didn't know what to do. If John were there he'd stop it, but he was over helping Harding. "Guys! Guys! Let's cool it, okay?"

"Shut the fuck up, white bread." Ladoor dismissed me and turned back to Cloninger. They glared at each other, then the Buzz turned and began walking toward Prevas' leg.

Ladoor fixed me again with a fierce glare. I held my rifle across my chest. If he raised his, should I shoot him? How the hell could I shoot another Marine? He turned and began to walk away. I forced myself to turn back to watch Cloninger, wondering if the last thing I'd ever feel was Ladoor's bullets hitting my spine.

The Buzz walked slowly, almost gingerly, searching for another booby trap. I wondered if he was also delaying reaching the leg. I knew I wouldn't be in a hurry to get to it. He finally did and stood staring down, water pouring in a curtain from his helmet. I couldn't tell if he was praying or trying not to throw up. Finally, he bent down and picked up the leg.

Cloninger began to walk back, carrying Prevas' leg by a handle of cloth like a grotesque duffle bag. He walked slowly, rifle in one hand, Prevas' long, basketball-player's leg in the other, careful of every step. Once in a while, he stopped, looked up, searched the rain for the medevac bird. Then he looked back down, guessing where he could put his feet next.

When Cloninger got closer, Prevas saw him carrying his leg. He started babbling. He wanted it, he needed it, he had to have it. He looked like a morphine-slowed imitation of a baby making slow-motion grasps in the air as he babbled and begged for something he'd just dropped. It was terrible to listen to.

I expected that someone would carry the leg to the chopper when we got Prevas aboard, hand it to the crew chief or tuck it in out of the way. But Matt took the leg from Cloninger and handed it to Prevas like someone presenting a mother with her newborn. He laid the leg on Prevas' chest, the boot just under his chin. The cleanly sheared, bloody thigh sticking out of the shredded trouser leg stretched down past Prevas' good knee.

I helped carry him to the chopper. We fought to keep our balance as we jog-walked through a rotor wash of water and mud. Even the raindrops hurled sideways felt like gravel pelting my face. Prevas clutched his severed leg to his chest with both arms like an oversized kid protecting a grotesque doll.

Harding didn't get on the helicopter. The explosion had picked him up and thrown him down, but he hadn't been hit.

We saw no enemy on the day Prevas lost his leg. No one to kill, no one to pay back. We were all scared. John and Corporal Harding and Woody and Gio didn't acknowledge that much, but even if they were braver than I was, I could see a hint of fear in their eyes. These guys will always run toward fire, I thought to myself. But they can't fight a booby trap, can't kill an inanimate object you can't even see.

That night in our hole, John and I were both quiet, absorbed in our thoughts. I couldn't figure out how an eighteen-year-old who dreamt of playing basketball in college and one day being a coach could make any plans for his life after losing a leg. I tried not to think of Cloninger carrying Prevas' leg, or worse, of Prevas clutching the bloody thing to his chest. I failed.

Those terrible pictures were joined by others: Cavett's bloody, flesh-filled boot dangling at the end of tendons stretching like slimy strings to his mangled calf; O'Grady, perforated and oozing blood from scores of wounds; Corrigan holding a bloody, shattered stump up in the air; those goddamn grooves in Jackson's thighs. I tried to get the images out of my head, but the more I tried, the faster and more vividly the kaleidoscope spun accompanied by echoes of screams and babbles and howls. I wondered again if I was losing my mind.

I didn't know I'd begun shaking with anger until John put his hand on my arm. "Mick," he said quietly. "You okay?"

I nodded, embarrassed, angry, and scared. "I want it to stop, John," I whispered desperately. "I want us to do whatever it takes to make them fucking stop."

Woody got a letter from Mike Jackson the next day. He read part of it to us:

"'I'm still here in the naval hospital in San Diego. Dottie used the money we saved for R&R to fly here and rent a room pretty close. The money ran out pretty quickly, but she found a part-time job doing hair not far from the hospital. She'll have to spend less time with me, but that's probably better for her. She's doing pretty well, despite everything. She takes really good care of me. As you know, she's wonderful.'"

Woody paused and cleared his throat, then looked down at the page again. "Listen to this." He shook his head as he read. "'They'll fit me for my new plastic legs pretty soon.'" Woody looked at us. I couldn't tell whether he was about to cry or burst out laughing. "Listen to this crazy SOB. 'I told them I want hollow ones I can hide beer cans in when the nurses aren't around.'"

Woody looked at us again. "Mike Jackson," he said, affection and awe and deep sadness in his voice. "Amazing."

"The man's got balls he could carry in a wheelbarrow," Harding said.

"Dottie, too," said Woody.

"Mmmm . . . maybe not," I said.

Woody smiled. It was the saddest smile I'd ever seen. "Good point," he said. "You know what I mean."

"She must be an amazing person," I said.

"Amazing isn't the half of it," Woody said.

"They're lucky they have each other," John said.

"Jackson's damn lucky," I said. I didn't know what I really meant. The man had no goddamn legs! Who knew what his wife would do? I guessed I meant he was lucky she was there with him now. It'd just seemed like something positive to say.

Woody nodded. "It's still the shits."

The responses from Corporal Harding and Pius John and me blended together like the chant of a dolorous chorus. There it is, man. There it the fuck is.

16

THE TREE LINE TO OUR FRONT ERUPTED, catching the lead fire team in the middle of a paddy. On point, Dasmund screamed "Gooks!" and let loose with a full magazine then spun and began running back to the low dike the team had just crossed. He was built like a tight end and probably could run like one too, but the water and mud slowed him down.

Gunfire roared from the tree line. Lieutenant Mangan yelled, "To the dike, to the dike! Return fire!" Bullets snapped above my head as I ran. Behind me, Gianelli yelled for Willis to keep up; Sergeant Gilles stood with his back to the enemy, waving his arm, roaring, "Move people, move! Get the fuck up there and get some!"

The point fire team tried desperately to get back to the dike. NVA bullets tore the water around them. Dasmund, farthest out, ran as fast as he could in the mud, arms flailing, bandoliers of ammo flapping, his M16 beating the air like a drum major's baton.

John and I threw ourselves down behind the dike. We couldn't fire because the point team was in the way. The two closest Marines got back and hurled themselves to our side of the dike. Burkotich and Dasmund still fought their way through the muck.

A burst of blood erupted from Tich's thigh. He crumpled to the ground. Woody jumped over the dike, ran out, grabbed Tich and half dragged, half threw him to our side of the dike. Dasmund suddenly bucked spastically and pitched face-down ten yards to our front. Corporal Harding jumped over the dike. His helmet flew off into the paddy. He ran to Dasmund, bullets chopping the water around him. He got to him without being hit, bent down and tried to throw Dasmund over his shoulder. The wounded man's helmet fell into the paddy. Harding stumbled, almost dropped him, then began struggling back toward us clutching the inert Marine to his chest. Dasmund's face was buried in Harding's neck, arms limp at his sides, his long legs splayed out on either side as though the two were groping their way through some perverse marathon dance.

Harding suddenly lurched midstride as though someone had pounded him in the back with both fists. A splash of blood painted the right side of his head. He stumbled forward a few steps and fell over the dike, Dasmund still clutched to his chest. Harding's helmet lay like a turtle half-submerged in front of the dike. Farther out, the rim of Dasmund's stuck up like a bucket abandoned in a swamp.

The lieutenant spoke into the radio handset. I couldn't hear what he was saying above the clamor of our gun. Then I heard him yell, "Slow it down, people! Conserve ammo." The call was echoed up and down the line. Firing slowed; John took more time between short bursts.

"Shot, out," the lieutenant said into the radio. He lifted his binoculars and looked toward the tree line, the handset still pressed to his ear.

"Splash, over."

Two artillery rounds slammed into the paddy between us and the tree line. "Right five zero. Add one hundred. Over." Long seconds passed before I heard, "Shot, out." And then, "Splash, over." Twin geysers of smoke and flame and debris exploded skyward from the trees.

"Open sheaf," the lieutenant yelled into the handset. "Fire for effect! Over." His eyes were glued to the tree line.

Six more explosions. Smoke, fire, dirt, debris churned skyward, tree limbs pinwheeled through the air as the 105 rounds blanketed one section of the tree line.

"Left five zero, repeat! Over."

More explosions bloomed up out of the tree line like filthy, mutated chrysanthemums.

"Roger that," I heard him say. "Bring them on. Over."

Two silver-winged A-4 Skyhawks banked in from the east. The lead plane dove toward the tree line. The air filled with the scream-ing roar of jet engines. The pilot released his bombs and pulled up sharply, chased by a line of green tracers that went wide of the roar-ing silver bird. John blasted two long bursts into the trees where the green tracers had started from. A pair of five-hundred-pound bombs zipped downward on an angled trajectory like large, winged iron darts. They blasted into the center of the tree line. Great eruptions of flame and smoke and chunks of trees filled the air. Roiling clouds of dirt and debris billowed like filthy geysers high into the sky, then collapsed almost lazily down as the crashing thunder of explosions roared in waves across the paddy, washing over us in spasms of deep, bellowing sound that drowned out our cheers.

The second plane banked and began its run. The Skyhawk stayed in its dive until it was closer in than the first plane. Two silver cyl-inders fell from its belly just before the pilot pulled up. The long canisters tumbled end over end through the sky as though they were somersault-racing to the ground. There was a massive, whooshing, rushing roar as the napalm exploded and thick waves of black-slathered bright red and orange flames billowed and surged through and above the trees, thrilling and awesome and beautiful. Thin, shimmery, gray purple waves of heat rushed across the paddy and washed over us like petroleum-pungent storm surge.

The roiling roar receded, and again I heard cheers and cries. "Get some, napalm!" "Crispy critters!" "Fry, you motherfuckers!" Payback at last.

Both planes circled tightly, made another pass, blasted the tree line and the area behind it with their 20 mm guns. Then they banked up and around and headed back toward Chu Lai. Good God, I thought. Such firepower. How can anybody fight us and expect to live? Take that, you bastards!

Then we were over the dike and walking forward on line, firing as we went. I couldn't tell if we were being shot at anymore. To my left, Corporal Harding suddenly bent double. I thought he was hit. He wasn't; he scooped his helmet out of the paddy, dumped the water in it and put it on his head. Water streaked the blood caked on his face.

Perspiration flooded my face, burned my eyes. I could barely make out individual trees in the smoking green tangle to our front, much less any men hiding there waiting to kill us. It couldn't have taken five minutes to slosh from the relative safety of the dike to the unknown of the trees, but it felt like time had stopped and frozen us in the open like two dozen mechanical bears in the target gallery at a fair.

The tree line cackled and hissed and snarled as we got closer. Trees and bushes burned, smoke hung in the air. My nose and mouth filled with the acrid bite of gunpowder and the pungent smell of charred wood and burned foliage. Then we were in the tree line. It was thick and snarled, a pandemonium of bamboo, twisting, climbing creepers, dark and smoking and burnt. I could feel the heat through the thick soles of my boots. Trees and bushes were shattered and torn. Room-sized patches of thick bamboo had been lifted and thrown down again to lie jumbled in mangled, smoldering clumps. Trunks of thick trees stood sheared off, roots bare, bark smoking, burned black.

"The gooks are gone," John said. "They've made their hat." He sounded disappointed and angry. I wanted to believe he hadn't been able to tell how scared I'd been.

Marines began to call back and forth: "Where are they?" "Where are the fucking bodies?" "Where did the fucking gooks go?" We searched the entire area; we didn't even find parts.

We had to have killed some. Where were the bodies? They couldn't all get out before the artillery, before the planes. Where the fuck were they? We found nothing. No bodies, no parts. No entrances to tunnels. If we'd killed anyone, the gooks had carried them off. A feeling of despair washed through me. Havey had been right: it was like fighting ghosts.

Harding looked like half his head had been dipped in red oil paint that had dried and scabbed. I wondered, *How could he lose that much blood and still stand?* The lieutenant saw him caked with blood. "You okay?" he asked.

"Not me, Lieutenant. Dasmund took one for me." He touched his cheek; his fingers came away red. He studied them as though they depicted some unfathomable truth.

Staff Sergeant Gilles met us as we walked back across the paddy. "What'd you get, Lieutenant?"

"Nothing." Mangan didn't try to keep the disgust out of his voice.

"Not even a body?"

"Not even much blood."

"Goddamn."

"How are Dasmund and Burkotich?"

"Dasmund's dead. Burkotich's shot through the leg. Doc says priority. Bird should be here soon."

"Fuck." It sounded more like deep disappointment than a curse.

Sweet Jesus. I hadn't seen a helicopter hurrying in, so I thought Tich and Dasmund would be okay. But oh my god, Dasmund was dead. I didn't know how to process that. Another eighteen-year-old kid who'd talked his mother into signing so he could enlist when he was seventeen. He'd only been with the platoon a couple weeks; to die that soon seemed cosmically unfair. I knew Marines got killed in combat, of course. I even knew it could happen to me, at least in theory. But Dasmund was the first Marine I saw killed.

His death was different from Havey's. That'd been terrible, but his own fault, an accident, stupid mistakes. This was the first Marine I'd seen killed in a firefight. This was different from the ones I'd seen wounded by booby traps, too. This was somehow more personal. The enemy had shot and killed Dasmund, and I'd seen him go down.

The lieutenant walked over to where Tich and Dasmund lay on the ground. He looked down at Dasmund's body for what seemed like a long time. He might've been praying. Then he went and took a knee beside Burkotich.

My stomach hurt. I wasn't even sure what emotions I was experiencing. Anger? Grief? Fear? Probably a mix of all those. I'd never dealt with such heightened feelings as a boy. But I thought about Jackson and Corrigan, O'Grady, Cavett and Prevas, and now Tich and poor Dasmund and how they'd been so horribly wounded or killed. And I knew, even if I wouldn't have been able to articulate the thought at the time, that a darkening brew was seeping into my soul.

A week after Dasmund was killed, as we dug our holes for the night a radioman from the CP trotted over to Corporal Harding to tell him the captain wanted him.

"Why's he want me?" Harding laid down his e-tool and climbed out of his hole.

The messenger was a skinny kid with a twitch at one side of his mouth. He acted like he couldn't care less. "Top's got a message for you's all I know."

"The first sergeant?" The color drained from Harding's face. "Bonnie!" He began running toward the command post before Woody or John or I'd even gotten out of our holes.

We caught up with him at the CP. Captain Brill handed Harding the radio handset. "First Sergeant needs to talk to you," was all he said. The captain's face was blank, but I saw a smile in his eyes. Harding looked stricken, like he'd triggered a booby trap and was helpless to do anything except wait for it to go off.

A slight smile began to twitch at the corners of the captain's mouth. He had his ear up to the handset of another radio tuned to the same frequency. I could catch most of what was being said.

Top Miller's gruff voice crackled over the air from Hoa Binh as he read the message from the Red Cross. "Baby," he said. "They've got a name here, but I'm not going to read it on the net. Baby born zero-one-thirty-eight this date. Mother and daughter"—he stressed the word—"doing fine. Congratulations. That's the end of the message. Congratulations from here, too, Marine. Over."

"Oh my God," Corporal Harding said. "Thank God, Bonnie's okay." He spoke not much above a whisper. "And the baby, too."

John and Woody and I and others in the CP pummeled Harding on the back, shook his hand, and cheered. The captain took out the battered tin of Robert Burns panatelas he kept in his pack and handed one to the new dad. "What's your daughter's name, Corporal Harding?"

"Hope, sir. Hope Frances Harding." He wiped a dirty hand over his face. "My wife picked the name. If it was a girl, Bonnie wanted to name her Hope. I thought it was going to be a boy."

"Disappointed?"

"Oh no, sir, Top said everyone's fine. That's the important thing. Frances is for my mother."

"She must be very proud," the captain said.

"My mother . . . yes sir. I'm sure she is. Hope's their first grandchild."

"Hope's a perfect name, Corporal Harding," Captain Brill said. "We all need hope, so I think that's a marvelous name."

Harding grinned like a kid anticipating treats. "I'm sure my wife will send lots of pictures. I'll show you some when they come, Sir."

"I look forward to that, Corporal Harding. Now you better get that cigar smoked before dark."

———

A few days after Hope was born, we spent the night in a graveyard again. The low earthen mounds could give us a little protection if we were fired upon while we waited to set up a blocking position at dawn. A platoon from Alpha Company was to sweep against us then, driving any enemy between into our guns.

John and I settled in behind a grave, the M60 trained on a trail approaching the cemetery. John took first watch. I tried to sleep propped up, my back to the mound. It wasn't easy; I was too keyed up. After the last couple weeks, the thought of killing NVA as Alpha drove them toward us across an open paddy filled me with bitter joy.

I slouched lower, leaning heavily on the ammo can under my arm, trying to get comfortable enough to fall asleep. I'd almost drifted off when I realized both cans I'd been carrying were on the other side of me, closer to John. In the dark, I could make out their shapes. Damn you, Willie, I thought. Now I've got three and you've only got one. If we get hit, you better come get it, because I'm not bringing your own damn ammo to you under fire. I rested my arm back on the can and eventually dozed off, thinking of tracers spewing from our gun toward waves of gooks caught in the open.

A burst of automatic weapons fire a few hundred meters to our west shattered the predawn quiet. The firing intensified, the *kak-kak-kak* of AK-47s intermingled with the *pap-pap-pap* of M16s, the low-pitched snarling cough of an M60, and *crash-booms* of RPGs. Our plan fell apart.

Lieutenant Mangan whispered furiously, "Let's go, people. Alpha's hit."

John and I had begun running across the graveyard when I remembered Willie's ammo can. I turned and saw him lugging two. Thank God, I thought. If he'd left it, gooks could find it and use it against us. I cursed Willie the dumb ox again, then was too busy to think about chewing him out.

We ran across an open space toward a thin stand of trees, threw ourselves down, and began blasting a thicker tree line from which the gooks now shot at us too. Lieutenant Mangan ran up and down the line, getting Marines in place, pointing out where he wanted them to fire. Bullets cracked and whirred above me, wood and leaves showering on me like foliage confetti. I fed ammo belts to the gun, linked them to rounds in a box, checked for twists in the belt, then grabbed up my rifle and began firing. I couldn't see an NVA to aim at, but there were a lot of them in those trees.

The roar and screech of gunfire and explosions became background bedlam for a dawn lightshow of red tracers flying from both Marine platoons toward the gooks, green blurbs of NVA tracers shooting back. Flashes of B40 rockets. The crash boom of LAAWs. A cacophony of all types of weapons filled the air. Abruptly the tree line around the gooks erupted in geysers of smoke and fire and debris. *Crump-boom crump-boom!* Two rounds. Then six. The earth shook and the tree line became shrouded in smoke. Deafening noise as volley after volley of 105 rounds exploded there.

Then we were on line and made it into the thick tree line without anyone getting hit. Down the line to my right, a deep echoing boom. Staff Sergeant Gilles' shotgun. Then the only sounds were the crackle of trees burning and the noise of Marines pushing through the brush and yells of "Here!" or "Got some here!"

This time our search produced bodies. And parts. And blood trails. Cloninger followed one gory wet track into a thicket then yelled, "Papa Sierra!" Staff Sergeant Gilles ran into the trees. There was another deep boom from his shotgun, then no more noise from there.

Next to a smoldering tree trunk, I saw the torso of a dead NVA. He'd been cut in half at the waist—skin, clothing and bone melted and fused into a gooey mass. John and I walked farther into the tree line, my rifle ready, John's gun cradled against his hip. I tripped on something soft and looked down at what was left of a leg. I moved on, looking for live NVA.

The gooks had carried off some of their dead or wounded, but we found seven bodies, or enough parts to count as a dead man, including the two Sergeant Gilles finished off.

I was with Cloninger and John when the lieutenant said, "No prisoners, Platoon Sergeant?"

The Buzz gave John a quick, sideways look. I couldn't read anything on his face.

"No sir," Staff Sergeant Gilles said firmly. "The two I killed looked like they had weapons." Two new brass tacks for the shotgun's stock. I wondered if Staff Sergeant Gilles would ever be able to add enough to avenge his brother.

Lieutenant Mangan studied Gilles' face for a second, then nodded slightly and said, "Let's go catch up with Alpha."

People around me looked even happier than when we'd found out Hope Harding was born. Seven kills and only one of our Marines had been hit. Lee, a swarthy, pock-faced guy from Second Squad, had his shoulder grazed. Doc Matheson said it was enough for his second Purple Heart, but he wasn't going to send him to the rear.

"C'mon, Doc," Lee bitched. "I been shot. Who knows what infections I could get? A few days in the rear's no skin off your ass."

"You're lucky I'm putting you in for a Heart, Lee. One more and you go home." Matt actually laughed at him then. "You nearly had to squeeze this one yourself to prove it bled."

"He didn't really do that did he, Doc?" Woody had been smiling before but looked now at Lee as though he'd kick his ass. It was unusual for Woody to be angry. I guessed he was thinking of Jackson. Maybe him and the others who'd been crippled or killed.

Matt shook his head. "Nah, I'm just pinging on him, Woody. It's not much of a wound, but it's a Heart." He turned to Lee. "But one I can fix up out here."

Marines smiled as we fell in to head back the way we'd come. Harding said Hope had been a good omen for us all.

I felt damn good. I'd been grossed out looking at the mangled and dismembered bodies. But Smitty was turning out to be at least partially right. I'd seen Marines horribly wounded and killed. I might not exactly enjoy looking at dead gooks, but there was satisfaction in it.

I had no way of knowing whether any of the bodies I'd seen were of men I'd killed myself. We'd probably killed some with the gun, and maybe I'd hit someone firing my rifle at shadows in the trees.

I had no way of knowing, but I hoped so.

17

WHEN WE GOT BACK TO THE GRAVEYARD, we took a break. People were in a good mood. Gianelli joked about heading to Hong Kong for R&R. Corporal Harding was happily anxious for pictures of Hope. Woody kidded Willis about going to Bangkok in a couple days. Lieutenant Mangan told me I'd take the gun while Gio and Willie were both gone. "It'll be good experience for you, McClure. Hopefully, you'll get us more kills."

"I'll sure try, Lieutenant." I felt like the coach just said he knew he could count on me, his second-string halfback, to score.

John and I went to the far end of the graveyard, where Staff Sergeant Gilles wanted us set up. I stayed with the gun and opened some Cs while John went off behind another grave mound to relieve himself. The platoon sergeant stood in the middle of the cemetery looking at a map with the lieutenant. I'd barely begun eating when Gilles roared at me. "McClure! What the fuck? That your goddamn ammo can lookin' like Joe Shit the Ragman's holding a yard sale?"

I jumped up and looked where he pointed. A filthy machine-gun ammo can sat against the grave mound where John and I'd spent the night. It must've been the one I leaned on while I tried to sleep. What the hell? Didn't Willie grab it when we ran toward Alpha? I'd have sworn I saw him carrying two. Maybe I'd been mistaken. In the daylight now, I could see this one was caked with dried mud. Fucking Willie! I was amazed Gio let him get away with filthy gear.

And didn't he know Willie'd left the ammo behind when we ran to the fight? Damn both of them.

It didn't take me ten seconds to realize I'd better get the can over to Willis or I'd end up humping the damn thing myself and that when we got back to the company perimeter Sergeant Gilles would have my ass. Maybe the lieutenant, too. After saying I could take over Gio's gun, he might reconsider if he thought I didn't keep track of ammo. Goddamn Willie!

The platoon sergeant and lieutenant were looking at the map again. I figured I only had a minute or two to find Willis and give him the can before Gilles made me carry it, and maybe the lieutenant did worse. I could see Willie across the cemetery where the lieutenant had sent Gianelli's gun team. Luckily, Gio was walking toward me just then, a grin on his face, a can of Cs held up in the air. He spotted my half-empty spiced beef can. "A lot of streets, McClure," he said loudly. "One way."

I didn't want to banter. "Willie left an ammo can over there last night." I pointed toward the grave mound. "Papa Sierra's on the warpath."

We walked toward the can. "Not Willie's," Gio said. "Looks like the way he treats shit if I don't keep on his ass, but he's got both his."

I looked over at Staff Sergeant Gilles. He was staring beyond me, scowling at the tree line we were heading to next. If the damn can wasn't mine and it wasn't Willie's, whose was it? No one in First Platoon besides us had humped M60 ammo that morning. Some other Marines must've been in that graveyard recently, but who? Second Platoon, Third Herd? Someone from another company? Whoever it was had made a terrible dumb mistake leaving an ammo can out there for the gooks to find. I didn't know if the enemy used 7.62 ammunition in any of their weapons, but even if they didn't, they could make one hell of a booby trap that would spew machine gun bullets for miles. And that can was full. It hadn't even jiggled when I leaned against it last night. It would've been a hell of a find for some lucky gook.

I hurried toward the can. "I don't think it's our platoon's, Sergeant Gilles," I called. I started to reach for the handle.

"Freeze, McClure!" the platoon sergeant bellowed. "Freeze!"

Bent halfway over, I stopped.

"Don't even breathe on that sonuvabitch!" Gilles yelled.

I was already reaching. I froze. I'd spent the night draped over that can. What the hell did he mean, don't even breathe on the son of a bitch?

Conversation around the graveyard stopped as people turned to find out what the platoon sergeant was yelling about. "Stand up slow," he said. "Slow and straight, and do not touch that fucking can. You hear, McClure?" It was a command, but his voice was quieter now, as though he didn't want to startle me.

"Yes, sir." The sweat soaking my back suddenly felt very cold.

"Step back, now. Back easy. Do not jostle that can."

I straightened up slowly. I took a step backward. Then another. It didn't take an IQ above single digits to see Staff Sergeant Gilles thought the ammo can might be booby-trapped. My eyes didn't leave it, even when I heard the lieutenant come up beside me and say something to the platoon sergeant.

"I don't know who the hell left that, sir. It's American, but we better not mess with it. We should blow it in place," Gilles said.

I backed up another couple steps, then stood very still. *Sweet Jesus, sweet Jesus.* I couldn't get my brain past the fact that I'd just spent the night leaning on it. It felt like my blood had coagulated in my arteries all of a sudden. I stood as still as a post, nearly paralyzed with the thought that if it was a bomb I could've been blown to bits. *Oh my god, oh my god . . .*

A half-dozen Marines had gathered around. They were all curious, but no one seemed particularly concerned.

"Who's got C-4?" the lieutenant asked.

Gianelli began bouncing up and down, an excited grin on his face. "Hey, I do, Lieutenant. I can get some. Right here, right here, sir. Let me blow it. Okay, sir? Okay?" The purple veins at his temples and in the center of his forehead bulged with excitement.

"I'll blow that hummer," Woody said. He already had a block of plastic explosive in his hand. He shook it at Gianelli.

Gianelli grinned like a chimp. "No way, José. This mother's mine."

I began to relax. The posturing, the contrast between scrawny, swarthy Gianelli and blonde, athletic Woodson was actually fun, like watching an argument between a little tough guy and an All-American Boy with gook sores on his arms.

"C'mon, Lieutenant," Gio said. "I haven't blown anything in a long time."

"Sheeit, Gianelli. You're headed off to get yourself blown on R&R in two days," Woody mocked. Then he played his ace. "Besides, I've got the C-4, my friend." He laughed as Gio good-naturedly flipped him the bird. I hadn't seen Woody that happy since Jackson was wounded.

"I'll get some, I'll get some," Gio argued. "I got friends in high places."

"Yeah?" Woody said. "Only if they been blowing dope."

Lieutenant Mangan shook his head. "Alright. Enough. This isn't choosing sides on the playground, people. What the hell, Gianelli? Get back over there with Willis like I told you before. What're you doing over here? Move. Now!"

The lieutenant looked at Woody. "Don't mess with it, Woodson. Just blow the son of a bitch. And be damned careful." The lieutenant turned to Smitty. "Tell Bravo Six we're going to blow a suspected booby trap in place. I don't want them all excited when they hear the explosion."

Gio took a few steps toward where Willie sat with the M60 across his lap. He stopped and looked back to watch what Woody was going to do. Woody had the brick of C-4 in one hand and det cord in the other. "Move back, people," he said. "The magician is about to make things disappear." He stuck his tongue out at Gio then turned back and bent over the can.

"Move back, people," Staff Sergeant Gilles yelled. "I want every-body behind a grave mound before I even hear 'fire in the hole.' Get your ass where it's supposed to be, Gianelli. Move now, people! When that shit cooks off, I want everyone safe."

———

Sometimes things happen so fast, in such brain-numbing fashion, that you don't realize what has really occurred. And then, for the rest of your life, there are times when your mind replays the film in the slowest possible motion, over and over again.

I turned away from Sergeant Gilles and took two steps toward where the gun and my ammo boxes and rifle lay a few feet away. In the next instant I was flat on my back, ten feet from where I'd been a second before. The roar in my ears, a freight train chasing an explosion through a tunnel. My mouth full of blood and grit and pain. All I could see was bright blue sky above me, and off to the side, wisps of black smoke rising toward a filthy brown cloud hovering over the ground.

I pushed myself slowly up onto my elbows. I turned my head very slowly. Something inside my screaming, hammering skull told me not to move any more parts of my body than necessary. I was terrified I would not find them all.

I spat blood and dirt and phlegm. It ran down my face and hung from my chin. I felt like I'd gargled with mud and blood. My nose and sinuses and throat were filled with its thick copper taste, burned with the harsh, caustic stench of gunpowder. Unable to form coherent thoughts, I wondered vaguely if the grit and filth in my mouth were bits of my teeth.

I looked around very slowly. A blue-gray haze hung like fog in the air. It burned my eyes. Where I'd just stood, Marines moved in the acrid mist in stop-start, kaleidoscopic motion, like zombies milling about. Just beyond them, off to the side, Doc Dorsey and two or three Marines knelt over someone on the ground. I couldn't see who it was. His legs and pelvis and torso writhed in the dirt like a crippled reptile. One of his arms rose an inch or two off the earth and fell back, as though he wanted to gesture, raise his hand to be called on, but the mangled limb wouldn't go any higher. To the left of that group, two more Marines lay spread-eagled in the grass. I couldn't tell if they were dead or alive.

A few feet away from me, Doc Matheson pulled himself to a kneeling position. One of the lenses in his glasses was cracked; it looked like a spider had built a web on one side of his lenses. He had a bloody gash from his temple down his cheek. He turned slowly in my direction. "You okay?" he said.

That's what he must've said, but I couldn't hear him. He seemed to mouth the words. He said again, "McClure. Mick. You okay?" I nodded very slowly; I thought so. Matt pushed to his feet. The blood flowed down his face and dripped off his chin. The air all around us seemed gray now, acrid and filled with low, guttural moans, a strange ringing hum pierced now and then by a shriek of pain. Matt hefted his corpsman's bag and staggered toward the two Marines in the grass.

My head felt like it was in a thick box filled with a dense thrum of noise. I looked beyond Matt at the Marines in the grass. Lawler, from Third Squad, held his thigh now, face contorted in pain. The train in my ears began to slow; I could hear him moan as he writhed. The other man, a new guy whose name I didn't know, lay facing me. His mouth gaped open, silent, his staring eyes wide. He was drawn up in a ball, blood seeping between his fingers where he held his belly. He stayed absolutely motionless, as though afraid the pain would increase or his wounds get worse if he moved. I knew he was alive, because he blinked.

I spat another mouthful of blood and dirt and slime. I had a vague feeling I should follow Matt to help out, but I couldn't figure out how. I couldn't concentrate, couldn't focus. My head was full of dense fog. Then the panicked thought hit me: *Do I have all my parts?*

Propped on my elbows, I began a terrified inventory, slowly, in no logical order. I was afraid if I jarred anything it might open up or fall off.

I could see. I could hear. I didn't know yet how well, but other sounds were coming through as the roaring and ringing in my ears decreased.

I moved my tongue around the inside of my mouth. It felt slippery and thick and tasted like warm, dirty pennies. My whole face hurt, but all my teeth seemed to be there. I spat more blood and drool. I raised one hand slowly and touched my cheeks, lips, and nose. My fingertips came away painted red. My face was coated with a film of blood, as though a bag of plasma had atomized into a scarlet haze and washed over my skin. Through the dull, muffled after-loudness of the explosion, I had a vague sense of onrushing pain where my face had slammed and scraped on the ground and where I'd bitten my tongue and lip and inner cheek multiple times.

I sat up slowly, raised my arms in slow motion, wriggled my fingers as though they were bound at their joints by arthritic vises. They worked. I looked down at my feet; both legs were still there. *Thank you, God, thank you,* I said, maybe out loud. I moved my toes inside my boots, lifted my heels off the ground. All okay. I closed one eye; I could still see. I did that again with the other; both okay. *Thank you, God, thank you.*

I looked down between the open halves of my unsnapped flak jacket. A piece of bloody meat the length and thickness of my middle finger clung to my utility blouse.

My vision blurred. I felt like I was moving very slowly down a long, dim tunnel. The thrumming, darkly effervescent sound that suffused my hearing grew louder, deeper in my ears. But no agony rushed through me. My head, my entire body, ached dully, my face burned from the scrapes and my mouth pinched where I'd chewed my cheeks and tongue. But I felt no terrible, piercing pain anywhere.

I stared at the raw meat on my chest. I was disgusted; I thought I might puke. Then I was terrified. I knew I couldn't touch it. There was no doubt at all in my screaming brain that if I touched that gory piece of flesh, it would be like pulling back the peel away tab on a can of guts and my entrails would spill out all over my thighs and I'd die.

I waited for the agony to strike. I waited for my innards to erupt against my clothes. I waited to pass out. Was this what it was to die? I stared at that hunk of bloody meat for a long, long time, then my fear mixed with stomach-churning disgust and weakening, exhausting relief, and I realized that those three or four inches of carrion adhered to my chest could not be mine.

I picked the bloody chunk of meat off me and flung it away.

Then I heard a sound I've never since been able to forget. A low murmur, a muted, awe-filled chorus that echoed and reverberated in the gunpowder and blood-stenched air. *Woody? Where's Woodson? Where in the name of God is Woody?*

I looked toward where the ammo can had sat against the grave mound where I'd spent the night. The earth in front of the mound was scorched; small fires burned in the grass that grew up the sides of the grave; a slowly dissipating cloud of bitter gray smoke hung in the air.

I slowly got to my feet. I wiped the blood and drool and snot from under my nose and off my mouth and chin. I stared at the scorched, smoky spot. Where the fuck did that filthy ammo can go?

Marines milled about, weapons in hand. Some of them stood and gaped at the place where Woody had been. The two corpsmen and John and Harding worked on wounded men. Smitty called for medevacs. The lieutenant paced back and forth, his face gray and sunken like a very old man's. "Where's Woodson? Somebody tell me where the fuck Woodson is!" His voice was a low growl, distinct from all the others I heard. He sounded as though he were afraid he'd find out.

I turned slowly in a circle where I stood and looked around the cemetery. Twenty yards behind me, in the opposite direction from where people worked on the wounded, eighty feet from where

Woody and the ammo can had been, I saw something lying in tall grass. I walked toward it hesitantly, praying I wouldn't find what I feared was there. Behind me, the fearful, worried chorus hung in the air as though the sounds of the words themselves contained deadly particles. *Woodson? Where's Woody?*

The grass obscured the thing until I was five feet away.

It was Woody.

My stomach churned and twisted and tried to fight its way up my throat. Somehow, I kept it down.

———

We never figured out what the booby trap was made of. We never figured out what triggered the explosion, either. Maybe Woody bumped the can. Maybe the booby trap was command detonated by someone hidden in one of the tree lines or snarls of bamboo around us. Maybe, though it seemed just short of impossible, Woody had been crazy enough to try to lift the lid.

It didn't matter. Whatever it was, it had propelled him nearly eighty feet through the air, ripped every limb from his body and flayed him open like a side of beef in a slaughterhouse.

I stared down at what was left of somebody's boy.

A few seconds before, he'd been a handsome, fun-loving young man whom others admired. A leader, a guy who seemed to have it all but was still kind to people like Willie; a brave comrade who cared deeply for others in the platoon and for friends like Mike and Dottie Jackson; a kid who got a kick out of the fireworks of explosions.

Now, the top of his skull was gone, and red, pulpy gray matter bubbled out of what had been his head and ran onto the ground. Where his face had been, there was no skin and very little flesh, just a red mass stretched over protruding cheekbones and across broken teeth bared in a hideous snarl under three dripping wet sockets where his eyes and nose had been. His arms were torn off jagged at the elbows, his legs ripped off above the knees. His torso and abdomen were completely open, exposed as though he'd been delaminated for a ghoul's anatomy class. What had moments before been Mrs. Woodson's son, Big Jim's pride and joy, guys' friend, girl-friends' lover, was now just red and brown mush from shoulders to thighs, lungs and organs bubbling out of the smelly slop, part of his intestines looping low beneath what had been his waist, circling around a bright red penis that poked straight up through the center of the pink brown coils like a bloody, fiery coal.

I gagged.

I wanted to call the others, but I couldn't clear my throat.

I did not want to look, not any longer, but I could not help myself. I could not make myself turn away. I was fighting my stomach, and my mouth tasted full of blood and sour bile, and my entire body flushed cold, and at the same time I was trying not to vomit, trying not to shit my pants. I was terrified and horrified, and I couldn't speak, I couldn't move.

Someplace in the dense distance, I heard the lieutenant's voice. He sounded like he was at the far end of a very long, dark tunnel. I stood there as if I'd been nailed to the ground, staring at all that was left of one of the best guys I'd ever known.

Finally, slowly, without turning back toward the people behind me, I raised my hand above my head.

"Woody ..." I gagged out the words. "Over here ... here's Woody."

18

BACK INSIDE THE COMPANY PERIMETER, I was surprised when Matt came and sat next to me. A blood-soaked field dressing covered the side of his face. I asked why he was still there. He shrugged and said he had stuff to do. He'd need a bunch of stitches but would go out on the supply bird the next day.

Matt held up his fingers and had me count them, had me touch my own to my nose, leaned in, and looked hard at my eyes. His chin with its two-day-old stubble looked like it'd been painted pink. "You might have a mild concussion," he said. "But you'll be okay." He turned my face side to side, then looked in my mouth. "How you feeling?"

"I'm okay. Wish I'd eaten less of my mouth." I couldn't have ached more from head to toe if a football team had used me as a tackling dummy; the inside of my mouth burned and pinched where I'd bitten my cheeks and tongue. My mind hurt more than anything.

"I'll write you up for a Heart when Dorsey and I do the report."

"What do you mean?"

"You were wounded." Matt looked like I'd asked something strange.

"I wasn't hit."

"But you were hurt when you got blown to the ground. Even if it was gravel and your own teeth that tore you up."

I looked hard at him. He was trying to do me a favor. "Matt, how could I wear a Purple Heart for what happened to me when the same medal's going to Woody's parents? And Dasmund's? And all the guys who lost legs or were otherwise wounded so badly?"

"The way I figure it," Matt said, "if Uncle Sam says anybody wounded three times gets to go home, any Marine who is, has more than held up his part of that bargain and should head back to the World, even if his wounds weren't that serious. You rate a Heart. People have gotten them for less."

Matt may have been correct, but on the day Woody was killed, I couldn't have accepted a Purple Heart if it'd been pinned on my chest. How could I live with myself if I ever met Jackson or Corrigan or Prevas or Cavett hobbling around on prostheses and they said, "How'd you get your Heart, McClure?" "Oh," I'd have to say, "I bit my tongue." Jesus. Matt reluctantly agreed not to write it up.

For days and nights I tried to shake the pictures of Woody out of my head. Nothing worked. The horror seemed to permeate my whole system, inflaming unanswerable questions that roiled in my mind. Why Woody? Why not me, when I slept on that fucking ammo can? Was a block of C-4 in Woody's flak jacket pocket all that made the difference between Gio living and him dying? Why had Woody been killed and others wounded, and me only knocked down? Twice now. How could you be coated with other men's blood, or worse, and be unscathed yourself? Did the randomness of it all mean you wasted your time worrying about getting hurt, or should you worry more? Did God have a plan? Did He give a shit? I had to believe God was protecting me, or I might've been too paralyzed to move. But then, hadn't each of those guys believed that too?

Despite the feeling of horror that clung to me, and the turmoil inside my head, I was excited about taking over Gio's gun while he was in Hong Kong. I'd miss my time with John, particularly our talks at night in our hole. He was the rock I clung to when things were really tough, though he too had been badly shaken by Woody's death. With Willie gone too, Glass was to be my A-gunner. He was from Detroit, the only one of three brothers who wasn't in jail. He'd been wounded pretty badly a few months before but wasn't flaky at all. He was Smitty's closest friend, though he tended to hang with the other black Marines, not the lieutenant's radioman. We got along fine.

One night while Glass slept, I stood watch. I fingered the rosary beads I now wore draped around my neck the way John wore his. The little black balls had lost the lacquered gloss they'd had when Mom pressed them into my hand the day I left for Vietnam; the tiny silver Christ figure on its cross had become sweat-dulled pewter gray. I recalled the nuns telling us if you prayed the rosary, you'd be saved from serious harm. Probably to your person, certainly to your soul. Mom believed that, too. She said the rosary every night I was gone. I appreciated that, and despite my doubts, I wasn't going to stop taking laps on the beads myself. I needed all the help I could get. Still, I wasn't sure those nuns, or my mother, had a clue. They hadn't been in Vietnam.

The waning moon passed like an illuminated ghost through the clouds. I strained to see if anything moved to our front. *Please help me be safe, God,* I prayed, holding the crucifix at the end of the beads. *And if any gooks are out there, help me kill them all.*

When I realized what I'd just prayed for, I wished John was there to talk with. Was the darkness he'd spoken of so long ago beginning to coat my soul? I had no way of knowing how much darker it could get.

⸻

A few days after Woody was killed, Smitty said, "I hope Gio and Willie are having fun."

John had had to talk Willie into keeping to his plans to go to Bangkok. "It's what Woody wanted you to do," John said. "Go to Bangkok like he did, forget this place, and have nothing but fun."

"Nothin' but fun," Willie said to himself. Over and over again.

Gio didn't talk at all after Woody died. People told him to have a good time in Hong Kong, but he didn't even smile when he and Willie got on the chopper to go.

"Willie's probably done havoc in immeasurable whorehouses by now," Cloninger said.

"Making progress in that dictionary, Buzz," John said.

"Gianelli's probably been high as a kite since he got off the plane."

"If I was in Bangkok or Hong Kong, I'd sure be gettin' laid," Carlton said.

"Shit, Carlton. You're never gonna know about Bangkok or Hong Kong," Smitty said. "You're an old married man."

"Yeah, and when I go to Hawaii after my baby's born, I'm definitely going to do my duty to the old lady."

"Regular Boy Scout," Smitty said with a slight laugh. "Get you a merit badge when you're back. I sure hope Gio and Willie are having fun."

"I hope so," Glass said. "They were pretty fucked up after Woody was killed."

"I keep thinking about him," Carlton said. "I can't help it. I wish I could, but I can't. What a lousy way to go."

God, how I wished they hadn't gone there. The pictures in my head pulsed. I really needed to keep Woody in a box now, not talk about him. Even if he'd been the best-liked guy in First Platoon, we needed to put him in a box and put that box on a damn high shelf. At least I did. But Glass said, "Maybe not." He looked like a gigantic praying mantis hunched down in the dirt, all arms and legs and long body. A black version of Prevas, except bigger. "If he had to go at all, it was quick."

"I guess," Carlton said. "Beats the shit out of a gut shot. Remember Lambert?"

"Don't," Landon said. "Enough."

"Gnat's Nuts is right," Glass said. "I don't even want to think about that. That took a long time."

"For Christ's sake." Smitty shook his head. "Can we talk about something else?"

I agreed with Smitty. I was suddenly exhausted again, too emotionally drained to argue or even stand up and walk away.

"No dress blues," Glass said. "And your momma don't even get a last look at you. Can't even say a proper goodbye."

"Just a sealed box in church," Carlton said. "A shitty way to go."

I didn't have the energy to ask them to shut up or to get up and leave. I sat there staring into the distance, trying to block the discussion out of my head.

"There ain't no good way to go, man," Glass said.

"There it is, man," Smitty said. "There it fuckin' is."

19

THICK CLOUDS MOVED OVER US, and a sliver of pocked moon prowled an angry sky. What we called a "witches' night" when I was a kid, only an occasional star hurrying through scant breaks in the clouds, shadows skulking everywhere. When the clouds huddled together, it was so black I couldn't tell Glass was on watch in the hole a couple feet from me.

I fell asleep in the middle of a lap on the beads and woke to a hellfire of earsplitting noise, blinding flashes, the earth bucking like a dragon trying to shake me off its neck. Geysers of steel and dirt and smoke and flame exploded everywhere as mortars and rockets crashed down on us.

I'd never been on the incoming end of mortar or rocket fire in the bush before. I panicked, writhed on my belly in the dirt like a reptile with a shovel through its back, scratched and clawed at the earth as though if I let go, I'd fly off the hill.

I got my bearings and crawled to the hole and fell in on top of Glass. A tangle of arms and legs, the two of us struggled to get free of each other, pushed, shoved, and swore, as though by separating one from the other we'd somehow be more protected from the descending steel than if we lay snarled together in the bottom of the hole.

We untangled while the blasts still reverberated and explosions still blazed across the hill. The barrage stopped abruptly, and all around me muzzle flashes split the night as attacking NVA and

Marines both opened up. I heard a long burst from John's gun fifty feet down our line—a yammering exclamation of angry sound so long I thought he'd burnt out the barrel. To my left, the precise, unhurried *pap* . . . *pap* of Landon's M16.

I thought every gook in the world was on us. Glass began firing his M16 in bursts. I grabbed up the machine gun, straining in the flash-split blackness to find a target down the hill. The muzzle flashes and reports from Glass' rifle buffeted my eyes and ears. All around me, a bedlam of noise. My eyes would not adjust to the dark, I could aim at muzzle flashes but could not see the enemy. What the fuck do I shoot at down the hill?

An artillery illumination round burst above us, a flare dangling high in the sky bathing the side of the hill in dim, yellow light. I saw movement then, black figures in the trees and boulders down the slope. NVA coming for us. The roar and rattle and crack of rifle and machine-gun fire grew louder and more frantic, and there were screams from down the hill and more from our lines. More illum rounds washed a thousand meters around the hill in eerie, quavering light.

I fired short machine-gun bursts at movement and muzzle flashes. Bullets cracked overhead, slashed angrily into the dirt around us. A B40 rocket roared and crashed farther up the hill behind us toward the CP. Metal and rock and debris flew all around. Glass slapped my shoulder, pointed down to our right. I turned the gun, blasted that area. Red tracers flew, streams of neon blurbs tore the air, hit the ground, careened up into the night like a death-dealing pinball machine gone berserk. I could see men running up the side of the hill.

The lead figure crumbled. Two behind him hit the ground. Immediately, one jumped back up and began to run toward us again. I blew him backwards with a laser stream of red-orange dots. He did a weird, jerking dance, like a jiver frozen in a pulsating strobe, then crumpled to the ground. I swung the gun back and forth, blasted anything that moved, shadows, muzzle flashes. The entire hill roared with gunfire, grenade blasts, screaming, yelling men. Thick, acrid haze. Dim yellow flare-light. Pounding, ear-shattering, reverberating sound.

A man rose from the ground down the hillside directly to my front. For a second, he was on one knee, hesitating. I swung the gun to shoot him. It jammed.

"Get him! Get him!" I screamed at Glass, but he was turned away, firing to our left, and didn't hear me.

I dropped the M60, grabbed my pistol, the thought screaming through my head: *you've never fired more than twenty rounds through a .45. Oh Jesus, I can't hit anything with this.* The man began to run directly toward us. In the flickering light I could see grenades in both his fists.

Please, God, please. I held the .45 with both hands in front of me, barrel wavering, the man only yards away now, one arm cocked back to throw.

I fired. The recoil threw my hands back up toward my face. The figure jerked to the left as though I hit him, but kept coming. He was so close I could see his mouth open as though he were screaming curses at me, his eyes straining, sweat covering his face. I brought the pistol back down in front of me and fired again.

The round caught him square in the chest, lifted him from the ground and threw him backward. One of his grenades exploded while he was airborne. His body twisted and lashed like rope in the air, then fell heavily to the ground. Behind him, the other grenade bounced down the hill and exploded in a quick, violent flash of light.

I laid the pistol in the dirt and fumbled at the M60's feed cover. And then, before I had time to fire the gun again, it was over. The NVA withdrew, dragging most of their dead and wounded with them.

They didn't get them all. Down the hill, cries and moans echoed through the thick night. Below to our right, a moan built to a cry of pain. A long, loud blast from Pius John's gun. The cry stopped.

Across the hilltop, inside our lines, a scream pierced the low thrum of moans and frantic whispers. I stopped glaring down the hillside long enough to look quickly around. Platoon leaders and platoon sergeants checked lines. Corpsmen tried to patch the wounded. Whispered, nearly pantomime activity under the wavering yellow light of more flares. A helpless feeling in the pit of my stomach as I glimpsed someone drag a body out of a hole.

I spent the next two hours soaked with sweat, shaking in the damp night cold, praying there would be no more mortars, no more gooks climbing the hill. I needed a cigarette so badly I almost lit one in the dark. Fortunately, there was no further attack. The only enemy gunfire came when a '46 landed very fast, loaded our emergency wounded, and lifted off again. The *whup-whup* and *thrum* of the rotors was still loud in my ears when a line of blue-green tracers sliced up through the black from somewhere quite a way from the hill. Streams of red ripped down through the sky from a gunship accompanying the medevac bird. In the dark, I hadn't known it was there until I saw the red slashes streak toward the NVA. The enemy had faded back into the black. Twice during the hours until dawn, there were cries of pain down the slope. Fire from several holes answered them.

At the first hints of dawn, the snap of Zippos grew to a metallic chorus. I lit a cigarette, floated on the dull, static ache it brought to my head and chest. As daylight began to tame the darkness, Marines emerged from the ground like trampled warrior ants.

The body of the man I'd shot with the pistol was only ten yards to our front. Beyond it, I could see other bodies the NVA had not dragged away. There were none where I'd shot the group earlier in the fight. I felt a sudden, irrational fear that the NVA I'd shot with the pistol might still rise up to kill me. I glared at the crumpled form, tried to will it to disappear. It didn't twitch.

In front of the Company CP, rows of Marines lay on the ground, corpsmen buzzing over them. There were no moans or cries of pain now, just the throb and hum of desperate activity. A row of poncho-covered bodies lay beyond the wounded. I counted seven, a pair of boots sticking out of the bottom of each. I felt like I'd just been sucker-punched in the gut.

Another medevac bird came in. More wounded Marines were carried or walked to the helicopter. The dead were next, wrapped in ponchos or inside black body bags, more than I'd first counted. Third Platoon had taken the brunt of the assault. The hillside in front of their position was littered with NVA corpses. One of Third Herd's machine guns had a dozen dead gooks strewn in front of it.

"Stacked on top of each other," Glass said, "like they couldn't wait their turn to get at us." He sounded astonished, still scared.

I lit another cigarette off the tip of the last, picked my rosary out of the dirt. "Thank you," I said. I kissed the crucifix then draped the beads around my neck. In the trees down the hill to our left, the lieutenant and Staff Sergeant Gilles and Second Squad searched for bodies. A voice called, "Papa Sierra! Sergeant Gilles! Over here!" A single, deep, echoing blast. A minute later, the shotgun roared again, farther down to the left.

Glass sat, legs dangling in our hole, blowing smoke rings. Smitty came over and sat down next to him. "How'd we do on casualties?" I asked.

Smitty shook his head, blew a cloud of mentholated smoke. "One KIA, a new guy in Third Squad. We were lucky. Talbot in Third Squad got gut shot, Eggers in Second, hit in the head. Both emergencies. We had a couple priorities, too, Akers and another new guy, I don't remember his name. Doc Dorsey and the lieutenant were wounded *tee-tee*. They'll stay."

We sat in the dirt then without talking, like school kids on a hillside watching the wreckers and ambulances drag cars and bodies away from a crash. Down our lines, Pius John sat like a stone Buddha in front of his hole. He didn't look over at us, just sat sharpening his kabar, staring down the hill, once in a while carving at his fingernails with the tip of his blade. I should've gone to talk to him, but I was too drained to move.

I scratched at the festering gook sores on the back of my forearm, lit another cigarette. I'd lit one off the tip of another since dawn. The soldier I'd shot with the .45 lay still thirty feet to our front. To our left, I could see another body, and a few feet from that, a severed arm lay in the dirt as though tossed aside as surplus in the NVA's retreat. I couldn't see any bodies over toward John.

"We got to have killed more than them," Smitty said. "Had to do a couple dozen."

"Someone musta drug them away," Glass said. He spat across the top of the hole, then lit another Kool.

Smitty nodded down the hill. "You guys get that one?"

"McClure did," Glass said. "Fuckin' forty-five." He sounded impressed.

"Decent," Smitty said. The lieutenant called for him then. "I'll let you know how many confirms we call in," he said.

Glass looked again toward the NVA lying to our front. "Damn good shot."

I nodded. I watched the crumpled body. Guarded it, wished it would disappear, feared it might. I reloaded the pistol. "Cover me," I said.

As soon as I said it, I felt foolish. Cover me. It sounded hollow, bullshit, John Wayne. But as I edged my way down the hill, my gut tightened, my finger caressed the trigger, and I kept the .45 trained on the prostrate form. *One motion, motherfucker, one breeze rippling in that shirt and I'll blow you apart.*

The soldier lay half on his side, half on his belly, facing up the hill. Dark stains soaked his torn shirt where the .45 round punched a large hole when it came out his back. One arm was twisted at a crazy angle beside him. I walked slowly around him, kept the pistol pointed at the body, waited for him to move. *Give me an excuse, asshole.* His face looked pressed into the ground. Then I realized it wasn't really a face at all, just flattened, mangled pulp. The grenade that exploded when I shot him had ripped open his skull and blown away the side of his head and face.

I turned and walked slowly back up the slope to our hole.

Pius John was waiting for me. He raised his head in a slow arc, indicating the body down the hill. "Yours?" he asked.

I stared at him for a moment. His face was blank. I looked toward the corpse again, then back at John. The first man I was certain I'd killed. I was too exhausted to contemplate the full meaning of that. I just knew I was relieved, and proud of what I'd done. "Yeah, mine," I said quietly. "That one's mine for sure."

John nodded, then turned and looked toward where he'd fired on the NVA at the beginning of their assault up the hill. There were no bodies; they'd all been dragged off.

"Mine are gone," he said. He shook his head. "I know I got some." He shook his head again, as though distraught by unfairness he couldn't explain. "Mine are all gone."

20

WE LEFT THE HILL TO SEARCH FOR the NVA who'd attacked us. As our column moved down the slope, I stared at the corpses strewn, mangled, and fly-blustered along our way. I couldn't help hoping none of them would move, hoping some of them would so I could shoot them again.

We searched for days, finding neither NVA nor any sign of a hidden complex. I thought again of the attack weeks ago on Delta and of Havey talking about fighting ghosts. The men who'd hit us hadn't been ghosts. At least not the ones whose bodies lay stinking on the hillside now.

A blocking platoon from Charlie Company encountered the NVA first. We were several hundred meters from the Charlie Marines when I heard a burst from an AK-47, then the roar of a full-pitched firefight. Lieutenant Mangan sprinted to the front of our column, and we ran toward the sound of fire. The ghosts had not vanished. Fury surged through me as I ran: this time, we'd pay the bastards back for what they'd done to us.

The Charlie platoon was in a graveyard, taking heavy fire from a tree line to their north. We were almost to them when rounds began cracking around us. We got to the edge of a stand of trees and dropped to the ground. Bullets tore through branches and tree trunks where we'd been standing moments before. I yelled for Glass to stay close with the ammo cans, then began firing.

Glass banged me on the shoulder and pointed up as a pair of Skyhawks banked in. The lead plane dove, dropped five-hundred pounders into the tree line, and roared up into the sky. "Get some, zoomies!" I yelled then began firing again. The thunder of the bombs bellowed like a thousand kettle drums in waves across the paddies. It mixed with the roar of my machine gun and the rattle and crash of the fight.

Glass cheered. Between bursts I yelled at him, "Pay attention! Keep the ammo coming!" Adrenalin coursed through me like electricity. I took a deep breath. Don't let the excitement control you, John had told me. Controlled bursts, don't burn out the barrel. Fire. Pause. Fire. Spent brass flew all around me.

The second A-4 banked in. Napalm canisters tumbled end over end into the tree line. A whoosh and roar and jellied gasoline billowing, roiling, belching toward the sky, a great splash of black-orange-red flames and clouds engulfing a long swath of the tree line.

I kept firing. Beside me, Glass fired his M16, yelling at the top of his lungs. I tried to make him hear me above the bedlam. "Ammo! Keep it coming, Glass, keep it coming!"

The roiling, whooshing blast of the napalm hadn't yet receded when the pilot of the lead plane banked around and made his own napalm run. The spectacle billowed through the trees again.

The wingman began his second run. The diving jet roared down, pickled, pulled up, and zoomed into the sky. I watched, terrified, as two winged bombs streaked toward the open space between us and the platoon from Charlie Company. "Incoming! Incoming!" I screamed. I pushed Glass' head down into the dirt and buried my own and wrapped my arms over my helmet. Glass clawed at the dirt.

Whatever the pilot had done wrong didn't matter to us at all. The five-hundred-pound high-explosive bombs detonated in front of Charlie, between our platoons. Above my head, steel screamed and howled as the bombs' blast rushed over us like jackhammer blows. The planes banked up and around and headed back to base.

We found no one alive in the tree line. Bodies cut in half. Unidentifiable heaps of meat and clothing and bone. Pieces of what had been men. We moved through the tree line and into the paddy beyond it, found more bodies, dropped by NVA trying to escape. At least a dozen, and no casualties for First Platoon.

My satisfaction evaporated as soon as we got to the Charlie platoon. I saw bodies of two Marines covered with ponchos. Two others sat nearby, one with a bloody bandage on his face, the other with a blood-soaked field dressing around his thigh. Their lieutenant sat leaning against a grave mound. On the other side of the mound, a smoking chunk of gray steel two feet long, thick as a rail, stuck out of the grave.

"No casualties from gooks," he said to Lieutenant Mangan. "But our own fucking air . . ." He stopped talking. He looked like he wanted to shoot someone.

John stood off to the side, looking toward the Charlie platoon casualties. "You okay?" I asked. I wasn't sure what I expected him to say. How could any of us be okay? We'd just had the satisfaction of a lot of kills with no casualties in our platoon ripped away by a fucking mistake. John's eyes looked like life had drained from them. "John. You okay?"

"Goodman," he said very quietly.

"Good man?"

He shook his head slightly. "Terry Goodman." He nodded toward the Marines' bodies. "My best friend in machine-gun school. Fuckin' gooks."

Father Mullin greeted each of us. He'd been ordered to Division Headquarters for the last months of his tour but complained so much about wanting to be with the grunts, they let him come back. He had gook sores on his arms and tatters of sunburnt skin hung from his neck. "It's been a while since I've been with Bravo," he said. "Corporal Harding, I hear congratulations are in order."

"Yes, sir." Harding grinned. "A little girl. Her name's Hope."

"Great name."

The priest admired half a dozen Polaroids while Harding watched like a kid wanting the teacher to pick his drawing for a prize.

"She's a sweetheart, Corporal Harding. Going to get her a tattoo to match yours and your wife's?"

Harding laughed. "Not Hope, Father. The lieutenant got me on next month's quota for Hawaii. Bonnie's bringing Hope to meet her dad."

"That's great," Father Mullin said. "Bring back some pictures of the three of you."

"I'll do that, sir. I've got a new picture of Bonnie here, too, Father." He pulled a snapshot out of the plastic bag.

"You're sure it's okay for a man of the cloth to see this, right?" Father Mullin sounded like he was joking, but you could tell he was more than half serious.

"Oh yeah, Father. This one's not like those others."

"Might not want to share those too widely, Corporal Harding," the priest said, smiling at the picture of Bonnie in front of the baby carriage.

"I don't show those around anymore. Not now," Harding said.

"Since Hope was born, he acts like her mother got transformed into the Virgin Mary's younger sister, Bonnie the Blessed." Gio laughed and dodged the punch Corporal Harding threw at his arm.

"Bonnie the Blessed," Father Mullin chuckled. "Still got the purple glasses and jewelry going I see, Gianelli. Where's that ring with the big purple stone with the cross in the center of it? I thought wearing that might show you had a vocation."

People scoffed. "Big Bang" Gianelli a priest! Gio had been unusually quiet since returning from R&R. He'd confided to John that he'd been so upset about Woody, he'd stayed drunk by himself in his hotel room the whole time. I'd hated to give him back the gun, but at least I was with John again.

"I gave the ring to Cavett when he was wounded," Gio said.

That surprised me. We clung to our talismans: my rosary, John's, Willie's rabbit's foot, Cloninger's raccoon's penis bone.

Gio seemed embarrassed now. "It always brought me good luck." He shrugged.

"Cavett. Too bad," Father Mullin said. "We talked about him losing a leg or his foot last time I was with you, right? He's the one who always bitched and moaned and said, 'I'm too short for this shit'?"

"Yes, sir," Gio said. "My A-gunner. His foot."

"Have you heard how he's doing?"

Gio shook his head. "Not a word, Father. I think he wanted to forget this place." He hesitated. "You know, as much as he could . . ."

"I hope he finds peace. We don't know why God lets bad stuff happen, but none of us can ever give up hope. I'll pray for him."

The priest noticed the engineer standing outside our circle. "Sergeant Weeks, what're you doing out here? Haven't seen you since Da Nang."

"Damned if I know, Chaplain."

He was a dour, frowning sergeant, usually stationed back at Division rear. For the past week, First and Second Platoons had been lucky, but two Marines in Third had been killed by a single booby-trap and one had tripped another that mangled his legs. The captain convinced someone to send us an engineer, at least for a while. We'd been skeptical it'd help much.

"If we could find the sons of bitches, we wouldn't set the fuckers off," Fullerton spat a stream through his teeth.

He was right, of course, but I wondered if Woody'd still be alive if the engineer had been with us then. Of course, the engineer himself might not be. "Maybe we'll finally find that damn complex they say is out here. He'd come in handy then, blowing stuff up." I surprised myself. I sounded as optimistic as Corrigan used to be.

Fullerton spat again. "We been looking for weeks. I think that complex is the figment of some pogue's imagination."

A few days later Sergeant Weeks had appeared. "How long've you been with Bravo?" Father Mullin asked now. The priest glanced at the engineer's clean uniform and unscuffed boots.

"Just got here yesterday. Hopefully, I won't be here long."

"Well, Sergeant Weeks," Father Mullin said. "I hope you can help us out here. We've had some terrible luck with booby traps."

The engineer shrugged. "We'll see, Chaplain. Not exactly what I'm trained to do."

The priest kept the smile on his face, though there was no longer one in his eyes. "I'm sure you'll do fine. And I'm sure you'll find being out here with the grunts more rewarding than fixing holes in the road or supervising burning the shitters."

Father Mullin didn't wait for a response. He seemed to remember everyone. He talked with Cloninger about where he was in the dictionary. They both used several words beginning with L. The engineer walked back toward the Company CP like he was going off to sulk. "How're the rest of you doing?" The priest asked. He turned to Willie. "Willis, right?"

Even before Willie answered, my mind took off in a sprint. How are the rest of you doing? I didn't know what to say about that. What the hell does that mean?

Physically? I live in the dirt, haven't had a shower in weeks. Eat once or twice a day, cold out of the can, as often as not. I've burned, blistered, peeled, and repeated more times than I know. When I get to sleep at all, it's in couple-hour stretches not knowing if I'll wake up alive. I'm bone tired and aching from walking endless hours in sun and rain. I've been knocked down, but I haven't been hit. When you think about all that, I'm pretty damn good.

Emotionally? I'm okay, I guess. Bored some of the time, scared nearly to death part of the time, wary in one way or another most of the time. I've gotten to hate gooks, and that's fine. And I've grown to love these guys and haven't even thought about that before. But I do love this mash-up of tough guys and wise guys and wrong-side-of-the-trackers and hillbillies and street thugs. And one warrior-philosopher-wannabe, not-wannabe-priest with the incongruous name Pius John. And Corporal Hard Ass, the lifer, and slow Willie and crazy Gianelli and all those other guys I wouldn't have hung with last year, but that I'm closer to now than even high school buddies like Spence. Yeah, I'm okay, I guess.

And how about spiritually, Father, now that you've asked? Well, I guess that's really your bailiwick, isn't it now? So maybe you can tell me. I'd like to know if God's made his hat, and I'm afraid to conclude that He doesn't give a shit because if He does, He might take it out on me for not believing in Him even if I really want Him to help.

I didn't say any of that, of course, but those thoughts flashed around like strobe lights in my head.

Willie's face lit up, thrilled that Father Mullin remembered his name. "Yeah," he said. Corporal Harding cleared his throat, glowered at him. Willie glanced toward Harding, then dropped his eyes. "Sir," he added.

"Hey Irish. What's so funny?"

I didn't realize I'd chuckled out loud. "Oh, not much, Father. I guess I was thinking that's really a complicated question."

The priest looked puzzled.

"I meant, how are we doing . . ."

"I see. Well, we'll have to talk about that." He smiled at me as if he thought the exchange had been fun. "So, Willis. I was asking how you're doing."

Willie grinned again. "Good," he said. He hesitated, then his grin widened. "I'm gonna get married."

"Jesus Christ," Gianelli said, only half under his breath.

Father Mullin glanced over at Gio. "Sure you don't have a vocation, Gianelli?"

"Sorry, Father."

"He's gonna marry a gook," Cloninger said.

Willie spun to face the Buzz. "I told you, she's not a fucking gook, Cloninger. She's from Thailand."

"Willis . . ."

"Sorry, Father." Willie glowered at Cloninger.

Father Mullin shook his head dismissively. "That's okay, but what's . . ."

John jumped in. "I think Willie might like to talk with you privately, Father. Have a little talk, get some advice. Right, Willie?"

Willie hung his head. "These guys always think I'm stupid," he said. He looked around like a big, slow, harmless dog being poked with sticks.

"Well, I don't think you're stupid, Willis," the priest said. "We can talk."

"He's sending his money to a whore he met on R&R," Fullerton said.

"Willie's willy's in love," Gio said.

John gave them both a piercing look.

Father Mullin scowled. "First time you ever got laid, Willis?"

Willie lowered his head even farther. "Um . . . well . . . come on, Father . . ."

"You're right, none of my business. But you come see me after chow, Willis. We'll figure this out, you and me. Right?"

Willie nodded without looking up.

"Yes, Chaplain," Corporal Harding growled.

"Yes, Father." Willie didn't look up.

Father Mullin turned to me. "McClure, right?"

"Yes, Father."

"Thought so. I don't usually forget another mick. Baltimore, right?"

"Yes, sir." I smiled, pretty amazed. Hundreds of Marines in the battalion, and he remembered my name and where I was from.

"So," he dragged the word out, a laugh in his eyes. "How are you doing, complicated question though that might be?"

I actually laughed at that. "Good one, Father," I said.

How'm I doing? I wasn't going to get into the accumulation of dark thoughts zigzagging through my head. I've worn part of a man I cared for a lot splattered on my chest. I've watched other friends killed or crippled and feel every one of them someplace inside me like a dull, sharp, empty ache. I was taught growing up that to take someone else's life was the greatest sin of them all, but I've killed gooks and I'll be happy to kill lots more. I live every goddamn day not knowing who's going to get killed or blown apart next, maybe me. So tell me, Father, how the fuck am I doing?

"I'm okay, Father," I said. "I'm doing fine."

I wondered if God punished people for lying to priests.

―――――

First Platoon led the Company deeper into the AO. We saw no enemy and found no booby traps. There was nothing for the engineer to do for several days.

Late one afternoon, we took five in an abandoned, bombed-out ville. Scorched, shredded hootches, scattered chunks of clay pots, a well, crushed and scattered like a mug smashed by a giant. The sour smell of decay.

The engineer had to take a leak. Instead of moving a couple feet away, he walked across the gutted ville toward a thick hedgerow. The booby trap was in a tree, face high when it went off. The only piece of him above the neck we found was one ear so intact it might have been removed with a scalpel. Doc Dorsey tucked it into one of the engineer's pockets before we wrapped him up.

No birds were available for routine medevacs, so the engineer had to spend the night with us. Having his headless corpse in a body bag inside our perimeter just behind our holes wreaked more havoc with my brain than his death itself.

The mine Glass set off several days later mangled his legs, groin, and arms. When the filthy gray cloud dissipated around him, he lay in a bloody sprawl, barely conscious, whispering, "Oh no, not again. Oh Jesus, not me again."

He seemed numbed to his pain as the docs and John and I worked feverishly to keep him alive. "Oh God, not yet," he begged quietly, as though he were praying in church. "Too young. . . . Not now, God . . . please not yet." His voice was choked, barely loud enough to hear. As though he were afraid if he prayed too loudly, God would say no.

We murmured kind stupidities to him, lying as we fought to save his life. *You'll be okay, man. We'll get you taken care of. We'll get you fixed up. You'll be okay.*

He looked like he'd been eaten by wolves.

Smitty finished his initial call for a medevac, then realized it was Glass who was wounded. He handed the radio to the lieutenant and rushed over to kneel beside us, stroking Glass' head. He wiped the spittle and the drool from the corners of Glass' mouth, tried to distract him from the carnage of his body. "You'll be okay, babycakes. Take it easy bro, we'll get you patched up." His tears fell into Glass' hair where they glistened in the dusty coils like dew on black ferns.

Glass' chocolate skin turned ash gray and his eyeballs retreated down into their sockets. The light faded from them like someone turned his rheostat down. He was dead before we saw the medevac bird in the sky.

Smitty began walking in circles, babbling and muttering until the lieutenant grabbed him by both arms and told him he needed to get hold of himself because he needed his help. Smitty stared at him as though he had no clue who the platoon leader was.

Staff Sergeant Gilles took a turn, put both hands on the younger man's shoulders. "Get hold of yourself," he said. "Don't let people see you like this, Smith. You're better than this. We need to find the fucking gooks who killed Glass. We need to kill some fucking gooks for him."

Nothing worked.

The *whup-whup* and *thrum* of the bird carrying Glass and Smith away was still in the air when we formed up to move out. "I see a fuckin' gooner, any kind, I'm gonna kill it," Cloninger said in his nasal twang.

"We can't find anybody out here, Buzz." My voice was a whisper. "We've seen nothing for days in this whole fucking place but little kids and mama-sans and old people."

"They set 'em, or they know about 'em," Cloninger said. "That's enough."

"I want to kill gooks, too, Buzz. But we can't just kill civilians." I still believed that, but I thought too that Cloninger was likely right about some of the villagers.

"Civilians, shit. No such thing out here."

"Women, kids are civilians," John said. For the first time, he didn't sound convinced by his own words.

Carlton stared at the laminated picture of his pregnant wife, tucked it behind the webbing of his helmet liner, hefted the radio, and began to walk a few paces behind the lieutenant as we began our long haul back to rejoin the Company. The rear third of the platoon hadn't yet started forward when he tripped a booby trap that blew him up in the air and sent Lieutenant Mangan tumbling through the grass.

The lieutenant wasn't hurt, but the explosion ripped up Carlton's legs and groin. He begged and pleaded to know if the family jewels were okay. "I promised my wife we'd have lots of kids," he whispered to Doc Matheson as the morphine took hold. Their first was due in a matter of weeks. Matt lied—he couldn't tell in the blood and goo—told him yes, your balls are okay, you're still hung like a bull.

Despite the morphine, Doc Dorsey had to tape Carlton's hands to keep him from probing his privates as we waited for the emergency medevac. He whispered in a high, dry voice as we slid him onto a poncho, "Oh sweet Jesus, my wife . . . Please Jesus, not my balls. . . ."

As the chopper lifted skyward, Corporal Harding ran back from the LZ to where Pius John and I knelt. As he stood watching the bird climb into the sky, a tremor began to twitch in his jaw, then in his hands. He broke a cigarette in half pulling it out of his plastic case. He shoved his hands in his pockets so no one would see. "Bonnie," I heard him whisper to himself.

John stared at the tarnished crucifix on the end of the rosary around his neck. I'd never seen a look like that on his face. It was as though the acids of terror and anger and horror had drained to the low point of the vat, and the fury brewing was going to be toxic and unconstrained.

We searched the nearest ville viciously. Pulled women and kids out of hootches and pushed them into a circle. Tore gaping holes in thatched walls and roofs with our bayonets and machetes and rifle butts, smashed clay pots, broke the legs off wooden stools, ripped apart sleeping mats, and overturned buckets of rice.

We didn't find so much as a tripwire.

When the search was over, Marines paced like beasts glaring hungrily at the women and kids huddled like trapped birds on the central path. The lieutenant wouldn't let anyone Zippo the ville. His voice was taut with anger and frustration. "I want every Marine in this platoon under control, people. You understand me, squad leaders? We will tear apart this whole fucking valley, but no one waxes a bunch of goddamn civilians."

"Civilians?" Corporal Harding shook his M16 in the air. He had six days to go before he left to see Bonnie and Hope on R&R. "All due respect, Lieutenant, but no fucking way are any of these fucking people civilians. At least none of them over ten. Every fucking one of them sets fucking booby traps or at least knows where the fuck they are!"

"Corporal Harding," Lieutenant Mangan said, "you know damn well what I mean. No one's going to shoot women and kids or old men."

"This losin' people without payback is bullshit!" The veins on Gio's forehead looked like they were going to explode.

"We're going to kill some gooks, people!" Mangan's eyes bulged like tumors in dark, sunken sockets. "They can't hide forever from us."

I realized John was nowhere around. I backed away from the group, couldn't see him anywhere. Maybe he went to take a crap, I thought. But that didn't make sense. He would've told me to watch the gun and just walked away from us and squatted at the edge of the ville. I went looking for him.

I found John behind a hootch across the ville. He had a young mama-san up against a tree, the tip of his kabar under her chin. Her eyes were wild, her teeth bared in a frantic grimace, nostrils flaring like rifle muzzles in her sweat-soaked face as she danced like a graceless ballerina up on her toes. The knife point dug in a fraction of an inch. Blood seeped a shiny red path down the blade. Tears streamed down the girl's cheeks; her entire body a tremor. A high-pitched, gasping squeal escaped between her clenched teeth.

"Who's doing it? Where are they, you whore?" John's whisper was a growl. "Where's your husband? Where are the men? Where are the bastards planting the booby traps slaughtering my friends?"

"*Khong biet*," she moaned. I don't know.

You're wasting your time, I thought, *she doesn't speak English.*

John pushed his face even closer to hers. "Who fucked up Glass and Carlton," he snarled. He had spittle in the corners of his mouth. "Who, mama-san? Who's setting booby traps?"

"John," I said quietly. I didn't want to startle him, kill the girl by mistake. She looked like she would slip off her tiptoes and impale herself on the blade. "John, the lieutenant."

His eyes didn't leave her, his nose only inches from hers. Her eyes bulged like red-veined golf balls. Every cord in her neck and vein in her face wanted to explode.

"John," I said again. He slowly lowered the kabar, still holding her by her shirt. He wiped the bloody blade on her trousers, then slipped the knife back into the sheath on his belt.

I lit a cigarette and waited. I could hear Sergeant Gilles yell for the platoon to form up. "We're leaving, John," I said.

He let go of the girl. She fell to the ground and shrank into a shuddering, moaning ball. John picked up the gun, put his arm around my shoulder. Neither of us said anything as we walked back to the center of the ville. I realized only later that watching John with that mama-san had been like looking at an image of myself in a dark, cracking mirror.

21

SMITTY CAME BACK ON THE NEXT supply bird, mortified that he'd fallen apart. We would've held it against most guys, but not him.

The same bird brought a new guy to First Squad, a wiry blonde kid with peach fuzz and an incessant grin on his face. He bounced when he walked, bubbled when he talked, and waved his hands more than Gianelli. Gio named him Fizzy. "Like one of those grape things you drop in water and it fizzes all up and makes bubbly Kool-Aid."

"What's up with Smith?" Fizzy asked John and me his first day in the bush. He gnawed on a loaf of date nut bread I'd traded him for the Marlboros he'd gotten in his Cs. "Dude didn't say a word on the helicopter ride out here. And oh man, that was a ride. We even circled around so the gunners could shoot some Charlies." Fizzy's hands jammered in the air, index fingers pointed like barrels firing. "I couldn't see if they got 'em, but, oh man, do those fifties work out. I'd never seen anything like that before." He shook his head, a wide grin on his face. "But Smith? He hardly even looked up, like he couldn't care less. That guy's cool or crazy, what do you think?"

"He's quiet," John said. "And his best friend just got killed."

"Smitty's a really good guy," I added. "But he doesn't say much, and right now he's got stuff on his mind. I'd just leave him alone, if I were you, you know?"

"Gotcha," Fizzy said. "Best friend. Man, that's the pits. You guys got any chow you don't want?"

"Tough week, huh, men?" Father Mullin was back with Bravo for a couple days.

I didn't say anything, just nodded in agreement. The understatement of the week, or whatever part of the calendar it was.

I didn't know what a week was anymore. It didn't matter, I wasn't short enough to count days. On the back of Gio's flak jacket, on either side of the peace symbol with the words "If I Die In Vietnam Bury Me Face Down So The Whole World Can Kiss My Ass"— circled around it—he'd inked columns of numbers—*99, 98, 97 . . .* down to a zero with wings on it. He'd crossed out *51* on the morning Father Mullin got to our pos.

"I was really sorry to hear about Glass," the priest said. "A good man."

Nobody said much. Smitty was off talking with the lieutenant. That was a good thing.

"A shame about Carlton, too. Anybody know how he's doing?"

All we knew was that he'd been flown to Okinawa.

"Anybody hear if his baby's been born yet?"

"He was waiting for word any day now," John said. He didn't try to hide the anger in his voice. The priest studied John's face for a moment, then nodded in understanding. I hoped he'd never find out what John had done with the girl.

"I'll pray for all three of them," Father Mullin said. He took off his glasses and wiped a hand across his sweaty face and up through the sparse hair on his head. "I knew that fellow, Sergeant Weeks, the engineer, too, you know. Another loss." The priest pursed his lips, shook his head slowly. "Don't get me wrong, I hate like hell to see any of our men die, but there's a positive lesson here, too."

I couldn't believe Father Mullin was going to feed us some priestly crap about God's will or some such. He didn't. "At least this will show the REMFs this is their war too, not just the grunts," he said. "You fellows face the tough stuff every day. They need to remember they're in this fight, too."

The day after Father Mullin left to be with another rifle company, we found out Carlton had died. Matt wondered if he'd lost his testicles in the blast and just given up. "Before you got to the platoon," he said, "I had two different Marines lose their balls or their dicks. Both of them begged me to let them bleed out. That was the shits."

I never asked, and Matt never said, what he'd done.

When Corporal Harding found out about Carlton, he went and sat by himself and studied his pictures of Bonnie and Hope.

John didn't talk much for a couple days after we found out Carlton died. I kept close to him whenever we went through a ville. I didn't want him ending up in jail. Then one night in our hole, as it began to get dark, he said, "I haven't had the courage to write to Gayle Carlton yet."

"What do you mean?"

"I don't know what to say."

"How well do you know her?"

John shrugged. "Met her a couple times is all, but I'd known him since ITR. I need to say something to her."

I pondered that as we stood silently for a few minutes. I had no clue what you said to an eighteen-year-old girl with a baby when her husband's just been killed.

"I guess I could tell her how much I thought of Ken."

"That seems like a good thing to say."

John was quiet again. After a while, he said, "I could tell her Ken was really happy he was going to be a dad."

"That would be good, I think."

"Maybe pouring salt in her wounds."

"Maybe. But she might like knowing he talked about it." I hesitated. "My guess is, you can't make her any sadder."

I hadn't given much thought to guys' families before. Even listening to the conversation about a closed coffin after Woody died, I'd mostly thought about him, not his parents. Woody, Dasmund, Glass, even Havey. I'd thought how terrible it was that they died so young. I hadn't thought much about what it did to their families. An empty, lonely feeling came over me, standing chest deep in our hole as the dark closed around us, thinking about Mom and Dad. I could only imagine how distraught they'd be if I were killed. I wished John and I weren't talking about it.

"I wonder if Gayle's had the baby yet," he said.

"Do you think they'd let us know?"

John shrugged. "It's not like Dottie Jackson writing to Woody. I don't think Ken's wife ever wrote to anyone else. I wonder if she had a boy or a girl."

"You could ask in your letter." I wondered if Dottie was still with Mike.

"He was hoping for a boy."

"I wouldn't say that."

"No. Of course not."

"I do think you could say he was thrilled he was going to be a dad."

"I guess you're right. He was, you know."

"Yeah. He was pretty excited."

"It's the shits."

"There it is."

John nodded. "I'll go see her when I get back to the World."

"See her? What do you mean?"

"You know. Drive there. It can't be that far from Chicago."

"I thought you only met her once or twice?"

"I've thought about it a lot. Friends who died, pay my respects to their parents or wives, you know? When I'm home on leave. Seems like the right thing to do."

"Jesus, John. After all this shit, won't you just want to forget it for a while, party, have fun?"

"Comfort the afflicted," he said.

"I think you're on your way back to the seminary."

"No telling. Got gooks to kill first. But right now, I have to figure out what to write to Gayle."

"She'll want to tell the kid about him someday. Might be nice if she can tell him his dad told people how happy he was he was going to be born."

"Yeah."

We were quiet for a minute, then John said, "I'm glad I'm nobody's father."

"Me too."

"I'm glad I'm not married."

"Yeah."

"My mother would freak out enough."

"To have you married?"

"If I get killed."

"Jesus, John! Don't even talk like that."

"Could happen, you know."

"I won't let it. I don't want to hump that damn heavy gun by myself."

I did, of course. I wanted to have my own M60, but definitely not because John got hurt. Gio was short now, due to rotate in a month and a half. I'd take over his gun then, unless one of the other gunners in the Company got hit first. I didn't want that either. Gio was the shortest gunner in Bravo; I was happy to wait for him to rotate home. And I couldn't imagine what I'd do if John weren't around.

"Gianelli's right," he said.

"How's that?"

"Lots of streets."

We crossed a wide, swift-moving river with water up to my neck, pushed inland a ways and dug in, in a tight company perimeter. The next afternoon, Captain Brill passed the word that everyone could bathe, thirty minutes per platoon, our platoon first. The first time in weeks. "Buddy system," the lieutenant told us. "Everybody pair up, no lone rangers in the water. Keep your weapons and boots close."

Soon, a couple dozen naked young men were in the water lathering themselves from callused feet to sunburned heads, splashing each other, laughing and joking and reveling in the most luxury we'd felt in weeks. For a few minutes, we were like teenagers skinny-dipping at a local swimming hole. It was as though we'd put our anxiety and anger in boxes and left them on the shore next to our rifles and boots.

I stood up to my waist in the river, trying to shave my several-day growth while not ripping chunks of sunburned skin off my face. The water was cool and a little fast. I washed both my T-shirts and my two pairs of socks. John floated nearby on his back. The water made the scar ropes on his chest gleam purple in the sunlight.

I finished washing my clothing, then lay back and floated, the tees and socks streaming like olive-drab kelp from my hands. For a few minutes, my usual anxiety was replaced by a seeping, almost physical, sense of calm. I began to think that with soap and water and clean socks and no immediate worry about someone shooting at us or a Marine triggering a booby trap, life was pretty damn good.

I floated on my back for another minute then had to walk back toward where John stood washing his clothes; the current had carried me downstream like a stick in a brook. Just out from us in the water, the two docs stood talking. Farther out, Ladoor and Askew crouched, only their heads showing like submerged hippos. I thought it was dumb for them to be that far out but shrugged it off. If the captain thought there was any chance we'd get shot at, he wouldn't have let us in the water at all. Screw them if they don't want to bathe with the white boys, I said to myself.

I waded in to shore and got my toothbrush and toothpaste and waded back out to where John stood talking with Gio and Cloninger and Landon. I spat just as Askew walked below me toward the shore. I hadn't seen him. The frothy white foam floated up against him and hung there for a few seconds, coating the bristly black coils of hair on his belly. "Goddamn, McClure, watch what you're doing."

"Sorry. Didn't spot before I spat."

Askew glared.

"Whitens teeth, not skin, Askew." Gianelli began laughing so hard at his own line he began to cough. "Oh man, better move upstream, Askew, I just peed."

Askew glowered at both of us. I looked to see what Ladoor's reaction was to the white boys laughing at the black dude's expense. I couldn't see him anywhere.

Askew was wading toward the shore again. "Hey, Askew," I called. He had big arms, a thick neck and delts that made him look like he wore shoulder pads. He looked like he wanted to wade over and punch my lights out. "Where's Ladoor?" I expected he'd tell me to mind my own business, but instead he turned and looked to where they'd both been in the water.

The lieutenant dove for him, and Corporal Harding dove for him, and the rest of us formed a chain and walked slowly back and forth in the water. The current pushed us and the mud sucked at our feet until our line looked like a serpent writhing in the river. No one knew where Ladoor had gone. Then John, on the far end of the line, fell into a hole in the river bottom and disappeared. When he came up, he was gasping for air. "Here!" he yelled. "I think I've got Ladoor!" He dove under again.

John and Harding and the lieutenant got Ladoor to the riverbank, lay him spread-eagled on his back in the dirt, and the lieutenant began to give him mouth-to-mouth. Doc Dorsey was still wading in from the other end of the line. Racing for his aid kit, Matt looked like a tall, skinny refugee from a nudist colony running on bad feet on a rocky beach.

Ladoor's eyes were closed; he wasn't breathing at all. Water dripped from his ears and the tight black hair on his head and glistened in the tiny black coils that covered his chest and belly and in the thick fur on his groin. His penis lay like a thick snake sunning itself across his thigh, and the sun glared off the pool of water in his wide navel like a taunting moon in an otherwise black sky. He looked strangely relaxed, like he'd drifted off to sleep on the beach.

His chest made a sudden, gross gurgling sound. The lieutenant sat up fast, and water and thick, gray, soupy stuff bubbled out of Ladoor's mouth and ran down his cheek. When it stopped, the lieutenant swiped his hand across Ladoor's lips, pinched his wide nose closed again, took a deep breath, and bent back down.

My stomach turned. I looked over at Cloninger. His eyes were wide as he watched the lieutenant put his mouth back on Ladoor's again. The Buzz looked like he'd throw up too.

Doc Matheson ran back to us. He knelt beside Ladoor and forced a trachea tube down his throat. Blood trickled from the corner of Ladoor's mouth. Matt breathed hard into the upper end of the tube, the purple scar on his face flashing with the effort. Ladoor's chest spasmed, Matt yanked the tube out and a stream of thin, watery fluid erupted from the unconscious man's gaping mouth and flooded down his chin onto his chest. It puddled like gray gruel on his skin.

Dorsey tried CPR, pumping Ladoor's chest over and over again. Then the two corpsmen took turns, pumping, breathing, trying to get Ladoor to come around. After a long time, Doc Dorsey sat back on his haunches. "It's no good, Matt," he said quietly. "He's gone."

Matt refused to give up; he kept doing CPR. I thought he'd crack Ladoor's ribs.

The lieutenant put his hand on Matt's shoulder. "It's okay, Doc," he said. "You did all you could. It's okay."

Matt ignored him, kept pumping Ladoor's chest. "C'mon, Ladoor," he said again and again like a cadence between labored breaths. "Fight, goddamn you, fight!"

The Marines who'd been standing naked in a circle around Ladoor and the corpsmen and the lieutenant began to peel away reluctantly, as though they were embarrassed by the drowned man, or, maybe, the frantic corpsman. They gathered their clothes and weapons and boots and walked up the slope. Then it was just the lieutenant and Askew and John and me and the two docs.

Matt finally, slowly stood up. He wouldn't talk to any of us. He just stared at the river in disbelief.

——

I found Matt later sitting by himself. We sat smoking without talking for a while, then I said, "You okay?"

Matt nodded. "I hate losing people I should be able to save."

"You did all you could, Matt. You and Doc Dorsey and the lieutenant." What else could I say? It was Ladoor's own fault; he shouldn't have gone out so far. What good would it do to say that?

Matt looked into the distance across the river. "I wish I hadn't cursed him," he said in a voice that wasn't much more than a whisper. "I hope to God that wasn't the last thing he heard."

——

We talked about Ladoor later, bitter and angry, at a loss to put his death in its place. John put it best: "Vietnam doesn't make the rest of life go away. We've all seen that. Babies like Hope are born; guys get dumped by girlfriends; friends graduate from high school and college; people get sick at home; grandparents die; brothers and sisters get married. But Ladoor? As much of a prick as he could be, he was brave and he'd survived months of combat. Man, when he drowned, life really sucked."

Corporal Harding said, "I wish to fuck Ladoor'd been watching what he was doing. Fucking waste. Drown on a swim call, for Christ's sake." He looked around at us, almost as if he expected a challenge. "What do they say to his parents? Your son went swimming in

Vietnam, Mrs. Ladoor. He refused to do buddy system. There were no gooks around, no one shot him, but now he's fucking dead?"

Nobody said anything.

"He drowned after all the shit he'd been through." Harding's voice quivered with anger. "Drowned. In Vietnam."

"Could've done that at home," Gio said. "Saved his ma all that worry about him being here."

22

THE BUNKERS IN THE VILLES WE came across now looked like they could withstand all but direct hits from artillery or bombs. Some of the villes had deep zigzag trenches dug around their perimeters, angles cut so a man could stand in place and fire in multiple directions with minimum exposure. Besides women and children and old men, now we saw younger men working the fields. At least that's what they appeared to be doing. We found no weapons or explosives or ammunition or other military supplies, but the trenches and reinforced bunkers were there because someone was expecting a fight.

We went through an abandoned ville, its hootches crumbled and rotted. There was no one around, but in a pile of straw where someone might have slept recently, Fizzy found a bullet.

"Look! Look at this, Corporal Harding." Fizzy held out the round. "This looks like it's new. Look at that hummer, man oh man, that's one big gun, isn't it Corporal?"

Fizzy almost never shut up. He'd talk at you about anything—movies, cars, food, even how tasty his C-rations were. He talked incessantly about racing stock cars after the Marines. Willie was the only one who'd listen to him for long. Gio'd once said, "Fizzy will go flat like the rest of you sad sacks. But it's gonna take a while, so enjoy the bubbles while you can."

There was nothing entertaining about what he'd found today. The round was longer than Harding's hand. "Jesus, Division was right," he said. "That's from a 12.7 heavy machine gun. There's a shitload of gooks around here if they've got something that big."

"If there's a shitload of 'em, we can really kick some ass, right, Corporal Harding?" Fizzy exclaimed.

"Right," Harding said. He didn't sound convinced. I realized I'd felt a little safer before Hope was born. Since becoming a father, Harding hadn't seemed quite as unflinching.

The next ville we came to was just three or four hootches centered around a well. Only women and kids. One very pregnant young woman looked like she had a basketball under her blouse. She was unusually tall for a Vietnamese and thin, except for her belly. She probably wasn't more than fifteen.

Fizzy gawked. "Holy Toledo, she looks like she's gonna explode."

"Stand back, Fizzy," Gio said. "You'll get hit if she goes off."

Fizzy grinned. He eyed the girl up and down. "Bet that was a ride. Must've been like screwing a grasshopper. So, where's her old man?"

"Somewhere waiting to fuck with us," Cloninger said.

"We'll probably make her a widow," Corporal Harding said.

"Let's hope so," John said. "There can't be any men around here on our side."

Harding nodded. "Kid will grow up without ever knowing his old man."

"Tell that to Glass' wife," Witt said. "Or Carlton's."

Harding nodded, then shook his head. He didn't say anything more.

The village didn't look much worse for wear when the search was over. We'd searched thoroughly and found nothing. We were sure the villagers knew more than they'd say when we questioned them in pidgin Vietnamese.

"Goddamn people. They're not deaf, dumb, and blind," Cloninger said.

"They're dumb if they think they can fuck with us," Witt said.

John didn't say anything. A few weeks ago we would've heard a lecture about why they were probably good people but couldn't rat out our enemy. I was glad he didn't bother now.

We hadn't gone a hundred meters beyond the ville when, behind me, Gianelli stepped off a low dike I'd just crossed and tripped a bouncing betty. The blast knocked me down, but I wasn't hurt. The metal tore through Gio's belly like a ragged meat cleaver. He crawled toward me dragging a pile of innards through the dirt and the smoke, his face purple and twisted and straining in a noiseless snarl.

He was dead before I could stand up.

We gently placed Gio's body in a body bag and sat beside him in silence waiting for the routine medevac bird. I smoked cigarette after cigarette and drained one of my canteens but couldn't ease the pain in my stomach. The Buzz sat silently hunched into himself like a stunned bird. John's eyes were closed, like he was in a trance. Except for his hands—they shook violently in his lap. We must've looked like three filthy, heavily armed priests trying to raise the soul of the dead.

Lieutenant Mangan finished on the radio and came over. John stuffed his hands in his pockets. The lieutenant looked down at the body bag, then at us. I'd never seen him look like he was going to cry before. He didn't; he began giving orders, a quaver in his voice. He switched the gun teams around. Willie would be John's A-gunner. Gianelli's gun was now mine. The Buzzard would be my assistant gunner.

Lieutenant Mangan looked at me hard. "You okay, McClure?"

I didn't want the gun. I wasn't supposed to get it this way. And how could John be with Willie tonight instead of me when we'd just lost Gio? I nodded. "Yes sir," sure he wasn't asking about my state of mind.

He squeezed my shoulder. "Good. We need you to be."

I nodded again.

"The gun." He gestured toward where I'd stood it on its bipod next to Gio's body. "Is it okay?"

"I think so, sir. Just dirty I think." My words weren't much more than a whisper.

"It's yours now, take good care of it."

The bird lifted off and the maelstrom of dirt and debris and heat-hardened air around us calmed. Pius John stood off to the side, staring at the flies shining on the wet spot in the dirt where Gio died. He started to shake. It began like a slight tremor, then grew to a shiver and then his muscles seemed to spasm into something like a convulsion, and a low, tortured animal sound came out of him.

I put my hands on John's shoulders. The noise and the shaking took a long time to stop. *Sweet Jesus*, John, I thought. *What will I become if you fall apart?*

A few days after Gio was killed, we came to three tiny villages, only a few hundred meters apart. The lieutenant sent a squad to search each. The Buzz and I went with First.

The only man in the ville was old, with corrugated brown skin, wide-set yellow eyes, and a wispy, stained goatee. His right leg was sturdy, knotted and weathered beneath baggy black shorts. His left was skinny, shriveled and bowed with a faded white scar that ran from mid-thigh down his pool cue–sized calf. I felt sorry for him until I wondered whose side he'd been on years ago when he was wounded, and where his sympathies lay now.

Corporal Harding grabbed him by the shoulder and put him out in front of the column as we prepared to leave the ville.

Fizzy looked at Cloninger and me. "What's he doing?"

"The old man's taking us to the next ville," Cloninger said.

"That isn't legal, is it?" Fizzy asked. "A civilian?"

"Legal? What the fuck?" Cloninger snapped. "There ain't no fuckin' civilians out here."

I didn't say anything. The Buzz didn't need my help.

"The lieutenant wouldn't do it," Fizzy said.

"Who the fuck made you an authority?" the Buzz snarled. "Legal. Jesus Christ."

"I don't think that's right."

"The lieutenant isn't here, is he?" Cloninger glared at him as though he were going to butt-stroke him with his M16. "You going to rat?"

"I'm not a rat, Cloninger. But it's not right."

"You want to tell Corporal Harding? You forgetting Gianelli?"

Fizzy shook his head.

I knew where he was coming from; I'd had the same qualms not long, or perhaps a lifetime, ago. But I didn't want any more of my friends to be crippled or killed. Sometimes a man must make choices, John had said. Corporal Harding had made his to try and keep us safe. "They know where the booby traps are, Fizzy," I said. "He won't get hurt, and neither will we."

I hoped I was right. But how many times had we seen people step over booby traps unharmed only to watch someone get blown up farther back in the column? If the old man didn't know where they were, I hoped he'd be the one to trip one, not a Marine. The thought occurred to me that the blackness John talked of so long ago was rolling in fast.

Corporal Harding pointed the old man in the direction we needed to go. He walked like he was heading to a meeting he was scared to attend. The way he put one foot down then swung the other around looked like his hips were playing a cello.

We followed him along the rice paddy dikes he chose himself. We encountered no booby traps. We came to a big dike bordering a wide expanse between us and the ville that the entire platoon would search next. We could see Second Squad and the lieutenant approaching across a field. Harding made the old man sit down. He spread the squad down the dike and told me to keep an eye on the papa-san.

The man's shirt was sweat-soaked. I sat and lit a cigarette. He licked his lips and slid his eyes slowly side to side, watching all of us, trying not to draw attention to himself, most likely worried we'd shoot him when he was no longer useful. Apparently satisfied I wasn't going to hurt him, he began a sing-song chatter of Vietnamese, then made a smoking motion with his hand. I could smell his breath and his sweat and the stink of nuoc mam.

"Fuck you," I said.

"Me?" Cloninger was surprised.

I shook my head. "Papa-san wanted a smoke."

"Fuck." The Buzz glowered at the old man. "I'll smoke him."

Fizzy walked up to the old man and took a pack of Marlboros out of his pocket.

"Don't do it," I said.

"What do you mean?"

"Don't give the gook a fucking cigarette. Jesus Christ, don't you think he and every other goddamn person over five years old know where the booby traps are? Don't you think the villagers knew where that was when Gio was killed, for Christ's sake?"

Fizzy didn't say anything, just turned and went back to where he'd left his gear.

"Give a fucking gook a Marlboro," Cloninger said in disgust. "And I'm smoking goddamn C-ration Kents."

The old papa-san stared at us like a small, wrinkled dog waiting to see whether he'd be kicked or thrown a scrap. Beyond him, Fizzy sat watching Second Squad make its way toward us. I hoped he wasn't going to say anything to the lieutenant about Corporal Harding. If Fizzy ratted Harding, I didn't want to think of what someone in the platoon would do to him one night.

The lieutenant came over and pointed to the old man. "Who the hell's this?"

Before I could answer, Corporal Harding was there. "Sir . . ." he said. I glanced over at Fizzy, hoping he wouldn't open his mouth.

"He's headed to that ville." Harding pointed to where the platoon was going. It had started to drizzle. The roofs of the hootches in the distant trees looked gray and wavy through the rain.

"What's he doing here?"

"We don't want him running over there," Harding pointed again toward the ville. "You know, give the alarm."

The lieutenant studied the squad leader for several beats. His expression said he didn't believe him. Usually, if he was going to have a piece of one of the NCOs, the lieutenant did it in private, not in front of the troops. But this wasn't a screw-up, this was deliberate. The platoon leader wanted the rest of us to know he wouldn't stand for it.

"We don't use villagers as mine detectors."

"They know where they are, Lieutenant. The fuckers set 'em or at least know where they are. You don't see *them* with their fucking legs blowed off."

"Corporal Harding, nobody in this platoon wants casualties to stop more than me. But we are not fucking using civilians as mine detectors. Got it?"

"Yes, sir," Harding said unenthusiastically.

That wasn't good enough for the lieutenant.

"Any more fucking with civilians, and you're out of a job, Corporal." Relieving Harding of his squad leader duties was about the worst thing the lieutenant could do to him. Mangan looked again at the papa-san. The old man looked worried; he knew they were talking about him. "Did you search him for weapons?"

"Yes, sir. Nothing on him."

"Leave him here when we move on that ville. I don't want him with us. You got that Corporal Harding?"

"Yes, sir."

"And, Corporal . . ."

"Yes, sir?"

"Make fucking sure none of your people think we can use civilians to walk point. No matter how many booby traps we hit. Got it?"

"Yes, sir." Through the rain running off his helmet, I could see the anger and embarrassment on Harding's face.

The lieutenant walked down the dike to wait for Third Squad to catch up with us. Fizzy didn't look up at him as he passed by, just sat staring at the ground, the water running off his helmet shrouding whatever expression was on his face.

I cupped my hands around my cigarette, trying to keep it dry. I was already soaked to the skin. I could see the outlines of the old papa-san's ribs beneath his wet shirt. His thin hair was rain-glued to his skull. He wiped a gnarled hand across his eyes, then studied the lieutenant and platoon sergeant and squad leaders looking at a map, probably wondering if they were deciding his fate. The squad leaders signaled us to get ready to move out.

A belching explosion hammered the air. I dropped down against the side of the dike. When I lifted my head, Fizzy was kneeling in the mud, helmetless, his hands covering his face. Blood poured between his fingers and flowed down his arms, further darkening his rain-soaked T-shirt and trou.

The docs sat Fizzy against the dike, pulled his hands away from his face. His eyelids flickered rapidly, as though they were fighting to either open or close. Rain like jellied hail made splotches and stripes in the blood on his face.

"I can't see," he cried. "I can't see at all." His voice rose in a panicked pitch. "I can't see I can't see *help me I can't see!*"

"There's blood in your eyes, man," Doc Dorsey said as he bandaged Fizzy's face. "That's all. You'll be okay."

"They'll get the blood out of your eyes in Da Nang, Fizzy," Matt added as he pulled the wounded Marine's hands down from his face. "Calm down now, let us work. You'll be okay."

After the medevac lifted off, I was by myself near the old papa-san. He looked like he was trying to decide if I was more likely to kill him standing there or running away. His withered leg began to quiver like a fiddle bow, then his entire body began to shake.

"You cocksucker," I growled. "You knew. You could've warned us, you son of a bitch!" I cradled the M60 on my hip.

Cloninger came up beside me. "Do the fucker," he said. "We'll say he ran."

I pointed the gun at his chest.

The old man pissed himself. It ran yellow and bitter-smelling down his crippled leg and glistened on the soaked ground until it became just another part of the wet at his feet.

I wanted to pull that trigger so much, see the bullets tear into him, taste the gunpowder, feel the violent, soothing recoil, hear the deep, insistent grunt of the gun. I wanted to do it for Fizzy. I wanted to do it for Gio, for Glass and Carlton and Woody and Dasmund and Tich and Corrigan and O'Grady and Cavett and Jackson and all the others I'd lost. I wanted to do it for poor, tortured Pius John. I wanted to do it for me.

The old man looked down at his piss-soaked sandal, then back up at me. He shook like he was terminally palsied.

"McClure! McClure! What the fuck are you doing?!" the lieutenant bellowed.

I lowered the muzzle of the machine gun and slowly turned away from the old man. The lieutenant and Smitty ran toward me. "Just thinkin', Lieutenant," I said. "Just thinkin'."

"Make damn sure you don't think wrong, Marine! Goddamned sure!"

I nodded. Lieutenant Mangan studied my face for a moment, then turned on his heel and started back toward the rest of the platoon, calling over his shoulder for Smitty to bring the radio as he went.

The radioman exhaled a stream of mentholated smoke toward the old man. "Would've felt damn good, wouldn't it, Mick?"

23

THE RAIN POURED OFF MY HELMET LIKE a curtain in front of my eyes. I could see nothing move in the ville or the tree line around it, heard no noise except the hammering rain and the suck and slosh of boots as we advanced on line across a wide, open area. I lifted the rosary around my neck. The soaked Christ figure at the end of the beads was tarnished, encrusted with dirt. *Help me,* I prayed. I wasn't sure what I was praying for. For protection against fire from the ville? From the darkness that had nearly let me kill an old, unarmed man? Then I knew. *Let there be gooks, God. Give them to me!*

Fire burst from the ville when we got closer in. We ran forward and threw ourselves down behind a low dike then lay half-submerged in the water firing back as the lieutenant worked up artillery. It seemed to take a long time before the 105s exploded on the ville.

The gooks made their hat. Two bodies were in the trench on the edge of the village, the one closest to me mangled by an artillery round. Down the trench, I heard the sudden deep boom of Staff Sergeant Gilles' shotgun.

"Maybe he wasn't dead enough for the sarge," Cloninger said. "Two fuckin' gooks." He shook his head in disgust. "The lieutenant waited too long to assault."

"The lieutenant's just trying to keep us alive, for Christ's sake," Corporal Harding said.

Pius John shook his head dismissively. "Killing NVA will keep us alive. We waited too goddamn long."

Some hootches were still intact, others burned or blown apart. Thatch smoldered in the rain casting an acrid, eye-watering vapor throughout the ville. Bits of clothing fluttered like desolate banners from burnt remnants of tree limbs and rooftops. At the lip of a shell crater already gathering water, a dead water buffalo lay, its horned head dangling over the edge, one glassy eye staring up at me in terrified curiosity. I felt bad for the animal.

"That'll cost Uncle Sam a hundred bucks," Cloninger said, shaking his head. "Could've saved seventy if we'd just killed a gook." In theory, he was right. A family could claim a hundred dollars if we killed their water buffalo by mistake, thirty for a family member. Out where we were, no one was going to submit a claim.

The lieutenant ordered the squad leaders to search the bunkers under the hootches.

Corporal Harding stood to the side of the opening to a bunker, grenade in hand. "*Lai dai, lai dai!*" he yelled. Come out, come here.

There was no sound from the hole in the earth. He pulled the pin, let the spoon fly, waited a couple seconds, then tossed the grenade into the bunker. "Fire in the hole," he yelled as he ran to the side. The entrance burped violently, smoke and noise, dirt, straw, cloth. Then Gnat's Nuts and Witt were down inside, rifles ready to kill anything that moved.

There was no one there.

Harding yelled *Lai dai!* into the next bunker. A frantic chatter of Vietnamese erupted from the hole. A woman's voice. Harding jumped back, raised his M16 to his shoulder. I covered the hole with the M60 on my hip.

"*Lai dai*, goddammit, or I throw a grenade!" Harding yelled.

I tensed, ready to gun down whoever came out of the hole.

From a couple hootches away, a gray-haired mama-san ran toward us waving her arms frantically, yelling in rapid, screeching Vietnamese.

Harding swung his M16 to her, then back to the bunker. Another burst of words came from the entrance. Harding pulled the pin on a grenade, kept the spoon depressed.

The old woman screamed. She looked like she was going to start hitting Harding. If she knocked that grenade out of his hand, we could all be killed.

Cloninger grabbed her by the blouse and held her to the side, arms and legs flailing, yelling at the top of her lungs.

"Lai dai!" Harding yelled again. "Five, four . . ."

The old woman stopped flailing; she appeared to be begging now. A crown of thick black hair appeared at the bunker's entrance. Cloninger threw the old woman to the ground and raised his rifle. I couldn't tell if it was a man or a woman coming out. Then a high-pitched flood of Vietnamese came from a young mama-san as she slowly climbed out, a young child in her arms. Blood trickled from the toddler's ears. Doc Matheson came over and held out his arms. The young mother stared at him fearfully, then let him take the baby from her. Harding waved Witt and Landon down into the hole.

We heard a muffled curse, followed by a child's whimpering sob, and then Witt handed another toddler up to Harding. "Jesus Christ," Witt said. "I saw something move and almost shot and then saw it was a baby. Don't know why I wasn't already shooting. Been a fuckin' gook, I'd been dead. That's one lucky kid."

"God damn you, mama-san," Harding yelled at the young mother. "You almost got your babies killed. Don't you know *lai dai*? Jesus Christ!"

The baby in Corporal Harding's arms began howling. The young woman held out her arms, crying something over and over. Both babies were wailing now. The older mama-san had gotten to her feet. She had a bloody scrape on the side of her face. She started yelling again, gesturing frantically at Matt and Harding. Cloninger looked ready to butt-stroke her.

"Buzz," I said. "Don't."

He grabbed her and threw her to the ground again. "Shut up, granny," he growled. "Damn near got them kids killed."

The woman lay on the ground, sobbing. *If Cloninger hits you in the face with his rifle butt, you'll have a lot more to cry about,* I thought.

We searched more bunkers across the ville. Cries of "Fire in the hole!" the muffled *crump-boom* of grenades exploding underground. Then shots inside a bunker.

In a few minutes, Matt rejoined us, a stricken look on his face. "Who's hurt, Doc?" Harding asked.

Matt shook his head. "None of our people." He hesitated. "Fullerton just killed a kid." Matt looked like he was about to cry. "It wasn't his fault. There was an old man and the boy in a bunker. It was dark. He shot them both." Matt shook his head. "Fullerton's really messed up. The lieutenant's trying to calm him down. You better go, too."

As we formed up to leave the ville, I saw both Harding and Pius John talking with Fullerton. He kept shaking his head, not saying anything. The old man and the boy lay outside their bunker. Except for the torn, blood-soaked shirt clinging to his chest, you might've thought the old man was asleep. The little boy with the single round hole in his forehead stared up open-mouthed, as though amazed by all he could see with three eyes. *How the fuck could you let this happen, God? I asked as I passed by.*

Father Mullin stood outside the Company perimeter when we got back that afternoon. Skinny, sunburned, thin red hair, and gray plastic-framed glasses, he looked more like a junior high science teacher than a priest who humped the bush with grunts. He greeted us one by one as we filed through the lines and invited us to the services he'd be holding later in the day.

"Hey, McClure, how's the Irish? Still doin' laps?" He pointed toward my rosary.

"Hi, Father. Some, I guess." The truth was, I wasn't. I still talked to God at night. But since Gio died, I mostly asked Him where He was.

The priest invited me to mass. I nodded; I didn't know if I'd bother.

Willie asked if he could go too. He'd been quieter than usual after talking with Father Mullin some time back. He hadn't told us what the priest had had to say. Father Mullin smiled. "Of course, Willis, of course. God doesn't care if you're Catholic. How you been?"

"Good, Father," Willie said. "They got that vee dee I come down with fixed with some pills." He hesitated and his loose, rubbery grin folded into a look of confusion and concern. "Guess you didn't know about that . . ." He hung his head.

"No, I didn't, Willis. You cured now?"

"Oh yeah, Father." Willie looked earnest now. "That was a couple weeks ago. It don't hurt no more, and I pee good again."

"Well, I'm glad to hear that," Father Mullin said.

"You were right," Willie said. "That girl in Bangkok didn't love me the way she said. She wouldn't have given me no clap, if she did. I don't send her my pay any more."

"That's good," the priest said. "Real good."

***

I sat in the dirt trying to write a letter home. Writing had been difficult for weeks. Once in a while I'd write some details to Spence, but I didn't want to tell Mom and Dad most of what I was seeing or doing. They'd worry even more than they already did, and they couldn't possibly relate to what I was feeling or how I thought now. I wasn't the Boy Scout or student-council-baskets-for-the-poor rep they'd known a year ago. That kid had disappeared, and I didn't know if he'd ever be back, even if I searched for him.

Sometimes I'd go several days without writing, too exhausted or terrified or horrified to try. When I did write, I mostly just commented on what they'd said in their letters to me. Even that was getting tough. Dad told me about ball games and movies, and Mom wrote about picnics and relatives and all kinds of stuff. But I'd forgotten how to care about such things. The World was too far away. I still craved the connection of their letters, but little they wrote about seemed real any more. My reality was dead or maimed Marines, a dead kid and his grandfather, bloody and bullet-riddled in front of their home. An old man I'd wanted to kill. I sure as hell wasn't going to write about any of that. John saved me from my chore. He came over to ask if I wanted to join him at mass.

"Come on, Mick," he said. "It'll do you good."

I shrugged. "I guess so. I'm not sure what to pray for anymore."

John smiled ruefully. "I've got a list."

The supply bird brought a new guy named Ayoub to First Squad. He had narrow, jet black eyes, a nose like a rhinoceros, and though he was just out of high school, looked like he needed to shave every few hours. Willie hooted when they were introduced. He couldn't figure out why anyone would name their kid Hey You.

"Goddamn, Willis," Corporal Harding said. "The man's name is Ayoub, not 'Hey fuckin' You.'"

Willie wiped his eyes. It looked like it would take a while for his rubbery face to mold back into place. "I could just see his ma leanin' out the back door yellin', 'Hey You come to supper.'"

It stuck. Ayoub said he'd been called a lot worse. On our way to see the priest before mass, John told Willie, "Gio would've been proud of you."

Sitting on a stump, a purple stole around his neck, Father Mullin heard confessions before mass. When it was my turn to take a knee beside the chaplain, his eyes were closed. "Please begin, my son," he said without opening them.

"Bless me Father, for I have sinned," I began the usual start to confession. "It's been . . ." I hesitated. " . . . at least a couple months since my last confession."

"Go on. Confess your sins."

"I threatened to kill a civilian, Father. At least I think he was a civilian. He might've known where the booby traps were. He was a villager, and old."

"You didn't kill the man, is that right?"

"Yes. I mean, no. That's right, Father. I might've if the lieutenant didn't stop me."

"Do you have any other sins to confess?"

I thought for a moment. "I didn't stop another Marine from knocking down an old woman."

"Did you do anything to her yourself?"

"No, Father."

"Do you have anything else you'd like to confess?"

I hesitated again. Then I spoke quickly, quieter than before, almost expecting a tongue lashing. "Sometimes, I question whether God even cares about us."

Father Mullin opened his eyes but didn't turn toward me.

"Don't lose faith, Irish." He smiled just a little. "God's watching over us, even if we can't understand why he lets bad things happen. We've no way of understanding his plan, or why he allows us to suffer. But know that God loves you and that we are all part of his plan. Okay?"

"Okay, Father." What else could I say?

The priest closed his eyes again. "Anything else to confess?"

I thought for a moment, just a moment, about telling him about the man on the hill I killed with the pistol. I'd shot at a lot of people, but he was the only one I was certain I'd killed. A picture of his bloody, mashed-in face flashed across my mind. I was sure there was no sin in killing the enemy. If I didn't kill him, he would've killed me. But what if God didn't approve? What did I have to lose confessing? "I've killed people, Father," I said. "At least one I'm sure of, probably a lot more."

"Were they NVA or VC? Enemy soldiers?"

"Yes, sir."

"In battle? They weren't prisoners?"

"No, Father. In a firefight."

"There's no sin in that, Irish." Father Mullin's tone had changed from pleasant but businesslike to consoling. "Killing our country's enemies is your duty, my friend. It's necessary and honorable. God makes exceptions to His commandment, Thou shalt not kill. You haven't sinned. Is there anything else?"

"No, Father."

It was time for him to come up with my penance. What could a priest do to a young man who's just confessed that he almost machine-gunned an old man? I would've sworn I could smell the piss running down the papa-san's leg.

"Now go find a quiet place and say the Act of Contrition and five Our Fathers and five Hail Marys. And I absolve you of your sins, in the name of the Father and of the Son and of the Holy Spirit. Amen."

"Amen."

"Go in peace." A phrase I'd heard every time I'd ever gone to confession.

I went off and said the formal words of the Act of Contrition silently to myself, then the Lord's Prayer five times and five quick Hail Marys. It was less than I'd had to do when I confessed in high school that I'd touched Janice Sanderson's breasts.

A hundred bucks for a water bull. Thirty bucks each for a grandfather and a little boy, not that anyone out here would ever make that claim. Less than ten minutes worth of rote prayers for coming within a trigger-squeeze of murdering a crippled old man.

Go in peace. I didn't think I'd ever know peace again.

I walked back toward our hole; I still had to clean the gun and stake out my field of fire for the night. *Go in peace*, I thought again. What a fucked-up thing to say in this place.

24

THE ENEMY SUDDENLY SEEMED TO BE all around us. Small groups attacked us quickly in the daylight, then ran. They hit us with mortars or B40 rockets or gunfire at night. Second and Third Platoons both had several Marines killed and others badly wounded.

First Platoon was mostly lucky. Brocato, a high school dropout missing part of an ear chewed off in a fight before he joined the Marines, was shot in the throat while on point as we climbed a hill. His dead, outraged eyes stared up at us as the gun teams rushed past his body. The shooter was gone before we were even in firing position. Two others, both with the platoon such a short time I didn't know their names, were badly enough wounded in a mortar attack to be medevacked and never return. Three other Marines on other nights were medevacked but came back in a couple weeks.

Two dozen young men made up First Platoon. One of them had been killed and five others wounded in the space of two or three weeks. I thought of all the dead and wounded in Second and Third Platoons and thanked my lucky stars.

Imagining the twenty-three boys in my honors English class today considering themselves mostly lucky if one died and five were badly hurt in a month is as unfathomable as picturing them sprouting wings and flying like crows.

Far off on our flank one night, Delta got hit hard.

"Dying Delta," Cloninger whispered. "Always in the shit."

"Let's hope it doesn't come this way." I unsnapped the holster for my .45. A picture of the man running up the hill at me weeks ago played across my mind. I prayed I wouldn't see a gook that close again.

We moved out at dawn with no idea where the NVA that attacked Delta this time had gone. Once again, they'd vanished like ghosts.

By afternoon, we were moving through head-high elephant grass, arms and necks and faces blood-flecked and raw from its blade edges. The point reached the edge of a wide, dry riverbed, and the platoon rippled to a stop. Lieutenant Mangan walked quietly to the head of the column and peered up and down the trough. We moved again, uncoiled, turned in column like the vertebrae of a snake, slowly inched our way above the riverbed, staying just inside the tall grass.

We crept a hundred yards, stopped again. The lieutenant passed the word down the column: "Guns up." As we moved forward, people silently mouthed the word "gooks," and palmed the air slowly, urging those behind them down to the ground.

The dry riverbed curved like the top of a horseshoe, a bend to our left, another to our right. The platoon lay along the curve just inside thick grass. Nothing moved below us in the trough; there was nothing large enough for a man to hide behind there. I wondered why we had stopped. Then I realized the point could see around the bend to our left.

Cloninger fished past his snaggled teeth with one dirty finger and flipped out his wad of tobacco. Beyond him, John turned and passed the word coming down the column, "No shooting until the lieutenant says."

I turned toward Harding and whispered, "No shooting until Magnet says." His eyes held some expression I couldn't read. I wondered if he were scared but dismissed the thought. Not Hard Ass Harding. I was scared and excited at the same time. If gooks walked in front of us, we could kill them before they even knew we were there. As long as there weren't too many of them. As long as they didn't have comrades coming up behind us in the tall grass. Harding nodded once, slightly, an almost imperceptible sign that he understood, then turned to pass the word to Ayoub: No shooting until the lieutenant says. The new guy's eyes were gigantic.

I saw nothing move below us. I still couldn't tell why we'd stopped, but it was clear the lieutenant thought something dangerous was up. I stared and listened so hard my head throbbed.

A column of NVA began to emerge from the far bend and walk down the long, wide curve of the trough. I couldn't believe what I saw. They trudged along slowly, silently, like tired old men limping back to the veterans' home after an overlong parade. One at a time, or in pairs or threes, rifles resting on shoulders or crooked under arms like hunters after the hunt. There were no signs of flank security. It was as if they owned the place.

Four of them. Then six, nine. One more, carrying a large pack and an RPG. Then two more, one man hobbling, his arm around the other's shoulders. I could see their faces, sweaty dull copper, black eyes sunken from lack of sleep. It turned out they'd been part of the force that hit Delta the night before.

Eighteen. Eighteen NVA with packs and weapons and no clue we were there.

Thank you, God, thank you.

But what if these are just the point? What if this is just the advance for all the gooks in the valley?

Fuck it. Fuck them! What a kill! Thank you, God. Please don't let there be more.

The sweat in my eyes burned like acid. I didn't move.

Eighteen gooks. Twenty-four Marines. No Marine moved or coughed. Feral cats eyeing prey. Eighteen dead men walking. Why the fuck doesn't the lieutenant fire?

Six more NVA came around the bend to our left. Then four more.

Shit a brick! Twenty-eight goddamn gooks! That's enough, God, don't let there be more. They stretched out the entire length of our position, only forty yards from the first of them to the far bend to our right.

Why doesn't Magnet shoot? Come on, man! Come on! I glanced to my left. *What the fuck's wrong?* John licked his lips, his jaw muscles pulsed. I read his mind: *Come on, Lieutenant, let us shoot before they get away. Come on, Lieutenant, it doesn't get better than this.*

Twenty-eight NVA. A nearly straight line parallel to where we lie. And they have no clue. *Thank you, God. Goddammit, Lieutenant, do it!*

The two at the head of the procession had almost reached the far curve. It seemed unlikely more would come around the bend to our left. *Come on, Lieutenant. Do 'em for Christ's sake!*

The deep, sharp howl of John's gun shattered the silence.

Every rifle in the platoon joined the machine gun's roar.

I raked the column end to end twice, then focused on individual soldiers. I blew one backward with a stream of bullets, followed him to the ground with a line of tracers. His body jumped and bucked and writhed in the red dirt until I swung the gun away. I fired and fired back and forth across my entire front, blasted a firestorm of tracers into the tangled, frenzied cluster in front of us. I cut a man in the center of the line nearly in half, vaguely aware as I did that NVA to the left and right of my own targets were falling, twisting and jerking in the bloody, filthy haze our bullets threw up.

A man crawling began to rise. He was kneeling upright when I turned the gun toward him. *Praying, asshole? You better!* His mouth wide open, he appeared to be screaming his astonishment into the din. My first rounds spat into the dirt in front of him. I walked the tracers upward, perforated him in a jagged line from his groin to his face, the bullets hammering him into a disjointed limbo dance until he was kneeling, leaking, torn, and bent backward from the thighs.

Then it was over. The NVA dead lay in the middle of the blood-soaked riverbed, all except three or four who sprawled against the far bank, shot trying to climb out of the trough. All twenty-eight were dead. Maybe not. One, splayed face down on the far bank, suddenly pulled his arms in under his chest as though he were going to do a push up or was reaching for something. Landon blew the top of his head off with one shot.

A gook in the middle of the column moaned, a low, stifled babble of agony and despair. "Damn," John said. He fired a short burst. When the machine gun's blast stopped echoing, there was no more noise from the riverbed. John shook his head in disgust, like he'd just killed a snake on the patio with a shovel. "Damn," he said again.

"First and Third Squads, search 'em," Lieutenant Mangan yelled. "Go with them, Sergeant Gilles. Get their weapons and anything Intel can use. Let's go people, let's go! This place could be crawling with gooks."

Then he was up in John's face. "You jumped the fucking gun, Garafano! You fired before I ordered!" His nose was only inches from John's. I heard the deep boom of the Finisher from the riverbed.

John's eyes narrowed in controlled anger; he knew he was wrong. "I just wanted the gooks, Lieutenant."

"We all want fucking gooks, Garafano. But I don't want to get Marines killed doing them. I decide when we goddamn get 'em. You got me?"

"Yes, sir." John stared at the officer. "I just wanted to kill them. I thought they'd get away, Lieutenant."

"You think I don't want to kill gooks?"

"No, sir. I just thought . . . I just thought they might get away."

"You want to run this platoon, Garafano?"

John hesitated slightly. "No, sir."

"Next time I'll have your ass, Marine, don't forget it."

"Yes, sir."

The lieutenant yelled to the Marines searching the bodies. "Let's go people, let's get outta here before this place is crawling with gooks."

John looked at me, shook his head as though the lieutenant's reaction surprised him.

"John," I said, "it's okay. We did 'em. The lieutenant knows that."

He hesitated, nodded, then turned to move out.

Cloninger clapped me on the shoulder. "Let's go, Mick, we're moving." He wore a broad, crooked grin. The Buzz nodded toward the riverbed. "Payback's a motherfucker."

I looked down at over two dozen bodies strewn mangled and rent in the trough, and felt happy for the first time in weeks.

25

THE CAPTAIN TOOK THE CP AND Second and Third Platoons to check out a distant ridge line. First Platoon was to search a ville, then wait there for the rest of the company. We felt better than we had in a very long time. All of us, except maybe Ayoub and Estes—the new guy who'd gone to the same high school as John and who'd joined the platoon in the days since the magnificent slaughter at the riverbed—knew it wouldn't last.

The big ville shimmered in the heat, waves of parched air hanging above scorched, barren paddies between us and it. The lieutenant spread us out in a wedge formation, the entire platoon a twenty-eight-man arrowhead providing maximum opportunity to bring fire to bear on the ville to our front or the distant hillocks on our flanks. We pressed forward across the open space, a thick, squat Marine named Ogala on point. I wished we'd reconned by fire, but Lieutenant Mangan wouldn't bring mortars or artillery down on a village where there might be nothing waiting for us but so-called civilians. He was in the middle of the spread-out triangle. Every once in a while he'd raise his binoculars, study the ville as he walked. Smitty stayed close to him. If the lieutenant saw any sign of enemy in the ville, I knew he'd have on-calls hitting it as soon as Smitty handed him the handset.

Staff Sergeant Gilles was on the other side of Lieutenant Mangan, the shotgun crooked in his arm like he was on a walk in the woods. He lipped an unlit cigarette and hand-signaled First Squad to keep their distance. Cloninger and I walked behind and to the right of the lieutenant, Pius John and Willie fifteen meters to our left, the two corpsmen behind us. Dust rose and billowed around our boots as though we were heavily armed wraiths floating forward on a thin, filthy cloud.

Sweat burned my eyes. I squeezed them shut hard. When I opened them, the trees surrounding the ville quivered and faded and came back again. *An oasis*, I thought, like in the Foreign Legion movies I'd seen as a kid. Open, barren spaces, blinding sun, stabbing pain in the eyes, shimmering waves of heat and then, presto, the oasis appears. Maybe this was ours, a village of thatched huts nearly hidden in thick, green foliage. I hoped the well was cool and clean.

I stepped down off a low paddy dike, the M60 resting on my hip, my thumb poised above the safety switch. Ogala was fifty feet away from another, slightly taller dike to our front. He held his arm high over his head. The platoon stopped. I caressed the safety. Ogala turned and stared at the lieutenant as if to say, "I don't like this." I heard John say, "Something's screwed up, Lieutenant. No kids, no dogs. It's too quiet."

An RPG hit Ogala in the chest; he disappeared in a blast of red, brown, and gray.

Marines in Third Squad began to crumple twisting and jerking to the ground. I barely heard their screams above the roar and screech and blast of machine-gun and rifle fire and RPGs erupting from the ville. Marines were in front of me; I couldn't shoot. I hunched down and ran toward the dike screaming, "You bastards! You fucking bastards!" Green tracers ripped past my head. Marines lay all over the rice paddy, some hit, some trying to get beneath the withering fire.

I started to grab someone lying on the ground. I didn't know who it was or even if he was alive or dead. Sergeant Gilles hit me on the back, pushed me forward. "Get to the dike," he screamed. "Return fire, return fire!" Then he ran in front of me toward a Marine crawling on his belly toward the dike. He kicked him, bellowed as he grabbed him by the collar of his flak jacket, "Stand the fuck up! Get to the dike. Shoot back!"

The Buzz and I'd almost caught up to the lieutenant in our surge for the dike. I was right beside Smitty when I heard Captain's Brill's voice crackling over the radio—"One Actual, One Actual, what's happening? What . . ." A heavy machine-gun round hit Smitty square in the chest between the open flaps of his flak jacket. The captain's voice stopped in mid-sentence like someone had torn the phone off the wall. The bullet went through the radioman, punched a hole in the back of his flak jacket and stopped in the middle of the PRC-25 on to his back. Smitty flew past me, his legs scrambling like he was long-jumping backward through the air.

Cloninger and I threw ourselves down behind the dike. Dirt showered us as fire from the ville clipped the low earthen wall. I pulled my legs in close, trying to hide every part of me. Beside me, the Buzz lay curled in a fetal ball.

I raised up enough to look toward the ville, then hit Cloninger on the helmet, threw the machine gun up on the dike and began firing. Cloninger tore open a can of ammunition. Bullets flew around us; dirt and debris blew up in small filthy clouds streaked by ricochets and careening tracers.

Beyond Cloninger, Lieutenant Mangan lay up against the dike staring at the ville, yelling "Smitty! Smitty! Radio! Radio!" Suddenly he jerked backward and sprawled flat out, his arm flapping like an electrocuted trout. He saw Smitty then. The lieutenant crawled back out into the paddy, one arm trailing blood in the dirt. He grabbed Smitty by his flak jacket and tried to drag him and the radio up to the dike. "Corpsman! Corpsman! Help me, help me!" he screamed.

I blasted a long burst at the ville. All along the dike, Marines returned fire. I stopped shooting long enough for Cloninger to link the ammo belt from the can to the one feeding the gun. His fingers fumbled with the links. Bullets snapped above our heads, slapped into the dike, but neither of us were hit. As soon as he was done, Cloninger turned away from me and began to crawl toward the lieutenant and Smitty. "Buzzard!" I screamed. "Cloninger, I need you!" He was already out in the paddy.

He was halfway to Smitty when a bullet tore his chin. He lay still, face down in the dirt, then he spat a stream of tobacco juice and blood and pulled himself forward on his belly again. The fire was like a steel blade above our heads.

Cloninger and the lieutenant pulled the radio off Smitty's back and rolled him over. Blood bubbles frothed and drooled from his mouth, sprayed over his chin, down his front. He was so close to me that between blasts from my gun, I heard gurgling sounds every time he gasped for breath. Cloninger pulled the battle dressing from the band around his helmet, tore it open and pressed it hard against Smitty's chest. I left the gun on top of the dike and crawled for the ammo cans the Buzz had left when he went after Smitty.

"Corpsman! Corpsman!" Cloninger yelled.

Nobody came. Both docs were working frantically on other people.

The radio's handset trailed by its cord out into the paddy. The lieutenant pulled it to him, keyed it over and over. Nothing. Not even static. He twisted the radio's dials with shaking fingers until he saw the hole in it, realized it was dead. He began yelling again, "Radio, radio, radio! Where's a goddamn radio!"

I fumbled as I tore open a can of machine-gun ammo. The Buzz kept pressing on the battle dressing against Smitty's chest. He looked like he was wearing shiny red gloves.

Smitty gagged. A long, choking, retching sound. He drooled a thin, foamy spit of blood and stopped breathing.

Cloninger spat away his own blood and the tobacco, wiped his blood-muddy palm across Smitty's lips and began mouth-to-mouth.

Corporal Harding was twenty yards down the dike from us. He pulled Second Squad's radio off a dead Marine and began to crawl along the dike toward the lieutenant, the heavy radio in one hand, his M16 in the other. Blood dripped from shrapnel creases on his forehead, ran down the ridge of his nose and into his mouth. He was halfway to us when an RPG crashed through the top of the dike above him. The blast blew him off the ground and slammed him down hard. His helmet tumbled into the paddy behind us. I thought he was dead, but the smoke and dirt hadn't even settled when he began crawling again.

"Here, Lieutenant. I've got a radio," Harding yelled as he crawled. He dragged the radio behind him; it hissed and crackled and squawked the captain's urgent, professional voice: "Bravo One Actual, we're coming to you. I have requested artillery and air, can you direct?" Blood ran from Harding's mouth and nose and ears.

The lieutenant crawled to meet him, grabbed the radio with his good arm, wormed his way back in next to the dike. "Bravo Six, Bravo Six, One Actual! My On Call, Tango Bravo One Seven One One, direction two two hundred, danger close. I need everything you've got, quick! Over."

Doc Matheson snaked to us on his belly. He pushed Cloninger away from Smitty, pulled back the radioman's eyelids, felt his neck for a pulse. He shook his head.

"Cloninger!" I yelled. "Help me! Ammo!"

Matt searched Smitty's pockets and canteen belt for more bandages, stuffed them in his own pockets and crawled farther down the dike.

Fire poured from the ville. Everybody in the platoon who was able to move was up against the dike now. Most fired; some of the wounded couldn't hold a weapon. One or two lay nearly flat, extended only their M16s above the dike and fired in the general direction of the gooks. Most leaned up, hugged the top of the dike, fired toward the ville, then ducked down to reload, forced themselves back up and fired again.

Cloninger helped me with the gun, then picked up his rifle. I fired burst after burst before I forced myself to slow down, afraid I'd burn out the barrel.

Harding lay on the other side of me, huddled against the dike, his rifle on the ground. He glared at me with fear maddened eyes. "My helmet!" he cried.

"Shoot, Harding, shoot!" I pounded him on the shoulder, pointed toward the ville.

"My helmet!" he cried again. He pointed back into the paddy where it lay a dozen feet behind us. The earth around it danced under the impact of bullets.

"Don't! Don't try it!" I pointed again at the ville. "Help us! Shoot!"

"I need it," he wailed. "Sweet Jesus, I need my helmet for Hope." In the din, I could barely make out the words.

"It's not safe," I yelled. "The gooks. We have to stop them." I gestured again at the ville. Harding's face was horrible, contorted with terror and indecision I hadn't thought him capable of. I thrust his rifle into his hands and turned back to the gun. I was firing again when he dropped the rifle and began to crawl into the paddy behind us.

I screamed at him to stop, but he didn't.

He got within a few feet of the helmet, reached for it like a drowning man struggling to grasp a raft. He lunged forward, got a hand on the helmet just as an NVA walked a line of bullets across the earth and blew the back of his head off. The helmet skittered away.

"Corpsman!" I screamed. I couldn't see Matt or Dorsey anywhere. I started to crawl toward Harding. Cloninger grabbed me by the leg, yelled at me to stop. Harding's brains spilled out of his skull. I scrambled back to the dike, picked up the M60, and fired as fast as I dared.

Lieutenant Mangan's artillery fire mission impacted on the edge of the ville. On the other side of Cloninger, the lieutenant screamed into the radio. "Fire for effect! Repeat! Fire for effect and for Chrissakes please keep firing!"

Six more 105 rounds blasted into the village. Geysers of smoke and flame and debris reached skyward. This time, the NVA didn't run. We were still taking tremendous fire. Another six artillery rounds hit. Then another six-round volley. Fire from the ville continued to rake us. Five more artillery rounds struck the trees. One fell short. It landed on the far end of our dike, beheading a new guy in Third Squad.

I fired furiously, swept the barrel of the M60 side to side. Cloninger spat great gobs of blood now, lifted more and more rounds from the ammo cans, fed the belt smoothly across his hands down into the gun.

Just down the dike from us, John and Willie blasted burst after burst into the ville. The fluorescent orange streams of tracers from our M60s pinpointed our position. Blue-green NVA tracers splattered across the face of the dike all around us, ricocheted and careened up over our heads. Cloninger and John and I dropped down trying to hide from the murderous fire, but Willie was hurled back, a hunk of flesh and bone ripped from his shoulder. His right arm dangled, splintered bone and ripped tendon gleaming through the blood. He writhed in the dirt like a wound-crazed animal.

Pius John dropped his gun. He crawled out to him yelling, "Willie! Willeeee!"

Willie began to kneel up. John grabbed him and threw him back to the ground. "Keep down, keep down!"

Willie howled.

John screamed for a corpsman. His cries mixed with all the others up and down the line.

Willie pulled John's hand away, started to inch his way toward the dike. "No, Pope," he yelled, "we've got to kill gooks." John forced him to lie still long enough to pack battle dressings on his wound. Then Willie pushed himself up next to John, lifted linked bullets above their gun's feed tray with his left hand, more focused and frenzied than he'd ever been.

The NVA machine gunner turned his attention to other parts of the dike. Tracers burst from his gun, a blue-green neon ribbon flashing out from deep in the hedgerow at the edge of the ville.

I studied his tracers for long seconds, aimed at the beginning of the green light stream that marked his gun, then pulled the trigger. John saw where I fired, then both of us slashed orange laser beams of bullets toward the gunner's position. The air screeched and whirled and screamed around us. I was almost oblivious to the terrible cacophony. I needed to kill the gooks. To kill was to live.

The line of green tracers suddenly jerked straight up in the air as though the NVA gunner fired at the sun. We'd hit him. I couldn't hear his screams, but in my head they reverberated with wondrous satisfaction. I fired burst after burst until those unheard screams stopped echoing in my head and I was certain we'd killed every man at that gun.

John stopped shooting. Willie slumped beside him, his good arm clutching the top of the dike, the torn one dangling loose at his side. John grabbed him by his good shoulder, pulled him down, rolled him over. Willie's head lolled backward; his helmet bounced into the paddy, coming to rest near Harding's feet. Willie looked like he was staring at it, trying to figure out how it got there.

But he wasn't. He had a gaping hole in his throat. The hair on his chest was drenched with blood; on the ground, a bloody pool glistened obscenely in the sun.

John held Willie to him, stroked his hair, cuddled him as tenderly as a man holds a newborn. Then howls exploded from him, tears etched the filth on his face. Around us the bedlam continued. Explosions, artillery rounds crashing into the ville, bullets screeching, men screaming, a deafening madhouse of killing and dying. John noticed none of it. He rocked gently, side to side. "Oh, Willie. Even you."

Farther down the dike, the lieutenant saw, or heard, that our machine guns weren't firing. He crawled toward us, dragging the radio, yelling, "Guns! Guns!"

An RPG screamed over the dike just above our heads. It exploded between us and the lieutenant, a violent, shattering roar that slammed us down into the earth beneath a storm of dirt and shrapnel. The lieutenant lay still. I thought he was dead. A panic greater than even my terror began to rise in me. How would any of us live through this if Lieutenant Mangan was dead? But then he was crawling again. "Guns!" he yelled. "We need the guns!"

John stared at Mangan as though he didn't recognize him, couldn't understand what was happening.

"Are you hit, Garafano?" Mangan shook him. "The gun, Garafano, the gun! Are you hit?"

John shook his head slowly. "No . . ." He stared at the lieutenant like a confused child. Then he looked at Willie, his glassy eyes, his raised eyebrows, his mouth hanging open above his torn throat. Willie looked as though he were trying to understand what all this meant, too.

Lieutenant Mangan yelled at me, "Fire, McClure! Return fire!"

"They've killed all my friends," John said. He patted the back of Willie's head with a hand bright with blood. "They killed Willie." He spoke like a child struggling to understand. "They killed Rudy, too, Lieutenant. And Woody and Harding. They're killing all my friends."

The lieutenant held John's face in both his hands. He yelled to be heard above the din, but somehow, despite the volume, despite the urgency, despite the actual words he was saying, he sounded almost tender. "I know, Pope. Now we've got to kill them before they kill more of our friends." He turned to me. "Shoot, McClure! For fuck's sake, shoot, Marine!" He turned back to John. "C'mon, Garafano. I need you. We all need you!"

John looked like he was thinking about that. His face began to grow hard.

"The gun, Garafano. Use the gun. Kill the gooks that killed Willis. We've got to kill gooks, kill them all before they kill all our friends."

John lay Willie down as though he were just sleeping, then rolled over and picked up his gun. Above us a flight of Phantoms began a run on the ville.

Even above the roar of my own M60, I could hear John's screams as he fired.

We sat propped up against the dike, surrounded by the debris of war, heaps of shell casings; strewn, empty ammo containers; torn, bloody bandages. Nobody talked. It would be dark soon.

I sucked water from my canteen, lit a cigarette from the glowing tip of the last. Cloninger sat on one side of me, a bandage across his chin. Willie lay on the other side. Smitty and Harding and half a dozen other dead Marines had already been carried to the LZ. I could see Second and Third Platoons searching what remained of the ville. A filthy pall lay above what was left. The only sound from there was the crackle and hiss of burning hootches and trees.

John had covered Willie's face. He sat beside him, staring into space, encrusted with filth and Willie's blood. The drying blood made grotesque patterns across the purple latticework of scars on John's chest. He looked like he'd lost his friends and his soul.

It seemed very quiet now, although the rest of the company surged around us, tending the wounded and the dead, searching the ville, preparing to dig in for the night. A mournful, urgent mutter had replaced the din of the last hours. It floated above the battlefield, broken only by occasional yelled orders and the roar of choppers taking the wounded and dead away.

After they took Willie's body away, John spoke for the first time since the fighting stopped. "Let's go see," was all he said.

I nodded, lit another cigarette. I didn't know what he wanted, but whatever John needed, I'd help him out.

We angled across the paddy toward the machine-gun position we'd wiped out earlier. Billows of dust swirled around our legs like an angry cloud. At the edge of the shattered tree line, a dead water buffalo, innards hanging from its belly, seemed to accuse us as we went past.

Second Platoon had dragged three NVA bodies from the bushes and laid them in front of the heavy machine gun. Two Marines neither of us knew, new guys from the look of their uniforms, stared down at them.

The gooks were mangled and torn. One split up the middle, another without a face. The third had the top of his head blown off. He glared at us, his mouth pulled back in an obscene grin. It may have been an agony grimace, but it looked as though at the instant of his death he felt satisfied with all he'd done to us.

John's face was a mask of frozen rage. He clenched his fists again and again, as though readying to beat someone to death. He stared at the grinning gook for what seemed like a long time. Then his entire body began to quiver. He began to rock back and forth, fists clenching at his sides, the bloody crucifix on the beads around his neck slapping against the blood coated scars on his chest.

Then he was stomping, his boots dancing on the dead gunner's face. Beyond him, I heard one of the new guys say, "Oh my God."

I let John go for a minute before I pulled him away. He didn't resist. He just stood staring at what he'd done, his boots gore slathered, the gunner's head stove in, the grin gone from his pulverized mouth, his nose and cheekbones and forehead smashed to pulp.

One of the new guys looked like he was going to throw up. "You okay?" I asked.

He looked up from the corpse, stared at John, then turned to me, horror and astonishment on his face. "I guess so," he said. "God, what a mess."

I nodded. "Yup." I took another deep drag on my cigarette and threw the butt down.

The new guy looked down again. "Oh God," he said, and he gagged.

I looked down then too. The cigarette butt stood upright, the bright tip still burning in the goo that had been the gook's face. It reminded me of Woody at the end.

I kicked the corpse in the head as hard as I could. Then I took John by the arm and turned away.

26

THE VILLE WAS THE GATEWAY TO all we'd been searching for. Behind it, headquarters and hospitals and supply dumps covered grid squares, most of them underground, all of them heavily defended. The day after our battle, Charlie Company found tunnels, and both Alpha and Delta came upon more heavily armed villes. More rifle companies joined in the fight. The battle for the complex would rage for days. Engineers would take two weeks to search the tunnels, digging things up, blowing them up, destroying everything.

But First Platoon was being pulled out, sent back to Hoa Binh. There were only fifteen of us left, including four walking wounded. We were told to move to an abandoned ville and hunker down to wait for a bird. On John's map, it looked like it should be less than a day's hump. We had no idea what lay between us and there. If we had, we wouldn't have gone.

Lieutenant Mangan had refused to be medevacked despite his wounded arm. He refused too to have Matt give him morphine, because it would make him lethargic, unable to lead us where we had to go. His bandaged arm looked like it'd been lacquered maroon then rolled in dirt. Staff Sergeant Gilles, a battle dressing taped to the side of his neck, had convinced the lieutenant he didn't need to be evacuated either. Blood oozed from under his bandage, made shiny streaks on his chest. His face was ash gray.

Cloninger's slashed chin hurt like hell and would need stitches, but he told Matt he didn't want to leave me. Matt and the lieutenant let him stay. "People been telling me my face is painful long as I can remember, Doc." The Buzzard winced when he attempted a smile. I thanked him for staying, more grateful than I knew how to express. He shrugged off my thanks, said I'd stick with him if I had a small wound, too. I wanted to think he was right, but it would've been tempting to get on a bird.

Matt had small shrapnel wounds in his face and one leg but was able to walk. Doc Dorsey, shot in the stomach, had been evacuated. The lieutenant didn't argue when Matt pointed out we knew nothing about what we faced next and might need a corpsman with us.

It seemed like a miracle neither John nor I'd been hit. As we walked away from the big ville, I thanked God for keeping me alive and in one piece. I thanked him over and over for sparing John. I was too sick about Harding and Smitty and Willie and the others we'd lost to know what to say to Him about them.

We made our way across open paddies, over small hillocks, and around or through tree lines. With our walking wounded, we had to move slowly. None of the four ever complained, but the effort glowed phosphorescent in their eyes.

Behind us, the battle for the complex raged. The din ebbed and roared, the gray whorl of smoke and filth pulsed higher and thicker beyond the big ville. The thunder of artillery and air strikes, the crackle and mutter and blast of machine-gun and small-arms fire never ceased, though they grew more distant as we pressed on. I looked back at the plumes of rising smoke, the ashen pall hanging over the place. The noises of men killing each other clung to the haze. Lieutenant Mangan had been right before we even came to the valley: all the gooks in the world.

The lieutenant and platoon sergeant looked worried as they studied the map.

"How much farther?" I asked John.

"A long ways." He pointed to his map. "We'll have to move parallel to these ridge lines. That's the shits." His fingers were crusted with Willie's blood.

I followed his finger across the contour lines. "Looks within machine-gun range."

John nodded. "Easy." He shook his head, didn't say more. If there were gooks with a machine gun on that high ground, we'd be sitting ducks crossing the open space beneath them.

"Lieutenant," John said. "Have you seen the long ridges this side of the extract point?"

"Yup."

"Any way we can go somewhere else? Or around them?"

"Not if we want to get out of here before Christmas. It'd take days to get around those fucking ridges."

He didn't really mean Christmas; that was months away. But the word hit me in the gut. I wondered if I'd live to enjoy another one.

"Good idea to get on-calls, sir?"

"I didn't get here yesterday, Garafano."

"No, sir. Of course not. Sorry, I just thought . . ."

"Maybe you fuckin' didn't," Staff Sergeant Gilles said.

"Sorry, Sergeant Gilles," John said.

"It's alright," the lieutenant said. "I'm going to request them." Without looking up from his map, he held out his hand. Nothing happened. Smitty would've slapped the radio handset into his palm. The lieutenant looked up, almost as if he'd forgotten that Smitty was gone. "Webster!"

The Marine carrying the only radio we had left looked up from screwing the lid back on his canteen. "Yes, sir?" He sounded like he had no idea what was going on. I wondered if he'd never noticed the teamwork between Smitty and the lieutenant. Maybe what we'd just been through had fogged his brain.

"Radio? You always need to be ready to hand me the fuckin' radio."

"Oh. Yes, sir." Webster fumbled in his flak jacket as though he were looking for a stick of Dentine.

"Today, Webster. C'mon. We need to move."

"Yes, sir. Sorry, sir."

Lieutenant Mangan explained to whoever he was talking to that he wanted to register on calls. He listened for a minute. Then, "Roger, I copy. Out." He handed the handset back to Webster. "Okay, men. Move out."

"Didn't sound like they wanted the coordinates, Lieutenant," John said.

"They're busy," the lieutenant said. He nodded back toward the big ville, as though the fight at the complex explained everything. It sure as hell didn't explain what we were supposed to do if a gook machine gunner caught us out in the open. The lieutenant shrugged as though it were no big deal. "We'll call if we need help when we're there." He tried to keep the concern off his face.

Ayoub had point. He'd been with us for the slaughter at the river-bed, but the big ville had been Hey You's first fight where the gooks shot back. He had fear in his eyes he hadn't had before. I could only remember him walking point once before. I hoped he knew what he was doing.

Just before we moved out, Pius John looked at my chest. "What happened to the beads?"

I looked down. The chipped black cross hung empty at the end of the string of worn black balls. "Looks like God's made his hat," I said.

John looked around us, a strange, sardonic expression on his face. "It'd be easy to believe, wouldn't it?" I couldn't tell if he was talking about Willie and Smitty and Harding and the others, or about what he'd done to the dead gook.

Ayoub started to move out. "But I don't believe it," John said. "I just don't know where to look for Him anymore."

Most of the half-dozen men in front of me threw themselves down when Hey You triggered the mine that hurled him through the air and flung him to the ground in a bloody heap minus half of one leg.

Matt quickly hunched his way up the line to beside Lieutenant Mangan. The lieutenant hadn't called for the guns, but John followed Matt, and Cloninger and I followed him. I tried to ignore the near-panicked looks from other Marines as we went past.

Ayoub was twenty or twenty-five yards out to our front.

Beneath the blood and dirt smeared wad of gauze and tape on his forehead, Matt's eyes were wide with fear. As always, he choked it down. He dropped his helmet and had gone several limping steps toward Ayoub before the lieutenant called to him. "Doc, wait. We'll clear a path."

Matt stopped. He looked at Ayoub lying face down in the dirt, silent, a bloodstain spreading beneath him. The corpsman shook his head. "There's no time, Lieutenant. Hey You could bleed out." He began walking again. The lieutenant didn't say anything more.

God, Matt, be careful, I said to myself. *Be careful, man.* I had a feeling everyone left in the platoon was thinking or praying the same thing. *Take care of him, God, he's the best.*

Matt moved slowly, watched every place he put down a boot. It seemed like a long time before he got to Hey You, set down his medical kit and bent over him. Matt was breathing so heavily, I swore I could hear the blood roaring through his veins. "I need help," he called without looking up.

"I'll go," John said.

"John . . ." I said. "You don't have to . . ." I spoke quietly, but I wanted to scream. Don't go out there, sometimes they come in pairs. It wasn't my finest moment, telling him he didn't need to help a wounded Marine. But I'd lost so many friends. I barely knew Ayoub. I didn't want to trade him for John.

John smiled as he shrugged off his flak jacket and gear. A genuine smile, the kind I'd seen on the old Pius John. "A man's got to make choices, Mick. He's a Marine. My turn to help Matt." John turned to the lieutenant. "All set, sir."

The lieutenant stared at him, then nodded. I saw deep appreciation in Mangan's face, and for a moment I recalled his very different expression after John triggered the ambush at the riverbed. "Be damn careful, Pope."

John crossed himself, kissed the dirty crucifix at the end of his beads, winked at me, and began to walk toward Ayoub and Matt. I'm sure he was convinced he was doing the right thing, what any one of us should've been willing to do to help another Marine. Maybe he was doing penance for what he'd done to the dead gook, or other sins, too. I began praying, hoping desperately God was still around.

The lieutenant looked at what was left of his platoon. Fourteen effectives now—stretching the term, given his and the platoon sergeant's wounds. "Everyone, take a knee," Mangan said. "Pay attention to the flanks and our rear."

Sergeant Gilles called individuals by name, told them where to look.

God help us. Don't let us be fired upon while we have two unarmed men trying to help a wounded one, I prayed.

I took a knee, looked around for cover if anyone shot at us. There wasn't much. I watched John walking slowly toward Matt. He barely took his eyes off the ground until he was there. I didn't stop praying until he was.

Matt already had a tourniquet on Hey You. He pulled bandages out of his bag and handed them across Ayoub's unconscious form to John. He cut what remained of Ayoub's trousers off him and began to sort out his other mangled leg. John started to bandage Ayoub's shredded stump.

Beside me, Lieutenant Mangan watched them in silence, then turned and looked down the row of scared faces behind us. "Fuck," he growled. "Webster, stay with me with the goddamn radio!" Webster brought the radio to him. The lieutenant called for an emergency medevac.

John seemed safe now. I felt a wash of relief. John and Matt. If they just carry Ayoub back the way they walked out, they should be fine. *Thank you, God, thank you. Thank you for taking care of them. Thank you for them.* I looked around again. We had very little cover anywhere near us. *Please, God, don't let us get hit.*

Pius John finished applying the battle dressings to Ayoub's stump. Matt jabbed another morphine stick into him, said something to John, continued wrapping bandages around Ayoub's other leg.

John took one crouching step backward out of his kneeling position and disappeared in a blast of flame, dirt, and smoke.

The explosion ripped Ayoub from the ground and slammed him down again. It blew Matt tumbling and sprawling in the dirt.

Behind me in the column, Estes began to holler and babble, and then he jumped up and ran full tilt toward the lingering haze around John's crumpled body. "John! John!" he yelled as he ran.

He got within two feet of John when the earth belched again—a terrible, flashing roar that threw Estes cartwheeling through the air and slammed him to the ground flat on his back twenty feet from where he'd just put his foot down. He lay there, eyes open wide, only his mouth moving and his chest heaving. He began to shriek.

Off to the side of him, John lay face down in a spreading pool of blood.

Beyond John, Ayoub lay on his back, eyes scrunched tight. He didn't move. His bloody legs, all one and a half of them, only partly bandaged, now coated with dirt. He moaned loudly through clenched teeth.

Matt raised himself off his belly to his elbows. His glasses were gone; he looked around like a mole suddenly exposed to sunlight. Blood from beneath the bandage on his forehead and from his nose and mouth streaked his face. He began to pull himself slowly back toward Ayoub.

"Doc! Doc! For God sakes, Matt, don't move! Don't even twitch, Doc! Lay still!" the lieutenant yelled.

Matt spat a mouthful of blood. He looked toward us, his face contorted as though all he could see were shapes where Mangan's voice came from. "I'm okay, Lieutenant."

"Don't move, Doc! For Christ sakes, don't! You're in a fucking minefield!"

Matt froze.

In front of him, Ayoub moaned loudly, a long, bubbly sound.

Pius John was silent.

Estes screamed. A wild, tortured, animal bawl of anguish.

Staff Sergeant Gilles stood up and glared fiercely around at everybody else. Some of the guys lay or crouched fearfully on the ground. Others had begun to pull themselves upright as though they couldn't decide whether to stay where they were or rush forward to help.

"Nobody move! Not a goddamn muscle. Nobody!" Sergeant Gilles roared.

Estes screamed again.

Gilles walked past me to Lieutenant Mangan. The platoon sergeant's face was so gray that, if he were on his back, I might've assumed he was dead. His eyes glowed with pain, and blood ran heavily now from beneath the bandage on his neck. "How we gonna get 'em, sir?"

Estes shrieked again.

The lieutenant closed his eyes. He was quiet for a moment, then he said, "I'll go after Estes." Estes was the farthest away from us.

"I'll get the Pope, Lieutenant," I said.

Mangan stared at me. Then he nodded.

Estes screamed again.

Ayoub continued to moan.

John was still silent.

Matt lay still, staring back at the lieutenant.

"Sir, you don't have to . . ."

The lieutenant held up a hand, cutting the platoon sergeant off. Mangan studied the men out in front of us. Then he turned three-sixty, looking all around. For a moment, he looked like he was trying to control a lot of frenzied thoughts, trying to make sense of everything around us. "Doc? Matt," he called.

"Yes, sir?" I could barely hear the corpsman.

"You're okay? You're not hit?"

"Yes sir . . . I'm okay, Lieutenant. Except I can't see real well without glasses."

"Can you get to Ayoub again? Awful fucking careful?"

The corpsman looked at Ayoub. Hey You let out another long, murmuring groan. Matt nodded slightly. "Yes, sir. But we've got to hurry. For him and the Pope." He got up on all fours.

"All right. You go to him. I'm gonna get Estes. McClure's going after Garafano." The lieutenant hesitated. "Careful, Doc. Goddamn careful."

Matt nodded again.

"Hey, sir," Sergeant Gilles said in a whisper only the lieutenant and I and maybe Webster could hear. "I can do it. You've got a messed-up arm." The blood oozing down the platoon sergeant's neck shone in the sunlight.

The lieutenant shook his head. He looked very old. "Thanks," he said. "I can still crawl. This makes more sense. You take Garafano's gun. Cloninger, you good with the M60?"

The Buzz said, "Yes, sir, I'm fine."

I wasn't sure if the lieutenant meant are you okay being responsible for the gun, or can you shoot well? I was scared enough thinking about crawling to John through a minefield. The thought of gooks discovering us and shooting at us as we did terrified me.

The lieutenant shrugged off his flak jacket and 782 gear. He paused, closed his eyes, thinking or praying or gathering himself. I hadn't stopped repeating, "Please God, please God," over and over inside my head. I was so scared, I felt like my innards had frozen. I might shatter like a flawed ice sculpture if I tried to move.

Lieutenant Mangan said, "We've got no idea how big this minefield is, Sergeant Gilles. We'll pull those guys right back here." He spoke with a calm I'm sure he couldn't feel. He pointed past the tail end of the column. "You turn the rest around and walk them back the way we came. Call the Six and see if we can get a Bronco, or anybody else, over us while we do this. Even if they can't stay, maybe they could at least tell us if there's gooks around."

"Yes, sir."

Estes shrieked again. There was nothing we could do to stop him. It was like summoning every gook within miles.

"Go, Sergeant Gilles. Come on, McClure." The lieutenant pulled his kabar out.

Jesus please help me, I prayed. *Hang in there, John, I'm coming. Choices, Mick, a man must make choices. . . .* Sometimes, there aren't any real choices. I needed to save John.

I pulled John's kabar from the sheath on the web gear he'd dropped before he went to help Matt. *Please, God, help me.*

Matt wiped a filthy, bloody hand over his face. It turned the red streaks into a mottled mask. He began to crawl on his hands and knees toward Ayoub. An inch at a time, he checked twigs, grass, clumps of dirt before he put any weight down. Ayoub gurgled and moaned. Matt called quietly, "Hang on Hey You, I'm coming to get you. You'll be fine, hang in there, I'm coming."

The lieutenant and I went down on all fours. Sweat burned my eyes, my T-shirt was soaked, my trouser legs clung to my thighs.

Lieutenant Mangan looked over at me. "Okay, McClure. Probe every inch with your blade. We need to get to them quick, but right now, slow is fast."

"Yes, sir," I whispered through a mouth that felt full of gauze. My tongue was raw against my chipped tooth.

"If you run into anything, you yell to me. All right?"

I nodded.

"Make the path wider than your body," the lieutenant said. "Dig up the dirt so you know exactly where to come back. You'll be bringing Garafano."

"Yes, sir," I said. I'm not sure it was loud enough for him to hear. I felt like I had a bale of cotton in my mouth. He stared at me. I nodded; he nodded back.

"Don't even start to move him until you've checked with me."

"Yes, sir."

It took me twenty minutes to get to John. The lieutenant and I started together, then diverged like the hands on a clock. I moved in a straight line toward John at the eleven; the lieutenant moved equally slowly and cautiously toward Estes at the more distant ten. At the one, Matt had reached Ayoub and was again bandaging his legs.

Twenty minutes. A third of an hour. A small part of a day. A lifetime. An eternity. I'd never been as terrified in a firefight, even the battle we'd just been through. Crawling in that minefield, seconds lasted forever.

Estes passed out five minutes after we began probing the dirt. He lay mercifully still for another five, then jolted back with a long, stabbing shriek. I dropped my knife in midprobe.

I picked up the kabar and resumed my slow, deliberate stabbing of the sun-baked earth. I blinked at the sweat in my eyes, rubbed filthy hands across my face, inspected every inch of the ground. Twigs, grass, reeds, rice stubble, clumps of dirt. I stared, I examined, I prayed. *Jesus, God, please help me. I promise I'll do whatever you want from now on. Please, Jesus, please.* I slowly pushed the blade into the earth, waited for it to hit plastic or metal, moved forward inch by inch, waiting to be blown to bits.

To my left, the lieutenant probed steadily, slowly.

Estes moaned.

To my right front, Matt chanted slowly to Ayoub, a sing-song cadence of quiet reassurance. "Hang in there, Hey You. Hang in there."

Ayoub moaned.

Straight ahead, Pius John didn't make a sound.

Pull again, thrust again, a line across my front as wide as my arms could reach. The lieutenant began yelling instructions. I stopped to listen, three feet from Pius John. He wanted Ayoub brought back the way Matt had gone out to him, Sergeant Gilles crawling out to meet them, searching for mines as he went.

"Keep going, McClure. You're good."

"Yes, sir."

Estes shrieked again, a high, shrill screech that flashed like an electric current, then evaporated in a gurgling babble. I closed my eyes, waited until the noise was over. I called softly, "John? John? It's Marty. Can you hear me? I'm coming, John, I'm coming." His back was to me. I couldn't tell if he was breathing. I was so close I could've put my hand on him if I dared to throw myself forward. He was so still.

The acrid smell of lingering gunpowder and the thick, sweet, coppery stink of blood filled my nose and my mouth.

"John? Pope? I'm coming."

No answer.

I probed the last two feet in blackened, blood-soaked ground. It darkened the blade of the kabar, stained my hands a foul, stinking maroon. *Jesus, John, so fucking much blood.* I was so close. I fought the urge to lunge forward, grab John, turn him over, help him be okay.

The lieutenant was three or four feet yet from Estes, who now alternated pitiful, incoherent babbles with high, piercing shrieks.

To my right, Matt was on his hands and knees, feeling the earth in front of him, then pulling Ayoub forward by the collar of his flak jacket an inch at a time. Matt looked terrified and focused at the same time. I wanted to throw him the kabar so he could probe the earth with more than his fingertips. But if I tossed the knife, it could land on a mine and kill them both.

I finally reached John. He lay on his side, facing away from me, arms outstretched as though he were reaching for someone's embrace.

"John? John?" I whispered, like I was trying to wake him up.

He didn't answer.

I took his shoulder and slowly pulled him toward me onto his back. His lightless, milky eyes stared straight into my face. From someplace inside him came a long, low, squishy rumble, a gelatinous murmur of deadness that echoed and rolled and roared inside my skull and for the longest time did so, much louder than every explosion I ever heard.

I looked down across John's disemboweled body, aghast at what the mine had done to him. I turned away and puked into the grass. Then I looked back at his face, his wide-open eyes, his parted lips pulled back over wide teeth under that Teddy Roosevelt mustache of his.

He looked like he was smiling at me, like he'd just discovered a wonderful secret, or had a story he wanted to share.

"Almost there, Estes, you'll be okay," I heard the lieutenant say. Off to my right, Matt was slowly pulling Ayoub to safety.

Estes screamed again.

I lay my head on Pius John's chest and sobbed.

27

WE GOT AYOUB AND ESTES AND JOHN out of the minefield without anyone else getting hurt. A CH-46 carrying
wounded from the complex diverted to us to pick them up.

Sergeant Gilles' wound had bled so badly while he helped Matt
pull Hey You in that he swayed like a drunk when he stood. The
lieutenant ordered him onto the helicopter too. Mangan refused
to go out himself, despite what had to be tremendous pain in his
arm. Matt wouldn't go either, even though without glasses he was
half-blind.

I put John's rosary around my neck and his kabar on my belt
when his body went on the bird. I watched the chopper carrying him
away grow small in the sky. I felt my soul would never again take up
as much space.

There were only eleven of us now, fewer than a normal squad. We
continued to move to the north, knowing that if we ran into any
sizeable enemy force we'd be deep in the hurt locker. I wished desperately the medevac had had room to take us with the wounded
and dead.

The sky turned black, and for a while we trudged through hammering rain. It stopped as abruptly as it began, sullen clouds reluctantly moving on. Steam rose from us and everything around us as

though we were walking through an anteroom of hell. Sometimes I looked down at the two sets of beads around my neck, one with a filthy Christ figure at the end of the strand, the other cross as empty as my soul. Despite being with ten other men, I was alone. I kept hearing John's voice: *A man's got to make choices, Mick.* Kept seeing his face, that smile he wore at the end. *Jesus, John, what do I do now?*

On point approaching a small stream, Lee bent down to push aside a branch blocking his legs. An NVA hiding against the riverbank cut loose with his AK-47. The rounds went above Lee, hitting nothing. He dropped to the ground and sprayed the top of the stream bank on full automatic.

We'd surprised four NVA. Probably because they were outnumbered, they'd hidden in the streambed hoping we'd pass them by. When Lee fired, they all ducked down, then sprang up again shooting, firing long bursts over the rest of us as we hugged the ground.

Fullerton crawled up close to Lee, ripped the riverbank on full automatic with his M16. Lee slapped a new magazine into his rifle and pulled out a frag. All four NVA crouched low again, ducking our fire, reloading. I knelt up to fire but couldn't get a shot off because Marines were in my way.

Lee let out a roar, jumped up, hurled his grenade, and tore toward the NVA at full tilt, firing his rifle as he ran. He was over the riverbank, screaming and shooting before the shrapnel from the grenade stopped whistling through the branches. Fullerton charged behind him yelling at the top of his lungs, then the rest of us were running forward screaming and snarling like jackals. Luckily, none of us were hit by shrapnel from Lee's grenade.

It was over in the seconds it took us to run to the stream. Lee stood panting, knee deep in the water; Fullerton above him on the bank. Four AK-47s were scattered in the mud. Two gooks lay belly down at the stream's edge, one with his head and torso underwater. A third was slumped against the bank, his shirt blood-soaked where shrapnel from Lee's grenade had torn his back, his face pressed into the dirt, hidden by a dirty straw hat. The fourth NVA lay on his back, eyes closed, the back of his head in the water. Blood dripping from his ears and nose and mouth ran down his face and thinned in the stream. His eyes popped open suddenly, he murmured in Vietnamese. Fullerton stitched him from his navel to his forehead. Chunks of bone and teeth and brain bobbed in the crimson water.

"Search 'em," the lieutenant told Lee. "Fast. Everything in their pockets, their ammo. Bring their rifles with you. I want us out of here before more show up."

Lee ransacked the pockets of the two facedown beside the water. Fullerton jumped down with him, laid his M16 on a rock, searched the man he'd just shot, then went over to the NVA lying against the riverbank. He grabbed the gook by the shoulder and turned the body over. The NVA moaned. I brought the machine gun up fast. "Get out of the fucking way, Fullerton," I yelled.

"Hold up, McClure," Lieutenant Mangan said.

The gook gasped for air.

"How bad's he hit?"

Fullerton tore the man's shirt up. "One in the side, Lieutenant. Some shrap metal in the face. Prob'ly not going to die if they find him."

Lee raised his rifle. "I'll do the fucker, Lieutenant."

"Hold it, Lee. Just fucking hold it!" The lieutenant gestured impatiently. "Webster, the goddamn radio. Now! Doc, how long's it gonna take the son of a bitch to die?"

Matt climbed down the bank. I could tell it hurt his leg. Without his glasses, he had to get his face very close to the wounded NVA. "Nothing fatal, Lieutenant."

"Fuck."

"Sir? If they find him, he'll tell them which way we've gone. How many we are." Matt squinched his eyes half shut trying to focus on the lieutenant. Blood from the shrapnel wounds on his forehead had dried in dark patches and streaks on his face.

The lieutenant nodded. He spoke for a while into the radio. Matt climbed back up the bank. For several minutes, Lieutenant Mangan paced back and forth as he talked to the captain. Then he said, "The Six is checking with Battalion to see if they want to send a bird out for him. He thinks Intel will want to interrogate him."

"Fuck," Cloninger said. "No bird for us, but they'll send one for him?"

"Maybe they'll take us all," I said. "I'll ride with a shot-up god-damn gook, if they'll get us out of here."

The radio rasped and crackled; Lieutenant Mangan listened to the Six again. His eyes bulged as though the pain from his arm was trying to escape through his sockets. He still hadn't let Matt give him morphine.

The expressions on the lieutenant's face changed like waves pounding a storm-lashed beach. Exhausted concern. Incredulity. Raging fury.

"You're kidding. . . . What?! . . . Do those idiots know how far we are from there? What's between here and there?"

Matt and I looked at each other. We'd never heard the lieutenant say anything disrespectful to the captain before.

Crackle. Crackle.

"I don't care, Six! Do they know what these people have been through yesterday and today?!"

Crackle. Crackle.

"I know. No, sir, I'm sorry. Do those people have any idea what they're doing to us?"

He paced back and forth, the handset to his ear, glared at the cord to the radio on Webster's back as though it were a tether to something monstrous and unreal.

"Can we at least get a Bronco to cover us?"

Crackle. Crackle.

The lieutenant lowered the handset then kicked violently at the earth. "Jesus Christ! Jesus fucking Christ!"

When he spoke on the radio again, it was with bitter resignation. "All right. Roger, Six Actual. Out."

He handed the handset back to Webster and stood staring into space.

"What's the story, Lieutenant?" I asked.

Mangan stared at Matt and me as though he hadn't quite processed what he'd been told. Finally, he said, "We've got to carry the fucking gook in. They want to interrogate him."

I was astonished. "Carry him in? What about a bird?"

The lieutenant looked away, almost as though he was looking for a helicopter on the horizon. He looked back at me with an angry scowl. "No birds. They're all running ammo and medevacs to the fight. We've got to carry him." The din of the ongoing battle behind us seemed to swell in the air.

Carry a fucking gook! It was absurd. I glared at the comatose soldier. A maroon stain spread on his shirt. His eyes were squinched shut like he was in great pain. His forehead was lacerated in half a dozen places. Blood trickled in rivulets from the wounds and ran down his face. I touched the hilt of John's kabar on my belt. I wanted to jump down into the stream and slash the bastard's throat.

"Jesus, Lieutenant," I said. "He'll slow us down. What if he makes noise? If we can't get across that big paddy fast and quiet because we're carrying him, the whole platoon"—I looked around, realizing that was only eleven of us now—"the whole fucking platoon, could get waxed."

"Lieutenant?" Matt glanced around to be sure no one except the lieutenant and I could hear him. He held my eyes for a second, trusting me with something. I'd never seen an expression on him like that before. It was terrible, like he'd just condemned his own soul. "If I give him three or four sticks of morphine, he'll just . . . he'll be gone. No one will know, Lieutenant. We won't have to carry him if he died, you know, of his wounds."

Lieutenant Mangan studied Matt for a long moment. I knew what the lieutenant was thinking: It would be so easy. A couple extra pops of morphine and the gook would be dead. Like he should be already if someone had just taken a better shot. Like he should be if I want to protect my men. But the Skipper said bring the son of a bitch in. Some asshole sitting in a bunker with no idea what could happen to us gave the Six his orders and he gave them to me. Fuck.

I could see the decision being made in Mangan's face. I'd never had any doubt that the lieutenant would do anything, including sacrificing himself, to save us if he could. But now he couldn't do it; he wouldn't kill the gook.

"Please, Lieutenant," I said. "Let Matt do it. For Christ sakes, Lieutenant, don't make us carry him. We're gonna get killed."

In the distance behind us, the violent din from the complex surged again.

"The Two doesn't need him, Lieutenant," I argued. "What the hell is one gook going to tell them we don't already know? We found what we've been searching months for and people are fighting their asses off."

It seemed like a long time passed before the lieutenant shook his head. "We don't kill prisoners," he said in a voice that couldn't be heard beyond Matt and me. "We'll carry him in. One stick, Doc. To keep him quiet. Just one, understand?"

"Yes, sir," Matt said quietly. "But even after that he could still yell."

———

Four Marines lugged the wounded NVA on a makeshift litter to the edge of the big paddy. The lieutenant scoped the area to our front. Broad fields and long paddies, flat, the entire area flanked by long ridge lines dotted with scrub and trees. The hills were too far away for us to put out flankers, but they were plenty close enough for any NVA gunners up there to shoot us when we tried to cross.

Mangan looked at his map, studied the area through his field glasses. Either hill could hide a lot of gooks. There was no good way to get across and no other way to get to where we could hunker down with some cover while we waited for an extract. The lieutenant plotted grid coordinates for potential artillery targets.

"Maybe they'll shoot covering fire for us as we go across," Cloninger said.

I looked at the open distance we had to cover within range of those ridges. It was a thousand times longer than the riverbed where we'd slaughtered the gooks. "They'd be shooting nonstop for hours, Buzz. It's going to take forever for us to get across there. Longer with that fucking gook."

We both knew there wasn't a battery going to shoot any place but into the complex. Please God, don't let there be gooks on those hills.

Fullerton had point. In the mud, it was almost impossible to look for trip wires, odd variations in the earth, anything that might mean we were walking into another minefield. He didn't bother to look for ambushes. Booby traps or land mines he might find and avoid, but it was too far across the open expanse to tell if anybody was waiting on the other end, and he couldn't do anything about the hills on our flanks. The rest of us were watching those hills.

In the open, the sun broiled the small bits of strength we had left. We moved slowly. Even so, walking right behind Fullerton, the lieutenant had to slow him down several times because the four men carrying the litter couldn't keep up, struggling through the mud.

Twice in thirty minutes Mangan brought the column to a halt. The teams carrying the litter set it down in the mud more gently than they wanted, fearful the wounded man might scream in pain and all hell would blast down from the hills to our flanks. Each time we switched litter bearers, the rest of us stood in place and stared through our sweat and the shimmering heat at those hills while a new cluster of four picked the litter up out of the mud. Then we all walked and stumbled and sloshed forward, cursing in frightened, furious whispers.

As fearful as I was, as focused as I was on the hills on either side of us, I couldn't stop thinking of John. As we pushed forward across the open space, I sometimes touched the hilt of his knife on my hip, felt his beads I'd taken off and put in my pocket so I wouldn't lose them. His kabar and his rosary were all I thought I had of him.

Our column stopped again. I pulled my rosary out from beneath my shirt, stared at the empty cross on my beads. *Where the fuck were You when we needed You? Look who's missing now, God. You. You and John. Did You really need him more than I do?* It is stunning to think of how I begged God for help and cursed him at the same time.

We began walking again. I stared up at the menacing hills off to both of our flanks. For some reason, I began to call a roll of the dead in my head. Maybe I was convinced I would be joining them soon. John. Willie. Smitty. Harding. Gio. Woody. Dasmund. Glass. Carlton. Ogala. Even Havey and Ladoor and that pissant engineer sergeant, whatever his name was. John's tremulous statement to the lieutenant during the battle at the big ville came back to me. *They're killing all my friends.*

My thoughts jumbled and tangled and freewheeled into a mess. John's smiling face came to me again. I half wondered if I was going mad. I squeezed my eyes shut to try to erase the pictures of John floating in front of my face. They would not disappear. I shifted the machine gun from one shoulder to the other. My hands were a foul maroon.

I jumped at every sound of a splashing boot, a muttered oath, a jostled weapon or piece of equipment. My hatred of the man we were being forced to carry increased with each noise we made. *They'll hear us,* I thought. *They'll find us all clustered up, and they'll squash us like worms in the mud.*

The Buzz walked behind me, in front of the litter bearers. I winced at the sucking sound my boots made every time I took a step. Behind me, Cloninger stumbled; his M16 banged against one of the ammo boxes he carried. I turned and glared at him. There was a silent apology written on his face, fear in his eyes. Blood seeped from beneath the bandage on his chin, spread along the creases in his neck. I looked past him at the wounded NVA. *You bastard*, I thought. *John wasn't enough? You're going to get us all killed?*

I began walking again, cursing the splashing noise I made.

A long moan rose from the litter. I spun and glared at the stretcher bearers as though I expected them to prevent the noise. From a front corner of the litter, Lee glanced hopelessly at me, then searched the surrounding hills with huge, terrified eyes. At the front of the column, Lieutenant Mangan studied the ridgelines through his binoculars. I sloshed back to the wounded NVA. The litter bearers set him down, trying not to jostle him into making more noise.

I stared down at the NVA's closed eyes. *A man's got to make choices, Mick,* John said from some place far away. "You'll get us killed," I hissed. "One more fucking sound, and I'll cut your throat!"

He was young, maybe my age, his eyes squinched shut against his pain, his mouth a thin slice of agony. Someplace under the surface of my thinking, how many faces like that had I seen? I could feel a tremor begin in my own. "We just want to live," I whispered. "You'll get us all killed."

My hand was shaking as I fumbled around my web belt where John's kabar and my canteens rode. I glanced back up the column. The lieutenant was shooting an azimuth to one of the hills. Everyone else stared at the ridgelines on either side of us as though they expected them to erupt.

I remembered something else John said in my early days in the bush: *Sometimes it takes more than guts to do what we must; sometimes it takes a very different kind of moral courage to make the right choices out here.* I looked at Matt and Cloninger as I fumbled at my belt. I didn't want more of my friends to die.

The wounded man spasmed in pain. His eyes flew open and I saw the fear and confusion I'd seen so many times before. His lips reluctantly parted, the cracked tip of his parched tongue squeezed slowly out. *Do not let him scream, God. Please. Do not let him yell, he'll get us all killed.*

"Choices . . ." I whispered. "I want us to live."

A bolt of pain or fear flashed across the NVA's eyes; his lips drew back in an agony-snarl. His mouth began to open wider, as though he were about to scream with all the strength he had left.

I found what I'd been reaching for on my belt. "Please don't scream," I whispered. "Please shut the fuck up."

My hand shook as I brought my canteen to his lips.

28

The ELEVEN OF US MADE IT back to Hoa Binh. We were all that remained of First Platoon. Matt, the Buzz, and the lieutenant were sent to Da Nang to have their wounds treated. Mangan's was bad enough that he was ordered to Okinawa to recuperate.

For several days, the eight of us who hadn't been wounded, at least physically, rested and ate and slept and took care of weapons and gear. I was too numb to find pleasure in hot food, warm showers, and canvas cots. I slept as much as I was permitted but even then couldn't escape my anger and guilt. Could I have kept John out of the minefield? Gotten to him faster? Prevented Harding from crawling after his goddamned helmet? When will they send us back to the bush? I didn't want to go back to face more bullets and booby traps, but I wanted to kill gooks to avenge my friends. I knew, though, that even heaps of gook corpses would never make up for them.

I heard First Sergeant Miller was rotating home, so I went to say goodbye before he left. The sign was there outside the tent.

BUSH BRAVO
WE COUNT THE MEAT

We had, but the price was way too high.

When I'd seen the Top in the bush a month before, there'd been a mischievous glint in his eyes. There was no smile in them anymore. I wondered if any of us would ever stop feeling damn near terminally sad. "You doing okay?" he asked. At the far end of the firebase, a battery of 155s opened up. The violent clap of outgoing artillery hung in the tent like ruptured church bells. More Marines in deep shit.

"It's not worth it, Top. All the guys we lost."

"It's an awful thing to lose friends," Top Miller began. "But let me tell you something, McClure. That complex was more important than you know. We killed a lot of NVA, seven, or eight, maybe more, for each of the Marines we lost. And we took a major staging area away from them, lots of gear and ammo and got some good intel, too."

His eyes hadn't left mine. I'm sure I didn't look convinced.

"But for what, Top?" I blurted out. "People in the villages don't even help us, and it's their fucking country. They're not worth Garafano or Gianelli or Corporal Harding or any of the others." I was inviting an ass-chewing, but I didn't care.

Top gave no indication he'd taken offense. "The Communists up north want to take over the free people down here. We're fighting Russia and China here, too, because this is where the Reds decided to turn the Cold War hot. People way above my pay grade decided we need to fight this war. They didn't get where they are being dumb."

First Sergeant Miller jabbed the air with his finger for emphasis, then he hesitated, and the look on his face told me he sincerely wanted me to believe what he was saying. "I'm not blowing party-line-perfumed smoke up your ass, McClure. I'm telling you what I believe, man to man, Marine to Marine."

I didn't say anything. I'd heard all that bullshit before, still wanted to believe it, maybe. But all I could think of was John and Harding and Willie and Smitty and all the others we'd lost. And I'd be damned if I could figure out why.

Maybe Top didn't expect me to respond. There seemed to be even more conviction in his voice when he continued. "What I believe even more, McClure, is that it's absolutely worthwhile to be part of a group of men willing to go in harm's way when our country tells us it needs us to, even knowing some of us will die. It's worth being a Marine. Very few men can claim that."

The company clerk, a twice-wounded rifleman from Third Herd, came into the tent with three new guys in tow. The scar on his neck looked like a purple noose. Maybe the Top only chose clerks with visible scars so new guys could see what they were in for. One of them gave me a quick, guileless smile. Like Willie looked when he hoped someone would be friendly to him. I gave him a quick nod, but I didn't smile. I didn't know if I ever would again.

First Sergeant Miller stood up. He looked at the new guys without smiling. "Welcome to Bravo Company, men. You're joining the best rifle company in the Marine Corps. You have a lot to live up to. I'm sure you will."

The Top turned and stuck out his hand. "I've got work to do here, McClure. Thank you for coming by."

"Thank you, Top. Have a great trip back to the World, sir."

"I'll do that," he said. "Keep up the good work in the bush." He gave me a hard look then, but there was kindness in his eyes. "Think about what I said. Only a few of us get to be Marines. People at home are going to respect you because you've done things most of 'em can't."

I wasn't convinced I'd make it home, but I didn't say that.

———

When I was wounded, everything that happened right then must've taken place in three or four seconds. Every one of them is expanded and freeze-framed in my mind.

It was our second day back in the bush, blazing hot before noon. My sunburned face and neck and hands felt like I was in a broiler.

Between the open halves of my flak jacket, my sweat-soaked utility blouse was plastered to my chest. I wore both John's and my beads around my neck.

I walked between Cloninger and Landon as we approached a ville on line, the M60 cradled on my hip, ready to shoot. A scrawny dog barked at us. Nothing else moved in the ville. To the side of the hootches, a water buffalo lowed a serrated moan. I heard a baby cry in the center of the ville; that meant people weren't down in their bunkers. No fight here, I thought just as an NVA popped out of a camouflaged hole to my front as though he'd materialized out of thin air.

His bullet hit just beneath my collar bone, punched its way through, clipped ribs and my shoulder blade, and lodged partway out of my back. I saw his face just before I fell. He was screaming at me, but I heard nothing except Landon's M16 explode twice in my ear. Two perfectly round holes appeared like extra pupils above the gook's eyes as the air behind his head filled with pulpy red mist. I never heard his AK-47.

———

Mom accepted my collect call from the hospital in San Diego. Her voice quavered as she told the operator, "Yes, oh yes. Of course I will." She had no idea then that I'd been wounded.

The operator said, "Go ahead, please" and I said, "Hi, Mom, it's me." She began crying. "It's okay, Mom. I'm okay."

She couldn't speak. I kept waiting, every once in a while, saying, "Mom? Mom? It's okay. . . ." For a moment, I thought the connection had dropped. Then I could hear Dad in the background, and finally he took the phone and said, "Marty? Are you alright?"

"Hi, Dad. Yes, I'm fine." I'd thought about how to tell them I was wounded without freaking them out. "I got shot in the shoulder, but I'm fine. I'm in the naval hospital in San Diego, but I'm coming home in a few days. . . ."

I checked my seabag through to Baltimore, then went looking for the gate for my flight to Chicago. Dress greens, new lance corporal stripes on my sleeves, my left arm in a sling that hid my ribbons and expert rifleman's badge. I lugged my duffel through the airport. My shoulder and chest ached, but at least no protestors had hassled me. In the hospital, I'd heard tales of vets, some in wheelchairs, being cursed, even spat on, but there weren't any demonstrators outside the terminal at 0530, and inside everyone simply ignored me, one more guy in uniform in one of the few parts of the country chock full of them.

The middle seat on the plane was empty. That was good, my arm wouldn't get jostled. A man in a suit and tie took the aisle. He glanced at my slinged arm but didn't look up at me. He opened his novel.

I didn't expect a hero's welcome, I wasn't that naive. But not even acknowledged? It'd only been a few weeks since I'd watched friends get killed or terribly wounded. Didn't anyone back here in the World even care about a wounded vet? How you doin', Marine? How's your arm? Nothing. I was invisible. I decided I wouldn't let it matter. *Tippecanoe and fuck you, too! I'm out of that goddamn place in one piece and headed home!* I tucked my head into my good shoulder and tried to sleep.

In O'Hare, I stood on a moving walkway heading toward the gate for my Baltimore flight. Despite the ache in my shoulder, I was in a great mood. Who cared if I was invisible, I was almost home. Besides, I'd never been on a moving walkway before. It was pretty cool.

A trio of girls moved toward me on the other conveyer. Except for uniformed nurses and the two gorgeous stews in their form-fitting uniforms on the plane from San Diego, how long had it been since I'd laid eyes on a pretty girl?

The three I spotted a ways down the belt looked about my age. As the walkways pulled us toward each other, they seemed like angels floating on an invisible cloud. Long, straight hair, two blonde, the one in the middle a brunette, laughing quietly among themselves. The brunette wore a miniskirt I swore wasn't much bigger than a belt. As they got closer, I saw all three were braless. *God bless America,* I thought, *it is good to be home.* One of the girls glanced at me, then said something to the others.

I smiled happily at them. *Oh yeah, McClure. It is so, so damn good to be home.*

As we drew abreast of each other, I was just about to say, "Good morning, ladies," when with drill team precision, all three flipped me the bird.

29

MOM LOOKED OLDER THAN I REMEMBERED; her dark hair was woven with gray now, and though she'd been slender before I left, she'd lost a lot of weight. She wore a crooked smile, and tears trickled down her cheeks as I came up the ramp. She studied my face, then glanced at my arm in the sling. Dad held her hand; I'd never seen him do that before. His hair was much grayer than I recalled. He smiled as though this were the best day of his life. I wanted to wave, but with one arm in a sling and the duffle in my other, all I could do was grin.

As I came through the doorway, Mom ran to me and threw her arms around my waist and buried her face against the uninjured side of my chest. I dropped the duffle and hugged her with my good arm as she cried quietly against me while people flowed around us. Dad stood behind her watching my face, a broad smile on his, his eyes filled with tears. When Mom finally let go, she still gripped my good hand while Dad came around her and leaned in and kissed me. He'd not done that in years. He kept rubbing my good shoulder, unable to speak. As I stood there, my parents holding onto me tight, I felt a joy, a sense of safety, I'd never recognized before.

When we got home, red and blue letters on a white bedsheet on the front of the house said: WELCOME HOME MARTY. Everything inside looked the same as I'd remembered—the furniture that had been there since before I was born, the faded rug with the cigarette burn in the living room, the shelves I'd made in high school shop filled with Reader's Digest Condensed Books, one of my parents' few indulgences. I only noticed two changes: my boot camp graduation picture now stood on the top shelf of the bookcase; it had been upstairs in my room when I left. Beside it was a plastic religious statue of a man in flowing robes I didn't recognize. "Who's the hippie?" I asked lightly.

"Saint Jude," Mom said. "The patron saint of desperate cases. He got you home."

I thought it was Landon and Matt, but I didn't tell Mom that.

———

Mom never asked me about the war, never uttered the word "Vietnam" in my presence the whole time I was home. She wouldn't watch any news about Vietnam, and if she were talking about something that occurred at home while I was in-country, she'd refer to that time as "while you were gone." The closest she ever got to even mentioning the war was on the Saturday after I came home.

I walked quietly into the kitchen after sleeping till nearly 11:00. Mom was bent over the counter rolling out dough to bake me a blueberry pie. "Good morning," I said, startling her. She spun to me, tears streaming down her cheeks.

"Mom, what's wrong?"

She put her arms around me, keeping her flour-whitened hands in the air, and laid her head on my chest, careful not to jostle my shoulder or arm. "I was so worried I'd lose you," she whispered.

———

Dad and I never talked about what I'd seen or done in Vietnam either.

A few days after I came home, I was helping him look for something in the garage. We'd been chatting about nothing in particular, when he said, "Marty, do you want to talk about what Vietnam was like?"

Probably much more quickly than either of us expected, I replied, "I'd rather not think about all that right now, if that's okay." That was the truth; I desperately didn't want to think about all I'd been through. What I didn't say though, was that I couldn't escape all the pictures that hung on the walls of my mind like grotesque paintings that made terrible noises in my sleep.

Dad's face showed concern and kindness. He'd lost weight too, and I'd noticed how tobacco stained his fingers were. Among the three of us, we went through four or five packs a day. "Of course," he said. "I understand. I'm pretty sure, though, it was a lot tougher than you let on in your letters. So, if it'd ever be helpful, just know I'm here to listen."

I wished later that I'd talked with Dad; he might've helped me deal with the loss of so many friends or make sense of what I'd done or become much sooner than I eventually did. It wasn't just Dad, of course; I didn't want to talk to anyone about the war who hadn't been there. How often have I looked back over that period in my life and realized help was there if I'd only known how to ask?

I had physical therapy several times a week at the naval hospital in Bethesda. On days I didn't, I slept in like a teenager. Mom took the bus to work; I drove Dad on days I needed to use our faded yellow Chevy Corvair to drive to Bethesda or run errands or go wherever I chose. What I really wanted was to go have a good time with Spence Burke. Since UVA was three or four hours away, I'd have to visit him on a weekend, when Mom and Dad weren't working and could plan around not having a car. Mom worried about me driving all that way with one arm in a sling. "But Ma," I argued, "with an automatic transmission and only three chipmunks in the rear propelling that car, how much trouble could anybody get in?"

"Don't 'Ma' me, young man. We're not the Beverly Hillbillies, you know." She snapped a dish towel at me. Then seriously she said, "I just want you to take care of yourself."

"I do, Ma," I said. She snapped the towel at me again.

"I think Marty's smart enough to know what he can and can't do, Peg," Dad said. "With that arm in a sling, he isn't going to try anything he shouldn't."

I stifled a laugh. Smart enough not to do anything I shouldn't do. Some contrast from what he thought when I dropped out and enlisted.

When I didn't travel to Bethesda, I mostly lazed about. I savored the peace and quiet and mundane comforts of home and tried to forget Vietnam. Food in the fridge, a soft couch, lots of TV. I didn't watch much news. I didn't want to be reminded of the war, or hear pundits and politicians debating it. President Nixon said he was going to end the war, achieve peace with honor, withdraw American troops as soon as the ARVN were capable of taking over.

I hoped desperately that "peace with honor" was going to be much more than a politician's phrase. Otherwise, what would John and Harding and Willie and Smitty and Gio and Glass and Woody and Carlton and all those other guys have died for? Why would Jackson and Corrigan and Prevas have lost their legs? I still couldn't figure out what could make their sacrifice worthwhile, but I was damn certain nothing would if the North Vietnamese had their way.

Despite wanting to forget Vietnam, I craved news of the platoon. I wrote to Matt and Cloninger and Landon but heard nothing back. I worried that they'd been killed or badly wounded. One evening I got home late after a Bethesda appointment and asked about mail.

"Nothing for you today," Mom said.

"Expecting something?" Dad asked.

"I wrote to a couple guys in the platoon. I'm just sort of anxious to hear from them."

A brief look passed between Mom and Dad. "You know, the round trip between sending a letter and getting one back can take three weeks sometimes," Dad said. There was no accusation in his voice. But I realized for the first time how terrible it must've been for my parents waiting to hear from me, particularly when I was too busy or exhausted or despondent to write for days.

"I'm sorry I didn't write more."

Mom put her hand on mine, tears in her eyes. "You're home now," she said. "Everything's fine."

Dad just smiled that peaceful smile he had. "I know you were busy," he said. He would've forgiven me anything now.

My relatives threw a welcome-home party for me a couple of weeks after I got back. Aunts and uncles, a handful of cousins. Uncle Dennis and Aunt Catherine were my favorites. They were in their late thirties, with kids in grade school. Dennis had been a Marine rifleman in Korea, though I'd never heard him talk about the war. They were at the front door when we arrived. "How you doing?" Dennis nodded at my slung arm.

"Good," I said.

"Good." He had a knowing, mischievous look in his eye. "You ready for this mob?"

"It'll be good to see everyone."

Dennis smiled and gave a half-nod, like he knew about something off kilter I hadn't discovered yet.

Catherine gave me a kiss. "I'm so glad you're here," she said. I complimented her on her short, curly hairdo. I liked Catherine; she'd always been the life of the party.

I looked forward to seeing all the relatives; it was flattering to have them come together to welcome me home. Everyone joined Mom, Dad, and me in the living room. I got a lot of awkward, careful hugs and handshakes; no one wanted to hurt my shoulder. They were glad I was home; a couple said they were proud of me, and several said they'd prayed for me. One or two of my younger cousins asked me how Vietnam had been. I got away with saying only,

"Hot days, wet nights, cold food, and all the dirt and mud you could want." Questions were mostly about my wound: Did it hurt much now? How long before I'd be out of the sling? All well-meaning and concerned and appreciated by me. And good to get out of the way early on as we all said our hellos.

People were starting to spread out a bit, refresh drinks, mingle, help themselves to food, when Uncle Gene asked, "What happened to the Charlie that shot you?" He took a gulp of his martini, hooked a thumb in his waistband and sort of tilted back on his heels giving him that self-important look some men of little consequence can affect.

I was so surprised by the question that I blurted out, "My friend killed him, I guess."

Mom flinched as though she'd been slapped.

"Good," Gene said, oblivious to anyone's reaction. "An eye for an eye, give 'em no quarter, is what I always said. That's how we did it in the islands, I'll tell you that." He finished the martini. He wore a self-satisfied expression, as though he'd just imparted a gift of great wisdom while pointing out he'd won World War II in the Pacific by himself.

I didn't know what to say. It was hard to think. The picture of an NVA's angry face with two sudden holes in his forehead and a red haze backlighting his head flashed through my mind. Uncle Dennis came to my rescue. "Marty, let me buy you a beer." We moved to Uncle Harry's study, where the bar was set up. Harry was an OB/GYN; his shelves were filled with medical books, and obstetrics journals were stacked on his desk. I remembered I'd been wanting to ask him a question for months.

Dennis handed me a cold Natty Boh. "Don't mind Gene," he said. "Sometimes he's a jerk."

I nodded. I didn't dare speak. All I wanted from this party, from my time at home, was some peace and some good times. I didn't expect I'd feel so angry, but I was boiling inside.

Dennis smiled; he seemed to study my eyes as though he'd found proof of something he knew was in there.

Harry came into the room. "You two reading medical journals these days? Some of them will keep you in stitches." He laughed at himself.

I said, "Uncle Harry, can I ask you a serious medical question?"

Dennis raised his glass. "Have at it, you two. I'm hightailing it before Harry dons his gloves."

"Of course, Marty," Harry said, smiling and nodding toward my arm in its sling. "But I warn you, I deal in lady parts and babies, you know."

"Luckily, I don't need advice on that." I forced a smile. "It's not about me; it's about somebody I knew. I've always been troubled by what happened after he was wounded."

It was months after Jackson lost his legs, but despite all I'd been through since then, I still thought about him. Two perfect, bloodless grooves in the hamstrings of a big, muscular guy, and you cut off both his damn legs? Why in God's name did they ruin his life? All I could imagine was some overworked doctor screwing up.

Uncle Harry studied me as I explained all that. I needed him to make sense of something I couldn't accept.

When he answered me, he seemed sympathetic, but spoke with a certain clinical lack of emotion. "I'm not a surgeon," he said, "but I know something about traumatic injuries. I've sometimes assisted when a pregnant woman's been violently injured."

Harry ran long, perfectly manicured fingers through his wavy silver hair. For a moment I thought of John's fingers, how he'd had almost an obsession about keeping his nails clean. And of how they'd been caked with Willie's blood at the end.

Harry explained that traumatically induced wounds, particularly from something as powerful as an explosion, can force debris you don't even see very deep internally, destroying tissue and arteries and causing tremendous damage not visible outside the body. He felt certain that was the case with Mike. "The doctors must've concluded they had no choice but to amputate to save his life. If they didn't, he probably would've bled internally in a way they couldn't stop in time, or he'd develop sepsis that would likely have been fatal. I'm so sorry for your friend, Marty," Uncle Harry said. "But I think the doctors had no choice, and they saved his life."

He was probably right, but it still made me angry and bitterly sad. I wondered again whether Dottie had left Mike yet.

I was surprised when Uncle Dennis and Aunt Catherine left early, claiming she was tired. I said I was disappointed to see them leave. "Enjoy yourself; it's your party, pal." Dennis winked. "Just stay away from John Wayne, I mean, Gene. Let's get a beer next week; it would be good to catch up." He gave me that studying-my-eyes look again.

Most of what people had to say the rest of the evening was just pleasant small talk: the latest movies, favorite comedies on TV, a good book, the Os and the Colts. Stuff of no consequence at all. But several times, the conversation turned to things that appalled me: Aunt Mary so aggravated by a broken appliance, how angry Uncle Gene had gotten at the poor service at the Chevrolet dealer, how upset Aunt Dolores was by the inability of the cleaner to get a stain out of a favorite dress.

What the fuck is wrong with you people? I fumed to myself. *Do you have the slightest goddamn idea what's really important? If you knew about Pius John or Gio or Woody or Corrigan or Mike and Dottie Jackson, or any of thousands of other guys, you'd be ashamed of your pissant concerns.*

I wanted to shake people, yell at them, make them understand. But I hid my anger instead. The party was for me, after all, and these were my aunts and uncles; I was supposed to be grateful, and in some ways, I was. Still, I found myself drawing inward, talking less as the evening went on. I was more than ready when Mom thought my silence was due to the pain in my chest and suggested we leave.

The following week, Dennis waved me to the bar from the stool where he sat. "Baltimore's best," he said to the bartender as I approached.

"The beer or the boy?" The florid-faced man behind the bar looked like a walking advertisement for Brylcreem, with a full head of white hair that didn't extend over his ears.

"Both," Uncle Dennis said. "Pull a Natty Boh, Sam, for my nephew, Lance Corporal Marty McClure, United States Marine, just home from 'Nam."

"Semper Fi," Sam said. He wiped his hand with a towel, then stuck it out. "Spent a little time in the Crotch, myself."

"Sammy was on Guadalcanal," Dennis said.

"With the old breed," the bartender said putting a tall draft in front of me.

"No kidding," I said. "That had to be tough." *How cool is this?* I thought to myself. Marines from three wars, all having a drink together. These guys had fought in legendary battles, Guadalcanal and the Chosin Reservoir, and they were treating me like part of their special fraternity. I guessed I actually was. I hadn't thought about that since I'd talked with the Top.

Sam glanced at my sling. "Most of them are," he said. He pointed at Dennis' empty glass.

"One more. I've gotta drive home."

"Afraid you're gonna pee in the car?" Sam asked. Over his shoulder, I saw a carved Eagle, Globe, and Anchor on the wall. The wood shone like a well-oiled rifle stock. He put a clear, fizzy drink in front of my uncle.

Dennis raised the glass. "And to you, Sam. Or is that 'up yours'?"

"Gin and tonic?" I asked, nodding toward his glass. I thought of Uncle Dennis as a beer-drinking man. I used to marvel at how many he'd consume at family gatherings to no apparent ill effect.

He held it up as though he were examining it. "Tonic," he said. He looked at me and smiled ruefully. "When Catherine had breast cancer, I told God I'd give up booze if he'd take care of her."

Behind the bar, Sam nodded. "Damn near put me out of business."

"She doesn't know. Only Sammy does. And now you."

"Aunt Catherine had cancer? When?" I was suddenly scared for her, and for him. She couldn't have been thirty-six.

"Last spring. May, June."

"Why didn't anyone tell me? Did Mom and Dad know?"

"Of course." Dennis smiled. "They didn't want you to worry; you had enough going on."

"Is she okay? She looked great Saturday night." They didn't want me to worry! I thought I'd been doing Mom and Dad a favor by not writing about things I'd seen or done. It never occurred to me they might be shielding me, too.

"Doing fine, thanks. Scared me half to death, but they believe they got it all. We're planning on her being fine going forward." He raised his glass.

"Hear, hear," said Sam.

"Wonderful. I'll count on that." I clinked my bottle against Uncle Dennis' glass.

"Speaking of Saturday night," Dennis said. "You do okay with the crew after I left?"

I shrugged. "Some things were a little hard to take."

He nodded as though he understood.

"It's pretty damn tough to give a shit about how inconvenient it is to have somebody's toaster go on the blink." I was surprised how angry I sounded. But it'd only been a few weeks since I'd looked into my best friend's lifeless eyes. Didn't my aunts and uncles have any clue there were much more important things to be upset about, for Christ's sake? "Sorry," I said to Uncle Dennis. "I didn't say anything to people at the party, but I was pretty pissed off by the time we left."

Dennis nodded. "No need to apologize. We've all been angry like that. It gets better the longer you're home."

"He's right, Marty," Sam said, "No need to apologize." He gave a little laugh—more like a snort. "When I got home from the Canal, I got in so many fights, smashed up so many bars, I had to finally buy one myself just to have a place where the owner would let me drink."

Sammy lifted a highball glass to the light and examined it. He had a gleam in his eye. Dennis and I both laughed a little at his story, but I guessed it was close to true.

"What's Uncle Gene's program, anyway?" I asked Dennis. "Did he win the war in the Pacific single-handed?"

"He was an Army supply sergeant on Kwajalein. After the battle. Gene never heard a shot fired in anger." Uncle Dennis had a disgusted look on his face. "It's the ones who saw the least who seem to talk about it the most. Guys like us . . ." he made a circle of himself, Sam, and me with his finger, ". . . we don't talk about it much, except sometimes with other guys who've actually been there, even if sometimes we still think about it a lot."

"Amen, brother," Sam said.

30

O N A SATURDAY MORNING, I tossed a duffel in the Corvair and drove to Charlottesville to spend the weekend with Spence. As I drove, I enjoyed thinking about good times we'd had together, late-night bull sessions expounding our eighteen-year-old philosophies, double dates, alcohol-fueled parties after home football games. That all seemed so inconsequential now compared to things Pius John and I'd talked of and done. But, I decided, inconsequential could be good. A weekend on the Grounds with not even college-boy cares would be just what I needed, nothing but fun.

As soon as I thought those words, Willie's rubbery, muddled face contemplating R&R after Woody was killed popped into my mind. John told him Woody would've wanted him to have nothing but fun. Willie had repeated that like a mantra over and over while he waited for the chopper to take him out of the bush.

I gave my head a hard snap. *Get out of the bush yourself,* I thought as I tried to push away images of Willie and Woody and John. *Forget Vietnam, McClure. Have a good time.*

When I got to the UVA campus, I felt pretty conspicuous with my short hair and arm in a sling. I'd seen clips of other campuses on the news, mobs of kids yelling antiwar chants. "Ho Ho Ho Chi Minh, the Viet Cong are going to win." Screw them, I'd keep my distance. I wasn't looking for anything but a good time with Spence.

Nobody hassled me on my way to his dorm. It felt good to be on campus again. Everything seemed more impressive than I remembered it from only a year before. Maybe at eighteen I'd been too focused on finding myself—or the next good time—to appreciate the impression a beautiful university makes. Maybe, too, patrolling through villages of thatched huts for months had given me an appreciation of brick and marble and manicured lawn. Everything seemed bigger and brighter than before, the red brick buildings sturdier, the massive white columns on Alderman Library more stately. I had no doubt I'd be back in college again when my time in the Marines was up.

On the bulletin board inside the dorm, a draft-resistance fundraising poster showed Joan Baez and her two sisters sitting on a couch. Above their heads in large letters it said: "Girls say Yes to boys who say No." They were really good-looking girls. That hurt as much as the poster's message. I hadn't even kissed a girl in almost a year.

Spence's dorm room looked like a hurricane had blown through. Heaps of clothes, empty beer cans, books, papers, notebooks, shoes, dog-eared copies of *Playboy* and *Sports Illustrated*. I laughed out loud as I looked in through the door. Staff Sergeant Gilles would've had a stroke. Or butt-stroked the occupants of the room with that shotgun of his.

Spence bounded out of his chair. "Martin McClure, welcome back!" We shook enthusiastically. He turned to the other three guys in the room; I didn't know any of them from my freshman semester. "This is my old high school buddy I've told you about, Marty McClure." He pointed to each of the other boys in turn. "Jim Barton, my roomie; he's from out in Roanoke. Tom Newton, Richmond. He could go home for lunch if he wanted."

"If his old man would let him," Barton said with a laugh.

Newton was slouched in a desk chair, legs splayed into the middle of the room. He shook his head, a disgusted look on his face. "An enlightened establishment type. He doesn't approve of long hair."

"And he's buddies with Agnew," Spence said.

"You don't choose your parents," Newton said. He was a big guy with the flaccid look of a high school football player who'd exchanged workouts for beer parties when he got to college. I wondered if he often wore that snobby look on his face. It didn't matter to me, nothing and nobody was going to get in the way of my fun.

"And this is Phil Trappini, our own New York Eye-talian," Spence said. I hoped my smile hadn't gone crooked. Behind Phil, I suddenly saw Gio snarling in the dirt.

Spence grinned. "One glance at that permanent tan and you can see why we call him Nig."

Jesus H. Christ! Smitty and Glass and Ladoor and Havey all paraded past my eyes. *Nig! Goddamn!*

Newton interrupted my apparition. "So you're the bad-ass Marine Spencer's told us about." A sarcastic tone in his practiced drawl seemed to be his specialty.

It took real effort to keep a smile on my face. I glanced at Spence. The dozen or more letters I'd asked him to save contained details I hadn't shared with anyone else, even Mom and Dad. I hoped he hadn't broken his promise to keep them private. Spence shook his head slightly, as though reading my thoughts. Whatever he'd said to his friends, I guessed he hadn't let them read my letters.

I looked at Newton. Hovering behind him I saw a whole squad of ghosts. I didn't want any hassles; all I wanted was a good time. I kept my smile, though I could feel it stiffening. "Just lookin' to have some fun," I said.

"Ever kill anyone?"

I was dumbfounded. I'd thought that someday somebody might ask me that, but to the extent I thought about it at all, I guessed it would be another Marine, someone who hadn't been in combat yet. Now, a total stranger who acted like a punk had just blindsided me.

"That's none of your business," I said.

"You did, didn't you," Newton exclaimed. He had a lewd expression on his face, as though he was getting a thrill watching the freak in the circus tent. "You are a bad ass. How did it feel? I bet you liked it."

I could see a kneeling man in a dry riverbed jerking and bucking as though he were caught in a strobe illuminated by lead. I held my palms up. "Enough," I said. "That's a personal matter." I could feel my face flushing angry red. I never imagined anything like this.

"I bet the people you killed thought it was pretty personal, too. Were most of them women and kids?"

I saw an old, withered man with a dirty goatee, the muzzle of a machine gun pointed at his chest and piss running down his leg. Then I saw a parade of my dead friends. John and Corporal Harding, Willie, Smitty, Gio, Woody, more of them, all waiting to see what I was going to do.

I stood up, my hand clenched in a tight fist. I wanted to beat the shit out of the son of a bitch.

Newton stood, moved closer to me. "What the hell do you think you're going to do with that arm, boy?"

"I'm going to kick your ass." I moved in; we were only inches apart. He was a little taller and with all the weight I'd lost in the bush, probably outweighed me by forty pounds. But if we fought, he'd have to kill me to get me to quit.

"Newton, stop being an asshole," Spence said.

"C'mon, Newt, you're out of line," Barton, Spence's roommate, chimed in.

"I'm wasting my time," Newton said. He stepped around me.

I sat back down. My shoulder burned as though I'd thrust a hot poker through my chest. My right hand was shaking. I hoped no one could see it; I didn't want them to mistake rage for fear.

"Screw yourself, Spence," Newton said as he walked to the door. "At least none of my friends are baby killers."

It was all I could do to keep from following him down the hall and punching him out, but Spence grabbed my arm and asked me to stay in the room. Barton and Trappini left us alone. It took me a while to calm down. After I had, Spencer said, "Newt's actually a pretty good guy, just kind of intense about the war. I apologize; I didn't expect he'd do anything like that with a friend of mine."

"But he's that big an asshole with vets who aren't your friends?"

"Truth is, I guess I don't know. We don't see many of you here."

Many of you. My best friend since we were kids. I felt a chasm open between us that couldn't be closed.

It took me a while to relax, but Spence and I tried to have a good time together. We walked into town to see *Butch Cassidy and the Sundance Kid*. It was a great flick, but watching Redford being the wise guy, having fun, I thought of Woody, then I wondered if Dottie Jackson looked like Katherine Ross, and how long she'd stayed with Mike. Four weeks out of Vietnam, six away from the minefield and the battle at the big ville, I wanted desperately to have fun, but I couldn't escape the war in my head.

We went to a party Saturday night. No one confronted me, but even after I was four or five beers in, I realized what a low standard that was for having fun. People talked about parties and rallies, professors who would or wouldn't let them cut class, sports rivalries and musical groups. The things they talked so fervently about seemed to occur in a distant place where I'd been a boy a lot of lifetimes ago. I found myself silently screaming: *What the fuck's wrong with you people? Don't you know there's a war on and guys our age are getting killed?* They knew, of course, and some of them wanted to stop the war, or at least prevent it from impacting them. But I could no more relate to those people than I could to the stoned girl I made out with later that night. She ran her fingers back and forth in my short hair, then slipped mine under her panties. "You're some kind of monk, aren't you?" she whispered against my lips.

On the long drive home Sunday, I felt mournfully adrift. I'd gone back to my old campus looking for fun. What I'd discovered, instead, was that I'd lost my youth. As I drove, I found myself dwelling on all that the war had taken from me. My friends, my innocence, my tranquility. I questioned whether I'd ever find peace again. I realized I would not around people who didn't know what I knew. At least for a while, I needed to be around other young men who did.

A week later, when the doctor at Bethesda said he'd discharge me to temporary light duty at Camp Lejeune, I was glad to be leaving home again to be with Marines.

31

I WAS ASSIGNED TO THE CHIEF of staff's office in the headquarters of the Second Division, essentially a gofer for the officers and staff NCOs. Skate duty, despite some long hours. After the bush, that was a gift.

I met the general one morning not long after I started work. A handsome, silver-haired, impeccably turned-out man with a chest full of ribbons earned in three wars, he was responsible for twenty-thousand Marines spread from the East Coast and Caribbean to North Africa and the far reaches of the Mediterranean. He and the sergeant major were walking into the briefing room as I was coming out. I'd seen the general going in and out of his office but had never been face to face with him before. He always walked fast, like he had things to do and didn't like wasting time.

"How're you doing, Lance Corporal?" he said. His piercing eyes fell to the ribbons on my chest. "Who were you with?"

"Fine, sir. Fifteenth Marines, sir. Bravo Company, sir."

"Bush Bravo," the general said. He smiled, the way an eagle would look if an eagle could smile. "I commanded Fifteenth Marines in nineteen sixty-eight. Bravo was one of the best infantry companies in the Marine Corps. When were you in-country?"

"Last year, sir. Nineteen sixty-nine." I could see the sign in front of the tent.

"Where were you wounded?"

"In the valley, sir."

The general smiled again. "I meant what part of you," he said.

"Oh," I said, a bit flustered. I put my hand on my chest, under my collarbone. "Here, sir."

"You look good. Healed up okay?"

"Yes, sir. Fine, sir. Almost done."

"Good."

"Reminds me, General," the sergeant major said, "when you saw the doc last week, he say anything 'bout that shrapnel from Inchon workin' its way outta your leg?"

The general shook his head as though he were amused. He had three Purple Hearts on his chest. The sergeant major had two. "Said it sometimes takes time. Twenty years isn't enough." He chuckled like it was no big deal.

"Itches like the devil when it comes out, though," the sergeant major growled. He looked like a bulldog when he grinned; I half-expected his tongue to loll out of his mouth. "But hell's bells, General, if it weren't for the shrap metal I carry around, I might blow away in a breeze."

The general laughed out loud at that. The sergeant major must have weighed two hundred pounds, none of it fat. It was like watching a movie star share secrets with a bulldog the size of a small bear. Two old warriors, they had a rapport I could only imagine. I wondered if John and I would have ever been able to set aside the horrors, even joke about our war. I doubted it. I didn't know if I'd ever finish searching for the peaceful part of my soul.

The general focused on me again. "Glad to meet another man who's served in the Fifteenth Marines," he said without smiling. "You'll be proud of that the rest of your life."

I wasn't so sure.

I hadn't been in North Carolina long when a storm roared up the New River and slammed into the barracks where I was asleep along with a couple dozen other Marines. Fierce, jagged flashes of light, the crash and roll of thunder. I hugged the polished linoleum deck, low-crawled away from my bunk, frantically searched for my fighting hole in the dim light of the squad bay. The only saving grace in my embarrassment when I finally stood up was that I wasn't the only guy who had scrabbled like a crab on the floor.

My dreams came in all shapes and sizes and relations to truth. Most times, I couldn't point to any given event that triggered a nightmare, but it wasn't hard to figure out where they came from. Except for the ghost dream, though, the friends I'd lost rarely appeared in any of them. Maybe that was because they were so often in my thoughts during the day.

A dream I had for months seemed to be a metaphor for all the gruesome pictures I carried in my head. A large, murky picture, a muted still life like a faded Renoir. A helmet, camouflage cover soiled and faded by months in the bush, four bullet holes in a line from the crown to where the left ear would be. The terrible sharp *whap* of bullets hitting metal. A short distance away, a pile of damp matter resembling hamburger gone bad—mottled grays, streaked red throughout, vapors rising from the small heap. When I could finally force myself to turn away from the picture, I'd come awake drenched in sweat, a bitter, metallic taste on my sore tongue.

Now that I was around other Marines, I didn't feel as angry as I had been. It was as though we all marched to the same muffled beat. Except for a few random dates, which were more about sex than anything, I didn't have much contact with civilians for months. I thought for a while about reenlisting just to stay in that womb but over time decided there were other things I wanted to do with my life. Maybe I'd try to go back to UVA.

The spurts of anger I'd felt seemed to be replaced by moments of guilt. I wondered again if I could have saved John, kept Harding up close to the dike, been as nice to Willie as Woody was, gotten Ladoor to come closer to the shore, warned Havey to never shit outside our lines.

Why I'd lived when my friends had died haunted my dreams as well as waking thoughts. Sometimes I dreamt of row upon row of body bags, like a black plastic version of the markers in Arlington. Some bags were packed full, others only in part. Some appeared to contain almost nothing at all. A solitary man in jungle utilities walked slowly, as though examining them. He stopped, looked down, an empty body bag at his feet. The man was me.

———

The dream that disturbed me the most for a dozen years began at Lejeune and has come to me, in one form or another, over the decades since.

Silence, an absolute vacuum of noise. Then a faint, distant sound, the continual *whup-whup* and *thrum* of rotor blades, a muted tremor of cries. A shroud of blue-gray fog, or smoke, perhaps. Dense, impenetrable, secretive, it swirled slowly, enveloped everything within sight. The faint, acrid smell of gunpowder and fire. Wet, stifling heat that evaporated suddenly, leaving in its place a void of such brittle cold, I felt stripped and naked before the eyes of the six figures who stepped from the silent, swirling pall.

I knew those young men so well, though the dream had transformed them. Their faces were pale, faintly lustrous. They wore faded, stained camouflage jungle utilities. Their uniforms were torn but clean, pressed and starched, with perfect military creases centered on each breast pocket and each leg of their trousers. They wore no hats or helmets and carried nothing in their hands, which, like their faces, were nearly translucent, except for their fingernails, which were radiantly black. Lacquered, or maybe, stained. Their jungle boots were dark but faded, caked with dried, gray mud from their thick rubber soles to their tightly laced canvas uppers.

On line, the Marines advanced toward me as the distant sound of helicopters pulsed like a heartbeat. The ghosts kept step with that cadence and with each other. Their eyes never left my face.

Then they stopped and looked at me from only paces away. Back then, none of them spoke, and I couldn't tell if they accused me or congratulated me for making it home. I worried about that for a very long time.

I bought a beat-up, faded-red Dodge Dart for two hundred dollars from a Marine deploying to the Med. It drank oil the way a staff sergeant guzzles beer, but the Smoking Strawberry got me some evenings and weekends to the beach where I'd walk by myself for hours then sit in the surf hoping the saltwater washing over me would fade the merciless pictures I couldn't escape.

Sometimes, if I had a ninety-six-hour pass, I'd make the seven- or eight-hour drive home to see Mom and Dad. They were always thrilled to see me, and vice versa, though I worried about Dad. He was only in his fifties but had developed heart problems, and I could see that the worry over that and their medical expenses had further aged Mom. They never complained about that or anything else to me, though they did sit me down one weekend for a talk.

Mom, who usually tried to be lighthearted around me, looked nervous. Her hands fidgeted in her lap; her hair seemed to have gotten even more gray. Dad looked at me with a mixture of embarrassment and chagrin. He'd lost weight; I braced myself for bad news.

"Marty, we know you want to go back to college when you get out of the Marines," he began. I wondered if they wanted me to come home to help take care of him.

"We've always wanted to help you out," Dad said. "We never expected we'd have so many medical bills."

"Dad, it's okay . . ." I started to say, but he shook his head.

"Our insurance hasn't covered a lot. We've had to take out loans."

Mom looked like she might cry.

"It kills me to say it," Dad continued. "But I don't see any way to pay for your college now."

I wasn't really surprised. It seemed to me they barely had the money to keep the aging Corvair alive. "Dad, Mom," I said, "it's really okay. I'll go to Maryland, I'll get in-state tuition, and I'll have the GI bill." Thank God, Dad would be okay.

Tears leaked down Mom's cheeks.

"Really," I said. "It'll be fine. Everything's going to be okay."

***

I made several friends while I was at Lejeune, though nobody I've stayed in touch with since. I thought I'd want to talk a lot about the war there, seek answers to all the questions I had or at least the comfort of knowing I wasn't alone in my turmoil. It turned out I was wrong. You don't talk about what's going on in your soul to people you don't really know, even if they look a lot like you. Still, just the rough camaraderie of other Marines was a small comfort in itself. Even if we didn't talk about it, those of us who'd fought knew we had something in common no one else shared.

***

I finally got letters from guys in the platoon.

The Buzz had thirty-seven days left on his tour when he wrote. Bravo was in a different part of the valley, Cloninger said, but it was mostly the same. "Nothing as traumatic as the big ville or after," he wrote, "but the shorter I get the more trepidation I feel." I wondered if he'd finish reading that dictionary before he got home. I lost touch with him after that.

Landon didn't write much more than he talked. "I'm okay. Mostly same, here. Be glad to go home. Hope you're good." He signed it, "Blessings, Virg." When I saw Gnat's Nuts again, at Lejeune, he wasn't really okay.

We met at the enlisted men's club. When he got several beers in him, Gnat's Nuts was damn near loquacious. He asked me if I ever thought about the men I'd killed. Landon was several beers in; I'd had a couple. The question startled me. I hesitated, then said, "Not much. I think more about all the friends we lost."

Landon was quiet for a while, then ordered another beer. "Dead people line up like it's roll call or something." He slurred his words slightly. "Sixteen of 'em, I know for sure." He drained half his glass, shook his head. "Dunno how many more I couldn't confirm."

"I think we both killed a lot. It was our job."

"The Bible says, 'thou shalt not kill.'"

"Well, I'm sure damn glad you killed that gook that shot me before he got off another round."

Landon lifted his glass in salute. "I'm glad you're not dead, Mick." He finished his beer. "But it's a commandment. I've sinned a lot."

"Killing people trying to kill you isn't a sin." I'd sinned plenty, I knew, but I didn't count killing gooks. Father Mullin hadn't either, I remembered, that day he'd heard my confession on the hill.

Gnat's Nuts held up two fingers to the bartender. I let it go; I could nurse part of one more. "I see a lot of their faces," he said.

If I wasn't careful, I could see faces of some of the enemy soldiers I'd killed, too. The man on the hill, the kneeling gook. The smashed-in gunners at the big ville when John and I finished. But I didn't need to waste my brain cells on them. I saw too many faces of dead friends. Landon knew all those same guys—Why wasn't he focused on them, instead of a bunch of damn gooks? I was getting pissed. But then I thought of that NVA with the two sudden holes in his forehead. Gnat's Nuts saved my life. Whatever was going on in his beer-addled head, I wasn't about to attack him.

"I think all the time about the Pope," I said. "And Corporal Harding and Willie and Smitty and Gio and Woody and Dasmund and Glass and Carlton and a bunch of others. And Jackson and Cavett and Corrigan, and Fizzy and that Irish kid with the shrapnel in his face. And there's more. But mostly it's the dead guys I was closest to I can't get out of my head."

I'd started off calmly, but as I listed our friends, my anger increased. "I don't have any fucking room in my head for a bunch of dead gooks I didn't even know, and oh, by the way, who were killing our friends and trying like hell to kill us." The left side of my chest felt like it was on fire.

"I know, but I broke the sixth commandment."

"Jesus Christ, Gnat's Nuts."

"Please don't say that."

"Don't say what, for Christ's sake?"

"You shouldn't take the Lord's name in vain. And I don't want to be called 'Gnat's Nuts' anymore. I'm ashamed of that."

"Ashamed? You saved people's lives."

"I took people's lives. That's wrong."

I clapped him on the shoulder. "C'mon, Virgil. Bottoms up. I've got to go to work in the morning. I'll give you a ride back to your barracks."

It was the least I could do, even pissed off; the man saved my life.

Matt and I kept in touch once he was home. He was stationed at the naval hospital in Portsmouth, Virginia, where he not only did all his work at that crowded place but took a lot of courses at Old Dominion in his off hours. He wanted to finish college and go to med school when he was discharged from the Navy. I hoped he would. It would be the start, or maybe the second act, of a tremendous medical career.

One weekend in May 1971 I had a four-day pass, so I threw some civvies and a case of beer into the Smoking Strawberry and drove to Norfolk. I told Matt I'd heard that Lieutenant Mangan had a company in Sixth Marines, and about Landon ending up in the brig at least once. Matt said Doc Dorsey was out, back in Idaho working for the phone company—a place, Dorsey explained, that had nothing to do with medicine and where people rarely got hurt. Neither of us knew about anyone else in First Platoon.

Matt looked good. The scar on the side of his face wasn't grotesque in the least. It gave him a bit of a rakish look he didn't deserve. We were sitting on the beach when he said, "It's been a year and a half, and I still think of what we did."

I'd had a few beers by then, had half a toot on; I think Matt had been nursing one can. I thought of how desperately he worked to save so many Marines, some of the time under blistering fire. "You were the best, Matt. A lot of guys owe you a lot."

He shook his head. "I should've done more. And there's certainly stuff I wished I hadn't done."

"C'mon, Doc. That's bullshit. You were the best."

Matt waved dismissively. "I'm talking about other stuff. How really decent guys did some of the things we did or threatened to do."

"Yeah. I've thought about that, too." I thought about the wounded NVA we'd been forced to carry, Matt's offer to finish him with a couple extra hits of morphine, how, scared and angry, I'd threatened to slit his throat. I sometimes wondered whether God would forgive a good man for doing something that in normal circumstances he would know was depraved. "It was war," I said, though that didn't seem like quite enough explanation of what I knew we were both thinking about.

"You can only push a man so far before he'll do things he couldn't conceive of before," Matt said.

"There it is."

"Both good and bad," Matt added. "I work with a lot of guys at the hospital who weren't there. I tried to tell a couple of them how crazy things, people, can get in the bush. They get a look in their eyes, like they wonder whether something inside you's about to go off."

Matt lit a cigar. The front of his Zippo had an EGA engraved on it. On the back, it said: "For those who have fought for it, freedom has a flavor the protected never taste."

He studied the lighter a minute. "Good guys," he said. "We shared some tough times with some really good guys. Too many of them didn't come home."

That's all I remember of us talking about Vietnam, though Matt did ask if he could see my scars. He studied them, probed their craters and ridges with a professional touch. I remembered him kneeling beside me in the dirt, bullets snapping around us, as he bandaged my wounds.

"The surgeons did a really good job," he finally said. "Damn lucky the gook who shot you didn't aim a couple inches to his left."

"You did a really good job," I said. "Inches, seconds. So much of what happened to us was so random."

Matt nodded. "I'm never going to leave anything I can control to chance again."

———

I ran into Sergeant Gilles at Lejeune not long after that. He'd been promoted to gunnery sergeant by then. We were in the PX late one Sunday morning; he and his family had just come from chapel. I almost didn't recognize him at first. He was in a tan suit and white shirt and sported a bright blue tie, shiny cufflinks, and tan-and-white shoes polished to a high gloss. He looked like a preacher leaving an A.M.E. church. When I came around the aisle, he was laughing and holding his little girls' hands. They appeared to be about five or six years old. He had a handsome young son too, a couple years older than the girls.

Gunny Gilles was happy to see me. The last time I'd seen him was the day I was wounded. By that time, he had nineteen tacks hammered into the stock of his shotgun. I remembered he put three in after the dried riverbed. Probably more after the big ville. I guessed he added more after I left. I wondered if that had been enough to avenge his brother.

The Gunny introduced me to his wife, Adelaide. "Please call me Addie," she said. She was pretty and soft-spoken with gentle eyes. She exuded calm around her husband and children, even when she made her son stop galloping up and down the aisle slapping the flanks on his imaginary horse.

"Lance Corporal McClure and I served together in Bravo Company. He was one of the good guys," Gunny Gilles said.

I thought that was a class thing to say: *we served together*, instead of something like, *McClure worked for me*. I was flattered too when he told his wife I was one of the good guys. *There'd been so many*, I thought.

The Gunny seemed genuinely happy and content, two words I'd never have associated with him in our prior lives. I wondered if he ever had nightmares or saw dead faces of Marines during the day like I did. I doubted he still saw the faces of the men he'd killed at such close range. When he thought of his brother or the Marines of First Platoon, he couldn't have had any of Landon's angst over his enemies' deaths.

I wondered, too, if Addie knew about the shotgun. I guessed not. Some parts of our lives are difficult to explain.

32

THE CHIEF OF STAFF ASKED me to step into the small conference room between his office and the general's. I rarely spoke with Colonel Branfort. I didn't need to; I got my assignments from one of his staff. I glanced at Sergeant Riker, my eyebrows furrowed. *Have I done something wrong?* He looked down at his desk.

I was surprised to see the division chaplain there. He looked very somber when he shook my hand. Senior officers didn't generally shake hands with enlisted men they were introduced to. *If the two of them want me to deliver a package,* I thought, *why didn't they just have Sergeant Riker or one of the lieutenants tell me to do it?*

Then it rushed at me like an RPG—Dad! He'd had a heart attack. Dear God, please let him be okay. A jumble of thoughts flooded my brain. I have to call Mom to see if he's okay. Can I use a phone in the office for a personal call? Who do I talk to to get emergency leave? God, it will take me seven hours to get home, even if there's no speed traps.

"Marty, sit down please," the Chief said.

Why would he tell me to sit down? *Oh Jesus, it must be Dad. No, no. How does the Chief even know my first name? Oh God.*

Colonel Branfort stayed standing across the table from me, his eyebrows knitted as he leaned in. It was like staring at a rottweiler tensing to lunge. *Dear God, please let Dad be okay.* Out of the corner of my eye, I could see the chaplain watching me, as though he expected me to do something but didn't know what.

"There's no easy way to say this," the Chief said, "so I'll just tell you straight out."

I went all icy inside. *Please God please don't let him tell me Dad is dead. Please, Jesus, please.*

"Last night, both your parents were killed in a car accident."

I clung to the table fighting to stay upright in my chair.

After the funeral, I drove back to Lejeune in a daze. Thoughts and pictures formed in my head, swirled and bumped against each other, ruptured and vaporized, and then, sometimes seconds, sometimes hours later, reassembled and churned again through my mind.

Mom and Dad hadn't stood a chance. The drunk came tearing over the rise in the wrong lane and hit the Corvair head-on. He got cuts and bruises and a couple broken bones.

"I can tell you they didn't suffer at all, Marty," Uncle Harry said. "I hope you can take some small comfort from that."

A pair of shiny coffins I wasn't allowed to look inside of. *What's better,* I said to myself with tears half-blinding me as I drove, *gut-shot or blown-up?* What had someone said after Woody was killed? A closed coffin means no chance to say a real goodbye.

I remembered very little else about their wake and funeral. The cloying smell of flowers, more people at the funeral home than I would've thought Mom and Dad had known. Uncle Gene was surprised I was in a suit. "In my day, we would've worn our uniform." *Fuck you, Uncle Gene.* Having only a few minutes to talk with Matt, who'd driven all the way to Towson from Norfolk but had to return for the late-night shift at the hospital. Uncles and neighbors as pallbearers.

I'd gone to Maryland National and Equitable Trust a couple days after the funeral to find out the balances on my parents' mortgages and took Dad's paltry insurance check to Commercial Credit to pay off their loans. I hadn't known how in debt Mom and Dad were.

I was grateful to Uncle Dennis and Aunt Catherine for taking charge of selling the house and giving away the furniture and everything else. I couldn't use anything that wouldn't fit in my locker in the barracks. The only things I took were Mom's photo albums, Dad's cufflinks, and a double-frame picture of them on their wedding day and their twentieth anniversary, the year before I went to UVA and then Vietnam. They looked so happy in both. Driving back, I remembered that morning in the kitchen when Mom leaned against my chest and sobbed, "I was so worried I would lose you."

So goddamn random, I thought as I drove, tears coursing down my cheeks. A Wednesday night. They'd been to a movie; they never did that during the week. A son of a bitch pickled in vodka at 9:00 p.m. on a weeknight. Both cars on York Road at precisely the same moment in precisely that spot. What are the odds? Life makes no goddamn sense. How can you be fourth in line and trip a booby trap?

33

I WAS SURROUNDED BY SHADOWS for the next several months. My Vietnam dreams didn't stop, and when I lay down at night I worried I'd have nightmares about crashes and vehicles on fire too. Thankfully, I never did. Instead, I saw Mom in her garden or baking pies or, a couple of times, reading to me when I was young. I saw Dad asleep in his chair, the Os or Colts on the TV, an open book in his lap, or I watched him raking leaves in the yard, or skiing with me. Sometimes, when I dreamed of them, I'd wake up, my face wet with tears. But despite the violence of their deaths, I was never horrified by dreams about them.

Maybe it was because I could grieve for Mom and Dad. People in the chief's office cut me slack, let me go off to the beach even during the day sometimes those first weeks when I needed to be by myself. None of them, at least the captains and lieutenants and sergeants, the younger people on the team, had lost a parent before.

I couldn't ask for slack when I thought of my dead Marine friends. All of us there were in similar boats. The aftermath of Vietnam was different from losing Mom and Dad, at least I thought then. A terrible time but something I simply had to endure, just push through. Like a firefight, a booby trap. Pull yourself together and move on no matter how many nights the ghosts march through your dreams.

I missed Mom and Dad terribly, but my memories of them were happy ones. The pictures in my head of my First Platoon friends were anything but.

Father Mullin was with Eighth Marines. He'd extended his tour in Vietnam, then when the Marines left was transferred to the Second Division and got himself assigned to a MEU headed off to six months in the Med. When 2/8 came home in the winter of '71, he wangled his way into another infantry battalion working up for another Med float. I heard he'd just gotten back to Lejeune, so I went to see him.

I told myself I was going simply because I respected him so much. I think I was really looking for help. Sort of like when I'd gone to confession in the valley after we'd been through hell and I'd been so angry and scared I'd nearly shot the old man. I wasn't angry or scared any more, and I had nothing I wanted to confess. But I needed help.

The priest's office was spartan, not much larger than a cell. Behind the beat-up metal desk, there was a crucifix on the wall. On one side of it, a picture of a drill instructor, face straining in barely contained rage standing nose to nose with a recruit. In very large print, the recruiting poster said: WE DON'T PROMISE YOU A ROSE GARDEN. Beneath that, in smaller print: The Marines Are Looking For A Few Good Men. On the other side of the crucifix was a nine-by-twelve photo of Michelangelo's *Pietà* that Father Mullin had gotten in Rome on the float.

He jumped up from his desk and shook my hand as though I were a long-lost younger brother. "Irish!" he exclaimed. "Darn, but it's good to see you!" It'd been over two years. I wondered if the man remembered every Marine he'd ever met.

Mangan had told him about Mom and Dad. We talked a little about the accident and how I'd been doing since then. "I'll keep them, and you, in my prayers. Sometimes I can't figure out what God's thinking," the priest said.

He was pleased to hear my wound had healed well, only bothered me a little on cold rainy days. I didn't mention that it seemed to burn deep inside when I thought about my friends. He was glad to hear I was going back to college.

We talked about people we'd seen since we got back to the World. We agreed Mangan was an officer on his way to the top. Gunny Gilles had been on the chaplain's first float. The priest shook his head. "Pretty tough for him, I'd guess. Home with a wife and three kids for only a few months and his company goes to the Med for six. Never complained. That's one staff NCO who's a pro."

I told him about getting together with Landon a couple times before he was discharged and went home. "'Gnat's Nuts' people called him, right?" Father Mullin said. "That man could sure shoot."

I didn't tell him Landon was ashamed of the nickname now. I was certain I knew the chaplain's position on that.

"I know the last several months have been damn tough after losing your parents. But how're you doing otherwise?" I knew he was asking about post-Vietnam.

How're you doing? That question again.

A disjointed tirade careened through my head, like that time he'd asked the same thing once in the bush. All my dead friends. All I thought we'd fought and so many died for made a mockery of in the daily news. Americans protesting the war now in droves. Vietnam vets throwing their medals on the Capitol steps. A Catholic priest charged with conspiring to kidnap the national security advisor and blow up government buildings.

If you believed the news, vets were all long-haired, bearded, drug-addled losers or worse. An army lieutenant named Calley who slaughtered women and kids by the dozens had become the symbol of everyone who served.

Congress passing resolutions calling for an end to the war. The Pentagon Papers, proving that our own government lied to us from the start. South Vietnamese generals saying their own government is so corrupt that democracy in their country has no chance. President Nixon claiming Vietnam is strong enough that American forces can leave, but when the ARVN go into battle the NVA kick their ass. The whole fucking thing is going down the tubes, and on too many days I see pictures of Pius John's dead, milky eyes, or Gio screaming silently in the dirt, or Woody in the grass. I ask myself what they died for and I come up as empty as the helmet just beyond Harding's reach.

How've I been, Father? To all outward appearances, I'm fine. But inside, I'm all kinds of fucked up, the worst I've been at any time in the two years I've been home from the war.

I didn't say any of that. Instead, I said, "It's been okay, Father. But I think I'm ready to go back to school." I forced a smile.

The priest chuckled at that, but there was concern in his eyes. "You'll do great."

We talked about his time with the MEU. Father Mullin had loved going to the Mediterranean for the first time. He described pulling young Marines out of bars in Naples and Istanbul before they got thrown in jail or worse. "Sometimes you have to protect knuckleheads from themselves," he laughed. He loved seeing Rome for the first time, going to mass in Saint Peter's. He saw me glance up at the picture of the Pieta.

"Do you know that sculpture? It's Michelangelo's masterpiece of a beautiful, youthful Mary holding her dead son draped across her lap. An amazing work of art," Father Mullin said.

"No, I don't," I said. My voice cracked.

I stared down at my hands. They began trembling, and then there were tears streaming down my face. The dam I'd tried so hard for so long to keep my emotions behind had cracked open as I looked at the sorrow Michelangelo had depicted so powerfully in Mary's face.

I thought of Mom. *I was so worried I would lose you.* Then John's mother, I imagined her dressed all in black, sitting on a hard chair in a funeral home in Chicago having just lost her beloved only son. I imagined Gio's parents in New York, both in black too, his mother dabbing her eyes with a handkerchief embroidered in purple, Mister Gianelli standing beside her, emaciated and stooped and devastated, a cigarette drooping from the corner of his mouth. I thought of Woody's parents in Delaware and Willie's in Vermont and Bonnie

Harding and baby Hope and Corporal Harding's mother and father, and Smitty's folks, all of them in black. Every one of them less accepting of their grief than Michelangelo's Mary.

I hadn't cried since some time after Mom and Dad died. I didn't want to cry in front of the priest, but I couldn't stop.

Father Mullin came around the desk, closed his office door and stood behind me, his hands on my shoulders. "I'm sorry, Marty," he said quietly. "I should have known after your mom and dad, that might've touched a raw nerve."

I stopped crying, spent and ashamed. "I'm sorry, Father," I whispered.

"No," he said. "It's okay. Really, it's okay."

"Marines don't cry," I said.

"Bullshit. Pure bullshit, Irish. We all cry at one point or another." He moved around in front of me and sat on the edge of his desk, facing me close.

Something inside me opened up then. "It's not just Mom and Dad. It's Pius John and Gio and Corporal Harding and Willie and Smitty and Woody and so many others who're always someplace in the front of my mind. There are times when it's like a gallery in my head of technicolor pictures of how horribly they died. I have no idea why I'm alive and they aren't. And I can't figure out what makes any of that worthwhile."

I rambled. It poured out of me. Finally, I stopped and sat slumped in the chair, drained and embarrassed and ashamed of what I'd just done in front of the priest. His eyes hadn't left my face. He understood and believed every word I said.

He went and sat back down in his chair. "They were wonderful young men," he said. He remembered Gianelli's purple glasses and the letters he wrote, how we'd called him our big bang junkie. "And Pius John Garafano," the chaplain said. "Naturally, I liked his nickname, the Pope. A good man. A heart full of love."

"That was John," I agreed. But we'd all changed by those last few weeks, too, I thought. I didn't say that. Father Mullin already knew a lot about the darkness that came over us in the bush.

He remembered the others we'd lost, too. Smitty and Dasmund, Glass and Carlton, Ogala. He remembered Corporal Harding and Bonnie and Hope. "Hope, what a wonderful name. We all need hope, no matter what bad shit life gives us. I have faith that God will take care of Corporal Harding's wife and daughter. I heard she remarried. I'm glad for that."

I didn't say anything, just stared at the top of that battered, gray metal desk. I didn't know how much real hope I'd ever muster again.

"I remember Willis." The priest laughed out loud, a happy laugh, nothing mean or belittling about it. "One for the books. Not the brightest bulb in the chandelier, maybe, but a good man in his own way."

"That was Willie," I agreed. "You couldn't help but sort of love him like a big, old dog."

"I shouldn't admit this," the priest said. His smile made him look like a conspiring leprechaun. "But part of me's happy for him that he got to have a good time on R&R before he died." He shook his head as though amazed at the admission. "Between you and me? I think God forgives Marines who've been in the fight for blowing off steam if they get a chance. I'll tell you one thing for darn sure, though. I would not have performed the sacrament of holy matrimony for Willis and that girl he met in Bangkok in a million years, unless maybe she swam all the way to the U S of A just to be with him."

I actually laughed at that.

He remembered Woody, too. "The really handsome guy, reminded me of that movie star, Redford."

I had to almost physically push the picture of Woody at the end out of my head.

"Really good guys," he said. There was tremendous kindness in his eyes. "Good people, good Marines. We should remember them, always." He paused for a moment, then went on. "But the truth of the matter is we'll go crazy if all we remember is what we lost, Mick." He held his hands out then. I remembered how he looked saying mass for us inside the perimeter out in the bush. "We've been given a gift, guys like you and me."

I could feel my eyebrows knit into a puzzled frown.

"We've been given the gift of life. Too damn many of our friends had that for too short a time. Why the good Lord gave us and not them that gift, we don't know. But one thing's for sure. How we use that gift, what we make of it, that's our choice. We can focus on the bad things or on the good."

I listened without responding. Coming from anyone else, that would have been bullshit. From Father Mullin, it sounded like a statement of fact. He looked me in the eye for a moment, then he went on.

"I don't kid myself, or certainly you, Mick. Focusing on the good memories instead of the terrible ones seared into our souls, is a lot easier said than done. But every one of those guys we've been talking about would rather we remember the really good things about who they were, the best parts of how they lived, not how they died."

"I don't know how to get rid of the terrible pictures my brain took but won't erase."

Father Mullin smiled gently. "I don't want to sound too much like a preacher," he said. "I know, too late for that, right?" His eyes flashed for a second. "I don't claim it's easy. But how we use the gift we've been given is up to us. Focus on what was good. Choose happiness, my friend."

———

I tried. I tried to think of Woody dancing in the dirt with Jackson. Of John being the good-humored social worker to all the Marines in First Platoon. Of Gio cracking us up with tales of becoming pen pals with Agnes Goodbody. Of Willie reading comic books and absentmindedly fondling that filthy blue rabbit's foot. Of Harding displaying new pictures of Hope. I thought of people's bravery in battle. Of Woody going after Tich under fire; Harding with Dasmund; even Ladoor scooping Cavett out of the flooded paddy while bullets splashed all around.

It didn't help much. I still had the terrible dreams, the reminders of the blood and the gore. When I worked to push the daytime images of death and devastation away to focus on the good parts of my friends' lives, as Father Mullin suggested, I often ended up with an emptiness in me that collected despair. They had each been, I knew, a good man, who deserved to live, or if he was bound to die, to have sacrificed his life for a worthwhile cause. I tried to believe they had, but from what I saw on the news about Vietnam, I often felt I was deluding myself.

I had no trouble following Father Mullin's advice when it came to Mom and Dad. But when it came to Vietnam and the friends I'd lost, I couldn't make it work.

Then the lieutenant suggested another way to cope that eventually did, but it came with a price I wouldn't recognize for years.

Magnet was actually a captain by then. After rotating home from Vietnam, he'd commanded a rifle company in Sixth Marines, then a few months before my enlistment was up had become the CG's aide. His office was just down the hall from where I worked. Sometimes, if he wasn't terribly busy, we'd talk a bit. He was especially kind after Mom and Dad died.

One day, the captain told me he'd recently seen Corporal Harding's wife and daughter. Hope would've been about two and a half then. "Bonnie stayed in Jacksonville after Corporal Harding was killed," he said. "I looked them up when I got here." His smile widened. "She remarried a couple months ago. A sergeant in Tenth Marines, cannon cocker, seems like a good man."

"Did Bonnie ever ask you how Corporal Harding died?" I hoped she didn't know. What would you say about a Marine who was great in the bush but panicked, maybe because of his daughter, and got himself killed?

The captain nodded. "All the relatives I've talked with ask that, once they know you were there when their Marine died." He was a man who didn't lie. I wondered what he'd said. "I told Bonnie her husband died a hero assaulting a heavily fortified position it was important for us to take." Mangan's eyes didn't leave mine. "And that he died instantly, didn't suffer at all."

"Yes, sir," I said. He'd told Bonnie most of the truth. At least all that should be important to her. "I'm glad I haven't had to talk to anyone's next of kin." Despite what John and I'd discussed, I didn't think I could put myself through that. Particularly not now, with Mom and Dad gone.

The Captain shrugged. "I thought it was the right thing to do."

"How do you deal with the guys we lost in the platoon, sir?"

"What do you mean?"

I wondered if he thought I was implying that the men we'd lost were his fault. Nothing could've been farther from the truth.

"I can't get them out of my head. I keep thinking of how they died and what a waste it all is."

Captain Mangan studied me for a long moment. I looked away. I didn't know what I expected him to say. It wasn't like he had a wand he could wave to help me forget.

He began very quietly. "I lost sixteen men killed in our platoon. You didn't know them all. Some before you got in-country, a couple after you were wounded. I can tell you every one of their names, and I can tell you how they died. I lost another twenty-one who were wounded badly enough they never came back."

He looked across the room. I wondered if he could see them there. His eyes were no longer sunk in his skull like they'd been after the big ville and the minefield, but there was pain there.

"I'm telling you this, McClure . . ."

"I'm sorry, sir. I was thinking about what you said. So many . . ."

He shook his head, indicating it was okay. "I'm telling you this because I know you can relate, and because it might be useful for you to know how I cope."

"Yes, sir."

"I can't relate, very frankly, to how you feel about your mom and dad. I can't imagine. I've got no advice there, except maybe to tell you I hope you can focus on your memories of happy times with them."

I nodded. I think he knew I meant, *Thanks*. I didn't expect anyone could know how I felt.

"But, as far as the Marines I lost, I deal with that using boxes, McClure. That's all I've got. All *we've* got, I think. It works for me, most of the time. I try very hard to focus on what I'm doing now. My job, working out, even just having fun, a movie, a book, a date. I try to keep things in their compartments. Some overlap. But I can't do anything well if I'm thinking of how those Marines died." He shook his head, "As for whether their sacrifice was worthwhile, I sure hope so, but I don't think that answer's clear yet. I think we need to see how the South Vietnamese do."

He opened his hands as if to say: There it is, that's the truth, that's all I have. I remembered how all of us had put bad things in their own boxes in Vietnam, rarely spoke of the way people died, tried to push the terrible pictures out of our heads. It was the only way we could stay sane, do what we did day after day.

Somehow, that seemed different then.

"I see pictures in my head."

Captain Mangan nodded sympathetically. "So do I. But I try very hard to keep them in their own boxes most of the time, shut the lids, and lock 'em so I don't have to look at them all the time. So I can do everything else I need to do."

"I don't know if I can do that, Captain."

"You can. You just have to practice. It's like pushups; the more you do them, the better you get at it, the more you can do. Same thing for keeping the lids on boxes closed. Sometimes you need to push down really hard."

"Do you ever feel disloyal, disrespectful for doing that?"

"No," Captain Mangan said. "I think it's what they'd want me to do."

34

I DROVE THE SMOKING STRAWBERRY onto the College Park campus in the fall of 1972, a twenty-two-year-old freshman with a handful of credits from my one semester at UVA. On one of my trips to the cemetery, I'd half-seriously told Mom and Dad that I wondered if I still knew how to read or write after three years of playing in the mud. I planned to hit the books hard. Maybe to prove something to myself. Maybe I wanted to make Mom and Dad proud. I was pretty sure they were watching, at least some of the time. Maybe Father Mullin's admonition to make something of the gift of life resonated more deeply than I knew.

I intended my return to college to be a new start. I would get on with my life, let go of a past replete with unanswered questions framed in horror and loss. I had concluded that following Captain Mangan's advice was the best I could do. If I was going to have any peace of mind, I needed to put Vietnam and all of my dead or maimed friends in a box and close the lid tight. So I did. It was like turning my back on people I loved.

I'd rented a tiny apartment a short walk from campus; at twenty-two, I would've been the patriarch in a freshman dorm. Besides, I was far older inside than my years. I didn't make any close friends that first year, sort of withdrew in plain sight. But despite all the time I spent in the library, or in my apartment poring through books, I wasn't a monk.

I avoided anything to do with Vietnam. There were a few anti-war demonstrations my freshman year, but they diminished in size and volume once the withdrawal of American troops was complete in November, and after January, when the secretary of defense announced the draft was ended, the shouting faded to a mutter at most. I kept away from all that. I had a confrontation only once, and that was because I said something stupid to a classmate who hadn't been old enough to drive when I was in Vietnam.

Several of us freshman, including a girl I'd been with the weekend before, had been sitting in a student lounge waiting to go into a class. Someone mentioned the Paris peace talks. Henry Kissinger, the national security advisor who was the principal American negotiator with the North Vietnamese, had just announced, "Peace is at hand." I didn't know what that meant, but I still clung to the hope that friends' deaths in Vietnam had been worthwhile. If Nixon's promise of peace with honor was true, South Vietnam would remain free and maybe they wouldn't have died in vain.

Beth said, "Why don't you ask Marty what he thinks. He was in the war." She gave me a conspiratorial smile. "He was even wounded." For some weird reason, my scars had turned her on in bed.

One guy said, "No shit, Marty, how'd that happen?" The wad of gum threatened to jump out of his mouth as he spoke.

I didn't want to get into a discussion of the peace talks or Vietnam, and I certainly wasn't going to say much about myself or my wound. At least Beth hadn't let on how she knew. I shrugged. "Not much to tell. A gook popped out of a hole and shot me. I shoulda ducked." I hoped that would stop any more questions coming to me.

The words were barely out of my mouth when Ruth Silver exclaimed so vehemently it was almost a yell: "Gooks? They weren't gooks! They were fucking human beings!" She was about five feet tall and probably weighed all of ninety-five pounds; I half-expected her to jump out of her chair and kick my ass.

"I know," I stammered. "But we called them gooks."

"Well, you shouldn't have! They're people, just like you. Not damn gooks or some other demeaning name! Maybe better than you!"

God Almighty, I thought. *People just like us.* I'd argue about that, but I half-thought that if I did Ruth would fly across the table, all fury and fang. "It's just what we called them," I said weakly.

"Well, that was ignorant," Ruth said in a tone that indicated she was talking to a cretin. "It's demeaning and a disgrace. Do you call me a 'kike' 'cause I'm Jewish? Are African Americans niggers to you?"

The class before us let out and the others, who'd been silent in the storm, all gathered their books and walked out. Ruth gave me a look like she had napalm behind her eyes, muttered something about "fucking stupid veterans" under her breath, then I was alone.

Ruth was right, of course, though she could've made her point without attacking me. I'd no more call a Vietnamese a gook today than I would call a Jew a kike or a black a nigger or a Hispanic person a spic.

But John was right, too, when he poked his head out of his box as I followed her down the corridor toward class. "Pretty weak, Mick," he said. "When we were trying damn hard to kill each other every day, calling our enemy names wasn't something we were going to worry about. Or that you should apologize for, or regret, now."

I met Patti my junior year. On Wednesday, September 18, 1974, to be exact. I tell people I remember the date because that's when I met the love of my life. And that's true. But, while I don't mention the fact, I remember that date too because it was two days after President Ford announced his clemency program for draft dodgers and deserters.

The ghosts marched front and center toward me that Monday night for the first time in months. They emerged from a dense shroud of fog, marching in step with each other and with a cadence I could barely hear. They halted and stood staring someplace beyond me in silence, then each of them slowly shook his head in disgusted disbelief. For the first time, Corporal Harding spoke for the bunch. "Life has consequences, McClure. So, what the fuck?"

Monday and Tuesday were the toughest days I'd had since I was discharged from the Marines. I couldn't focus in class; when I should've been studying, I stared into space while a parade of dead and crippled friends marched slowly past.

I kept thinking Harding was right: life has consequences, but what price did those bastards pay? Break the law, refuse to serve, desert your fellow soldiers, and all it costs you is a few months of community service? What about the guys who did serve, who did the honorable thing and now lie in the goddamn ground or push themselves around in wheelchairs? I wanted to scream: What kind of values does this country have? But I had no one to scream at. All I could do was mourn the parade marching silently through my head.

I didn't sleep very much Tuesday night, even with the help of my friend Jim Beam. When I finally fell off, I dreamt of rows of poncho-covered bodies and bloody heaps of severed legs.

I woke up on Wednesday with a headache. As I drank coffee alone in my apartment, I told myself to get a grip. Two weeks into the semester, and I had a job to do. Boxes, McClure. Focus. Move ahead. I'd set my sights on a 4.0 semester and wanted it badly. Fortunately, I only had two classes that day: an 11:00 American lit seminar with Professor Ormandy and Professor Lister's 3:00 math class.

I loved Max Ormandy; Professor Lister was a different matter. He was the only professor I ever had who kept a seating chart. Lister's List. He had an ironclad rule: any class missed without prior permission would cost two points on the student's semester grade. If you weren't in your seat when he reviewed the roll, you were absent, even if you slid in one minute later. I'd never been late to his class and wasn't going to be that afternoon.

I tried to force myself to concentrate in Professor Ormandy's class that morning. If my attention wavered at all, the ghosts appeared whispering "consequences; consequences," shaking their heads in dismay. After class, I went straight to McKeldin Library to work for a few hours on a term paper. When Patti Marshall walked through the door in front of me, it was like watching poetry flow into the room.

She wore blue jeans and a sweatshirt with a red Maryland terrapin on the front, and her long blond hair was pulled back in a ponytail. She was a few inches shorter than me and moved with an athletic, feminine grace. The sweatshirt did not hide her figure. She was beautiful. She stood in the middle of the room looking at a small paper in her hand, then up at the signs above the doors to other rooms. No one else was there at the time, but I suddenly felt like a high school freshman at the teen center walking across the floor to ask a girl to dance. I remembered how wide a room could feel if I got shot down in flames.

"Can I help you?" I asked.

"Do you work here?"

"Too much of the time."

She cocked an eyebrow. "Well, maybe you can."

My God, what a smile. "What do you need to find?"

"This book on Steinbeck." She smiled again, a little embarrassed. "It's my first time in the library." She showed me the paper.

"One of my favorites."

"You know this book?"

I laughed. "No, sorry. I meant Steinbeck's one of my favorites."

"Thank God for librarians."

"Yup. But I'm not one. Come this way."

"You said you work here." She looked a little skeptical as I led her into the stacks.

"I'm a grind. I put in a lot of hours here."

We introduced ourselves. I found the book, then asked if she'd like to get a pizza and beer.

"Tonight? It's a weeknight. I have class tomorrow and a paper due, too." She had a soft, slightly husky voice that felt like velvet inside my head. I think I was already falling in love.

"Welcome to college." I held out my hands like I was a professor imparting some bit of wisdom. Huckster was more like it. How many weeknights ever found me doing anything but hitting the books? I gave her my best smile. "Ain't it nice to be free?"

Patti laughed, sort of, at that routine, but she looked pretty dubious. My God, she was pretty.

I didn't give her a chance to respond. "C'mon," I said. "Pizza and a beer, or a coke. We'll go early. I've got to hit the books tonight too. How about 5:00?" Lister's class finished at 4:30.

"Well . . . I guess I don't have any classes this afternoon."

"What dorm are you in?"

"Annie A, what about you?"

"I've got an apartment right off campus. We can meet in the lobby of your dorm. It's a short walk to the pizza place."

"That sounds nice. I could use a break from the freshman meal plan, and pizza shouldn't break my budget."

"I'll buy."

Patti shook her head. "Dutch treat."

"I don't mind paying."

"Nope. Dutch." She raised her chin. "What year are you, by the way?"

"Junior." I glanced at my watch, thinking of Lister's List. I thought I heard her whisper, "Daddy will kill me," under her breath.

"Why?"

She shrugged. "You have an apartment, and you look older than most of the freshmen I've met."

"Methuselah."

"Gesundheit." She giggled at herself. I laughed too. "Okay, five in my dorm lobby," she said. "But I absolutely have to be back by seven. Paper to write tonight."

"That's a plan. Five it is."

Patti looked out one of the reading room's tall windows. "Wow. It's pouring. And me without an umbrella."

"Take mine."

"You'll need it."

"I've got a poncho in my pack." I pulled it out, then started grabbing books off the table, cramming them into the backpack.

"Late for a class?"

I glanced up. Patti looked puzzled. The clock on the far wall said 2:45. "Sorry. Yeah. A crazy professor. I'll tell you about him tonight." I bolted for the door.

———

I walked very fast; the rain ran in sheets off my poncho, seeped down my neck, soaked my shirt. My pants were mud-splotched and drenched to my knees. Halfway to the math building, I wondered what'd possessed me to loan my umbrella to a pretty girl just because she'd agreed to go with me for pizza and beer. But I wasn't about to skip Lister's class, even if I'd be miserable sitting there in clinging, wet clothes. I'd spent plenty of days, and nights, soaked and cold with no hope that the next day or the one after that would be different. As I splashed along the walk, I told myself I'd be damned if a rainstorm was going to wreck my chances of getting an A.

In the downpour everything across campus was coated thick gray; I could barely see where I was going. For a moment, I was reminded of a twilight cloudburst in the bush. Harding slipped out of his box. "Deserters? Really, McClure? What the fuck?" *Jesus, Corporal Harding! It's not my fault.* I pushed the lid back down on him. *Focus, McClure, or you're going to be late.* I bent forward and began to jog down the sidewalk, my books and notebooks clutched beneath my poncho, my shoes splashing spray further up on my legs.

A figure came toward me through the gray sheets of rain. As we got closer to each other, I could see he wore some sort of helmet, a hard hat that a construction worker or electrical lineman wears. He walked slowly, leaning forward, as I jogged toward him.

I was only a few yards away when I saw that in one hand he carried some sort of short pole; from his other dangled a long, thickly bent object, maybe drawings or plans or something else wrapped in canvas or oilcloth to ward off the rain.

I stopped as though I'd been pinned midstride in place by the shards of lightning splitting the sky. I gawked at him as he continued to walk toward me through the storm. Then I bolted from the sidewalk and ran and slipped and splashed across the lawn and down the hill. The guy in the hard hat must've thought I was nuts.

I went into the little bar directly across the street from campus. I stripped off my poncho and dropped it in a wet heap just inside the door, then squeaked and squished across the worn wooden floor, past the unoccupied pool tables, the silent jukebox. I tossed my damp books and notebooks up on the bar, pulled my soaked shirt loose across my chest and shoulders, then wiped my face with a paper napkin.

A tortoise with a fierce expression on its face and a bright red M on its breastplate glared at me from the face of the clock across the bar. It was two minutes before 3:00 p.m.

"Filthy day," the bartender said.

I nodded.

I was into my fifth or sixth beer before I stopped hearing Prevas begging for his leg.

35

I STAGGERED OUT OF THE BAR SOMETIME that afternoon and to my apartment, where I lay down to rest my eyes. I didn't wake up until the next day. I was on my third cup of coffee at the kitchen table when there was a knock on the door. My head hurt. It was 9:00 a.m.; whoever it was, I didn't want to see them.

When I opened the door, Patti stood there, my umbrella in her hand. She thrust it toward me. "You forgot this."

I took it from her. She glared at me in my baggy sweatpants, unshaven, my hair looking like I'd combed it with a Mixmaster. It took me a half-minute to remember I'd stood her up. "I'm really sorry about yesterday," I said.

"Right. I guess that's what freshman girls should expect from upperclassmen."

"It's not like that. At least not with me. I mean . . . I'm sorry. I made a mistake. Something unexpected came up."

"Right," she said again. Even laced with sarcasm, her voice was velvet. "I can see that. You look like you got hit by a truck."

"Sort of," I said.

Patti turned to go.

"Do you want to come in? I've got coffee."

"Hell no," she said without looking back.

———

The next day I waited nearly three hours in her dorm's lobby before I spotted Patti coming back from class. "I'd still like to take you out for pizza," I said. "I owe you that much."

"No, you don't," she said. "We were going to go Dutch." She didn't sound angry, just matter of fact. "Thanks, but I don't think so."

———

I ambushed her in her lobby again several days later. "Look, really, I don't treat girls that way. I made a mistake and I want to make it up to you." Patti didn't say anything, but the skepticism in her expression seemed to mingle with curiosity.

"I know an inexpensive Italian place that makes authentic lasagna, just a block off campus. Let me buy you dinner, it's the least I can do."

"You don't have to. Dutch, remember?"

"I want to."

"Pizza, lasagna. For an Irish guy, you sure like tomato sauce."

———

Patti never asked why I'd stood her up, and I didn't know if I could trust her enough to tell her the truth until we were on our fourth date.

"I had something really weird happen that afternoon," I said. "Years ago, when I was in Vietnam, I had a buddy lose a leg." I suddenly hated that I said it like that. As though he'd just set it down somewhere, misplaced it, couldn't remember where it might be. The word did no justice to the violence with which life and parts of it were ripped from my friends. But what could I do? I sure wasn't going to tell her at dinner how Prevas begged us to put his sheared off leg on the bird.

Besides, she knew what I meant, she'd sort of winced when I'd said it. "I'm sorry," she whispered and put her hand over mine on top of the restaurant table.

"I hadn't thought about him much in a long time, but I saw a guy carrying something through the rain and I thought of him. I sort of freaked out. I ran away from him and next thing you know I'm in that bar hammering back the beers, and then I go home and lie on the sofa to rest up before meeting you and don't wake up until Thursday morning."

"I'm so sorry," Patti said.

"No, I'm the one's who sorry."

"Why didn't you tell me when I brought you the umbrella? Why not before now?"

I shrugged. "I didn't want you to think I was one of those drug-crazed Vietnam vets you read about in the paper."

"Are you?" There was mischief in her eyes.

"Well, I did take a lot of aspirin the morning you brought the umbrella to me."

Patti laughed. I figured then that we'd be okay. But she did have questions. She waited until we'd finished eating before she said, "How often does the flashback sort of thing, or whatever it was, happen?"

"That was the first time."

Patti sipped her coffee. She didn't say anything.

"It really was. I don't think it could happen again."

Patti didn't look convinced. "And . . . why couldn't it?"

I hesitated, then decided to just go with it. Or at least part of it. "It's not exactly table talk. Let me just say we had to find my friend's leg and put it on the medevac helicopter with him. It was hammering rain. The man I saw in the mist and pouring rain was wearing a lineman's hard hat and carried something big." I shrugged. "I think it's pretty unlikely that kind of thing is going to happen again, send me into a panic like that."

"I'm sorry," Patti said again.

"Why?"

"I'm sorry that happened to you. Both things. In the war and three weeks ago."

"Thanks. I'm fine."

Patti waited a moment, then said, "Do I need to worry about you being violent?" She looked me straight in the eye. Her expression was thoughtful but not worried.

"God, no." I knew there was a darkness in me capable of nearly unimaginable things. Hurting Patti was not one of them.

"I didn't think so," she said.

Saint Rita's cemetery unfolds in gentle undulations up the hill across the road from the small stone church with the sharp steeple where Mom, Dad, and I used to go to mass. White marble tombstones climb the slopes beside a hoary stone wall bordering the graveyard. On an unusually warm Sunday in late February, the five old sugar maples that stood like aging centurions alongside the wall were beginning to bud out, and the lichen coating the stones was beginning to green up. Mom and Dad's graves are on a small rise, where half a dozen markers sit peacefully in the overcast light. Patti and I stood quietly for a moment in front of my parents' gravestone. "So young," she said. "Your mom would only be forty-eight next month." She put her arm through mine and leaned in.

The drive from College Park had taken us an hour and a half. I told Patti I'd done it every few months since I'd gotten out of the Marines. "I call it visiting the folks. I guess I did it at first more out of a sense of duty than anything. But later, I found it brought me comfort. It's hard to explain. Kind of like I can talk with them here." I shrugged. "Some kind of weird Irish mysticism or something, maybe. I guess you think I'm crazy." We'd known each other five months then.

Patti squeezed my arm tighter and put her head against my shoulder. "Not crazy. Sweet, and thoughtful. Maybe it's helped you get over some of the hurt."

I told her then for the first time about Pius John and Woody and Gio and some of the others. Not detail about them, and certainly not about how they died, just that they had. "I cared about them more than I cared about anyone else. Except, I guess, Mom and Dad. But even that was different from how I felt about those guys. They were like brothers I never had. That's a cliché, but it's true."

"You've lost so much," Patti said softly. "You said it's sort of healing to come here, visit your folks. What do you do that helps you heal from losing so many friends?"

I didn't know how to answer that. I keep them hidden away, each in his own little compartment, my series of safety deposit boxes, so to speak. I keep the lids down tight on the boxes so the memories don't escape and come for me.

That's what I thought. What I said was, "Coping with the guys' deaths is more difficult."

Patti looked surprised.

"I just try not to think about them. I was right there when every one of them was killed. For a long time, I couldn't get the horrible pictures out of my head, even when I tried to think of all the good things I knew about each guy. So now I just try very hard not to think of them at all. Sometimes I feel pretty guilty about that, but it's how I cope. It took me a long time to get to that point."

Patti didn't say anything. She probably didn't know how to respond. She squeezed my arm tighter.

"Feels like it's getting chillier again," I said. "Want to head back? We could stop for a bite on the way."

"Okay." Patti's voice wasn't much more than a whisper.

I slipped my arm out of hers and put it around her waist then looked back at Mom and Dad's gravestone. "This is Patti Marshall," I said. "She's very important to me."

"I'm very pleased to meet you, Mr. and Mrs. McClure. Your son's very important to me, too."

I kissed my fingertips, touched them to the granite. "I love you guys," I said out loud. "I'll be back soon."

We started to walk to the car, then I stopped us and turned back toward Mom and Dad's grave. "If you see John and the other guys, tell them 'Hi.'"

It was hard not to think of the guys, try as I might. In the next month, Quang Tri, Hue, Chu Lai, and Da Nang all fell to the North. I wondered how many Marines died over the years defending those places. Boxes, I told myself. Put all this stuff in one the size of a goddamn packing crate, cram the lid shut, and focus on school and time with Patti!

That only worked some of the time.

The ghosts visited me a lot in those weeks. To the *whup-whup* and *thrum* of rotor blades, they stepped together out of the turbid pall and marched toward me, in step. Sometimes they just stood front and center and stared. One night, no one spoke, but Gio spit. It hung in the air like globular disdain. The night Da Nang went down, Pius John spoke for them all, a sorrowful chagrin on his face. *It wasn't worth it, Mick. It wasn't worth us at all.*

On April 23, 1975, President Ford gave a speech. Vietnam, he said, is "a war that is finished as far as America is concerned."

I had a feeling the war inside me would go on for a very long time.

Saigon fell on April 30. The last ten Americans in-country, Marines guarding our embassy until the end, were evacuated from Vietnam.

I felt sick to my stomach as Patti and I watched the news. Helicopters took off from the roof of the American embassy; Vietnamese who'd worked with us fell to their deaths from the skids. At the gates below, throngs pleaded for escape. Overloaded helicopters flew away from the city to American aircraft carriers off the coast, unloaded on the flight deck, then were pushed overboard into the sea to make room for more.

We sat on the couch in front of the TV, Patti gripping my arm. She gasped as a Huey went over the side of a ship then sunk reluctantly into the depths. "It's like a damn metaphor for America's involvement in Vietnam," I said quietly. I felt like I was watching a movie caricature of what our country had done to so many who'd served. I hadn't felt such despair, such loss, since Mom and Dad died.

Later, we walked to the pizza place not far from my apartment and sat at a table outside. I hadn't said anything on the way there. After we'd ordered a pizza and pitcher of beer, Patti said, "Do you want to talk, Marty? We don't have to, but I'm here if you want to."

"I don't think I can," I said. Up on the campus, I heard cheers from gatherings of students. I didn't know whether to be wildly angry or bang my head on the table. Why were they cheering? There was no victory, only defeat. What was going to happen to all the people we left behind? And why, dear God, for what, had so many Americans died?

A noise woke me later that night. It made no sense. No one in First Platoon sounded like that. A scared, pleading whisper—a soft, husky voice.

I was sitting upright, my back against the paddy dike, the map spread across my thighs, the handset up to my ear. I couldn't read the grid coordinates. Frustration and anger and fear coursed through me.

The noise sounded like Patti's voice, frightened, querulous, someplace off in the distance beyond the gunpowder- and blood-reeked mist. "Marty? Marty . . ." it whispered. "Marty . . . please."

I needed a medevac bird. Now! Immediately! Emergency! Stretcher bearers. Corpsmen. Why won't anyone help me? Sweet Jesus, how can I save them if no one will help?

"Marty . . . Sweetie . . ." She sounded closer now, whimpering, gasping. "Marty . . . it's okay. Please . . ."

Not now! No! If I can't save them, they're all going to die. Die for nothing, nothing at all. Please someone, please help me. I don't want to be all alone.

A brilliant flash of light. I tensed for the concussion, the roar, and the pain. My muscles knotted up tight; my body clinched into itself.

The light stayed on; steady, not pulsing or flashing like a gun or a bomb. I felt no hammer blow to my body, no pain. I heard no explosions. The only sound I could actually hear was the whisper, "Marty . . . please . . . sweetheart . . . It's okay . . . It's a dream . . ."

I stayed upright where I sat and turned slowly to my right. In the far corner of the bed, Patti sat, one hand holding the sheet above her breasts, her hair tousled and sleep-mussed across her face, down over her bare shoulders. She was reaching toward me with her other hand, afraid to touch me, surprise and fear merged on her face.

I took my hand down from my ear. Sweat-soaked and clammy, I sat naked and shaking against the headboard of our bed. I stared down at Patti's pillow on my legs.

"It's okay, Marty," she whispered. "It's okay, you had a bad dream."

She dropped her hand to the mattress, close to me, but not touching yet. The light on the nightstand beyond her hurt my eyes. I closed them and nodded at her. "I'm sorry," I whispered. The old bullet wound was on fire.

"It's okay, Sweetie. It was just a dream."

I nodded again, suddenly terribly chilled. I tried to catch my breath.

Patti took the pillow from my lap, pulled the sheet up to my chest. "You're soaked," she said.

"I thought your pillow was a map. I was trying so hard to get a medevac in. I was trying to save all my friends."

Patti rubbed my arm gently, moved closer to me on the bed.

"It was terrible," I said, my voice still a whisper. "People all around me were dying, but I couldn't get anyone to help. All my friends were dying, and I was going to be all alone. I couldn't get through to anyone on the radio. I couldn't do anything to save them, and no one would come. No one would help me."

Patti edged closer to me. She put her arms around me, laid her cheek on my shoulder. Her breasts were warm against my side.

"I'll always help you," she whispered. "Whatever you need, I'll always be there."

36

We WERE MARRIED IN THE UNIVERSITY CHAPEL six months later. Just the two of us, a few college friends, and Patti's parents and sister were there. Patti wore a calf-length white dress and fall flowers in her hair. Her parents didn't approve. They liked me okay the few times we'd met, as much as you can like a man six years older than your daughter whom she's known just over a year.

When we told them we were going to get married around Thanksgiving, they tried to talk us out of it. "You're only a sophomore, Patti," her father said. "Wait until you graduate."

"We don't want to wait, Dad. We're ready now. And it's not like I'm dropping out of college. I'll keep going. I'll graduate with the rest of my class."

"Ready now?" her mother exclaimed. "Patti, you're only nineteen."

"I know I'm young, Mom. But we've thought it all through. We're committed to each other. We're not going to wait. We'll make it work."

"What are you going to live on?"

"I have the GI Bill, and I work part time on campus." It was the first time I'd spoken in the conversation.

"That doesn't give you much," Mr. Marshall said.

"No, sir. But I'll get a full-time job after graduation."

"Why don't you wait until then?"

"We're not going to wait, Dad. I can work part time, too. I'm hoping you'll still help with my tuition."

"What if the job you get next fall is someplace too far away for Patti to commute to College Park?"

"Dad, don't worry so much," Patti said. "There are plenty of schools in the area Marty's going to apply to in the spring. We're not worried about that."

She was a beautiful bride.

I'd never been happier in my life. I tried to set aside the questions that gnawed at me about Vietnam and the impact the war had on me. For the most part, I was able to keep the lids on my boxes closed tight. I still felt guilty about turning away from my friends, but it seemed necessary to have the peace Patti and I deserved in our new life.

I was beginning to really focus on the future I saw for us. Patti was looking forward to her remaining years of college; I was raring to graduate in June and get to work. I was sporting nearly a straight-A average and had fallen in love with American Lit. I'd talked with Doctor Ormandy about a teaching career. I wanted to do something helpful to young people, and if my love of literature dovetailed with that, what more could I ask? I'd begun to dream of teaching in a private school. The students would be eager to learn the life lessons I'd help them find in the stories we read, and, with my great grades and dedication, the headmaster and my fellow teachers would be happy to have me join their team.

When I look back almost forty years later, I laugh at how naive I was. Still, I've gotten more than I hoped for from my career, even if I still suffer over what I did to get my job.

Early in March, I came home from a late afternoon class. We were still in the apartment I'd had since my freshman year. It was so tiny, I'd had to get rid of the bedroom door to leave enough room for a double bed. I could see Patti's legs on our bed as I came in the front door.

"I'm home," I called. "Eaten yet?"

"No."

Patti spoke so quietly, I barely heard the word. I went to the bedroom; she was staring up at the ceiling. "Are you okay?"

She shook her head. I knelt down beside her. A tear ran down her face into her ear. "What's the matter, P?" A range of possibilities zipped through my mind: bad day in class, a fight with one of her parents, some sudden illness, though she looked perfectly healthy except for her red eyes and nose. "Are you sick?"

She shook her head again and began to cry harder.

I took the soggy tissue out of her hand and put my face on the damp pillow next to hers. "Tell me, Sweetie. What's wrong?"

"I'm pregnant." She began to cry harder. I felt like I'd just had the wind knocked out of me. "How . . . ?" was all I managed to say.

Patti kept crying. "I knew you'd be mad."

"I'm not mad, just really surprised."

"I must've messed up the pills. I'm probably ten weeks along. Are you sure you're not really angry with me?"

"Honest, I'm not angry. Just worried. What will we do about your school?"

"I don't know; I don't care. I'm just glad you're not angry at me."

I could just imagine the conversation I'd be having with her father: "You've gotten my nineteen-year-old daughter pregnant? She has to drop out of school? Didn't I caution you about this?"

It took less time than I would've expected for us to get used to our news. Patti was first to decide to be happy about expecting a child, even though the baby would change her plans the most. She's always been ahead of me in seeing all the good in our lives.

I was worrying one night about what we'd do about her school. "Marty," she said, gently admonishing me. "You worry too much. It's pretty simple. I'll finish this semester and take a couple summer courses to build up my credits. Then I'll take a leave of absence from school. You'll get a good job teaching and we'll be careful and save as much of your paycheck as we can." She held up her hands as if to indicate how straightforward this all was. "When the baby is a year or two old, he or she can go to daycare and I'll go back and get my degree."

I put my hand on Patti's belly. It didn't feel any different to me yet. "Got it all figured out, haven't you Mrs. McClure?"

She gave me a kiss. "Our little family will be just fine. Count on it, Mr. McClure."

What we didn't count on was the trouble I'd have finding a job.

By late spring, with a wife and a baby due in the fall, I was just weeks from graduation but didn't yet have a job for the upcoming school year. Teaching high school English at one of the preps around D.C. or Baltimore was what I really wanted to do, but I would've taught first grade math at an inner-city public school if it meant I could support my family. I submitted my resume to several private schools. When I got any response, it was a form-letter rejection. I applied to public schools in all the counties near College Park and got nothing. I couldn't figure out why. My grades were stellar, and I was older and more mature than most students graduating with a teaching degree. I tried to hide it from Patti, but I was nearer to panic than I'd been at any time since I'd freaked out over the chimera carrying Prevas' leg.

Then Professor Ormandy called me into his office one afternoon. He handed me a slip of paper. On it was the name, John Stark Burden, PhD, Baltimore Country Day, and an address I assumed was the school's.

"Jack's the head of the English Department," Max said. "Young man, maybe ten years older than you. Really smart, really ambitious, really opinionated." The professor stroked his beard and smiled, amused by either Burden or his opinion of him. "He was one of my best grad assistants when he was a student years ago. I helped him get his job at Country Day. He could have been an excellent college professor if he wanted, but he really loves teaching the teenagers. Using literature to help form their thought processes, he says."

That's exactly what I want to do, I thought to myself. What I wouldn't give to teach with that man.

Max arched one eyebrow knowingly. "Actually, what he really loves is being a large fish in a very small pond. He demands a lot from the teachers in his department, but you wouldn't have any problem with that. He's going to have a teaching position open in the fall, freshman and sophomores, I believe." I stifled the urge to clap my hands. Professor Ormandy continued, "I told him I had a student I thought would be great for him. You have to make it through his interview, and, I suppose, be approved by the headmaster too. But if Jack wants you, I'm quite certain he'll get his way. The interview is important, but he said if I recommended you, he was sure you would be more than good enough for him."

The professor smiled in sort of a self-satisfied way. "If you're interested, all you need to do is send him your resume, and his secretary will contact you to schedule an interview."

Interested? I damn near wanted to hug Professor Ormandy. A decent salary and health insurance to cover our baby's birth? I'd been thinking seriously about applying for construction jobs; I'd dug enough holes in my life, and the chances of someone shooting me in one now were pretty damn slim.

"Thanks, Professor," I said. "That's the best news I've had in a long time. I really do appreciate it, Professor. I can't tell you how much."

"I wouldn't have given Jack your name if I didn't think you'd do a really excellent job."

"I promise, I won't let you down, Professor. I really appreciate it."

I've never told Patti, or Corrie, or anyone else, what Professor Ormandy said next. Or what I did in response.

I stood and stuck out my hand. We shook, then his smile faded, and he got a somber look on his face. "Marty, can I give you a word of advice I'm pretty sure you won't like?"

"Sure." I sat back down. I couldn't imagine what he could say that I wouldn't like. I'd dye my hair Marine green for that interview, if he told me it'd help me get the job.

"You've had no luck in your job search so far." He knew I hadn't even gotten an interview anywhere. It seemed a rather odd, unusually awkward, introduction to whatever the professor was going to tell me.

"No, sir. That's why this is so great. That, and that teaching at Country Day would be like my dream job."

"You'll have to get your master's, you know. Night school at Towson or Loyola or Goucher, I'd guess."

That certainly wasn't advice I wouldn't like. "Oh, yes, sir. I figured that. I'll apply to start in the fall."

Doctor Ormandy nodded. "That's not the advice I want to give you."

I waited for him to tell me what he wanted to say.

"Jack was very active in the peace movement, part of the antiwar crowd. Not just as a student; in the years since. Op-eds in the *Sun*, rallies in Baltimore, marches in Washington, all of that stuff. I doubt he's mellowed much since the war ended."

"Okay . . ." I guessed that meant I shouldn't tell war stories. I was never inclined to anyhow, and I'd learned to get along with antiwar types at school, even if I didn't like them much. I needed that job. If that meant not debating the war, that was my preference, anyhow. So what the heck. "I'll try not to push his buttons," I said halffacetiously. "I just want to teach English."

Professor Ormandy steepled his fingers in front of his chin. "I expected as much. But this is more serious, if you want that job."

"I do, Professor, I can promise you that. I need it with a wife and a baby on the way."

He looked at me, and he didn't blink. "I assume you have your Marine Corps service on your resume?"

I probably looked puzzled again. "Yes, sir. Of course."

"I would take it off. It would be a real negative with Jack."

My chest suddenly felt sore. I didn't know what to say. Or even how to begin thinking about that. It felt like I'd just been told to deny what—at least until Patti and our baby—had been the most important part of my life.

I must've sat just staring at the professor for some time. I knew there were a lot of people who didn't like vets. It seemed to me that any time a guy did something wrong, if he was a vet, that was in the news article's first line. "Marine Corps Veteran Robs Store," or "Army Vet Sideswipes Guardrail." I'd never seen "Man with Four Draft Deferments Convicted of Drunk Driving" or "Former War Protestor Embezzles from Bank." It pissed me off, but it'd never occurred to me that being a Marine could keep me from getting a job.

I didn't do anything with Jack Burden's address for the next couple days. I finally told Patti about Professor Ormandy's opening the door at Country Day. I didn't tell her what he said about my resume.

"That's so fantastic!" Patti actually clapped her hands.

"It's not a done deal, you know. Max thinks some Vietnam vets haven't had a lot of luck getting good jobs."

"That's so unfair. Does he think that's why you haven't yet?"

I shrugged.

"But Doctor Ormandy thinks you're a shoo-in with his recommendation, right? Just think, a steady paycheck and insurance. Teachers have good health insurance, right?"

"I guess they do. But I'm not a shoo-in. The professor just thinks I have a really good shot."

"Of course you do. They'd be lucky to get you."

I almost asked Patti's advice about my resume, but I knew what she'd say. Do what you think is best, what you think is right, Marty. You always do.

If only she knew.

I justified leaving my Marine Corps service off my resume by semi-convincing myself that all a school would really be interested in anyway was my college transcript, Professor Ormandy's recommendation, my grades. I made up my mind that I wouldn't lie; if asked, I wouldn't deny being a Marine. But fuck Jack Burden, if he didn't ask me about being in the service, that was going to be his problem, not mine. I had a family to feed.

The ghosts came again the night I mailed off my new resume. They kept pace with a faint beat I could barely hear as they marched front and center to stop only inches from me. Woody had disappointment etched on his face. "Damn, Mick," is all he said before he turned and began to walk by himself into tall grass. For several days, I had to stomp hard on the lids to keep all the guys in their boxes.

I've loved Country Day. Teaching there's been a great career for me, and it's been good for Patti and the kids. This year I'll retire after forty years of teaching and coaching and lots of activities with the students. I think I've done a pretty good job for them. It's been a great fit.

When I go home at the end of my last day of school, I'll take with me the little American and Marine Corps flag set that's spent thirty-three years on the front of my desk.

37

I N THE SPRING OF 1980, Douglas was three and a half, Katie one. Patti had taken a handful of classes at Loyola and worked part-time as a teachers' aide but was mostly a stay-at-home mom, which, for the time being, suited her fine. I'd been teaching at Country Day for almost four years, helped coach football and lacrosse too. The headmaster had turned out to be all I could've wanted, and Jack Burden had left to be a bigger fish in a bigger pond. Life was good.

Then I ran into Corrigan.

Actually, he ran into me. I'd cramped up half way through a 10K in Hunt Valley and abruptly slowed to a jog. A guy with an artificial leg was running along in the middle of the pack, so tied up telling the runner beside him a story, he wasn't paying attention and nearly knocked us both to the ground.

"Sorry," he said. "Gotta watch those abrupt stops. Some of us don't have great brakes." He grinned and the sheaf of straw thatch on his upper lip jumped up and down. "Shall we?" He swept his hand forward as though ushering me onto a ballroom floor.

"My fault," I said, "should've gotten to the side when I cramped up. You go ahead."

He was tall and rail thin and beginning to lose his hair, and he wore a prosthesis where his lower leg should've been. I tried to imagine what the "Professor" must look like now and what he'd be doing running in Maryland. "Corrigan?"

He cocked his head. "One each." He studied me, the grin on his face getting broader. "I know you, don't I? Vietnam?"

"McClure," I said. "Bravo One Fifteen, First Platoon. Guns."

He grabbed my hand, pumped it up and down like the handle on a well spouting friendship. "My God, it is indeed. Damn but you clean up good." His voice was deep and full of mischief, like I remembered, though for years if I thought about Corrie at all, I'd heard him screaming at the bones sticking out of his shredded leg.

He'd gone to law school in D.C. and was a junior partner now in Russell & Stephens, a prestigious Baltimore firm. He and his wife and three kids lived in Lutherville, close to where Patti and the kids and I were in Towson. I agreed to join him the next week for the ten mile out and back he ran most Sunday mornings at Loch Raven Reservoir.

At Loch Raven, Corrie wanted to talk about guys in the platoon. He hadn't been in contact with any of them since he was medevacked, for the most part didn't know who'd lived or died. He'd done physical therapy at Bethesda with a Marine from Third Platoon who'd lost a leg on the third day of the battle at the big ville. The Marine had known Pius John and Corporal Harding, and had told Corrie they'd been killed.

"The Pope. Damn, I couldn't believe it. I thought nothing could kill him. Corporal Harding, too."

"Willie and Smitty were killed there too," I said. "And a new guy you didn't know, Ogala. A bunch of others from the company, I don't remember their names. John was actually killed the next day. A lot of people were badly wounded. It was a fucking terrible two days."

"Willis and Smitty," Corrie said quietly. "Jesus Christ, I hadn't heard about them." His Nikes made a two-beat sound on the pavement, the soft heel-to-toe thud of his left alternating with the sharper slap of the right, tightly laced to its plastic foot.

He knew Gio was dead. The Marine in Bethesda had known Gianelli too. Everybody in the company knew Gio.

I didn't want to go through my roll call of the dead, but Corrie wanted to know who was okay, who we'd lost, and he had a right to know. I told him about Dasmund and Glass. No details, just that they'd been killed. He didn't ask how. He didn't know Brocato. He'd been so new when he died, I'd hardly known him myself. I told him about Ladoor.

"The guy fucking drowned on a swim call?"

"Unbelievable."

"What the hell do you tell his parents?"

"I know." The way the war had ended, I didn't know what you could say to anyone's parents.

We reached Peerce's Plantation and turned around in the restaurant's parking lot and began our run back to where we'd left our cars. Five miles out and five miles back. How Corrigan did it I didn't know. I was amazed how fast and steady he was with that prosthesis. As we ran under the big, fragrant pines on the three-mile flat stretch along the water before the steep climb up toward the top of the dam, we were both buried in thoughts of lost friends.

"How about Woody?" Corrie's question blasted me out of my thoughts. In the last few years, when I'd thought of Woody at all, I worked very hard to picture him laughing and handsome and funny. I wasn't always successful, but I tried. Now all I could see was what was left of him in the tall grass.

"He was killed," I said. "Booby trap." It was suddenly hard to breathe, but I kept running, trying unsuccessfully to get rid of the pictures in my head, trying to keep my wrenching stomach from cramping me up.

"Goddamn! Woody, too?"

We ran on without talking for a while. When we reached the long bridge to the other side of the reservoir, Corrie said, "Did you know he and Jackson were from the same town in Delaware?"

"Yeah. Played on all the same teams."

"Both legs is the shits."

I didn't know how to respond to a one-legged man about that. Fortunately, I didn't have to, because Corrie asked, "Ever hear how he did back here in the World?"

I couldn't remember if Corrie had still been around when Woody read us Jackson's letters. I listened to the *thud-slap* of his Nikes and watched his strange gait out of the corner of my eye and decided not to mention Jax wanting hollow prostheses so he could hide beer cans from his nurses.

"Dottie, his wife, flew out to California to be with him at the hospital. Beyond that, I don't know." It'd been over ten years; I still wondered how long Dottie stayed with him. I guessed there was some chance they'd stayed together. Corrie and Sheila had been married six years and had three kids. That was probably different, though. As he said, both legs was the shits.

We were almost across the bridge, the sun high in the sky making cats' eyes along the rippled water beneath us. A slight breeze carried the clean scent of pine. A perfect spring day for two friends to be out on a run. I wondered what Mike Jackson did instead of dancing and sports.

Corrie was happy to hear I'd seen Father Mullin and Gunny Gilles and Captain Mangan ten years before at Lejeune. I hadn't seen them since, but I'd gotten Christmas cards from Mangan. "He's a major now," I said.

"I'm really glad they got home okay."

"For damn sure. I saw Landon then, too."

"Gnat's Nuts? How was he?"

"Pretty screwed up. Drinking too much. Said he was really upset about all the gooks he killed."

I thought then of Ruth Silver for the first time in years. I didn't feel bad using the term with Corrie. "Landon didn't want to be called 'Gnat's Nuts' anymore. Said it made him ashamed, because it was a sin to kill. Can't say as I had much sympathy for him."

"No shit, Sherlock," Corrie said angrily. But then, he actually sounded somewhat sympathetic. "I guess there's lots of guys with booze and drug problems."

"I hope Landon's okay, not shambling the streets in dirty cammies, so screwed up he can't find his ass with two hands, much less a job, like some of the guys we see on the news."

I told Corrie that Prevas lost a leg. "The pits," he said. "He wanted to be a coach, didn't he?"

"He talked about it a lot."

"I wonder if he ever went on to college?"

"Dunno."

"It would take a hell of a principal to hire him to be a basketball coach."

"Not likely, I guess." I didn't tell Corrie what I'd done to get my teaching job. I've never told anyone, until now.

"How about Cloninger?"

I didn't know what happened to him.

"Good guy," Corrie said, "but a strange motor scooter."

"Buzzard, the Buzz."

"Looked like one, didn't he? And that dictionary of his. Could almost tell how long we'd been in the bush by the words he used."

We were on the front side of the long hill heading down past the dam. Corrie was still going strong, though the steep uphill and downhill sections clearly hurt his leg. Our breathing was more relaxed now as we approached the short flat that led to where we had parked.

"Did he ever tell you how he came to enlist?" Corrigan began chuckling.

"The 'Blondie in a coma' bit?"

"Oh, yeah. I can hear the Buzzard now. 'A coma's a funny thing. Blondie never moved a muscle when I tickled his feet.'"

"That was funny. Sick, I guess, in a way."

"I wonder if he checked on him again when he got home."

"I wonder if Blondie ever got out of that coma."

"Cloninger probably tickled him again."

"Sick, Corrigan. You're a sick man."

"Tell me you haven't wondered about that yourself, McClure."

"A hell of a thing."

Back at the parking lot across from Sanders' store, Corrie got two Heinekens out of a cooler in the bed of his pickup. He popped the top on both and held one out to me. I'd pulled off my wet T-shirt and was rubbing the sweat off my face with it. "Damn, Corrie. It's ten-thirty. On a Sunday morning."

Corrigan made an exaggerated show of looking at his watch. "Well, hot damn, so it is. After watching you run in that 10K, I thought this little excursion might take us 'til noon." He shook with laughter. I took one of the beers.

He frowned, looking at the puckered indentation in my chest. "Turn around." He made a spinning motion with his hand. He whistled at the size of the scar on my back. "Damn, McClure. You were lucky with that one. A couple inches to the right. . ." He let that hang.

"Luck of the Irish," I said.

"Here's to that," Corrie raised his bottle in toast. "Speaking of us being lucky," he said. "I sent five hundred bucks to the memorial fund yesterday. You contribute yet?"

"Memorial fund?" A small group of vets had been trying to raise money for about a year for a Vietnam veterans' memorial of some sort to go in D.C. I figured he meant that but wasn't sure. From what I'd seen in the paper, they weren't having much success. I hadn't really been paying much attention, part of my effort to keep the lids on.

Corrigan nodded enthusiastically. "The Vietnam Veterans Memorial Fund. There's going to be a monument on the Mall in Washington."

"I don't need a monument."

Corrie dismissed that as though I'd just uttered nonsense. "Of course you do, we all do."

"The government's not going to pay for it, right?"

"You know that's not going to happen."

"So vets are supposed to build a monument to ourselves?"

"There'll be donations from lots of people, not just vets. The public's going to honor us for our service."

"They're never going to get the money. No one cares." I couldn't remember the last time I'd even heard the word "Vietnam" used around school. I studied the remains of the Heineken label I'd shredded, surprised how bitter I sounded.

"I think you're wrong; I may send in another five hundred bucks. You ought to send something. If enough people contribute a little, it'll happen."

That was fine for the lawyer to say. I had to clothe and feed two kids on a teacher's salary. I couldn't afford to throw money away on lost causes. My country had thrown away enough in Vietnam. "I'll save my money. I don't care about a memorial."

Later that day, the lids rose off the boxes more than any time in the last few years. Pictures kept appearing in double-hinged frames. John, head thrown back laughing, purple latticework of scars on his chest dancing in the sun, then his slight smile at the end, dead milky eyes, and, down below, eviscerated parts. Gio laughing too, purple veins on his forehead writhing mirthfully above purple granny glasses; in the frame beside that one, every vein on his face, neck, and arms straining as he writhed in the dirt alongside his innards. Woody, easygoing and handsome, then the ghastly remains no one should ever see.

Once we had the kids in bed, Patti came and sat next to me on the couch. "You've been off someplace most of the time since you got home from your run." She raised her eyebrows in mock surprise. "Smelling of beer, I might add."

"Corrigan always has a beer after his runs. Carb replacement, he says. Breakfast of champions."

"He forced you to join him, right?"

"Twisted my arm."

"I have a feeling the two of you are going to be trouble."

"Hope so."

"So what gives? Something's been bothering you."

"Sorry if I've been quiet today. We spent most of our time talking about guys from our old platoon. He wanted me to tell him who did what after he left. A lot of the guys we both knew are dead or wounded as bad or worse than him. It brought back some tough memories I've worked hard to forget."

Patti gave me a hug, and we were quiet for a moment. Then she said, "I'm sorry that was hard for you. Maybe it will just be the one time."

"I hope so. I don't know. He's all excited about a memorial to Vietnam vets some people are raising money to build in D.C."

"Sounds like a worthy cause. Did he ask you for any?"

"He asked me to send a contribution."

"I think we should."

"I don't need a memorial."

She gave me one of her gently skeptical looks. "It might be a nice way to honor the friends you lost. You haven't mentioned them in a long time."

———

Patti threw her arm across my chest. I stopped thrashing and jerked upright on the bed. All I could hear was my own shallow gasps and her whisper, "It's okay, Marty; it's okay." But it wasn't, of course, because the ghosts were sending me signals again.

I finally felt calm enough to throw my legs over the edge of the bed and sit, holding my head. I listened for noise from across the hall. Patti knelt up behind me, gently kneaded the back of my neck. Sweat enveloped me like a wet shroud. I raised one hand slowly, pressed my fingers hard against the deep ache of the old bullet wound. My heart battered my ribs. Patti whispered "It's just a dream, Marty. A bad dream. You're okay."

I nodded slowly. I wasn't sure I was okay at all.

"Do you want to tell me about it, Sweetie?"

"Did I wake the kids?"

"Douglas would be in here by now. I'll look in on them in a few minutes. Can you tell me about your dream?" Patti's a big believer in getting problems out in the open, talking them through.

I shook my head. "I don't know," I finally said. "Vietnam, guys I was with. I don't know what it meant."

Actually, I probably did. It was as though the ghosts had listened in on my conversation with Corrie that morning. Maybe they had.

The dream began as it had for a decade, in silence, the same absolute vacuum of noise. Then only that distant sound, the *whup-whup* and *thrum* of rotor blades. The same shroud of blue-gray fog or smoke. The thin bite of gunpowder and fire. Wet, stifling heat this time. The figures looked almost the same as before. Pale faces; faded, stained jungle utilities, torn, but pressed and starched. No hats or helmets, jungle boots caked with mud.

This time, each of them carried something in his left hand. John carried a rosary; the silver crucifix gleamed bright. Gio held a stack of envelopes, each stamped "free" in bright red. Smitty held a full pack of Kools. Harding had pictures fanned out like poker cards in his hand. Woody held a single 45 rpm record, no doubt the Ronnettes. Willie grasped a rabbit's foot, clean and gleaming blue.

The six Marines advanced toward me on line, marching to a cadence I thought only they could hear. Others marched behind them, too far back to recognize who they might be. The six stopped and stared at me. Then in unison, they raised their right hands and waved.

I couldn't tell if they were saying hello or goodbye.

38

THE FIRST TIME CORRIE AND I TALKED about the Americans held hostage in Iran was at a cookout at his house that Fourth of July. We hadn't talked about Vietnam on our last several runs, but we'd argued about Jane Fonda that morning.

We'd just started our climb up the hill that rises steep and winding past the top of the dam. As we shortened our strides and leaned in, I was telling him that Patti and I'd seen *Electric Horseman* the night before. "You'd enjoy it, I think. Kind of a fun story about a washed-up rodeo champ who steals a twelve-million-dollar horse that's been mistreated so he can set it free."

"Fonda's in that, isn't she?" Corrie's voice held none of his earlier humor.

"Willie Nelson, too," I sang a line from "Mamas Don't Let Your Babies Grow Up To Be Cowboys" in a nasally, flat whine, trying to divert Corrie from the rant I suddenly saw coming on. His Nikes made a *shup, slap* sound as he ran.

We recovered our breathing on the short flat before the last steep curves up the hill. "I'm surprised there, McClure. You went to a 'Hanoi Jane' movie?"

"A Redford movie."

"Shit."

"Look, she should've been thrown in jail for treason, but I'm not going to let her keep me from seeing movies I want to see."

"I wouldn't cross the street to lift my leg on Jane Fonda."

I laughed out loud. "I don't know, Corrigan. I'd pay good money to see that on the evening news. Particularly if you wore those green shorts and that Marine Corps tee." I pictured him on a New York sidewalk, balanced on his plastic leg, the other cocked in the air as Hanoi Jane walked by.

That solved whatever problem might've been developing, though at his cookout that afternoon, Corrie asked his youngest daughter in a stage whisper, "Maeve, what's a Jane Fonda?"

"A fat ugly pig," she said, a matter of fact expression on her three-year-old's face. She went back to her corn on the cob.

Through the screen door, I heard Sheila ask Patti, "Now do you see why I still smoke?"

Later, Walter Cronkite signed off the evening news. "And that's the way it is, Friday, July 4, 1980. And as today they enter their ninth month as prisoners, it is the two-hundred-forty-fourth day of captivity for the American hostages in Tehran."

When the two of us got outside again, Corrie's voice quivered with anger. "Fifty-two Americans and we're helpless to get them out. Nine months! A botched rescue, our people dead in the desert, us a laughingstock to the world. Two hundred forty-four days they've been locked up by that fanatic asshole. God, my heart breaks for them and their families."

Almost seven months later, the hostages finally came home. They'd been held captive in the U.S. embassy in Tehran for four hundred forty-four days.

They were treated like returning heroes. Yellow ribbons tied everywhere. Church bells across the country pealed for hours. President Reagan greeted them at the White House after a motorcade down Pennsylvania Avenue, where people stood cheering six deep on the sidewalk for twenty blocks. A thousand tons of ticker-tape fell on their parade in New York. There were parties and receptions; they were given lifetime passes to sporting events, presented keys to cities.

Every bit of it was covered on the nightly news.

Corrie and I ran the next Sunday. It was cold, but a beautiful day. Ripples on the reservoir sparkled, the sun painted the pines a bright gleaming gloss. Corrie's breath formed ice crumbs on his mustache.

"Did you see the bastards?" he asked.

"Which ones? There's a lot of 'em." I was in a great mood, enjoying the run. I assumed he meant politicians on the early Sunday shows, which I'd skipped.

"The hostages. Fucking ticker-tape parade, the White House, keys to cities. The whole nine yards."

"I'm glad they're back," I said.

"We get our asses shot off in Vietnam and people spit at us, call us names. We got fucked. Those guys sit around playing board games or rereading old *Reader's Digest*s, and people call them heroes and throw them parades like they were damn astronauts."

"Not really the hostages' fault," I said. I hadn't thought about the girls in O'Hare or Spence Burke's friends at UVA in a long time.

"Of course not, damn it. Not at all. I'm glad they're back too. But I'll tell you this, things are just plain fucked up. We fought for our country, not just sat in some goddamn room. Where was our ticker-tape parade? Who did one fucking thing for veterans when we got back to the World? It's like we never came home!"

I thought later that day about my flight home from San Diego, how nobody, including the man in the seat next to me on the plane, even noticed that I was alive. I thought too about the thousands who weren't.

I sent a check for a hundred bucks to the Vietnam Veterans Memorial Fund the next day.

39

MY FIRST YEAR AT MARYLAND, I'd sent Captain Mangan a Christmas card in care of the CG's office. I wasn't sure if he was still the aide, or whether he'd have the time or the interest to respond to my note. As befit a Marine writing to a senior, I'd addressed him as "Captain" in my card. He'd only known me as PFC or Lance Corporal McClure. I got a letter back congratulating me on adapting to college and telling me that if I got up to Baltimore, I should have a piece of strawberry pie at Haussner's for him. He started his letter "Dear Marty" and signed it "Mark."

We've kept in touch over the years. I enjoyed following his career, mainly through the notes in his Christmas cards. We aren't close friends, but much more than simply acquaintances. Two men who shared an experience that changed them forever when they were once young.

In 1981, Major Mangan was the commander of the Marine Corps recruiting district in Philadelphia. In October, I received a formal invitation to the command's annual Marine Corps Birthday Ball. On the back of the invitation was a handwritten note:

Marty—
I hope you and Patti can make this. It will be nice to have a couple
of us from our old First Platoon.
Semper Fi,
Mark

"That's a Tuesday," Patti said when I showed her the invitation.

"I know," I said. "I'd have to take Wednesday off; you'd have to skip class."

Patti was still working toward her degree at Loyola. She didn't like missing class. "Is it that important to you?" she said. "Is it worth you taking a vacation day and me missing school? You don't even talk about the Marines much anymore."

She was right, but I was surprised how important the invitation felt.

On November 10, we walked into the Philadelphia Sheraton, me in my rented tux, Patti looking great in her old bridesmaid's dress. We were the first of the couples assigned to our table to arrive. My place card read, "Mr. Martin McClure"; Patti's said "Mrs. Patti McClure."

The card at the seat next to mine read "Mrs. Dorothy Jackson." I stared at it, momentarily stricken. I hadn't thought about Mike or Dottie Jackson in a long time. The next place card said, "CPL Michael Jackson, USMC (Ret.)."

"Marty . . . ? Are you okay?" Patti was studying my face as though something were terribly wrong.

"I . . . I know this guy."

"Is that a problem?" Patti asked just as a voice like a roll of thunder ten feet behind me called out, "McClure! Major Mangan told me they might let a shaggy-haired civilian come to the ball."

Mike Jackson walked toward me, hand outstretched. He moved like he had tight hinges for hips. I half-expected to hear a clicking sound with each step. Six-three or -four, he still looked like a lumberjack, though he no longer rolled like a sailor. He wore dress blues, his Purple Heart and Bronze Star medals on his chest, corporal's insignia on his sleeves. A very attractive young woman in a shimmering gold dress held his other hand.

Dottie Jackson was exactly as Woody had described her, only a dozen years older. A thirty-year-old cheerleader with a knockout figure and wavy, brown, shoulder-length hair framing the smile on her face. The deep lines etched around her eyes didn't distract from how pretty she was or how happy she looked.

My thoughts flailed about. Was I supposed to tell Mike I was sorry about his legs? Tell Dottie I could only imagine how tough life must've been for her? Despite all the time I'd spent around Corrie, I had no idea what to do or say. Do you express sympathy and remind people of their infirmities, their difficulties, or pretend there's no elephant filling the room? Maybe I should let them try and forget their troubles for an evening? Do people like the Jacksons even have to try to forget their troubles, or is their version of normal such a part of their lives that the abnormality strikes their consciousness only when someone else brings it up? I had no idea what the right answer was.

I didn't say anything right away. Standing still, you couldn't tell Mike's legs weren't real. I'd never mentioned his legs to Patti, never had reason to bring up his name. How would she react if I suddenly said something? How would Dottie react? As we stood making introductions, all that careened around in my head.

Dottie saved me. We'd no more than introduced ourselves and talked about where we lived when she asked, "Do you have kids?"

"Two," Patti said. "A boy and a girl, five and two."

"Wonderful! We have three. Or we did when we left home this evening. The eleven-year-old, the boy, is a wise guy like his father. He lips off too much, and the babysitter may throw him out the window."

An eleven-year-old! Jackson could hardly have been out of the hospital! I fought to stifle my imagination.

"If she could lift him, she would," Mike said.

Dottie laughed. "The girls are nine and six. Fortunately, they take after their mother." She poked Mike in the ribs.

"Damn lucky thing," Jackson agreed. "Mike's a good kid, too," he said. "Beginning to play golf with me, and he got his Scout troop to raise seven hundred and thirty-eight dollars for our memorial in

D.C. Helped me with the fundraisers we had for it at the Legion and D.A.V., too."

"Good for him," I said, and meant it.

"I'm really glad you came," Mike said. "The Major told me him and you keep in touch and you live in Maryland. I thought about contacting you. But, you know how it goes."

"Trust me. My mother used to tell me the road to hell's paved with good intentions, and there's a stretch called the Martin McClure Memorial Highway. I had no idea you were in Philadelphia. I've lost touch with everybody except the Major and Matt. You remember Doc Matheson?"

"Sure. He and Doc Dorsey saved my life. Where's Matt now?"

A picture of Mike sprawled bare-ass over the thorn bush, two grooves carved in his thighs flashed through my mind. I pushed it away in time to say, "Boston. He's a doctor." Two goddamn little pink grooves scooped clean out of tree trunk legs. I could see them almost as clearly as I did twelve years before. I pushed the bitter feeling rising in me back down. "Oh, and Corrigan," I said. "How could I forget Corrie? I run with him almost every Sunday morning. Remember him?" I felt myself flush, suddenly mortified that I'd talked about running.

Mike didn't seem to notice my face. "Corrigan? The guy we called 'Professor'?"

"That's the one."

"The major told me he lost a leg too. Sounds like he's doing okay."

Jesus Christ! What'd I just done?

If Mike noticed my discomfort, he didn't let on. He was probably pretty used to people being uncomfortable around him. "Corrigan lives in Baltimore? He should've come too."

"Yeah. I was going to ask Mark, Major Mangan . . ."

"I call him Mark too. Just not when we're doing Marine stuff." Mike grinned as though he'd let me in on a secret.

". . . but Corrie was going to be away. He's a lawyer, travels a lot."

Mike turned to Dottie. "The last time I talked to old Marty here was just before I was wounded. I was trying to con him out of his spare socks."

I tried to keep a calm look on my face. Dottie smiled at me as though she were expecting a story. Goddamn socks. The man didn't even need socks after all.

Patti sat quietly, listening to the conversation, concern for me in her eyes. She can take my temperature with a glance. Inside my head, I could hear Jackson's urgent whisper: *Please, people . . . please hurry. . . .*

"I was sorry about all that," I said. I almost said "to hear about your legs," but that would've felt like slapping them both in the face. Suddenly I remembered Woody's tales of the three of them dancing on weekends.

"Thanks," Mike said quietly. "Worse things happened to other people." That seemed to close out the subject.

Dottie inconspicuously patted her husband on the back. That and the slightest pursing of her lips were her only reaction to our brief exchange. It occurred to me that maybe I was the one who hadn't come to grips with what had happened to Mike. I couldn't help it; no matter what Uncle Harry had said about medical necessity, I wasn't ever going to get over Mike and Dottie Jackson losing his legs because of two little goddamn bloodless grooves.

We moved away from Vietnam then, talked about our families, jobs, the towns where we lived, the handful of guys with whom either of us had kept in touch. I was glad I didn't need to talk about all the guys we both knew who'd been killed or wounded after Mike left. I guessed he and Mark had done that.

Major Mangan stopped by our table a couple of times. Cheryl was even prettier in person than in the family pictures in Mark's Christmas cards. He looked like I expected he would in his mid-thirties: handsome, still youthful, athletic, and trim. A recruiting-poster image of a Marine officer with his gleaming gold major's oak leaves on his shoulders, his Silver Star and Purple Hearts and other medals on his mess dress. Still an innate intensity, though I was struck by his eyes—they looked much younger than I recalled. I guessed his advice about keeping lids on boxes worked for him.

It had turned into a very pleasant evening. After dinner, before the cake cutting and toasts, Patti excused herself to go to the restroom.

"Good idea," Mike said, "rented a little too much beer, myself." He slid his chair back in a couple of jumps, then leaned forward, his hands flat on the table, and pushed himself up.

I started to offer him a hand but saw that Dottie didn't move, just gave Mike a sideways glance, unobtrusively checking to see if he was okay. So I sat still, trying to pretend the way he moved was the most normal thing in the world. I suppose it was in theirs.

When it was just the two of us at the table, Dottie lit a cigarette. She and Mike smoked a lot. "Mike told me you were there when Woody passed away?"

Her question hit me like a spear in the chest. I didn't expect we'd be talking about him. I should've, of course; they'd been best friends. Maybe Mangan had told Mike I was there when Woody was killed. Passed away? Jesus! I nodded at her. It wasn't her fault; some people just talk like that. "Yes," I said quietly. "I was."

"Mark said he didn't suffer." Her face sought reassurance.

I tried to draw a curtain over the terrible picture of Woody that filled my mind. I shook my head slowly, hoping the horror inside my skull wasn't showing on my face. "No," I said. "He didn't suffer at all."

Like Mark told me once long ago, people want that assurance; it's a small comfort they need in their grief. I did when Mom and Dad died. God knows, I'd told Dottie the truth.

Her smile was serious and thankful, a little crooked. "I'm glad," she said.

I nodded. What more could I say?

"He was the best friend we ever had, Mike and me. I still miss him."

I nodded again. "I know. I do too."

Major Mangan used his sword to make the first cut in the giant sheet cake with the EGA in the middle above the words "Happy 206th Birthday, Marines."

Mike leaned toward me as the oldest Marine present was given the first slice. "Did you meet Sergeant Major Valentino?" The senior enlisted Marine looked like a bulldog with silver hair. "Great guy," Mike said. "Been a Marine since Christ was a corporal. A grunt in Korea and Vietnam."

I thought of First Sergeant Miller as I looked at the ballroom full of Marines. The Top had been right: I was proud of being a Marine, even if I did all I could to avoid the painful part of my memories. He'd been dead wrong, too: the people above our pay grade who'd sent us to war didn't know jack shit.

I pushed that angry thought aside as the youngest Marine, a PFC, was introduced to the crowd and handed a slice of cake. He was eighteen. I looked around at all the young Marines in the ballroom. They looked so eager, so confident, so proud. I smiled. I envied their unsullied commitment. The Few, The Proud, The Marines.

"Looks like they're letting kids play with guns these days," Mike said.

I laughed. "Were we ever that young?" I didn't mention Corrie's theory of vet years: like dog years but longer. For every year you spend at war, you age twenty inside. I intended to enjoy the party again, and being with Mike.

After the cake and coffee were served, the disc jockey took over. Young Marines and their dates surged to the floor.

"Ready?" Mike asked Dottie.

"Ready and rarin'."

Mike pushed up to his feet.

Patti started to move her chair back. We love to dance; at weddings and reunions we're often among the first on the floor. But I put my hand over hers and we sat and watched.

Mike shuffled stiffly trying to keep time to the music, his legs moving woodenly, causing even his torso to be a half-measure off the beat. His hands and arms and head were the only parts of him in rhythm at all. I thought of watching him and Woody dancing in the dirt like *Bandstand* contestants. Now he looked like a gigantic, tight-jointed doll in Marine blues, just wound up and released as Dottie swirled around him, all rhythm and grace. They watched each other's faces, laughing like love-struck teenagers at a CYO dance.

A tremendous sadness welled up inside me. They deserved so much better. Still, they'd made a good life together, despite what happened to Mike, what happened to them. What had John told Woody so many memories ago? A man is so much more than his legs.

As I watched Mike Jackson try to dance, I began to think of Woody again and John and Gio and all the others I'd lost and whose memories I'd worked so hard to push away. I didn't want to think about them, about how they died. My brief conversation with Dottie had been difficult enough. I didn't want to be angry or sad or to wrestle with my unanswerable question: What in the name of God could make all the deaths, all the cripplings, worthwhile?

But as I watched the Jacksons in the middle of all the young Marines on the dance floor, I wondered for the first time in what felt like forever whether I should sometimes try to remember the good things about my old friends' lives, not pretend they'd never been part of mine.

"You okay?" Patti said quietly. "What're you thinking about?"

"Old friendships," I said.

She indicated the Jacksons. "Ready to join them?" She began to push her chair back again.

"I'm not sure," I said. "Let's give it a try."

40

THE FOLLOWING SPRING, I was in Boston for a conference and met Matt for dinner at Faneuil Hall. Like with Mark Mangan, we'd kept in touch with Christmas cards and an occasional note, but hadn't seen each other in over ten years. Matt was still rail thin; the scar on his cheek had faded to a line drawn with a silver sharpie. He was just thirty-five, but his shock of brown hair was threaded with gray. He had a web of wrinkles around his eyes, and he looked bone tired, but he seemed happy. He was a trauma surgeon at Mass General, spending most days and nights trying to save victims of car accidents and shootings and other violent events. It was the first night he'd taken off in a couple weeks.

I was the one who brought up Vietnam during dinner. "I was surprised when you decided to specialize in trauma surgery. After all you'd done and been through as a corpsman, I kind of figured you'd be ready to be a dermatologist, or GP, or something, not practice where you'd have to make life-or-death decisions every day."

Matt sipped his Glenfiddich, then gave a little chuckle and shrugged. "It just seemed like what I should do."

"Isn't it stressful as hell?"

He looked like he was getting ready to deliver a punchline. "I claim I don't really have stress, even though my team thinks I'm a carrier." He laughed again, then added, "It isn't the practice for everybody, I know. But it's like I tell my team, we've been given a gift, we get to save lives." The look in his eyes turned wistful, sort of sad. "We just can't ever save enough."

After dinner we walked to his townhouse, not far from the hospital. His den smelled like a smoke shop. Two leather easy chairs, a large television, a sturdy oak bar with several bottles of single-malt scotch, and a shiny walnut cigar humidor on its top. A large glass ashtray on the table between the easy chairs held ashes and cigar butts. The tables and the floor next to one of the chairs were strewn with magazines with names like *American Journal of Emergency Medicine* and *International Journal of Surgery*.

"A surgeon who smokes," I said, and immediately felt badly for sounding like I disapproved. I'd given up cigarettes but didn't lecture people who smoked.

Matt didn't take offense. "I practice not preach," he said. "Besides, I get my Cubans from my pal, an anesthesiologist, who goes to London a lot. I do my patriotic duty by burning the contraband he brings back."

He got a kick out of using that line. I'm sure I wasn't his first audience.

A *Boston* magazine on the floor had pictures of Matt and three other men on the cover. "Boston's Most Eligible Bachelors," it proclaimed.

"Fightin' 'em off, I guess," I said with a flick of my eyebrows.

Matt shook his head, embarrassed. "They talked me into doing that for some charitable thing. I've broken more dates than I've kept. They ought to call me the 'medical monk.'" He laughed, didn't sound disappointed at all.

I took the cigar he offered. "I'm going to need to double my laps around the Commons tomorrow morning after this." I told him about running with Corrigan on Sundays and about seeing Mark Mangan and dancing with the Jacksons at the Birthday Ball.

"I do a lousy job of keeping up with anybody," Matt said. "You and Mark with Christmas cards is about it. I wish I did more. Corrigan's running; that's great. Doing it with a prosthesis can give you joint issues, though. You guys may need to cut that out, or at least the Professor should, pretty soon."

Matt took a long pull on his cigar. "I'm really glad to hear Jackson's doing well. I worried about him. But that man always had guts. He was a hell of guy."

"Still is," I said. I didn't know what to make of Matt saying Jackson was doing well. I guessed it was a relative thing, or a doctor's perspective.

"I still think about the guys a lot," Matt said. "Particularly the ones we lost. We had a lot of good guys in the platoon. Some crazies, for sure, but then most of us probably were a little, one way or the other."

"I've spent years trying not to think about the guys we lost," I said. "Because when I do, I can't get how they died out of my head. The pictures are still there, and they're terrible. And given how the war turned out, I can't for a minute justify why they died." I tapped the ash off my cigar. "I don't think I'm ever going to get past that."

Matt blew out a big puff of smoke. "Sometimes dealing with stress after a trauma can take years."

"Are you saying I've got some sort of PTSD?" I bristled a little. The only people I'd read about who'd been diagnosed with that seemed to be jobless or homeless guys running around in their cammies.

Matt put up a hand. "I'm not saying you've got any kind of disorder, Mick. And believe me, I don't need to be a psychiatrist to know about stress; I've dealt with it enough." He stood up. "More scotch?" He poured more for both of us. I stared at the golden liquid in my glass and waited for him to say more.

"You couldn't teach the way you do or be the kind of guy you are if you had a disorder. It's not like that." Matt relit his cigar. "But you can't do what we did in Vietnam without having some sort of post-traumatic stress. We all just deal with it in different ways, over different periods of time." He blew out a stream of smoke. "Look Mick, I'm not trying to give you advice, but it's like I tell the families of patients I've lost: I hope there comes a time when you'll be able to focus on what you loved about them, the times you enjoyed being together, not on how they suffered or how they died."

41

CORRIE UNSTRAPPED THE PROSTHESIS from around the stump of his leg and stuck it in the bed of the pickup between the cooler and his duffle bag. Upside down, it stuck straight up in the air, quivering like the latest discard on a surgeon's carnage pile for amputee robots—a waxy, jointed polymer leg with a blue and white Nike laced tightly to its plastic foot.

"How you doing?" I asked, nodding toward where he held a chunk of ice.

He took a pull on his beer then barked a long belch. "Good," he said. "Old Stumpy gets a bit irritated now and then, but we do okay."

He paused as though something had struck him for the first time. "Kind of like Sheila, come to think of it," he said with a straight face. I laughed and joined him on the tailgate. Late October of 1982. Already, colors were turning, and the pines along the banks of the reservoir smelled crisp and clean. A perfect day for a run, and we'd pushed hard.

"What can I do to convince you to go with me to the Salute?" Corrie asked.

The Vietnam Veterans Memorial Fund had raised over seven million dollars in private contributions, not a dime of federal funds. The Memorial was going to be dedicated in two weeks. A gleaming black granite wall engraved with every one of the almost fifty-eight thousand names of the dead. There'd be a parade, a candlelight vigil. It was being called the National Salute to Vietnam Veterans. Some commentators called it a belated homecoming; a couple hundred thousand vets were expected to show up. And parents and widows and children of men whose names were on the Wall.

There was no way in the world I could look at fifty-eight thousand names.

"How do you deal with it?" I said. "All those names. And they all died for nothing? I don't know how you can go there and deal with the insanity of that, the absolute waste."

Corrie looked off in the distance, into the trees. For a moment, I thought of sitting inside a company perimeter waiting for a patrol that had taken casualties to come back in.

"I'm never going to figure it all out," he said. "The big picture, I mean. Should we have seen it through? Did we help the South stay free for a dozen years? Was that worth the price we paid? Or was the whole thing fucked from the start and all those guys on the Wall died for a lost cause? I don't know if anyone's objective enough to really figure that stuff out. I'm not that guy."

Corrie got another piece of ice out of the beer cooler. "You know what I am, Mick? I'm just a guy who believes most of the men on that Wall died for each other, and for guys like you and me. Maybe they believed in a bigger cause." He shook his head. "I did once. But when the shit hit the fan, I think we all fought and bled for each other, not mom and apple pie, or the flag, or the South Vietnamese."

He stared off into the distance again. He took a long pull on his beer, then said, "I used to think the Memorial was just about the guys who didn't make it home, but I was wrong. It's about you and me, guys who lived and are doing fine. And it's about the guys who saw so much bad shit they could never quite get over it." He snorted a brief, humorless laugh, glanced at me, then looked down at the beer bottle as though the label might have answers on it. "Might be all of us, truth be told." He smiled a little. "That's okay too."

Corrie stopped talking, took the last swig of his beer. "That was a long speech. Sorry."

I waved the apology away.

"What it comes down to, what it always comes down to, is the guys." Corrie said the words almost like a prayer. "We share something no one else can with an awful lot of good guys. Fifty-eight thousand of them have their names on that wall."

We sat quietly then, each of us absorbed in our thoughts. Three other runners jogged into the parking lot and began doing post-run stretches behind the line of parked cars. Corrie recognized the oldest of them. He wiped his face on his sleeve. "Glad you folks are here, Steve," he called, face split in a broad grin. "Otherwise, we'd have to drink all this stuff ourselves."

The three came over. Steve introduced the younger couple. I shook hands, said "Hi," but nothing else. I was tied up in a jumble of thoughts about the Wall and the war. "Help yourselves," Corrie said, pointing toward the cooler. Steve did.

"That's beer," the younger man said. He wore an expensive warm-up suit, and even after a run he had perfectly coifed hair.

"Damn," Corrie said. "I told my wife gin for breakfast today."

"It's eleven o'clock," the young woman said. She wore makeup and had very shapely legs. She saw Corrie's rubbed-red stump and swallowed hard.

He shook his head. "Can't be helped," he said. "It takes McClure here longer to do ten miles than it used to. I damn near had to carry him in today."

I forced a smile and just shook my head.

We sat on the tailgate and watched them walk to their cars. "Nylon running shorts," Corrigan said. "*Mmm, mmm, mmm.* Just think of the possibilities." He opened another Heineken. "Ready?" he held the bottle out to me.

I shook my head. "Thanks, no. I've got to grade essays this afternoon. I don't want to put forehead prints on the kids' papers." I finished my beer. "I'm not going to the Salute," I said. "I remember the guys we lost in First Platoon, and I will as long as I live."

"It's more than just the guys in our platoon," Corrie said quietly. Then he brightened. "It's going to be like the welcome home we never got."

"Thirteen years after I got home. I don't need it now."

"Come on, Mick, that's bullshit."

"I didn't expect a parade."

"You didn't expect people to flip you the bird, did you? Admit it, Marty, it would've been nice to have people say 'thanks for your service,' instead of ignoring you or treating you like you were some kind of drug-crazed baby killer. Right?"

"Sure, but I've been home a long time. It's kind of like throwing yourself a graduation party a dozen years afterwards, and you're on your way. Big whoop."

"A lot of vets aren't on their way. If we're honest, I doubt any of us have really come to grips with that war. The Salute's going to be a way for people to say thanks for serving in a tough time."

I thought about that, and I thought about my conversation with Matt. For years, being a Vietnam vet was like carrying a virus people could immunize themselves against only by silence. No one wanted to be reminded of that war. In the past, if I mentioned I'd served in Vietnam most people seemed uninterested or embarrassed or uneasy, as though that time in my life weren't something I should be talking about. So I didn't. And after a while, that became fine with me. And now I didn't need a parade, and I sure as hell didn't need to go to Washington to remember all the friends I'd lost for no good reason I could fathom! With all the news about the Wall or vets' groups around the country gearing up to travel to the Salute, the ghosts were coming to see me a lot.

Since the ball and then talking with Matt, I'd been tempted once in a while to let myself think about the guys in the platoon. That usually hadn't worked out very well. I'd had to push down hard on the lids again since my thoughts invariably turned to how my friends died and what a waste their deaths were. I, surer than hell, wasn't ready to look at the names of fifty-eight thousand dead guys. I shook my head. "I'm just not going to go."

"There's going to be thousands of vets there. All of us are going to march in the parade. We'd probably see some of the old guys from First Platoon."

I'd pretty much convinced myself there wasn't going to be anybody there I'd have anything in common with anymore. The major was back in the Second MarDiv in the Med on a float. Matt was undoubtedly too busy at Mass General. I hadn't kept up with anyone else. Why the hell would I want to spend a couple days with a bunch of cammied-up guys with nothing better to do with their lives than dwell on what Vietnam did to them?

———

Patti and I'd disagreed about that weeks before when I'd told her I had no interest in going to the Salute. We'd been doing the dishes after dinner; the kids were playing in the family room. "I just don't want to hang with a bunch of guys wearing their old camouflaged uniforms like they never moved on from the war. They give the rest of us a bad name."

"Maybe they haven't moved on," Patti said. "Maybe the war's still the most meaningful thing they've ever done. That doesn't mean they're bad guys, Marty."

"I know that, P. Being a Marine's important to me, too. But I've done other important things in my life. I'm a husband and father, a teacher. I don't define what's important in my life around being a Vietnam vet."

"Maybe a lot of them don't either."

"Then why do they look like they do?"

"Maybe it's just their way of honoring the friends they lost. Maybe it's not just about them; it's about their friends who didn't come back."

That had given me pause. I'd attempted to take Father Mullin's advice, but too often that failed and the images embedded in my brain were so painful I would try again not to think of my old friends at all. I still felt guilty about that, but what could I do?

Patti thought I should go to the Salute. "Why don't you want to go, Sweetie? I worry if you don't, you'll be missing something you'll regret later."

"I've just, you know, moved on with life. I don't need to focus on Vietnam anymore."

"I don't think you've totally moved on."

I didn't want to hear that. "What do you mean? I've got a great life with you and the kids. Things are really good at school. Of course I've moved on."

"Of course you have. You're a great dad, a wonderful husband, a terrific teacher . . ."

"Don't forget I'm nice to the dog."

"That, too."

"So, I've moved on."

"You have, Marty. But not totally. You haven't really come to grips with your friends' deaths, have you? Every time Corrie's brought the Memorial up, it's put you in a funk."

"I'm sorry. I didn't mean to be in a funk around you."

Patti gave me the eyeball. "That's not what I meant."

I knew that.

"I just don't like it when you're upset. I want you to be happy."

"I am happy."

"But there's something missing, too. I don't know, maybe going to the Memorial would be like visiting the folks."

"It's not the same, Patti. I was right there when my friends died. And there're fifty-eight thousand names on that wall, and I can't, for the life of me, understand why."

"Do you need to, Marty? Do you need to make sense of their deaths to remember the good things about them? We can't understand why your parents died; there's no way to make sense of that. But you find it comforting to visit them, to remember their lives."

Patti stuck her head around the corner to check on the kids. She came back to the sink and said, "I remember you told me the first time I went with you that it was really painful your first few times. But then it got better, and there's been something very positive about going there for years. It's not like you don't still miss them or don't wish they were alive today. You do. But you always say it's good for you when you go there, that it makes you feel good."

"I just don't think this is the same."

"It's not, I know. And it would be tough to go there, I don't doubt that. But in the long run, maybe you'd feel better, maybe you'd make peace with what seems like a hole in your heart."

I didn't respond to that; I didn't know what to say.

But running on Sunday, I knew. I said "no thanks" to Corrie. "I'll take a pass, parade and all."

Corrie wouldn't give up. "Even if you don't care about the parade, you can bet with all the guys there, it's going to be party time."

Corrie was pushing me too damn hard! How the hell could anybody party after looking at fifty-eight thousand names on that Wall? I drained my beer, didn't say anything about the supposed party.

"Well, give it some thought," Corrie said. "You might change your mind. Even if you don't think so now, you're going to want to see the Wall. That's going to be wonderful."

Wonderful! Fifty-eight thousand names of men who died for nothing right in front of my face? My God! I lost it, then.

"I don't want to think about it, goddamn it!" I jumped down off the tailgate, accidentally knocking Corrigan's leg to the ground. I picked it up, slapped the Nike and the plastic foot to get the dirt off.

"Jesus H. Christ, Corrie! I don't need to see it!" My fingernails clawed at the dirt in the folds of the cup at the top of the plastic calf. I didn't mean to sound so harsh to my friend, but it was just too damn much. "Corrie," I said, and slapped the plastic-filled running shoe again, hard. "It's the last place in the entire goddamn world I want to be."

I slapped the Nike again. Harder. *Whap! Whap!*

I stopped slapping the shoe as abruptly as I started. Neither one of us spoke for a minute, and then I went on, more quietly, less frantically. "For ten years we fight a war and guys die every day. We're fighting global communism, we're fighting to keep the people of South Vietnam free, we're fighting for peace with honor, we're fighting for this, we're fighting for that, we're fighting over the size and shape of the fucking table at the Paris peace talks. And one day the president comes on television and says, 'I declare the war over. We've achieved peace with honor.' Jesus H. Christ!"

I looked at the other cars parked near us. No one was around. It wouldn't have made any difference if they were. I barreled on.

"And then the tanks roll south and we watch all those people we claimed were our friends claw at the embassy gates then spend the next ten years in concentration camps, if they weren't shot. Is that all it takes? Fifty-eight thousand guys in body bags and then people in pin-striped suits say 'Aw fuck it, we don't need this war, let's let 'em have the goddamn place,' and we just call it quits?"

I pressed my fingertips hard into my throbbing shoulder. "Jesus Christ, Corrie. Why wasn't it over before then, if it was going to be over at all before anything really got done? Did we have a goddamn quota before Johnson or Nixon or somebody would finally say, okay that's enough guys in bags? Let's just give up and go home. All those kids killed. My good God."

Why couldn't Corrie understand? He left his own goddamn leg in the dirt. He had known those same guys I tried to avoid in my head. Didn't he ache for them just like I did?

I took a deep, gasping breath. I looked over at Corrie and then, in a very quiet voice, said, "Corrie, I'm sorry. I don't mean to yell at you. But what the hell do I need to go to the Vietnam Memorial for? What is there that would change things, that would make the pain worthwhile?"

During my entire outburst, Corrie had just sat staring at the ground, rubbing the red tip of his stump with a big chunk of ice. He stopped rubbing his leg, dropped the ice in the dirt beside the truck, and looked at me. "It's the guys, Marty," he said. "They did their best, and we loved them. They're what counts in the end. No matter what the outcome of that war was, they matter to us."

Corrie looked away, as though he could see something off in the distance again. He went on quietly. "We may each have had different reasons for serving. But at the end of the day, what we fought for was each other. We were part of a brotherhood—we still are—that believed in courage and discipline and loyalty. No matter what we thought, or think now, of our political leaders or their decisions, we believed in America and each other. That was the cadence we all marched to, Marty. You, me, all the guys with their names on the Wall, even the kids who serve now. And something inside us is going to march to that quiet cadence the rest of our lives."

42

"IT WAS THE MOST POWERFUL THING I've ever seen." Corrie came back from Washington talking as though he'd had a glimpse of salvation. He began as soon as I pulled up beside his truck and opened my door. Before I'd retied my Adidas he'd given me an outline of his days at the Salute. The parade, the Wall, the reunions, the impromptu parties.

I knew something about it from the news. I was glad to see that the crowds of vets looked, for the most part, like you'd expect any gathering of men in their thirties to look, clean cut, well dressed, respectable. In a word, normal. There were field jackets, and parts of old uniforms, but they were the minority, and under the circumstances, they weren't out of place.

The morning paper on Veterans Day ran a feature article about a soldier who'd overcome heroin addiction and been sober two years. In his boonie hat and camouflaged fatigue blouse, his craggy face and haunted eyes made him look like he'd just escaped from the crypt. It was supposed to be a success story. I guess it was, in a way. But it was also a back of the hand to the thousands of vets at the Salute who'd never had those problems. From what it looked like to me watching TV, most who came home and got on with our lives, raised families, paid taxes, coached Little League, never made the news.

I was angry as hell when I read that article. I'd had a different reaction when I watched a news report of volunteers who, day and night, from mid-morning Wednesday until midnight on Friday, slowly, solemnly read aloud all fifty-eight thousand names on the Wall. It'd been all I could do not to cry.

Before Corrie and I'd reached the hill that rises up past the top of the dam, I'd heard about vets who'd walked from Vermont to Washington; a vet who came home one night from his second job to find his wife had returned her new dishwasher to Sears and used the money to buy him a round-trip ticket to D.C.; the vet on his way to the Salute whose car broke down and was fixed in a small-town garage for no charge when the owner found out where he was headed.

"The parade was something else," Corrie said. "People lined the streets, three or four deep, cheering us as we walked. More amazing than when the Iran hostages came home. Probably over a hundred thousand of us marching. Most of the states had a row of guys in wheelchairs leading their contingent." Corrie paused for a few seconds, then said, "You see stuff like that, it makes you realize how lucky guys like you and I are." The one-two slap of his shoes on the pavement seemed louder and faster than it had before.

He knew the stats about the Wall. Fifty-seven thousand nine hundred thirty-nine names. Three sets of fathers and sons. Thirty-one pairs of brothers. Eight women, all nurses. Sixteen chaplains, including two priests posthumously awarded the Medal of Honor. He didn't see Father Mullin at the Salute.

"We got to the Memorial," Corrie said, "and there was a brief dedication ceremony, and then the fence in front of the Wall was taken down and people went to touch the names." He was still amazed. "It took me over an hour in the crowd to get my turn. I couldn't find everybody that first time, it would've taken too long. I found Pius John, and Willie, and Harding, and Smitty. They all died on the same day, I guess?"

"John was the next morning."

"I couldn't get to Gianelli or Woodson or anyone else then because I wanted to let other people have a turn. There were so many mothers and fathers and wives there. So many kids looking for their fathers' names. It broke my heart."

He didn't expect me to answer.

"I'm telling you, it was sacred, Mick. That's the only way to describe it. Like a shrine, but when you're close to it, that black granite's like a mirror, too. You catch yourself looking back at yourself, surrounded by all those names on the wall. It's the most powerful thing I've ever seen."

There'd been places where vets who'd served in the same unit could meet. We were running back from Peerce's when Corrie began to tell me about the guys from First Platoon he'd seen.

Landon was there, sober now for five and a half years; the first six or so that he'd been home had been rough. He told Corrie, "'Then I realized the good Lord would forgive me for killing all those people, and he was more important than me, so I forgave myself.'"

"I told him he saved Marine lives," Corrie said. "That, by the way, was more words than I'd heard him use the whole time in Vietnam."

"Damn straight," I said.

"In fact, he's a lay preacher now," Corrie said. "Can you imagine him in a pulpit? What would you get, one-word sermons?"

"Best kind."

"Repent!"

"Pray!"

"Salvation!"

"Damnation!"

"You wouldn't know if he was warning you not to sin again or sending you to hell."

"Cloninger was there, too."

"Really? I would've liked to see him."

Corrie gave me a sideways glance.

"How's he doing?" I asked.

"He's great. Still looks like a vulture, beak might be even bigger. He's got five kids, if you can believe that."

"Damn. Has he figured out what causes that?"

"He runs a Sears store close to where he grew up. Must be pretty well respected; got himself elected to the county school board."

"His kids probably make up a third of the students. Good for him."

"His wife was there too."

"Laura? Of 'New Year's Eve at the Manor on the Mountain' fame?"

"Same one. Seemed awfully nice."

I glanced at Corrie. I remembered her picture. "Did you ask the Buzzard about Blondie?"

"I didn't, but Matt did. Apparently, Blondie woke up, didn't remember a thing. He's a changed man, according to the Buzz. Teaches the Cloningers' kids in Sunday school."

"Matt was there?"

"Sure was. He was flying somewhere for a medical thing, did a layover in D.C. for the night. He was surprised you weren't there. Said to say hi and tell you if you're ever in Boston, he knows where they keep the Scotch and cigars."

I laughed at that. Matt was the other guy from the platoon I still kept in touch with, though like Mark Mangan, it was mostly through Christmas cards. I promised myself then that with Matt I'd do better than just once a year.

"I would've liked to have seen him," I said.

"Yeah. I wish you'd been there."

At least he didn't say "Told you so." "How's he doing?" I asked.

"Matt's doing well. Looks worn out, but otherwise good. He didn't say much about it, but I got the impression he works like a dog. Said he loves it, though. He couldn't buy a drink the whole weekend. I don't think any of the corpsmen there could."

"They deserve the best they can get."

"Amen, brother. I think the gathering was a little tough on him, and I don't mean his liver. Sunday morning, a bunch of us got together to have breakfast and clear our heads. We were talking about how powerful the Wall was, and how beautiful, and sad, and sort of overwhelming. The Doc was silent as a brick. Then Cloninger said, 'What're you thinking, Doctor?' Matt had this faraway look in his eyes. He just said, very quietly, 'I wish I'd been able to save more guys.'" Corrie shook his head. "Pretty amazing after all that man did."

"We couldn't have asked for a better corpsman," I said. "Or a better guy."

"Amen again."

"Mike Jackson was there too, and Dottie. They're great."

"Yeah, I really enjoyed seeing them at the Birthday Ball last year. We haven't kept in touch, but they sure seemed good then." I thought for a moment. "She's terrific. You know, after we found out Mike lost both his legs, I wondered whether she'd stay with him. You know, a nineteen- or eighteen-, or whatever she was, year-old girl. That had to be tough."

"I'm sure it was."

"God, I'm sorry, Corrie. That was stupid of me."

"You've said stupider, McClure, shake it off. Speaking of legs, Prevas was there, too. Would you believe it, he's a damn basketball coach. A high school in Ohio. Good record, too."

"No way, José. That's great. How's he doing?"

"Great," Corrie chuckled. "We got into a pretty interesting argument."

"Wait. You haven't seen the guy since 1969, and the two of you have an argument?"

"Well, let's say an intense discussion."

"Lawyer."

"You're welcome. I'll tell you about it. There was some crazy stuff that went on. Remember a guy from the platoon you all called 'Fizzy'? Lost an eye in the valley?"

"I do, yeah. He wasn't there long. Gianelli named him that because he never shut up, like he was bubbling all the time. I remember when he was wounded. Didn't know he lost his eye. Too bad. He wanted to be a stock-car driver."

"Not so fast there, Kemosabe."

"What's this got to do with your argument with Prevas?"

"I'm getting there. But I've got to tell you about your man Fizzy first. He races!"

"What? How's a one-eyed man drive race cars?"

"Stock cars, dirt track. Apparently, there aren't many rules in Arkansas. It was his left eye he lost. Says he doesn't need it to drive counterclockwise on a track."

"Good for him. That's crazy."

"Oh, that ain't all."

"That's not enough?"

"Oh, no."

"And this ties to you and Prevas getting in an argument?"

"Of course."

"Are you one of those lawyers that bill by the word?"

"Sometimes. The shorter the better. I like four letters the most."

"So how did Fizzy cause an argument between you and Prevas?"

"He didn't cause it; he stopped it."

"I'll bite."

"I think his real name's Jim Fitzpatrick, or something like that. But he introduced himself as Fizzy, and that's what Cloninger and Landon called him all weekend. He liked that. Anyhow, Fizzy usually wears an eyepatch, he says, but sometimes he puts in a glass eye."

"Okay."

"Well the crazy son of a bitch has one he got made special for holidays, you know, the Marine Corps Birthday, Veterans Day, Memorial Day, Fourth of July. He wore it last weekend. Bright scarlet with a gold Eagle, Globe, and Anchor in the center of it where the pupil would be."

"No shit?"

"I shit you not. Do you know what the crazy man did with it?"

"Wait, he wore it. That's great, but isn't that crazy enough?"

"Oh no, no way. Saturday night, we're in this bar, and Prevas and I get into this argument."

"Oh good," I interrupted. "I thought you guys never would."

"Yeah, yeah. So Saturday in the Dubliner, we're all there, Matt, Landon, the Buzzard, a gazillion other people, all Marines, or corpsmen, a few wives. Prevas starts arguing with me. He hates the term 'handicapped,' says it sounds like you're retarded. Prevas says he's not goddamn retarded, just not able to do some things, or do some things the same as other people do them. Not able. Dis-abled." Corrie shook both hands for emphasis as we ran.

"I prefer 'handicapped,' myself. I can do almost anything you can, so I'm able, but I do it differently, or slower, maybe. That's my handicap, just like racehorses have handicaps, and golfers have handicaps. It just means how you do something, not that you're not able to do it. You'd think Prevas would agree, he's a coach. He should know about handicaps."

"Different strokes, I guess." I was thinking it must've been funny, in a bizarre sort of way, to see two one-legged guys arguing about whether they were handicapped or disabled. I wasn't sure if I could've had a conversation like that if I'd been that badly wounded.

"Exactly," Corrie said. "I admit it was beer fueled, but it was fairly good natured until Prevas begins to get a little pissed. He wouldn't let it go, and he was getting louder. All of a sudden, Fizzy comes up beside him, and Prevas doesn't even see him because he's arguing at me, and old Fizzy pops that red eyeball with its EGA out of its socket and puts it on Prevas' shoulder and holds it there like he was balancing a marble. 'You better calm down,' he says ''cause I'm keeping my eye on you.' Prevas didn't know whether to shit or go blind, to use his favorite phrase."

I let out a roar of a laugh. "You win. You're right. That's as crazy as it gets."

"Oh, no, it gets crazier."

"No way."

"Oh, yeah. After that, we left the Dubliner and packed into a couple of cabs. Cabbies wouldn't take a dime because we're Vietnam vets. So off we go to a strip club on M Street, a dozen Marines and Matt, and another corpsman he knew named Searles." Corrie laughed, then went on. "Searles is blind—sunglasses, cane, and all." Corrie began laughing again. Even as irreverent as he is, I couldn't imagine what he found humorous about a blind corpsman.

"So, Matt pulls out a wad of bills and talks one of the strippers into giving Searles a performance in braille. I wish you could've seen the look on his face. Christmas in November. I thought Matt might have to perform an emergency grin-ectomy before the smile killed Searles." Corrie shook his head. "A true patriot, that girl."

"That's fantastic. And you guys are crazy."

"Yep, crazed Vietnam vets, thank you. I wish you'd been there. All the guys wanted to be remembered to you. Where but the Corps could you come up with people that great?"

I wondered if I could've gotten together with the guys from the platoon and avoided the Wall.

43

THE PERSON I REGRETTED NOT SEEING at the Salute more than anyone else was Matt. Our Christmas cards crossed in the mail that year. In them, we both promised we'd try hard to get together in 1983. It was a couple years more before we actually did, though Corrie almost saw him that June.

He'd gone to Boston to take depositions. He and Matt planned to have dinner, but shortly before Corrie was going to leave the Parker House to meet him, he got a call from Mass General saying that Doctor Matheson apologized but he'd been called into surgery and couldn't meet his friend.

Corrie did, though, come back with another article about Matt he'd seen in the paper. It wasn't a puff piece, though it referred to Doctor Matheson as Boston's "Medical Marathon Man." Matt wasn't a big runner, but the writer apparently enjoyed analogy, even mentioning Heartbreak Hill once. The author called him the Medical Marathon Man because he never gave up, often saving the most badly injured patients, sometimes on his feet performing multiple surgeries on multiple patients for an amazing number of hours. When I read that, I thought of all the times I'd seen Matt kneeling in the dirt, sometimes under fire, trying to save a Marine's life. I remembered him working on me as bullets flew around us.

"Being a trauma surgeon means functioning under excruciating pressure," the article said. "Every day, patients' lives literally depend on the decisions you make and the actions you take in a very short moment of time. I asked Doctor Matheson how he coped with such stress. I expected him to tell me he listened to music or meditated or did yoga, or something like that. The look in his eyes when he answered, I can describe only in contradictory terms: haunted and serene. 'If I do my job right,' he said, 'if I leave nothing I can control to chance, I can save someone's life. What can be more soothing than that?'"

I put the paper down for a moment, recalling how Matt had looked anything but serene when he couldn't save people like Dasmund or Glass or Ladoor.

The writer went on to praise Matt's work and dedication but seemed slightly bemused at what she described as his ascetic lifestyle. Thirty-six years old and not yet married, he'd been named, the article noted, a year or two earlier one of Boston's most eligible bachelors. The author asked if he still was. He laughed, saying he couldn't be, since he seldom went anywhere that didn't require him to wear scrubs. "Besides work," the author said, "Dr. Matheson's only interests appeared to be the Sox, single-malt whiskey, and Churchill-size cigars. 'Strange health risks for a doctor,' he admitted, 'but I practice, not preach.'"

When I finished the article, I found myself wondering if Matt was happy and how long he'd keep up such a pace. I had little doubt about what drove him so hard.

I got an answer to my question a dozen years later. Matt had been asked on short notice to fill in for another speaker at a conference at Johns Hopkins. Patti couldn't join us for some reason. She was disappointed, since she'd never met him. Corrie was disappointed too; he was on the road for a big case again.

Matt wasn't yet fifty, but he looked ten years older, with his creased, angular face and thatch of steely gray hair. Except for his eyes. For someone as intense and focused as I guessed he still was, he had happy eyes. He'd married the widow of a colleague who'd died of cancer several years earlier. I'd seen Sally's picture in the Christmas card they sent the year they were married. A pretty, refined-looking woman with silver hair and a hundred-dollar hairdo, she appeared to have an easy smile. She and her late husband had known Matt for over twenty years.

"She's trying to broaden my horizons," Matt said with a broad smile. They had tickets then to the symphony and the theater, as well as the Sox, though Sally often ended up going with a girlfriend or by herself. "She understands completely if I have to be at the hospital. The only things she complains about at all is the cigars and that I don't exercise or sleep much." Matt shook his head. "But there's so many patients. There's plenty of time to sleep when we're old." He grinned. "I tell her I get all the exercise I can stand jumping to conclusions. She says the only conclusion I've ever jumped to was when I said yes as soon as she suggested we get married."

Matt raised his hands—*What can you do?* He pushed his glasses up onto his forehead and rubbed his eyes. The smile that blanketed the crevasses of his face was the happiest I ever saw on him.

I saw Matt for the last time in 2010. I was in Boston for a meeting again. Patti was teaching, so she couldn't come, and Sally was visiting her son and family in Austin, so it was just me and Matt. I joked that it was like we were shunned, the only attendees at a high school class's every-ten-year reunion. "Yeah," Matt said, "and our math isn't too good at that."

I'd just turned sixty, Matt sixty-three. I'd been at Country Day for thirty-four years, hadn't coached for a dozen, and had relinquished the chairmanship of the English Department to enjoy the last few years of my career just teaching, without having to focus on the administrative side too. Douglas and Katie were grown with kids of their own. Patti would retire the next year from teaching French at Towson High. Life was good. The family was great, and I was doing what I loved, at a pace I enjoyed.

Matt hadn't slowed down a bit. "I got Sally interested in the Red Sox, and I can tell the difference between Vivaldi and Brahms, now," he said with a laugh. "But I still miss the Sox's home games and the symphony and theater more often than not, 'cause I'm operating or attending to patients or lecturing somewhere. Couldn't ask for a better wife, though," he said happily. "Sally understands what's important to me, even if she thinks someone our age should begin to slow down."

We toasted each other's good fortune in marrying wonderful women and promised that someday we'd all finally meet.

We were halfway through dinner when Matt asked me if I thought much about Vietnam any more. "Not much," I said. "Why?"

"I don't either," Matt said, "but a lot of our vets seem to be refocused on the war. You see a lot more bumper stickers and gray-haired guys wearing 'Vietnam vet' ball caps."

I hadn't paid a lot of attention, but when Matt mentioned it, I realized he was right. I'd seen quite a few bumper stickers with the Vietnam Service Ribbon on them, and often guys wearing hats with Vietnam campaign ribbons embroidered on the front.

"You didn't see that ten years ago, much less twenty or thirty," Matt said.

"I guess the way the troops coming home from Iraq and Afghanistan got treated kind of opened it up for Vietnam vets too," I said.

Matt agreed. "But it's more than just that it's okay now," he said. "I've been talking to the docs at the VA hospital about it. They're seeing guys like us, sixties, maybe seventies, who're talking about Vietnam, sometimes for the first time in decades. It's like as we get into our senior years, if we don't share what it was like, the memories will be gone forever and no one will ever know about a really important time in our lives."

"Do you mean guys are having PTSD after all these years?"

Matt shook his head. "No, it's different. These guys've been fine, led normal, functioning lives. They're fine now, in fact, you know, other than the physical reason they're at the hospital—diabetes or arthritis or a whole host of things. Nothing psychological or emotional awry. But when the staff talks to them, they're finding these guys are thinking about combat a lot more than they have since the years right after they came home. They've seen it in Korea vets, too. Absolutely normal guys, but forty or fifty or sixty years after they fought they want to open up about what they did at Khe Sanh or Pork Chop Hill."

Matt drank some of his wine. "The head docs are calling it LOSS. Late-onset stress symptomatology. Nothing to worry about, but if we think more about Vietnam in a few years than we have in a while, that might be what that's all about. Makes sense, it's an important part of who we are, even if we've never talked much about it."

I agreed with that.

Matt smiled. "I've had a dream for years. Always the same, always crawling toward someone wounded. Blood everywhere, rivers of it. Tremendous, silent noise. Dream noise, you know? You can tell everything's blowing up, but it's kind of visual noise, not aural."

"Like in the movies where stuff is blowing up in slo-mo, but all you hear is the music," I said. "In my dreams, there's no music."

"I can never get to them, and I can't tell who they are. It's like I'm in a quagmire, and I can never move fast enough to save whoever needs me out there."

Matt poured more Chianti for both of us. "I don't need a shrink to translate that one for me." He smiled. I didn't detect the slightest regret.

Two months later I flew to Boston for Matt's funeral. Sixty-three—two years younger than I am now. He'd dropped dead of a heart attack between operations. "I guess it's fitting he went out in his scrubs," Sally said with a sad, crooked smile. She seemed to have no self-pity, just gratitude that she'd had Matt as long as she did.

"Matt was the best man I've known," I told her.

"I know," Sally said. "I've known Matt since his residency. He was a kind man, and brilliant, but he never slowed down, from then until, well, you know, last week." Her eyes filled then, but she quickly regained her composure.

"You'd probably appreciate this, or maybe *understand*'s the better word," she said. She paused for a moment, as though forming her thoughts. "Matt never talked much about Vietnam, just to say he'd been a medic in the field in some very tough times with some guys he'd really cared for a lot. He did say he'd decided to become a doctor mostly because of that experience. I don't think he ever told anyone any details about that time; he certainly didn't talk about it with me. I'm certain, though, that something about it drove him at the pace he kept up all his life."

"Matt never quit," I said. "He did everything humanly possible to save lives."

Sally smiled. "That was the Matt I knew," she said. "He never gave up."

———

I know it can't happen, but ever since Matt died, there's been a part of me that's thought his name should be on the Wall with the others, even if it took him over forty years to join them.

44

A COUPLE OF MONTHS AFTER CORRIE showed me the June 1983 article about Matt, I went to see Woody's parents. It was more than a dozen years after I got home from the war.

Patti and the kids and I spent a few days with friends in Rehoboth Beach. Country Day's football practice began on Wednesday, so early on Tuesday evening I drove home to get a good night's sleep before the first session. At thirty-three, I was proud of still being able to outwork and outrun most of the kids.

It was a beautiful late August evening on the Eastern Shore, so I decided to meander cross country rather than contend with traffic on Route 50. I drove on two-lane roads through flat expanses of corn and soybeans, the radio tuned to a station playing oldies, laughing to myself thinking of Douglas and Katie in the waves with Patti and me.

I came to an intersection where an arrow pointed toward Seaford, Delaware, and remembered that Woody and Mike Jackson had been from there. Without any real thought, I turned and drove into town. There was a James Woodson listed in the phone book in the booth outside a gas station. The teenage attendant with a cigarette perched behind his ear gave me directions to Cherry Lane. I had no intention of doing anything but driving by the house. I wasn't even sure why I was going to do that.

I convinced myself I was just curious about where Woody had lived. John and I'd talked about how we'd visit the families of friends who'd been killed. More pavement laid for the McClure Memorial Highway. I'd never even visited John's mother. Maybe by just driving by the Woodsons' I'd feel better about not keeping my promise. Fourteen years, John, far too late to comfort the sorrowful, my friend. What would I say? *I knew your son fourteen years ago; he's been dead damn near as long as he lived. Just thought I'd drop by and stir up your painful memories, 'cause I still think of him.*

I shook my head in chagrin. *Jesus, McClure, you're a case.*

I pulled up across the street from a modest Cape Cod with a closely mown lawn and well-tended flower gardens on either side of the front steps. At the end of the driveway, behind the house, a one-car garage had a basketball hoop above the door. There was no net. I wasn't sure what I was doing there.

I sat staring at the Woodson house, trying not to think about when Woody was killed, trying to remember Father Mullin's advice. I tried to imagine Woody growing up in that house, riding his bike on that street, shooting hoops in the driveway, playing catch with his dad. I thought about him hung over, his hands covering his ears in the helicopter going out to my first day in the bush. Running out under fire to save Tich. Laughing with Gio and Willie and John and me. Kidding Harding about his pictures of Bonnie.

Screwed, blewed, and tattooed. A phrase for the ages. I smiled at that; I could hear Woody saying it. Then I heard him say, "Move back, people, the magician is about to make things disappear."

Jesus, God, take that away. I tried hard not to think about Woody at the end, but the pictures sat off in the peripheral vision of my mind. Never quite out of sight, like something barely hidden in tall grass that you don't want to see.

I sat with the car running, pushing the pictures back and forth inside my head. A small woman, probably well into her fifties, came out the front door. She stood with her back to me, spraying her garden, then turned the way people do when they get the feeling someone's watching them. It dawned on me that it must be frightening for a woman minding her own business on her front lawn to see a strange man sitting in a car across the street staring at her. I switched off the ignition and opened the door. I didn't know what I was going to say, but I didn't want Woody's mom to be scared of me.

I stopped at the curb before stepping onto their lawn. She didn't look scared at all. She looked as though she expected me to ask which house on the street belonged to someone.

"Mrs. Woodson?"

"Yes?" That took her aback, a strange young man calling her by name. "Can I help you?"

"Ma'am, my name's Marty McClure. I was in Vietnam with your son."

She dropped the hose. It sprayed up against the bay window, a harsh sound like the crackle and rip of a firefight someplace off in the distance. Her hands went up to her mouth; I thought she was going to cry. It seemed like a long time before she said anything. I felt so guilty bothering this poor woman. I wanted to back away, retreat to the car.

"You knew Tommy?" Not much more than a whisper.

"Yes, ma'am."

"Oh my. I have to call Jim."

"Mr. Woodson? I'm sorry, please don't bother him. I didn't mean to intrude . . ."

"Oh, no. Yes. He just went back to the shop to work on someone's tractor. They need it tomorrow. I'll get him, he's only five minutes."

"Mrs. Woodson, I don't want to be a bother. I just . . ." I didn't know why I was there.

"Oh no, he'll want to come. To meet someone who knew Tommy then. Please come in while I call him. Please." She sounded as though it'd be cruel if I left.

She sat me in the living room and went to call her husband. In one corner, a table held a vase of fresh flowers and a dozen photos in unmatched frames. An 8x10 picture of Woody was in a gold frame on another small table, above it on the wall a crucifix with a frond of dried palm.

I picked up the photo. Dress blues, high, stiff-collared tunic, gleaming brass buttons, white dress cover, its brim polished to a radiant sheen. PFC Woodson's official boot camp graduation picture. You couldn't tell that the buttons on the blouse were permanently sewn in place or that the uniform was split down the back, fastened with eye hooks so that recruit after recruit could shrug it on, sit at attention on a wooden stool, scowl at the camera, all in the matter of seconds allotted each new Marine. Woody looked rugged and handsome, the sides of his head cropped so short you couldn't tell he was blond. He wore the required Parris Island tough-guy glare, but the DIs hadn't been able to erase that trademark gleam in his eyes.

The old Marine Corps recruiting slogan came to me then. The Few, The Proud, The Marines. *Jesus, Woody, I'm so sorry,* I said inside my head. I clamped my teeth together, feeling the muscles tighten throughout my face. In the kitchen, I heard Mrs. Woodson say, "Oh yes, please hurry. I don't know how long he can stay."

A matching gold frame sat beside Woody's picture. Inside it, a sheet of parchment-like paper, a pencil etching: *Thomas J. Woodson.*

My stomach clenched tighter looking at that. I still hadn't been to the Memorial, but I'd seen pictures of the etchings people did of loved ones' names on the Wall. How do you stand that? How do you touch, how do you make a rubbing of your boy's name and not lose your mind? A picture of Douglas laughing, knee deep in the surf, gesturing for me to join him, wandered in front of my eyes.

On the other side of Woody's Marine Corps picture was one of him with a beautiful girl in a prom dress and Mike Jackson and Dottie. Woody's blond, curly hair reached almost down to his shoulders. The girl wore a sweet, slightly mischievous smile. Dottie was a younger, even prettier version of the woman I'd met almost two years before. Mike looked like Paul Bunyan in a tweed sports coat. Both boys' smiles said, Man, it doesn't get any better than this. I wondered who the girl was. The table looked like a shrine.

Mrs. Woodson came from the kitchen to ask if I'd like coffee. She was calm, though her eyes held a sadness I guessed would never go away. She did a wonderful job of pretending not to notice how upset I was. I said once more that I didn't want to be any trouble. "Trouble?" she said. "You're certainly no trouble, Marty. It's so good of you to stop by."

While she made coffee, I looked at the other pictures in the room. A wedding picture of Woody's parents. Mrs. Woodson had been very pretty then, shoulder-length blond hair and a waist you could get both your hands around. Her husband was in uniform with corporal stripes on his sleeves and a number of ribbons. I recognized the Purple Heart and the Presidential Unit Citation. I guessed they'd gotten married during or right after World War II. Mr. Woodson was good-looking, with high cheekbones and a strong jaw. He wore a broad smile, but his eyes looked older than the rest of his face. Woody couldn't have avoided being handsome if he'd wanted to. I had to work again for a moment to keep the picture of him at the end out of my head. It seemed to sit in a spot dimly lit by a red bulb off to one side of my brain.

There was a photo of Woody's sister in a wedding dress; another with her husband; several of their kids. Other framed photos of Woody, too. As a very young boy. In his high school football uniform, his blonde hair in wet ringlets, a ball under one arm. In his basketball uniform; in his baseball togs. One in his high school graduation cap and gown. His whole life before Vietnam was all there in frames.

I was still looking when Mrs. Woodson came back in the room. "We got that at the Wall," she said, indicating the etching. I nodded, didn't say anything.

"That one is Tommy and Emily Stephens at their senior prom."

"They were a good-looking couple."

"Weren't they? Tommy dated a lot of girls." She rolled her eyes a little and smiled. "But I think Emily was a real favorite. She's married now, with a beautiful little boy. She still comes by to talk with me sometimes." Mrs. Woodson picked up the picture. "The couple with them is Mike and Dottie Jackson. Mike was with Tommy in Vietnam too. Did you know Mike? They enlisted together. Terrible what happened to him."

"Yes, ma'am, I knew Mike. I mean, I know Mike, and Dottie. I knew him in Vietnam, only a short while before he was wounded. I actually saw him and met Dottie at a Marine Corps event in Philadelphia two years ago."

"They're a wonderful young couple. So strong, the two of them."

Woody's sister's name was Carol. "I wish she could've met you; it would have meant a lot to her. These are our two grandchildren, Susan and Tommy." Mrs. Woodson smiled. "Tommy's named after his uncle."

"That's wonderful," I said.

She nodded. There didn't seem to be anything else to say about that.

They insisted I call them Ellen and Jim. Woody's dad looked like a man who could crank a gigantic wrench all day long. His face and arms were sunburned the color of wet sand, and the creases on his knuckles still had grime in them when he got home from the shop. When we shook hands, I saw a faded Eagle, Globe, and Anchor on his upper arm. I wondered if Woody would've grown up to look like him. I wondered too how many times in the last fourteen years Big Jim Woodson had wished he hadn't set such a powerful example for his son.

"Thank you for coming," he said. "We've never met anyone who was in Vietnam with Tom."

"Mike," Mrs. Woodson said.

"Of course. Besides Mike Jackson." Mr. Woodson nodded. "Did you know Mike, too?"

"A little. Like I told Mrs. Woodson . . ."

"Ellen."

"Yes, ma'am, Ellen. I got to the platoon shortly before he was wounded."

"Hard to believe, from the same high school class." Ellen stared at the floor for a moment, shaking her head.

"Best friends. He and Tom were best friends since they could walk."

"I saw Mike and Dottie, like I told your wife, actually met Dottie for the first time, at a Marine Corps Ball in Philadelphia a couple years ago."

"It's been longer than that since we've seen them, I guess. Hasn't it, Jim?"

"I think you're forgetting Mother's Day last year. They stopped by then."

"Oh, you're right." Ellen turned back to me. "That Dottie's quite a girl. Mike's mother and I are good friends. Margaret says they're doing pretty well." She paused and looked down at the floor again. I couldn't imagine what she was thinking. I wondered if she envied Mrs. Jackson; her son was home, even without his legs. What John had told Woody came to me again: a man is much more than his legs.

"It's really terrible what happened to him," Ellen said.

"Yes ma'am. I was really glad to see he was doing okay." I wanted to say how special I thought Dottie must be, but talking about the Jacksons seemed like it might be pouring more salt in the Woodsons' wound.

"Are you okay?" Jim Woodson seemed to study my eyes. I wondered if some tortured expression had just crossed my face. He must've realized I didn't understand what he meant, because he said, "I mean, were you wounded, too?"

"I'm fine," I said. "I was, but not badly." I felt strangely guilty about saying that.

"Tell us about Tommy," Ellen said.

That caught me by surprise. It shouldn't have, of course. Why was I there if not to tell them about their son? But the way she put it, what was I expected to say? What could I tell someone's parents about their own son? I wasn't about to tell them how he died. Tell us about Tommy. I'd never called him anything except Woody, or Woodson. Tell us about our only son, our late son. What could I tell them that they didn't know? That I was willing to say?

"We called him Woody, you know." I tried to smile. Maybe I could keep this light. "I always remember him as kind and brave, and he had a terrific sense of humor." I always remember him that way. Jesus Christ.

Ellen nodded vigorously. "That boy was a rascal," she said. Jim nodded, too, a slight motion that said he agreed with me, but he hurt too much to act enthusiastic.

"He called me 'McClure of Arabia.' It was so hot and blistering sunny where we were most of the time, and this Irish skin of mine fries in no time, and we didn't have decent sun lotion back then, if we had any at all." I glanced down at my hands. How many times had I rubbed machine-gun lubricating fluid into their backs to loosen them up enough that I could clean the gun? "I took to draping a green towel under my helmet to hide the back of my neck and my ears and the sides of my face from the sun." I indicated with my hands. "Woody, Tommy, thought that was funny. He started calling me 'McClure of Arabia,' you know, like the movie with Peter O'Toole? Fortunately, it didn't really stick."

They both smiled at that. I felt like I was talking too much, as though I were rushing through a story in the hope of fending off a worse inquiry. It came anyhow.

"Were you there when Tom died?" Jim asked.

Jesus. A fist in my stomach. But what did I expect? Of course they'd want to know that. I nodded. "Yes, sir. I was."

Jim looked like he'd just turned to stone.

Ellen's hands began moving in her lap. She seemed to study them, then she looked up with tears in her eyes for the first time that evening. "Can you tell us about when he passed away?" Her voice wasn't much more than a whisper.

I struggled to keep my composure. I couldn't imagine what she was feeling, this little, gentle-voiced woman whose only son had been killed. The thought flashed through my mind: I don't know how I'd live if Douglas or Katie were taken from me. For what seemed like a long moment, I didn't speak. Passed away. Jesus Christ. They should never be told.

"Woody was always very brave," I finally said. "That morning, he tried to protect the rest of us from a booby trap, but it went off."

Phosphorescent pictures flashed through my head like scenes through the window of a train careening into hell. They didn't need to hear how I'd spent the night sleeping with my arm on that goddamn booby-trapped ammo can. They didn't need to know that their son had argued with Gio about which of them would blow it in place. They did not need to be told that Woody stuck his tongue out at Gio or that he yelled, "Move back, people, the magician is about to make things disappear." They didn't need to have me describe the bloody hunk of their son stuck to my chest, or have me tell them what their handsome boy had turned into in the grass. But sweet Jesus God, how could I ever get those things out of my head? How could I tell them without that picture distorting my words?

Ellen's hands were busy in her lap. She stared at them as if there were answers in the way they moved. Jim studied me intently, as though he were trying to extract some hidden truth from my face. He sat absolutely still, his hands on his knees. He looked like a sand sculpture at the beach. I half expected his face, maybe his whole body, to crack and crumble to the floor. I wanted desperately to say anything I could to help them in any possible way.

"It went off," I said again quietly. "Woody died instantly. He didn't suffer."

People always want to know that. The good news in this bad news is that your loved one didn't suffer. Your son is gone, but he didn't suffer. With Woody, that much was true. I felt so inadequate saying it, though.

Ellen was crying softly. Jim's eyes were full of tears, but he held them in. He was staring beyond me into some distance I couldn't see. Looking at his face, it was all I could do to keep from breaking down.

We sat for a while, none of us saying anything, then Ellen stirred first. She asked if I'd like more coffee. I was exhausted. I wanted to get home, to get to sleep, but she pleaded with me to stay for her peach pie. "It's the least we can do," she said, "You've been so awfully good to stop by."

Maybe it was the pie that got Jim talking about the casualty call. He'd been fairly quiet, anguished but stoic, until then. But as we sat together at the kitchen table, something broke loose, as though he'd never spoken of the details of that day to anyone else but had to tell me.

It had been a Sunday afternoon. A government gray car out in front of the house. Two Marines, a gunnery sergeant and a corporal, and Father Rivers, the local priest. The worst day of their lives.

Ellen had been in the kitchen, Jim in the living room reading the paper, waiting for the game to come on. He and Tom always watched the Os if they played on Sunday. He heard a car door shut in front of the house, then saw them start up the walk. He got up quietly and went to the door, trying to decide whether to throw the deadbolt so they couldn't get in. He didn't want Ellen to hear, so he opened the door before they rang the bell.

"Jim, I'm so sorry," the priest said. Only a few hours before, they'd joked about the Os-Angels series on the church steps after mass.

"In the kitchen, I heard the voices," Ellen said. "The whole time Tommy was gone, I hated whenever someone came up those steps." She called, "Who is it, Jim?," but he didn't respond. Something was wrong.

She was still carrying the raspberry pie she'd been about to put in the oven when she walked into the living room. When she saw the two Marines behind Father Rivers, she dropped it on the floor and ran upstairs.

The priest and the gunny helped Jim up the stairs. "I could barely stay standing," he said.

He kept pushing gently on the bedroom door, the whole time whispering, over and over, "Sweetheart, please let me in." But Ellen was slumped on the floor against the door, softly crying, "No, no, please God, no." Maybe if she were hidden enough, quiet enough, the terrifying news wouldn't follow her into the room. It took a long time for Jim to get her to move enough for him to go in.

"It was so terrible when they came to tell us," Ellen said as she dabbed a Kleenex at her cheeks. "I was terrible."

"Now, Ellie . . ." Jim reached over and took her hand. His eyes were filled, but I had the feeling that Jim Woodson was a man who never cried in front of people, though I guessed he'd cried at his son's funeral. I hadn't seen such anguish on anyone's face since I was in the valley. We were talking about Woody, of course, about one Marine, but I thought then of all those I'd lost. I thought of Mom and Dad, too. On a gleaming black screen behind all the faces parading through my mind, fifty-eight thousand names seemed to quiver in bright light.

Tears leaked down my cheeks. Ellen put her hand over mine. "I'm sorry," she said. "Do you want us to stop?"

My God, Woody's mom apologizing to me? Me crying in front of his dad? "Oh, no, no, I'm sorry, please don't," I whispered.

"Sometimes I think it helps to talk about things. And to cry." Ellen dabbed again at her eyes. "They wouldn't let us open his coffin, you know."

"Yes, ma'am." Under the table, I clenched my hands together so hard I thought I might break a finger. I thought of Mom and Dad's sealed coffin, tried not to imagine why, tried not to think of Woody in the grass, prayed I wasn't about to throw up on the Woodsons' kitchen floor.

"It was terrible not being able to see my boy for the last time."

"Sometimes they know best, Ellie," Jim said. He reached across the table and put his hand over hers again. The EGA on his bicep was faded and seamed. I remembered Woody saying he'd fought at Peleliu. It had to be horrid, knowing the damage combat could do to his boy.

"I know, but still, even now, fourteen years later, there's a tiny part of me that wonders whether it was really my Tommy in that coffin."

Jim patted her hand. "Ellie . . ." was all he said. All the creases on his face seemed to have deepened.

"I know," she said again. She looked at me as though she thought I'd understand. "Mike's mother told me that after they amputated his legs, he had phantom pain. He was certain he was feeling real pain in his legs, even though the poor boy didn't have them anymore. I think sometimes it was like that with me not seeing Tommy again. I couldn't help myself, sometimes, I was just positive he was going to come in that door."

Ellen looked past Jim toward the kitchen door. He watched her eyes, then he looked down at the table as though it held a hatchway to escape. He didn't say anything.

"I guess I was angry he didn't, wouldn't ever," Ellen said. She shook her head as though she were disappointed in herself. "I guess everyone grieves differently. For a while I was so angry, I took it out on people I had no right to. Even ones that I loved. Poor Carol, she was grieving too, of course, for her brother, just different from me.

Poor girl. I blew up at her once when she couldn't find the color shoes she wanted for some event. It seemed such a trivial thing to worry about. Then I got so I hardly could get out of bed. For a long time, I didn't want to run into anyone who'd remind me of our loss."

Jim hadn't raised his eyes from the table. I wanted to tell them I could relate, but how could I say that to Woody's mom when she was talking about her dead son? I didn't say anything, and Ellen went on.

"Tommy would be thirty-four now, a grown man. Like you," she said, and she actually smiled. "But I still think of him as a boy. I suppose we always will. Sometimes, even now, it seemed almost hourly back then, I catch myself looking out the back door, waiting for him to get home from school. Sometimes when I'm at the sink, I look at the basketball hoop half-expecting to see him there. He and his dad used to love to shoot hoops."

That struck some chord in Jim. I thought then he might cry. He didn't, but his eyes filled again and at the same time seemed to grow duller, as though a light inside him had dimmed.

"For a long time, I didn't want to let go of the idea that Tommy was not in that casket. I almost believed it had all been a terrible mistake, and that I would see him at our back door again one day. It was kind of comforting, you know? Looking out back for him, walking out to see if he'd gone around the garage. Jim did that for a while, too. Didn't you, hon'?"

Jim nodded. I don't think he could speak.

"But I guess we move on a little," Ellen said. "It's what Tommy would want. I don't do that much anymore."

Jim seemed to need to change the subject away from looking for his son. He got up and got the etching from next to Woody's boot camp graduation picture. "We went on Tom's birthday in January," he said. "It was so cold and windy that day, we could barely hold the paper against the panel."

"Some vets helped us with it," Ellen said. "It took some courage for us to go there, even after all these years. We'd been to the cemetery a thousand times. Probably more. Tommy's buried here, the cemetery's right near the church. It's somehow comforting to go there."

I could imagine them going to his grave nearly every day. I knew I would if Douglas or Katie were dead, God forbid. Even though it'd been ten years since Mom and Dad died, I still visited them at St. Rita's once in a while. I'd gone a few weeks before; no special reason, I just wanted to say hi.

"The Memorial's different," Ellen continued. "I didn't know if I could face all those names."

That is for damn sure, I said to myself.

"It's a special place," Jim said. "We'll go back, Veteran's Day or maybe November 10."

Ellen reached across the table and took the framed rubbing from Jim. "I just kept rubbing my fingertips into his name in that shiny black granite. Like if I pressed hard enough, maybe I could feel his hand in mine, like when he was a little boy. Silly, I know . . ." Her voice tapered off; she dabbed a Kleenex at her eyes.

Jim reached over once again and this time patted her hand. I tried not to move a muscle. In a stronger voice, Ellen said, "There's something sacred about that wall. Maybe it's because all those boys are there together, their names, I mean. That's so important. It's a place for everyone to honor all their sacrifices, to remember every one of them lived. There's a comfort in that, too, remembering but still going on, maybe even finding a little peace. Don't you think so, Marty?"

"I do," I said, praying that neither of them would ask me when I'd been there.

45

I HAD TERRIBLE NIGHTMARES FOR the next couple of nights. I dreamt of Woody in the grass. The dream was different this time, though—in the grass, what was left of him wore his gleaming white dress uniform hat. I dreamt of Mike Jackson too, his bare white ass flashing in the sunlight, but instead of the scooped-out legs I'd seen, he showed me his stumps. Worst of all, I dreamt of seven-year-old Douglas wearing Marine Corps dress blues, lying in our living room in a closed wooden box while a casualty-call team with Pius John dressed as a priest pounded on our front door.

The kids kicked my butt in wind sprints during practice on Wednesday and Thursday. I kept looking at those fifteen- and sixteen- and seventeen-year-old boys, so full of spirit and promise, and thinking of all my friends whose names were on the Wall. I'd never thought of my refusal to go to the Memorial as an act of cowardice before, but as I thought about Ellen and Jim Woodson, I began to wonder if I should.

I couldn't get over how Woody's mom had actually tried to comfort me. I was embarrassed by that but appreciative and nearly awestruck by her courage at the same time. The last thing Ellen said to me as I left her and Jim to drive home was, "Come back and see us any time, Marty. And between now and then, we hope you have a good, happy life. It's what Tommy would want, you know. For all of us."

For the next couple days, I kept picturing the Woodsons' house, the photos that had so happily recorded Woody's life. There had to be photos, or at least memories, of happy times in Pius John's mother's house, and in Gio's, and Willie's, and my other friends' parents' too.

I drove to Loch Raven Reservoir on Thursday evening after our coaches' meeting. I parked at Peerce's, intending to go for a run to clear out my head. But when I run, my thoughts tend to freewheel, jump about, and I needed to think, so I walked instead, for over two hours. I thought about my friends. Not how they'd died, but how they'd lived. And about how much I missed them. I thought too about what Corrie had said back around the time of the Salute. How all of us marched to the same quiet cadence of belief in each other and America and in the value of serving something bigger than ourselves. I'd felt for a very long time that I'd lost more than my friends: I'd lost something else that I'd never admitted to myself—what it meant to have served alongside each of them.

By the time I'd walked by myself through the tall, quiet pines along the reservoir bank and back to the car, I realized I'd not lost that belief. I'd just hidden it by mistake in the boxes where I'd tried to bury my bad memories.

———

The ghosts came to me that night for the first time in a while. They stepped forward out of the swirling mist to the quiet chord of distant helicopters. They walked toward me in step with each other and with a cadence I thought in my dream that I too could hear. Behind them were many others, hundreds, perhaps thousands, stretching to the periphery of my vision and back into the mist. They were all marching in step.

The six friends who've always been there smiled as they approached. As before, they stopped only paces from me. Then they all beckoned me forward, toward them.

When I got back to Rehoboth on Friday evening, my gang was having a last romp on the beach. Patti knew something was up when I had tears in my eyes as I hugged the kids.

"A little sand in my eyes," I said. She gave me one of her *Okay, we can talk about this later* looks.

Katie scampered off to play at the water's edge. Douglas stood next to me watching her go. I grabbed him again and hugged him until Patti thought his ears would pop off his head.

Later, when we were alone, Patti said, "You doing okay? You got a little emotional with Douglas on the beach."

"I'm good," I said. "I've just been thinking a lot the last couple days about how lucky we are with our kids. I want that to last forever."

"That's sweet. We are lucky. What got you thinking about that? Miss us?"

"I did. But other stuff, too." I told Patti then about how, on impulse, almost inadvertently, I'd visited Woody's folks. "He was Mike Jackson's best friend. They grew up together and were both in my platoon. Woody was killed a couple months after Mike was wounded. He was a really good guy, sort of the All-American Boy. Funny, brave, kind. One of my favorites.

"His parents were amazing. So sad, but so strong. Being in their home made me realize how much I'd forgotten about Woody and a lot of the other friends I lost. How much I pushed their memories away, the good as well as the bad I wanted to escape from. For a long time, I think, I forgot what was important that we shared."

Patti gave me a hug. "It's probably like you've said about your parents, it's good to remember the good parts of their lives."

"I'm going to the Memorial on Monday after practice."

"That's kind of short notice, but I can try to get a sitter. I guess we could bring the kids."

"Thanks, but I think I should go this first time by myself."

"You'll be okay? Maybe you could see if Corrie can go."

"No, Sweetie," I said. "This is something I want to do by myself. I'll tell him about it next time we run."

"He'll be pleased."

I nodded. He would be. But I wasn't going to do it for him.

46

THE FORECAST ON MONDAY MORNING WAS warm with a chance of rain. Patti asked if I wanted jeans and a rain jacket to change into before I left school to drive to D.C. I said no, I'd grab an umbrella, but I was going to wear my coat and tie. She smiled at me and nodded. She didn't need to ask why.

I drove to Washington, recalling names. There were so many I remembered and more that I'd known once before but couldn't recall. John, Harding, Willie, Smitty. Gio, Woody. Dasmund, Glass. Carlton. Ogala. Brocato. Ladoor and Havey, too.

Too many names. Fifty-eight thousand waited; I knew only a few. Too many pictures, too much pain. Images tumbled through my mind like kaleidoscope pieces, in random patterns, jagged sharp edges here, softened round edges there. John grinning over a can of bubbling hot Cs; John staring at me glassily in a thick pool of blood. Gio bent nearly double laughing; Gio snarling in the dirt. Woody dancing with Jackson; Woody lying unrecognizable in the grass. By the time I got to New York Avenue, I was exhausted, my stomach ached, and my shoulder was on fire. I got in the right lane so I could turn onto Florida Avenue, make a U-turn, and head home.

But I didn't turn; I kept going. I compromised with myself as I finished the drive into the District. I knew too many guys whose names were on the Wall. I couldn't handle focusing on every one of them; I'd find the names of those I'd been closest to, the six who always came in my dream. The others would wait. If I came back, they'd always be there.

I crossed 17th Street and walked slowly down the sidewalk between Constitution Gardens and the reflecting pool. It was just after 5:00 p.m.; the September sun was warm and bright, though the breeze carried a hint of rain. When I spotted the Memorial a couple blocks away, I put on my beat-up red baseball cap with the Marine Corps emblem on the front.

I didn't look for the guys right away. Instead, I got a brochure about the Memorial from a park ranger and read it as I went slowly down the walk and stood on the neatly manicured grass in front of the Wall.

Set in the middle of Constitution Gardens between the Washington Monument to the east and the Lincoln Memorial to the west, the Wall, from where I looked up at it, was a chevron rising to over ten feet in the middle, at the apex, and stretching, tapering out two hundred forty-six feet on each side to a height of inches above the ground at the ends.

At the very top of the Memorial it says:

IN HONOR OF THE MEN AND WOMEN OF THE ARMED FORCES OF THE UNITED STATES WHO SERVED IN THE VIETNAM WAR. THE NAMES OF THOSE WHO GAVE THEIR LIVES AND OF THOSE WHO REMAIN MISSING ARE INSCRIBED IN THE ORDER THEY WERE TAKEN FROM US.

The listing of names begins there on Panel 1E at the vertex, after the engraved date "1959," and continues down the gleaming black granite wall until the names seem to disappear into the earth at the east end. Then the roll resumes, the names of the dead and missing arising from the earth on the west side, continuing full circle to the

middle of the Wall, to the bottom of Panel 1W and the date "1975,"
where it says,

OUR NATION HONORS THE COURAGE, SACRIFICE
AND DEVOTION TO DUTY AND COUNTRY OF ITS
VIETNAM VETERANS. THIS MEMORIAL WAS
BUILT WITH PRIVATE CONTRIBUTIONS FROM
THE AMERICAN PEOPLE. NOVEMBER 11, 1982.

Names. Fifty-seven thousand nine hundred and thirty-nine
of them, then. Three hundred thirty-seven have been added since.
Black granite panels and gray engraved names. Pure, simple, stark.
So powerful, I would've been speechless if anyone had started to
talk with me. Almost fifty-eight thousand names listed by date of
death, without regard to rank, race, religion, or branch of service.
Over twelve hundred of the names servicemen still missing, POWs,
or MIAs, or "whereabouts of remains unknown."

I hadn't gone close enough to read any names, but the six repeated
over and over in a soft refrain in my mind's ear. Woodson Gianelli
Smith Harding Willis Garafano. Woody Gio Smitty Harding Willie John.

I spotted an elderly black woman shuffling down the macadam
walk in front of the Wall. She was alone and leaned heavily on a cane
as she walked, head down, the inky veins on the back of her hand
straining as if they wanted to burst from her loose, dusky skin. She
moved as though every joint in her thin body complained each time
she took a step. Occasionally she looked up at the panels, then put
her head down again and continued her slow shuffle. She carried
a black purse, its cloth faded and worn shiny, the lacquer long ago
rubbed from its flat wooden clasp. It was large, almost like a shop-
ping bag, though it appeared to be light on her arm.

The woman stopped several panels to the west of the vertex of the
wall. She stood only inches from the panels, resting on her cane. Her

shoulders were slumped; she seemed to breathe heavily, as though exhausted, though not defeated, by a weight far worse than whatever physical pain walking caused her. I was near enough to see both her image in the gray-etched black granite and the reflection of the Wall on her own etched, ebony face. I thought of Smitty and Havey and Glass and Ladoor, wondered if any of their mothers were old and worn like her. A tear, unexpected, trickled into the corner of my mouth, the salty taste vaguely unpleasant. I reached a hand up slowly, worried any movement I made would disturb her quiet, and rubbed both my eyes, then chased tears, or the feel of them, down my cheeks. Jesus, what we do to our mothers, I thought.

As I watched her, she leaned again heavily on her cane, balancing herself while she fumbled in her purse. Then, slowly, painfully, she leaned farther forward and dropped a single red rose at the base of the gleaming granite. She hesitated then, as though studying the rose, or perhaps praying, or maybe she was simply unable to summon the strength to stand upright again. I wanted to go help her, but the moment seemed too private, too sacred for me to interfere. If she stumbled, I'd rush over, but not otherwise.

After a long, agonizing moment, the old woman slowly pulled herself back up, regained her balance on the cane. She reached to just above her height on the Wall and touched her fingers to the engraving. My breath caught in my throat as her fingertips stroked the carved letters of a name so gently I imagined her recalling touching her little boy's cheek before he grew up and died. I stifled a sob when she leaned her forehead against the Wall and her slumped shoulders shook as she cried. *My God*, I thought, *what have we done?*

In a few moments, she composed herself, pulled herself upright, or as upright as her bent shoulders would allow. She took a handkerchief edged in black lace from her purse and wiped her eyes and her nose and her cheeks. She looked up again toward the name on the Wall, then she lowered her head and turned very slowly and walked back up the walk. My chest felt like it was going to explode.

I wasn't able to force myself to go closer to the Wall. Fifty-eight thousand names in straight gray lines in the gleaming black granite. It was not possible for me to think of going close enough to see the lines create letters, form individual names, compose memories. It had to be enough for the time being to stand back, to think. Pius John, Gio, Woody, Smitty, Willie, Harding, all the others. I remembered each of them then as young men, boys really, dirty and ragged and sunbaked and smiling. But their eyes didn't laugh. They were nineteen and twenty and already old.

My God, they were special, I thought. *I missed you guys.*

The Wall itself seemed to stare back at me. The late afternoon sun glanced off the polished granite, created pinpoints of light like cats' eyes in patches of black around the gray etched names. Fifty-eight thousand pairs of eyes that looked back at me. Eyes that smiled once, I thought, but saw too much, and in the end, way too little, too.

I rubbed beneath my shoulder as I looked up and down the length of the Wall. Partway down the west side, a bouquet of flowers leaned against the gleaming black base; here and there, a rose or red carnation was stuck beside a line of names in the spaces between the panels. At other places there were tiny American flags, a Navy flag, a Marine Corps flag. The brochure said that notes, photos, pictures of friends and relatives, medals and other mementos left at the Wall are collected and stored in a warehouse someplace.

I finally decided I had to go closer. Not for all I saw written across that wide V but for six special names. I turned and walked to the Washington Monument end of the Memorial. The park ranger spoke quietly, like an usher with friendly but sober respect for the place in which we stood.

"One hundred forty panels, sir," he said.

I looked at the man's face but could read nothing. He was as composed and considerate as a funeral director. It felt all at once like it would definitely rain. I asked the ranger to help me find the six names. Garafano, Harding, Willis, Smith ("There are six hundred and forty-four, sir"), Gianelli, Woodson. There were so many others, but those would be enough for now.

The ranger searched an alphabetical index. Fifty-eight thousand names. The entire phone book for Towson isn't half that long. He wrote panel numbers on a small slip of paper and handed it to me. I thanked him and turned to walk back to the Wall.

A few feet down the sidewalk a large man stood to the side. He wore faded jungle utility trousers and blouse and faded and cracked, but clean, jungle boots. His brown hair, gray streaked, billowed over his ears and down his neck, his bushy beard mottled with gray. "USMC" was stenciled in faded black above his breast pocket, from which dangled a Purple Heart and a Combat Action Ribbon and Vietnam campaign medals. He had lance corporal chevrons and crossed rifles on his collar.

The vet was muscular, like someone who worked heavy construction or some other physical labor. He reminded me some of Mike Jackson, though from his movements, he had his legs. I felt to see if the knot on my tie was straight in my collar. One more drug-crazed, baby-killer Vietnam vet for the press, I thought sarcastically as I got closer. Pal, you're painting us all with that brush. He watched me as I approached. He had a handful of Memorial brochures like the one I'd gotten from the ranger when I first arrived. Self-appointed helper and tour guide, I said to myself. I wondered if he had a real job. Then I felt guilty as Patti's words from some time back came to me. "Maybe it's just their way of honoring the friends they lost." Still . . .

He took in my coat and tie and glanced up at the emblem on my baseball cap. He smiled as I got closer. "Semper Fi," he said.

I smiled back. "Semper Fi."

"Who were you with?"

"Bravo One Fifteen. Nineteen sixty-nine. You?" I was surprised at the pride I felt saying I'd been part of Bush Bravo of Fifteenth Marines.

"Golf Three Nine," the other vet said. "Sixty-seven, sixty-eight."

I was struck by his eyes. I expected something hard and faraway in them, maybe dazed or somehow off-kilter. They held nothing of that. His eyes were very gentle, even peaceful, but at the same time they held a sense of something else, a purpose, perhaps. Maybe like a stoic monk who'd experienced the dark side of the world and then found his quiet calling.

"You've got one of these?" He held up his fistful of brochures.

I held mine up. "And some panel information the ranger gave me."

"Need anything else?"

"I'm good. Thanks."

"Let me know if I can help." He smiled, seemed to study my face for a moment.

"Thanks," I said. I half-wanted to say, "You could put on real clothes," but of course I didn't. For a second, I remembered again what Patti had said and felt guilty for having had the thought.

"First time here?"

I nodded. He seemed to study my face once more, then nodded himself and stepped aside.

I moved slowly down the walk. As I got closer to the low end of the Wall, I began to feel apprehensive, nearly panicked, as though I might turn and walk away without ever seeing what I'd come for.

Ahead of me, a woman, fifty or fifty-five-years old, held her finger to a name, her face wet with tears. A man the age my father would've been if he were alive pressed close to her, aimed an Instamatic camera at her trembling finger and the letters etched in the granite above it. My chest grew tight; I felt a roiling in my stomach as though I'd been groin-kicked. It was hard to breathe. I slowed my pace even more, kneaded my shoulder hard as I walked by the couple. Just past them, leaning against a panel was a framed picture of two young kids, perhaps a few years older than Douglas and Katie, maybe sixth or seventh grade. Behind the picture, a piece of white construction paper, hand-drawn red hearts in the three corners I could see, had written across it, "We Love You Daddy." There were two names printed below that, partly obscured by the picture frame, and by my tears.

———

The first name I found was just above eye level in the middle of a line. I thought of Ellen and Jim, how painful it must have been to see, to touch, their boy's name. I reached up, stroked the letters with my fingers. THOMAS J. WOODSON. It felt like the engraving was being etched in my mind. An image came to me then. Woody on the first day I met him, not at the end. So handsome, so hung over, so happy showing off his new bulldog tattoo. Tears leaked down my cheeks as I caressed the cold granite. Woody, I whispered the words to myself. I am so, so sorry. My lips moved, but I made no sound.

RUDOLPH P. GIANELLI. I stared up at the name at the beginning of a line a few inches above eye level. The sun was hiding now, and a soft rain had begun to fall. The water mixed with the tears on my cheeks and dripped into the corners of my mouth.

A deep red, almost purple, carnation was stuck in the crack beside the line of names. It could've been for any of the people in that line, but for me, it was Gio's. I thought of the purple rings and purple granny glasses and how the veins stood out purple on his temples when he laughed. Rudolpho, I thought, a lot of people loved you. And the best part of it is, I think you knew that. We missed you, Gio. I still do.

Two panels away. HECTOR J. OGALA.

Damn, Ogala, I barely even knew you. How long were you in-country, a dozen days?

At the end of that line. MARION D. HARDING.

A sob escaped me despite my efforts to choke it back. *Jesus, Harding, we were so goddamn sorry.* I wondered where Hope was then. Harding's daughter would be fourteen. I could see the grin on his face as he showed us her pictures. I hoped her stepdad treated her well, loved her as much as Harding would've. I hoped he was good to Bonnie, loved her as much, too. He was probably a gunny by now. I wondered if he had an Eagle, Globe, and Anchor tattoo as well.

I moved up the same panel to the next line. I didn't need the ranger's slip of paper any more.

THOMAS R. SMITH.

A steel band coiled around my chest. *Hi Smitty*, I whispered, or maybe I just said it in my head. For a moment I thought I could almost smell mentholated tobacco. *You were a good man, Smitty. One of the best.*

EVERETT P. WILLIS.

Aw, Willie, I said. *You too. I can't see a rabbit in a pet store or drive past a cow without thinking of you.* I started to shake. Tears blurred my vision; their salty taste mingled with the blood from my rubbed-raw tongue. I moved my fingers back and forth on the panel, caressing the letters, the names, the memories, again and again. MARION D. HARDING. THOMAS R. SMITH. EVERETT P. WILLIS.

Jesus guys, that was a terrible day.

I moved down to the next panel.

PIUS J. GARAFANO.

"Oh, God, John," I whispered.

I pressed my fingers into the etching as hard as I could, trying to get the letters closer to me somehow. I rubbed the name over and over, almost as if subconsciously I could sculpt the words into my hand like they were engraved on my soul. I thought of John talking and laughing, pontificating or telling a tale, his head thrown back in that Teddy Roosevelt grin, the rosary I'd had for ten years in my desk drawer skipping across the scars on his chest. "Ah Pope," I whispered out loud. "One of a kind. I'm sorry it's taken me so long."

And then my head was against the carved surface of the Wall, and I was sobbing, then sliding falling kneeling on the wet pavement with my face pressed against the wet black granite, my arms outstretched against the base of the panels, unable to move, half-dead weight against dead names.

"Oh John, oh guys, I am so sorry. I love you guys. I've missed you so much."

I felt pressure under my arms then as someone very strong began to lift me from the ground. From someplace that seemed far off in the gentle rain, there came a deep rumbling, like the muffled sound of distant friendly artillery firing for effect. It seemed to repeat over and over: "It's okay, man. It's okay, it's okay." The big vet got me to my feet and I turned and fell against him, sobbing into his camouflaged chest.

And all I could hear above the sound of the rain picking up in the trees were my diminishing sobs and the deep rumble of the other Vietnam veteran's voice.

"Welcome home, Marine. Welcome home."

About the Author

A Naval Academy graduate, **Mark Treanor** was a Marine rifle platoon leader in Vietnam, an artillery battery commander, and leadership instructor who later served on the boards of the National Defense University and the Naval Academy. A lawyer, corporate executive, and leadership coach, he has participated in national security fact-finding missions in Iraq, Yemen, Africa, and the Caucasus. He lives in Maryland and Vermont.